Advance praise
RECIPE FOR A GOOD LIFE

"Reading *Recipe For a Good Life* was like being on the receiving end of an enormous hug just when you need it most. Bursting at the seams with heart and humour, this book is a most glorious love letter to the amazing women of rural Cape Breton. I now want to get a time machine and move to South Head Road!"

–**BIANCA MARAIS**, *The Witches of Moonshyne Manor*

"Fans of the delightful Lesley Crewe know that she can skillfully make you weep or laugh at the drop of a noun. In her latest novel, *Recipe for a Good Life*, she weaves loneliness like silk into the soul of a person with a stitch of humour. This clever author knows that the heart can teach you more than you will ever teach it."

–**BEATRICE MACNEIL**, *Where White Horses Gallop*

"Lesley Crewe has done it again! *Recipe for a Good Life* absolutely delivers, with vivid characters, and plenty of moments both hilarious and touching. Lesley's writing with lots of love, here, and it shows."

–**STEPHANIE DOMET**, *Fallsy Downsies*

"I fell arse over tea kettle in love with the characters in this book, and now find myself missing them on a daily basis. That's the sign of a good story!"

–**NANCY REGAN,** *From Showing Off to Showing UP*

"*Notting Hill* meets Cape Breton—if Julia Roberts was a bestselling author and Hugh Grant a clandestine baker instead of a bookseller. With Crewe's signature wit and a cast of cheeky characters, lolloping dogs and heaps of food, this is a warm hug of a book.."

–**NICOLA DAVISON**, *In the Wake*

Praise for **LESLEY CREWE**

NOSY PARKER

Globe and Mail bestseller, Indigo's Top 100 Books of 2022

"From Montreal-born, Cape Breton-based author Lesley Crewe comes a delightfully authentic novel that provides the perfect feel-good distraction.... *Nosy Parker* is as entertaining as one could want."
–**WINNIPEG FREE PRESS**

THE SPOON STEALER

Globe and Mail bestseller; Canada Reads 2022 longlist

"I loved *The Spoon Stealer* so much, for so many reasons....I laughed, I cried through scenes both charming and horrifying, and I was emotionally attached to every character. Like with every one of Ms. Crewe's books, each scene and character was expertly crafted, and I was left wishing the story would never end. An absolutely wonderful, heartfelt story of family and redemption, forgiveness and love."
–**GENEVIEVE GRAHAM**, bestselling author of *Bluebird*

"Lesley Crewe artfully threads history and humour through this touching story of family, friendship, and the preciousness of memories. With its indomitable spirit, down-to-earth wisdom, and a dash of gutsy sass, *The Spoon Stealer* might just steal your heart."
–**AMY SPURWAY**, award-winning author of *Crow*

MARY, MARY

Leacock Memorial Medal for Humour longlist

"A funny and charming story of a dysfunctional Cape Breton family, and the irony of the "white sheep" who stands out like a sore thumb."
–**ATLANTIC BOOKS TODAY**

Recipe for a Good Life

LESLEY CREWE

Vagrant
PRESS

For Aunt Edie and Uncle Bill
I miss you

Vagrant Press is an imprint of
Nimbus Publishing Limited
3660 Strawberry Hill St, Halifax, NS, B3K 5A9
(902) 455-4286 nimbus.ca

Printed and bound in Canada

Editor: Penelope Jackson
Editor for the press: Whitney Moran
Cover design: Heather Bryan
Typesetting: Rudi Tusek

NB1668

Library and Archives Canada Cataloguing in Publication

Title: Recipe for a good life / Lesley Crewe.
Names: Crewe, Lesley, 1955- author.
Identifiers: Canadiana (print) 20230226485 | Canadiana (ebook) 20230226493
ISBN 9781774712047 (softcover) | ISBN 9781774712092 (EPUB)
Classification: LCC PS8605.R48 R43 2023 | DDC C813/.6—dc23

Description: Indigo exclusive edition.
Identifiers: Canadiana 20230227155 | ISBN 9781774712481 (softcover)
Classification: LCC PS8605.R48 R43 2023b | DDC C813/.6—dc23

Nimbus Publishing acknowledges the financial support for its publishing activities from the Government of Canada, the Canada Council for the Arts, and from the Province of Nova Scotia. We are pleased to work in partnership with the Province of Nova Scotia to develop and promote our creative industries for the benefit of all Nova Scotians.

"If you have any young friends who aspire to become writers, the second greatest favor you can do them is to present them with copies of *The Elements of Style*. The first-greatest, of course, is to shoot them now, while they're happy."

–Dorothy Parker

Author's Note

Dear friends and neighbours,

As you know, I live only three minutes from the top of South Head Road. With my writer's wand, I've changed the locations of the properties in the story so that they are closer to the actual road itself, only because it suits my purposes. The gorgeous vistas from the coastline and cliffs overlooking Morien Bay, Long Beach, South Head itself, with Flint Island and the ocean beyond, would not be seen unless you went further in. So forgive me for that. This story takes place in 1955, but I do not mention the devastating fire that completely wiped out Waddens Cove and many of the houses in South Head on August 20, 1935.

Although this book is a work of fiction, I am using the real names of the Homeville Women's Institute members in 1955–1956, at one particular meeting held in the fictional character Bertha Bailey's house, as a tribute to the many, many, wonderful W. I. members over the past seventy years. Fine souls who embody the word "good." I use their first names instead of their husbands' because I want them recognized for their own sakes. They are listed in the order given in the record of attendance. This amazing organization has been a driving force for "Home and Country" in our part of the world since 1951 and is still going strong to this day. My mother was a member when she lived here briefly, and my grandmother Abbie (Mrs. Kenzie Macdonald, as she signed it in the W. I. N. S. Branch Minute Book), was president in 1959–1960. I was also a member in the mid-1980s and 1990s. They had the very good sense to never give me the title of president. However, they did elect a pregnant me to drive to the Valley and stand in the sun for three hours waiting for Princess Margaret to attend a luncheon being held in her honour. She smoked from a cigarette holder during all three courses and actually spoke to me as she was leaving, asking me how far I'd travelled. I babbled something and she moved on.

I hope the love I have for Mira Gut, Round Island, Homeville, South Head, Waddens Cove, Black Brook, and Port Morien, as well as the people who settled here, both living and remembered, will shine through.

Chapter One

Montreal

1955

Gaynor Ledbetter was fed up to the back teeth, so she asked her secretary to call her hair stylist near the Windsor Hotel downtown to see if she could squeeze her in. It's not like the woman had to do anything complicated. She scrubbed Gaynor's hair to within an inch of its life, fastened grey metal rollers in the thinning strands, threw her under the dryer, and then teased it into a monstrous beehive, before using enough hairspray to keep it as hard as a rock for a week. Simple.

Her secretary, Dolores, was new, which was part of the problem. Gaynor waited for two minutes, and when nothing happened, like her phone ringing, a knock at the door, someone popping their head in, she wearily got up out of her chair, a cigarette firmly planted between her lips, and jerked her office door open. There was Dolores, looking panicked at her desk.

"*Well?*"

"I'm sorry, Mrs. Bedwetter...Betterletter..."

"*SPIT IT OUT!*"

"I can't find the number."

"Kill me now." She slammed the door shut and called the hair salon herself. "This is Gaynor Ledbetter. I have a standing appointment with Mitzi every Tuesday at noon, but I wondered if she can take me right this very minute? Yes, I'll hold."

She blew smoke rings up towards the ceiling and realized that the tiles above her desk were the colour of tobacco. Easy solution. Stop looking at the ceiling.

A voice came back on the line.

"I see. Tell Mitzi I'm very disappointed, seeing as how I'm a very generous tipper and have sent many new clients her way...what? I'll hold."

A voice came back on the line.

"Brilliant. Tell her I'll see her in twenty minutes."

Gaynor grabbed her sizable alligator purse, threw her smokes and lighter into its depths, and shut it with a satisfying click. Then she grabbed her sweater and scarf from the coat rack and opened the door. Dolores was at her desk looking flushed and teary.

"For God's sake, whatever you do, do not let anyone know where I am. Do you understand?"

"W-what if it's your husband?"

"Use your noodle. Obviously, you can tell him. I'm talking about my needy and pathetic writers who demand constant handholding. 'Become an editor,' they said. 'You love books,' they said. I do love books; I just hate the people who write them."

An hour later, Gaynor was happily lying on a beach in Maui, the hot sun baking the back of her neck. The roar of the ocean filled her ears as she drifted off. A lovely calm overtook her frayed nerves. This was just the ticket.

And then some kind of hermit crab kept pinching her shoulder. Her eyes flew open and she sat up, hitting her forehead on the front of the hair dryer with a thwack. "OW!"

Gaynor pulled up the dryer and gave the young woman in front of her a look. "Kitty, is it asking too much to have some peace? How did you know I was here?"

"I bullied your new secretary into spilling the beans. I think she's quit. Last I saw her she was running down the stairs sobbing. What do you do to these poor souls?"

"Can't this wait?"

"I'm afraid not, seeing as I'm about to have a breakdown and may never write again."

This is why Gaynor hated writers. They always said they'd never write again. And they always did. Gaynor had heard this particular song and dance seven times before. But Kitty did look especially agitated, and she was Gaynor's number-one client, so as inconvenient as it was, she'd have to gird her loins.

"Fine. Go get a cup of coffee and we'll walk back to the office together when I'm finished here."

"May I bum a smoke?"

Gaynor pointed at the purse at her feet. "Why do you never buy your own cigarettes?"

"You always have some."

Writers.

They walked down the Metcalfe Street sidewalk back to a large grey office building where the Empire & Bloom Publishing Company took up the entire third floor. It was a blustery day. Not that Gaynor's hair moved an inch, but her scarf did flap in her face from time to time. Kitty grabbed her arm as if she was an old thing when they crossed on a green light; to someone Kitty's age, Gaynor probably did seem ancient.

Montreal was full of stylish ladies, but many of them tried too hard. Kitty attracted attention despite her brunette waves always being in a tousled mess. No hairdressers for her. An alluring woman who never acknowledged it. Maybe she didn't know, or even care. It seemed to Gaynor that she was forever hiding. Her head was always down. No one would suspect she was married to a well-known actor. She didn't fit the part. Today she had on her usual capris, buttoned-up sleeveless shirt, and flats. No earrings, high heels, or lipstick. And still she looked better than most of the women around her. Gaynor decided life wasn't fair.

They trudged up the stairs instead of using the elevator. Kitty insisted. "You're going to dry up like an old prune behind that desk if you don't lubricate your joints with a little exercise."

Gaynor's feet stopped moving, causing Kitty to bump into her. "This is what you want to say to me? Keep it up."

When they got back to the busy workplace, the desk in front of Gaynor's office was empty. "Well, shit." She snapped her fingers at the desk one door down. The secretary, Iris, looked up. "Could you find me another—"

"Victim?"

Iris wasn't afraid of her. Gaynor wished she could steal her away from Mel Bloom, but the world would crumble. Besides, an Iris should work for a Bloom. "If someone comes looking for me, tell them I'm in a meeting with this brat."

"Righto. Hi, Kitty. Loved the latest!"

Kitty waved and disappeared into the office, Gaynor shutting the door behind them. If she had to describe her space, a cluttered grotto would suffice. Four walls of floor-to-ceiling books sucked the light out of the room. Heavy blinds took care of the rest. They were closed for most of the day, since the afternoon sun through the large window burned a giant sizzling hole in the back of her skull.

Gaynor draped her purse, sweater, and scarf back on the hat rack, and Kitty fell into the upholstered chaise longue in front of the far bookcase. She actually put her arm up to cover her eyes as she crossed her legs and shook her foot until her shoe fell on the carpet. "Could I trouble you for another cigarette?"

"I know what I'm getting you for Christmas." Gaynor lit two and handed one to her. She then settled back in the swivel chair behind her desk. It fit her ample bum perfectly.

"So, you're never going to write again? A familiar refrain."

"I knew you wouldn't believe me."

"Funnily, no I don't. You have seven bestselling Inspector Harry Gunn novels under your belt. Do you know how many writers would kill for that kind of readership? Not to mention talent?"

"And I am going to slit my throat if I have to write number eight." She looked at the lit end of her cigarette and was about to put it back in her mouth when she waved it in the air instead. "Or maybe I'll stab myself or jump off a cliff. How about I drown in a vat of chicken fat? Which do you prefer, being buried alive or strangled with a shoelace?" Kitty paused and took a drag. "Why didn't I make my detective a woman? Harry Gunn does nothing but nick himself shaving, clean his dratted pipe, mumble, and scribble on napkins. A grumpy bachelor who shuffles around in slippers drinking port. He's driving me mad."

Gaynor felt a small stab of panic, which made her almost reach for another smoke before she realized she had one between her lips. Kitty had never gone into this much detail before. Maybe she was fed up. Who wouldn't be, after living with the same character for years? Gaynor always waxed poetic about Harry Gunn, only because he and he alone was responsible for Gaynor and her husband Simon going to Florida every February. She wanted the character to live forever. The thought that he might not was upsetting.

"Why not give him a sidekick? Some wisecracking dame who gives him indigestion?"

"Shall I call her Gaynor?"

"Your wit is astounding."

"Because he'd still be there driving his Volvo to crime scenes and unnerving suspects with his steely gaze. Not to mention the fact that I've run out of ways to gruesomely kill people. Crucifixion? Check. Eaten by pigs? Check. Head stuck in a giant pickle jar? Check. I'm done, I tell you."

This sounded bad. Gaynor tried to remain calm. Kitty was C. J. Faulkner, the biggest fiction writer at this firm. Gaynor's husband had discovered Kitty quite by accident when she took his English class at McGill University. He handed Gaynor an assignment she'd done and Gaynor was blown away by her voice, so she brought it to Mel Bloom's attention. The rest was history. Mel had been eternally grateful. Especially since Kitty was a speed demon. It only took her two or three months to write one of her novels.

"Okay. Why not let Harry drive off in his Volvo and disappear over the horizon for a while? Not forever, mind you. Your readers would be up in arms. But write something else. It doesn't have to be a murder mystery, although you are brilliant at it. Is there anything else you'd like to try? Romance?"

Kitty jumped up and paced back and forth, kicking her shoe every time she did. "Romance? Ugh. What do I know about romance?"

"You are married to Robert Chandler, leading man extraordinaire."

Kitty's cigarette ash fell on the rug as she moved towards the window and peeked out through the blinds. "I'm married to Kurt Wagner, mama's boy, narcissist, and womanizer, in that order."

Now this was something Gaynor did not know. How was that possible? Probably because Kitty never talked about him. But then she never asked, either.

"If that's the case, why don't you send the louse packing?"

Kitty sighed and turned around, stubbing her smoke out in the ashtray, wasting a perfectly good cigarette, before draping herself over the chaise again. "I don't know anything else. He's been in my life forever, and he's always gone anyway; he's leaving for New York to do a small movie. Should be away for six weeks this time."

A crazy idea popped into Gaynor's head. "You should go away too."

"Where?"

"Anywhere! You need to recharge your batteries. Just get out of Dodge. Paris. London. Madrid?"

"Huge, miserable cities full of artificial, self-important people. How can I think when there's always so much noise? Our old apartment building only has three floors, but we are sandwiched between a tuba-playing member of the Montreal Symphony directly above us and an operatic diva below us."

"Oh. Now I get why you killed off an opera singer in your latest book."

"She had her head bashed in with a tuba, remember? I'm slowly losing my marbles. Nothing is fresh or exciting. I'm stale and flat and unhappy. The only thing I love is writing, and now I'm afraid to go near my desk."

To Gaynor's horror, Kitty covered her face with her hands. Oh hell. Gaynor didn't have a maternal bone in her body, so for a few miserable moments she stayed on her chair, but then it became obvious she was expected to do something. She got up and sat next to Kitty, tapping her fingers on Kitty's back as if testing the doneness of a cake. "There, there."

Kitty leaned against her and Gaynor had no choice but to take Kitty's hand in her own. Thank God there were no tears. "Look, go home and have a hot soak. I'll talk to Simon tonight and see if we can't come up with a solution for you. You know how good he is at solving other people's problems. 'Simon says' and all that. I'm glad you came to me. There's no need to suffer alone."

"I had to come to you. I have no one else."

"Your dad?"

"He hasn't noticed I'm not talking to him."

Gaynor wasn't sure what else to do. "Ciggy?"

⋙⋘

Gaynor told Simon over a serving of veal scallopini what was worrying her before pointing at her plate. "This is delicious, by the way."

Simon sipped from his wineglass. "A new recipe. We had a great time making it, didn't we, Jersey May?"

They both looked at their basset hound, who had placed herself exactly between her owners' chairs, in case a crumb of French bread hit the floor.

Simon was a content soul, five years away from retirement. He and Gaynor shared a love of literature, good food, and great wine. Jersey May completed their family.

He put down his fork to take another slice of bread, slathering it with a thick layer of butter. "So, you think this is serious and not just the usual fretting?"

"It's definitely different. She's such a lovely young woman, but today she seemed frazzled, with circles under her eyes, like she's not sleeping. Her noisy neighbours are driving her mad, her husband is gone all the time, and she's not talking to her father, who is apparently the only family she has, not that she ever goes into great detail."

Simon chewed his bread and slid his round glasses back up his nose with the side of his hand. "Okay. Rest. Silence. A change of scene. Which means getting out of the city into the country. She's an independent soul, so I don't think the idea of travelling alone bothers her."

Simon took another gulp of his red wine to chase down the bread. "Interestingly, at lunch today Larry mentioned our golf trip to the Highland Links in Cape Breton a couple of years ago. That is one beautiful island and pretty remote. Maybe she should head somewhere like that for a while. Tell her she needs to go on a writer's retreat to get her juices flowing again. And tell her Empire and Bloom will pay for it."

"Pay for it?"

"If Mel Bloom finds out Inspector Harry Gunn is going the way of the dodo bird, he'll cough up the money. You're going to have to tell him about this. If Kitty suddenly decides to chuck her whole writing career, you'll be the one explaining why you didn't do everything you could to keep her happy."

"You've got a point."

"I always do."

"Cheeky."

⊸❦⊶

As soon as Gaynor got back to the office the next morning, she was surprised to see a new secretary sitting outside her office door. Iris was a wonder.

8

She gave her the once-over. "You're the new replacement, I see." And what she saw was a trim little woman with a buttoned-up blouse tucked into a wool skirt, her hair in a bun, and a pair of glasses hanging off a chain around her neck. Did she come out of central casting?

"Yes, Mrs. Ledbetter. Dolores."

"That was the name of my former assistant, and she lasted two days."

"A good thing. Otherwise, I wouldn't be here changing your life."

Gaynor smirked. A new Iris? "We'll see." She opened her door and threw her belongings on the desk before she left again to thank Iris for her great work as she knocked on Mel Bloom's door.

"Enter."

Mel Bloom was a large, balding man with thick eyebrows, who chewed the ends of cigars. He spent his life with his feet up on his desk, barking orders over the phone. Iris was the real power behind the throne. She got things done by actually putting her feet on the floor.

"Gaynor! Has to be trouble. You only come in here when things are dicey. Sit down. Would you like a drink?"

"At nine in the morning? Actually, maybe I will, because things are dicey. C. J. Faulkner is talking about packing it in."

That got him up. "What? Bloody hell. Tell me everything."

"The poor child has been burning the candle at both ends for the last decade with Harry Gunn. I think we've taken her for granted. She's so quick to come up with another novel that we just assumed she'd be willing to do it forever, but at this point, she's fed up with the stories, the character, maybe even the genre. I think she's done. It might even be too late."

He slumped in his chair and took the cigar out of his mouth. "This is a disaster. She is our shining star, the reason we keep getting other great writers in our stable. They want her success and think we're the reason for it. Which we are, but let's face it, not many writers are as talented as she is. That opera singer's head being bashed in by the tuba was horrifying and magical, all at the same time."

"I'm hoping to approach her with an idea, but I'd like your approval."

He nodded. "Okay."

"I think she needs to go away on a retreat. Two months. A change of scene might perk her up."

"Great idea."

"And we should pay for it."

Mel put the cigar back in his mouth. "Seriously?"

"We can't afford not to. If we tell her to make her own arrangements, she might not have the will to bother, but if she knows that we're behind her, no matter what kind of story she comes up with, she's more apt to do it. Don't you think?"

He twisted the cigar around with his fingers. "Perhaps. It will be costly."

"Not necessarily. Ever heard of a place called Cape Breton?"

Chapter Two

Cape Breton

Bertha Bailey never stopped from morning till night. At the age of seventy, the only time she sat down was to pee or knit a layette for the newest grandchild. Number thirty. A not unlikely number, seeing as how she had ten kids of her own. This knitting business was a cottage industry thanks to her eleven great-grandchildren as well.

But it had to be said she also loved a good murder mystery and put her feet up to read a few chapters at the end of the day while crunching on pink candy Chicken Bones before turning out the lights.

She lived in the country along a dirt road in a ramshackle farmhouse in South Head, Cape Breton. Her husband, Donald, had died ten years earlier, in 1945. A heart attack after too much celebrating.

"The war is over and the boys came home. I can't believe I've lived to see this day!"

He spoke too soon.

The only reason Bertha was able to manage was her youngest son, Wallace. He was the only one of her kids who had never married, and so slipped seamlessly into maintaining the property after they laid his father to rest.

And he did it with great ease. Whereas Donald had been a wiry string bean, Wallace took after his mother's people. Six feet six inches tall and three hundred pounds of pure muscle. Everyone said it was a good thing he was a placid soul; like Bertha, the calm in everyone's storm. If he had had a temper like Donald, people would've run a mile.

But Wallace never ran, he lumbered. Many thought that was the reason for his nickname, Walrus, but the real story was because his beloved nieces and nephews could never pronounce Wallace when they were little.

Bertha was feeding laundry through the wringer washer with six young grandchildren around her feet when the phone rang.

One long. One short.

Not her ring. She continued with her wash. Soon enough the phone sounded again.

One long. Three short.

Drat, that was hers. It never failed. She wiped her hands. "Hold on, hold on."

She went into the dining room, picked up the earpiece, and didn't even get a chance to say hello.

"Bertha?" Ethel shouted.

Ethel was a bit hard of hearing.

"Good morning, Ethel. Is it urgent? I'm in the middle of something here." She put the phone receiver up against her enormous bosom, the spot her grandchildren loved to cuddle against. "You sweeties stay away from Nan's washing machine, do you hear me?"

"It's okay, Nanna," Ruby answered. "I'll take the younger ones into the garden to pick peas."

"Thank you, sweetheart." Bertha loved this child. A sensible girl.

"You there?" Ethel squawked.

"Of course, dear. Where else would I be?"

Bertha was incredibly patient with everyone, but poor old Ethel was a bit of a handful. That's because Ethel had no life, and so she spent her days listening in on the party line to hear about everyone else's life and then passed that information on to her neighbours. Or she tried. Bertha was the only one who didn't hang up on her.

"You're not going to believe it!"

"What?"

"The Campbells' place down from you has been rented by some outfit in Montreal!"

"Outfit?"

"A big company of some kind. Donna's husband didn't say."

"Donna's husband? I didn't know you were friendly with him."

"Er...sure...didn't you know?"

Bertha did know. Everyone thought old man Campbell's son in Toronto was foolish for trying to rent that little house, but there you go. "Good for him."

"I know! But who on earth would want to come here?"

"Why wouldn't someone want to come to God's country? But that property needs work."

"Imagine! Someone from Montreal! I've never met anyone from Montreal. Will they speak French, do you think?"

"I haven't the foggiest, dear. Look, I have to run. I'll drop off some tea biscuits on my way to Morien."

Bertha never could hang up on a person without offering some kind of reward. And her baking was legendary. She knew Ethel would enjoy it. The poor soul needed a treat now and again.

Bertha went out onto the covered back porch and resumed her position hunched over the wringer washer. She waved to Ruby to thank her for her good work with the kiddies. Every summer day a different group of grandchildren found their way to their Nan's house. Most of the time Bertha forgot who belonged to who. It didn't really matter. They all looked the same: towheads with faces full of freckles.

A few of her own children had a reddish tint in their blond hair, but only Wallace was a true auburn. Donald declared he had to be the milkman's son. Bertha knew he was only half kidding, while she only half wished it was true. But nowadays he was a sea of glorious ginger because of his colourful mop, mustache, and thick beard. Bertha would shake her head as she doled out his bacon, eggs, sausages, and stack of homemade toast first thing in the morning.

"Will you trim this animal? You're thirty-five and you look like Old Man Moses."

Wallace would crinkle his eyes and wink at her, so she finally stopped bugging him. You can't argue with someone who won't argue back.

She heard the roar of the tractor coming along the back field. Wallace had the front loader full of sawed-up logs, which he'd pile against the back shed to chop later. The grandchildren rushed out of the garden like mischievous gnomes and surrounded him, begging for a ride. He nodded to Ruby and she reached down and put the kids in the bucket one after the other, then sat in the middle with her arms around all of them. Wallace drove around the yard slowly but purposely went through pot holes to make it extra bouncy. The youngsters squealed with delight.

Bertha took her laundry basket and hung out the wash, keeping her eye on them. They loved their uncle Walrus more than anyone. But then again, everyone loved Wallace, including every animal he had ever came across. His two enormous Newfoundland dogs, Argus and Pride, rarely left his side, and the chickens in the yard would run after him until he sat down and held them in his lap, much to the dogs' dismay. He absolutely refused to kill a chicken.

"You eat chicken!" Bertha would point out.

"I don't know the ones from the store personally."

"Lord love a duck."

"I do love me some ducks."

From the age of twenty to twenty-five Wallace had been fighting for his life on the Atlantic in convoy ships, so girls were the last thing on his mind, but when he came home Bertha was sure he'd be snapped up. There was certainly enough interest from the fairer sex, but Wallace never made time for them. Always content to spend his days outside gathering apples from their orchard, picking black currents, digging potatoes, pulling carrots, and making hay for their two horses. He helped his neighbours haul lobster traps on occasion, fixed machinery, was an ace with plumbing and carpentry. You name it, Wallace could do it. He was a true handyman, with ham-sized hands strong enough to help a cow in distress when calving, gentle enough to wipe a three-year-old's nose when they were left out of a game of hide-and-seek.

While she knew that Wallace would make a great husband and father, after several years of nothing brewing, Bertha realized she was quite content to have him remain an old bachelor. She certainly slept better at night hearing his snoring through her bedroom wall.

Clothes hung up, she went back into the kitchen and put a dozen biscuits in a used paper bag. Then she took off her apron and patted her white hair in the mirror, pinning back a few tendrils that had escaped her bun. She adjusted the girdle under her flowered housedress, which was no easy task, and pulled her rolled stockings up to her knees before grabbing her change purse and the truck keys.

She stood on the front porch. Wallace stopped the tractor and waited.

"Who wants to go to the store?!"

Six kids jumped off the tractor loader and scrambled up and into the open back of the truck. "Ruby, make sure the young ones are in the middle."

"Yes, Nan."

"Need anything?" she shouted over to Wallace.

"I'm good."

"No! You're great!" Ruby yelled back.

And with that Bertha got in the cab, turned on the ignition, and ground the gears noisily with the stick shift. She knew Wallace was grimacing, but she never did get the hang of doing it smoothly. Wallace had taught her to drive after Donald died. He wanted her to be more self-sufficient, and she was grateful to him. She'd never had freedom like this before. She blasted the radio as she bumped her way down the dirt road, careful not to be in a hurry and stir up too much dust. She'd just remembered that one of that bunch back there had asthma.

Bertha was great at a lot of things, but singing wasn't one of them, which was why finding herself alone was always a thrill. No one to tell her to pipe down.

Ethel's house was closer to the highway, which was a good thing. Since her husband had died, she'd depended on her son to shovel her and her older sister out in the winter. Everyone agreed that if she lived further down the road, they'd be marooned until spring, as she and her son didn't get along. But sometimes he'd have no shame, and Wallace would end up plowing the driveway and picking up a few groceries before her own flesh and blood would show up with some excuse or other.

Bertha pulled into the yard and stopped rather abruptly. Ethel's black cat ran in front of the truck, just daring her to hit him. It was a constant game of Chicken with that critter.

"You kids okay back there?!"

"YES!"

She picked up the paper bag and scooted her ample hips closer to the door. It was becoming obvious that this truck was too high for her and her hips, so her descent was not graceful.

"I'll be right back. Everyone stay put and listen to Ruby."

"Yes, Nanna!"

Bertha walked up the steps, grabbed the screen-door handle, and pulled. Ethel came with it and ended up lurching against Bertha's famous bosom.

"Merciful heavens, Ethel!"

"Sorry, Bertha. Saw ya comin'."

"No harm done. Here are your tea biscuits."

"Bless you."

"Do you need anything at the store?"

"More marmalade."

"Nonsense. I'll have Wallace bring you over a jar. I made plenty."

"You're a dear. Listen to this. I just got off the phone with Donna to ask her about the Campbells' place and she was very huffy with me. Wanted to know where I got my information. I said you told me."

Bertha was now sorry she'd offered up her delicious marmalade. "Ethel, you have to stop blaming me for everything. Soon people will stop talking to me, too."

"What do you mean? Have people stopped talking to me?"

Ethel's stricken face made Bertha's big heart twinge. Surely the woman had noticed. "Of course not. But some people don't like gossip."

Her friend snorted. "If you don't like gossip, what in the name of God are you doing living in this part of the world? It's the only pleasure we have here in the sticks."

Just then a ruckus flared up involving the kids and one very irritated cat who was now perched on the roof of the truck's cab, hissing for all he was worth.

"Leave that poor cat alone!" Ethel yelled at them.

"Leave those poor kids alone!" Bertha yelled at the cat. She turned back to Ethel. "Must dash."

The black cat threw a few swipes at Bertha as she opened the truck door, before he jumped down onto the gravel and streaked past Ethel, who tried to pick him up. Bertha didn't know why she bothered. The cat never let anyone near him.

Reassured that all was well within her little group, she set off again, this time taking the one who had asthma into the cab with her just to be on the safe side. He was four. His name was John, or Jimmy. Something like that.

"How's Nanna's boy?" she asked him as she put on her turn signal and looked left before proceeding right down the road towards the village.

"Goods."

"Did you eat all your supper for Mommy?"

"Nos."

"Why not?"

"It's not goods like yours."

Bertha knew he'd say that. They all said it. That's why she liked asking. Totally selfish, but it always made her day.

Down the road they went, past a few fields, lots of trees, the long cove, and on over the green Black Brook bridge to the cemeteries and up past the beautiful sandbar, where birds of all kinds gathered. By the time they entered the village of Port Morien, the bay on the right was full of whitecaps. Good thing lobster fishing was over for the season. It would have been a rough day out there today. The colourful boats were tied up at the wharf.

The houses were dotted around the harbour for the most part, but all the churches were on the other side of the main road, United, Catholic, and Anglican. The village also had three stores and they did a roaring business. Everyone had their favourite, and once you picked one, you didn't often stray.

Bertha counted heads to make sure she hadn't lost a grandchild on the way over, then handed Ruby a dollar and told her to let the kiddies pick out penny candy for the ride home.

She pushed open the door and a bell jingled. The owner, Hopper, who always sat on a stool by the cash register, greeted her with a "Mornin', Mrs. B.," and then got busy doling out gumdrops, black licorice, candy necklaces, Atomic FireBalls, and Pixy Stix.

Bertha happened to see Donna at the back of the store, trying to figure out what can of soup she wanted.

"Hi, Donna. Lovely summer day."

"Hey, Bertha. Got your usual crew with you."

"Always. Realized I didn't have two tins of tomatoes for the goulash tonight, and didn't want to use my fresh ones. Didn't have ground beef either, so I should've just made something else, but the munchkins over there like goulash."

"Just so you know, that dratted Ethel listened in on hubby's long-distance call earlier and then had the nerve to blame you for spilling the beans, which is nonsense, of course."

"I know. She told me."

"Can you believe that woman? No shame, I tell ya."

"Not that I care, but she said an outfit is renting Campbells'? What's an outfit when it's at home?"

Donna looked around and lowered her voice. "Junior Campbell called and said an agency got in touch asking if they could rent the house as a retreat for someone for two months. They wouldn't say who. Junior is hubby's cousin and wants him to mow the lawn and tidy up before they get here, but he seems to forget that hubby is getting long in the tooth. These Toronto types give me a pain. Come down here and straighten it up yourself, I say."

"Wallace could do it."

"You volunteer that boy too often. If he's willing, I'll make sure he's paid."

"Ethel said this someone is from Montreal?"

"Apparently. Can you imagine some city slicker stuck in the boonies? And what kind of retreat? Religious? That's all we need. A bunch of fanatics wandering around."

"A retreat could mean anything. Maybe someone is recovering their health. I hope not, because the drafts in that old place will kill them for sure."

Just then Old Lottie Murphy wandered nearby, so the conversation stopped. The ladies knew that once Lottie opened her mouth there was zero chance of her ever closing it, so with a quick wave, Bertha grabbed her canned tomatoes and hustled to get the ground beef and pay for her purchases. Her brood were chomping on candy as they happily followed her out the door and into the back of the truck. She put the four-year-old beside her in the front seat.

She smashed through the gears as Earl Butts walked up from the wharf with his rubber boots on. He put his hands over his ears and smirked. Bertha honked and waved as she chugged away.

She glanced over at the little fella pretending to smoke his bubblegum cigarettes. "Goods?"

"Goods."

⊰❦⊱

Wallace whistled a tune as he took a knife and a bucket and stood in the jumble of vines hiding zucchinis. His mother didn't like them to get as big as canoes; the peel was too difficult to remove at that stage. He did as he was told because he loved zucchini loaf and his mother made the best. His was a close second.

Only Wallace and his mother knew that he loved to bake. If his brothers ever found out, he'd be frigged, so they kept it a secret. They spent many happy evenings going through old recipe books. Wallace had a habit of talking to his dough and his mother never laughed at him. Kneading was his relaxation, and with those hands, his bread dough was as smooth as a baby's bottom in a matter of minutes.

He only started to bake after the war, when his dad died. Donald would have been horrified at the sight of one of his boys in the kitchen.

"Ever think about becoming a baker?" Bertha asked him once as he took a pan of cinnamon rolls out of the oven.

"Nah."

"But you're so talented."

"I know that and you know that. Who else do I need to impress?"

"If you could do anything, what would it be?"

"Someday I'd like to take a university course in philosophy. Axiology, to be specific."

If Bertha had dentures, they would have fallen out of her head. This boy of hers was a complete mystery. "I have no idea what that is. Nothing to do with chopping wood, I gather?"

"It's the study of values. How does a person decide that something is good? What is good?"

"And when did you come up with this?"

"Night after night on the ship, keeping watch on the Atlantic for U-boats under the stars. Stars that were completely untouched by the insanity here on earth."

Bertha hid her face in her apron. Wallace went over and put his arms around her. "Being home is good."

Wallace was completely serious about this ambition, but it wasn't necessary for him to do it now. It could remain a burning ember in his pocket. In the meanwhile, he used the bookmobile. The librarian did her best to find books that might interest him. It's not like anyone else in the neighbourhood was looking for philosophy texts on axiology, ethics, or aesthetics.

He had about seven zucchinis in the bucket when he heard a vehicle pull up. He waited for the usual crescendo of voices from the small ones, but there was nothing, so he wandered around the house, his chickens and dogs strolling along with him. It wasn't his mother or the kids but Mrs. Wadden. She always asked him to call her Dolly, even though she was a good fifteen years older than he was. Dolly was the councillor's wife, who fancied herself a bit of a celebrity as she was the one who put on all the local plays and variety concerts, as well as acted and sang in the rotary shows in Sydney.

She was definitely a good-looking woman who had a spectacular figure and she loved to wear red lipstick. His mother's friend Ethel called her a tarted-up tart.

"Yoo hoo! Anyone home?"

"Just me, Mrs. Wadden."

"It's Dolly! Please! How are you, young man?" She held out her manicured hand and Wallace had to wipe the dirt off his fingers onto his overalls before extending his. She took hold and didn't want to give it back, which felt mighty awkward.

"Mother will be back soon. She took the kids to Morien."

"It's not your mother I want to see. It's you."

"Me?"

"Yes, and while I have you here, any chance you'd be interested in the theatre, Wallace? You'd make a marvellous leading man."

"No, ma'am. Not even one tiny bit."

Her face fell a little. "Oh dear. That's a real no, isn't it?"

The dogs helped him out by standing too close to her. That's when she noticed their slobber. "Oh my. Well, tell me, would you be interested in my plumbing?"

"Plumbing?"

"Someone said you did that sort of thing and I'm afraid my husband isn't at all handy. I'd like to fix up a few things in the bathroom and wondered if you were free? I'd pay you handsomely of course."

"Always willing to be paid handsomely. When do you want me to start?"

"The first of the week? But perhaps you could come over tomorrow and take a look at it, to see what needs doing? Do you know where I live?"

Everyone knew where she lived. In the biggest house in the village.

"Yes."

"Splendid."

Just then his mother and the kids came down the road and turned in, a trail of dust behind them. Mrs. Wadden waved her hand in front of her face, and Wallace could tell his mother was annoyed, but she'd never give herself away.

She opened the cab and the little fella crawled over her lap to join his cousins who were now running around the front yard.

"Dolly. How lovely to see you. To what do I owe the pleasure?"

"Hello, Bertha. I came by to talk to Wallace, actually. I'd like him to fix our bathroom and he kindly said he would. I hear he's very good."

"Oh, he is that. None finer. Would you like a cup of tea?"

Dolly glanced at the squawking chickens, the screaming gang, and the drooly dogs. Her face gave them the answer. "Thank you, but no. I must go. See you around two tomorrow afternoon, Wallace?"

"Surely."

They watched her get into the sedan and waved when she beeped. The dust billowed behind her car as she drove away.

"I bet she asked you if you'd be interested in her plumbing?"

Wallace looked at her, amazed. "How did you know?"

"A wild guess."

Mother and son stood in the yard for a moment, enjoying the salty ocean breeze that cooled the hot August sun. The clothes on the line waved to and fro as the kids ran under the sheets. There was an eagle at the top of one of the big fir trees down by the water, its favourite spot, and the neighbourhood crows were none too happy about it, doing their best to irritate it with their squawks and dives, but the eagles ignored that sort of thing. If it got too much, they just silently soared away and flew higher than the rest of the squabbling mob.

Walrus knew there were many lessons to be learned just by observing life around him. Eagles were good.

And so was this spot. He never tired of it. The farmhouse sat on a hundred acres, fields and trees, overlooking the shoreline. The Baileys never had much extra, seeing as how they had ten kids to feed, but the farm gave them everything they needed, with odd jobs thrown in.

The house was tall, shingled, and painted white, with two stories and a small front porch where everyone threw their boots, jackets, fishing rods, pails, and toys. A covered porch ran across the entire back of the house. It was screened in halfway up, but in the winter, shutters closed it off. Wallace asked his mother if she wouldn't rather have her old wringer washer in the kitchen than use it in the frigid porch, but she never agreed.

"I need to sit at least ten around this kitchen table, and if I bring that monstrosity in here, we'll only get six."

"We do have a dining room."

"It's easier for me to dole out food here, dropping mashed potatoes in a circle like I'm playing Duck, Duck, Goose."

"Only you and I live in this place," he teased.

"When was the last time we ate supper alone?"

That was true. Thanks to Wallace's nine siblings, Mary, Annie, Helen, Jean, Lizzie, Ruth, John, Charlie, and Bill, and the fact that none of them lived more than ten miles away, two or more were always over every night of the week, picking up their kids, having endless cups of tea with their mother, and consulting her about everything from knitting patterns to favourite recipes to who was related to whom in the family.

Mary, the eldest and bossiest sibling, was always pointing her finger at Wallace. "When Ma is talking about this stuff, you should be writing it down. Someday she's going to forget and then none of us will have a clue."

His mother came to his defense. "He's got enough on his plate. If you're that interested, do it yourself."

"Ma! Wallie lives here. You could be prattling away at night, when it's just the two of you. What else is there to do?"

"I read my detective stories. Who cares if Great Uncle Leroy married his first cousin?"

"Great Uncle Leroy married his first cousin? Well, that explains a lot."

Bertha headed into the house with her cans of diced tomatoes and package of ground beef, while Wallace picked up an old bike thrown in the scraggly flowerbed by the gate. Good thing marigolds were hearty. Then his mother turned around. "Oh, I forgot. Would you be interested in fixing up the old Campbell place?"

"Fixing it up? I'd be there for months."

"Actually, just clean it up. Someone from Montreal is renting it."

"Imagine that."

"The son in Toronto needs someone to mow the lawn and spruce things up a bit. Donna Smith said he'd pay you."

"When are they coming?"

"That, I don't know. I can ask Donna or get Ethel to listen in on her." Bertha shook her head. "Imagine having nothing else to do all day but eavesdrop."

Her kids Ruth and John were over for goulash that night. Ruth was picking up helpful Ruby and her sister Polly, John was fetching asthma John and Jimmy as well as his sister's Lizzie's twins, Paul and Jane, since she didn't drive. John also brought over a small metal doohickey from his boat engine that he wanted Wallace to take a look at. They stayed in the shed with the little fellas while the girls rolled out cookie dough and listened to their mothers talk their Nanna's ear off at the kitchen table.

The phone rang. One long. One short.

They knew that wasn't their ring so they ignored it. Ten minutes later it rang again. One long. Three short. Bertha jumped up.

"Wanna bet it's Ethel? That was Donna's ring earlier."

Ruth rolled her eyes as she sipped her tea. "What a surprise."

Bertha walked out of the kitchen and picked up the handle, putting her lips near the candlestick mouthpiece. "Hello?"

"Bertha? Just found out that the people from Montreal are coming next weekend."

"That so."

"Something to look forward to."

"Ethel, you never leave your yard. How is this exciting?"

Just then they heard a click and Donna got on the line. "Ethel Macdonald! How dare you listen in on my private conversations. And why are you bothering Bertha with all this? She's not remotely interested in whether someone stays at that old house. If you don't stop this nonsense, I'm going to call Tootsie and report you."

"Don't call the operator. I don't mean no harm."

"And by the way, everyone on this party line knows you listen in. Your darn budgie is always tweeting in the background. So don't think you're fooling anyone!" Donna hung up.

Bertha heard Ethel sniffing. "She's right, dear. You can't keep doing this."

"It passes the time. I don't get company anymore."

"Then why don't you take your turn hosting Institute? We never go to your place."

"Because I don't want people in my house."

"People have to actually cross the threshold in order for you to have company."

"Can't be bothered."

"Then volunteer at the country fair. Or go visit the elderly."

"I don't know any Beverly."

"Elderly!"

"I'm elderly! I'm all alone."

"No, you're not. Your sister lives with you."

"Oh, that one. She never opens her trap. Who can talk to someone who has their eyes on an easel all day? I mean, how many flowers and trees can one person paint?"

"You need a hobby, dear."

"I have one."

"You need another one."

Chapter Three

In truth, it was a great relief to get out of the city—and that lasted until she was in the middle of New Brunswick after driving along the highway and seeing nothing but trees for hours.

Kitty turned to her dog, an apricot toy poodle, moping in the front passenger seat of her Morris Minor. "I'm sorry, Pip. I had no idea just how far away this solution was."

When Gaynor called her two days after their meeting to tell her that Empire & Bloom were offering her a writer's retreat in rural Cape Breton for two months, all expenses paid, including gas and food, she was floored.

"Wow."

"I know. It was Simon's idea and Mel agreed. That's how much you mean to us, Kitty. Mel Bloom is not going to take any chances on losing you. He wants you to get your head together, enjoy this time away, and write whatever you damn well please. Create that new woman detective you were talking about. Or not! It doesn't matter. You just need to rest and think and enjoy the solitude of living in the country. I'll miss you, of course."

"No, you won't. You hate it when I barge into your office."

"You're confusing me with someone else."

Kitty laughed. "Well, thank you, Gaynor. You're a good friend, and thank Simon and Mel for me too. I think this might be just what I need."

"I'll send along the details later today."

Kurt was in their bedroom packing. What else was new. He didn't acknowledge her when she sat on the edge of the bed, so she took a good long look at him. A chiselled face with sandy hair and blue eyes. Dimples for days. But he always looked bigger on the screen than he actually was. He was only five feet nine inches tall. The one chink in his armour.

He went back into the walk-in closet and brought out another suitcase.

"That's mine."

He put it on the bed anyway. "I need it."

"Actually, it's coming with me."

Kurt finally looked at her. "What do you mean?"

"I'm leaving you."

"Oh, good one," he said, smirking. "You should be an actress."

"I am leaving. I won't be here when you get back."

He gave her a dirty look and sat in the upholstered chair on his side of the room, crossing his legs with a dramatic sigh. "I'm fed up with these little tantrums you throw every time I have to go out of town. I'm a working actor. How long have we been married? Fourteen years? This shouldn't come as a big surprise."

"Typical of you to assume that this is about you."

"What's it about then? By all means, enlighten me."

"I'm going away for two months on a writer's retreat. Gaynor is organizing it for me."

He seemed puzzled. "Your writer's retreat is the study next door. You've done very well in there. Why change things?"

Just then the tuba madman started practicing through his open window. Kitty pointed. "That's one reason."

"Give me a break. Buy some earplugs."

"And here I was hoping you'd be happy for me and wish me well on this little adventure."

Kurt leaned back into the chair. "You always make me into the bad guy. If you're determined to go, then go. I'm just surprised you feel the need. You obviously have a winning strategy going on. Seven novels in ten years would seem to suggest that."

"I cannot write one more Harry Gunn book."

"Nonsense."

She sighed and rubbed her forehead. "Would you like to play the same character over and over again for ten years?"

When he didn't say anything, she continued. "You're gone a lot, Kurt. And even when you're here, you're not here. You party non-stop."

"I always ask you to come with me but you never want to. It's part of the job. It keeps my profile up to be seen in the right places with the right people."

"When was the last time we had a date? A dinner and a movie? Just the two of us?"

"I can't remember. Yikes." He got out of the chair, put the suitcase on the floor, and crawled on his hands and knees across to her side of the bed. He reached out and put his arm around her. She put her head on his shoulder.

"Two months. Where exactly are you going?"

"Cape Breton Island, Nova Scotia."

"Sounds remote."

"That's the idea."

"And boring. How much is this going to cost?"

"Nothing. Empire and Bloom are picking up the tab. That's how much they don't want me to leave."

"Did you threaten them?"

"I told Gaynor I didn't want to write anymore and that frightened her."

They listened to tuba man go through what was presumably his scale. That's when the opera singer started practicing the "Queen of the Night" aria from Mozart's *The Magic Flute*.

"Want some earplugs?" she asked him.

"Christ. How about a pistol?" He kissed her nose and got up to start packing again. Kitty leaned on her elbow and rested her head on her hand as she watched him.

"The break will do us good," she said.

"Speak for yourself. I'll starve to death."

"Hardly. You're going for six weeks. I'll be gone for eight. You won't waste away in two weeks. Not with your mother still alive and in this city."

"You better explain it to her. The idea of a wife leaving her husband is not something her generation understands."

"And yet she's always so happy for you when you swan off to movie sets endlessly."

"That's different, my love. I'm her only child, and a male at that, and a movie star. There is nothing I can't get away with."

Kitty rolled over and stared at the ceiling. "I think you truly believe that."

⋇

Whereas Kurt called his mother to bid farewell and said he'd see her in six weeks, Kitty actually drove over to Milton Park. Not that she'd get extra credit, since it was only a four-minute car ride, but at least she was delivering her news in person.

The house was a Victorian greystone duplex, with black wrought-iron stairs leading up to the wide, green front door. A solid and sturdy place. Martha kept it very tidy, if unimaginative.

Kitty rang the doorbell. She would never barge in. When Martha opened the door, she looked surprised. She was a round, short women with a beautiful complexion. Not a wrinkle on her. If Kitty were closer to her, she'd ask the name of the face cream she used.

"Oh, you brought the dog. Wipe its feet on the mat."

"She has no dirt on her paws. I carried her from the car."

As Martha moved down the hallway to the kitchen she looked back. "Why are you here?"

"Nice to see you too, Martha."

"No need to get your back up. I didn't expect you, that's all. You never called." She sat at the kitchen table, so Kitty sat down too, Pip in her lap. She looked around. The kitchen never changed. Still the same faded wallpaper featuring endless flower vases and tea sets. The lace curtains had been hanging around forever and there was no pattern left on the tiled floor. Martha had scrubbed it off years ago.

Kitty had promised herself she wouldn't start talking first. She wanted to see how long it took Martha to say something.

A good thirty seconds. "Would you like a cup of coffee?"

Martha knew she didn't drink coffee.

"No, thank you."

"Kurt is in New York, I hear."

"Yes. Six weeks of filming, as far as I know."

"He's very popular. You're a lucky woman he's so famous."

"Well-known in certain circles, yes."

Martha gave her a smug grin. "Still jealous, I see."

Kitty turned her head to gaze out the kitchen window.

"He married so young. Just eighteen."

"As was I."

Martha leaned forward. "Let him go. Let him marry someone young and she can have his children."

"How many times are we going to have this conversation, Martha?"

"A woman who can't have a baby shouldn't expect her husband to suffer."

Kitty took a deep breath. She never learned. Always hoping for something to change. "I told him to go, but he hasn't. If he really wanted kids, he'd have them by now. Stop blaming me. It's getting old."

Martha folded her arms across her chest. "I see the way you look at each other. There's nothing there, so why insist on staying together?"

"Habit?"

"Frech."

Sighing, Kitty looked down at Pip for moral support. "How's my father?"

"The same."

Martha was her dad's housekeeper. She arrived soon after her mother died, when her father realized he couldn't cope with a seven-year-old alone. Martha happened to have a son, Kurt. It was an odd arrangement. They lived downstairs. It got complicated when Kitty and Kurt became close in high school, more out of loneliness than anything else. They decided to elope rather than live in the same house, divided only by a set of stairs. When they moved out, Kitty assumed Martha would too. But that didn't happen.

That's how naïve she was.

"I tried to call him at work, but they said he was in Quebec City for a few days. I want you to tell him that I'm going away for two months."

"You're not! What did Kurt say to that?"

"'See ya later.'"

Martha rose from her chair and stalked to the kitchen sink. "Do you take nothing seriously? No wonder you don't have a marriage. You treat it like a joke."

"This is the first time I've ever gone away. If we don't have a marriage, it's because Kurt loves being an actor more than a husband."

"My boy has to make a living, like every man. And yet you resent that. You are a spoiled brat and always have been."

Kitty stood as well. "Tell my father I'll send him the details of where I'll be in case he remembers he has a daughter."

"You blame your father for everything!"

Kitty took a step forward and pointed at Martha. "No! I blame you! He actually loved me once upon a time, but you have poisoned our relationship for no reason. I'm not a threat to you. You can live here until you die. I don't care. I'm not after this house or his money. But the man I used to love? I'd like him back."

She banged the door of her childhood home on the way out.

⁂

It took Kitty three days of driving to finally come to the brand-new Cape Breton Canso Causeway. It seemed to be a very big deal. It had only been open for seven days. She kept hearing about it on the radio as she motored along, so she honked the horn as she cruised underneath its ironwork, before she stopped at a gas station in Port Hawkesbury to fill up, grab a bar of chocolate and a Coke, and let Pip out to do her business. According to the map, she'd arrive around suppertime if all went well. Hopefully she wouldn't have any trouble finding the place.

Twice on the trip she'd almost turned around and headed back. All her problems were still in the car with her, and after talking Pip's ear off for three days, she was no closer to solving anything. She'd told Gaynor she wanted to get away to think. But she couldn't think. A numbness had descended a long time ago. That's why she hated writing Harry Gunn novels. She could write them in her sleep. She was asleep. Somewhere deep down, she knew she needed to wake up.

And as she drove the last few hours to her destination, the spectacular view of the vibrant green rolling hills, navy-blue water, rugged coastline, and cirrus clouds did lift her spirits. Even Pip raised her nose and sniffed the air blowing in the window.

"You can smell the ocean, Pippy. You've never seen the ocean." That's when Kitty realized she'd never seen it either. A very depressing thought.

She was bone tired when she turned from the Louisbourg Highway onto Horne's Road. It wasn't paved. That couldn't be good. It seemed endless until she turned left at the stop sign. Mira Bay was in front of her, the water shimmering in the August sun. It was beautiful, but she didn't dare stop. Farther along there was a sign for Round Island, and according to her map the next community was Homeville, where South Head Road was located. She eventually found it, and the directions Gaynor gave her said the house was a few miles down this gravel road. The owner had said he'd arranged for someone to tie a red cloth to a tree on the right-hand side that would indicate the house a little farther in. When Gaynor had said this was remote, she wasn't kidding. Kitty wanted quiet, but not drop-off-the-face-of-the-earth quiet. For the first time in her life, she realized that if she was in trouble, not a soul would hear her. The optimism brought on by the gorgeous scenery faded quickly. That, and the fact that she'd never driven on dirt roads before, made her feel like she was in another world and out of her depth.

Luckily, she hadn't gone very far down the road before she saw a white house on the left, with a big chimney at the front. It had a rock wall around a large yard. There was a car, but no one seemed to be around. At least that meant people lived there. Maybe they'd hear her scream.

Densely packed spruce and fir trees interspersed with white birch and alders seemed to go on forever, but they would be difficult to walk through with so many bare, dead branches close to the ground. The broken, fallen trees were strewn around like pick-up sticks. She drove over a small bridge with stretches of water and marshy land on either side and came to a flatter section that looked quite barren. But the road was very hilly in spots. There were a few laneways with no sign of anyone. This was too remote. And then she saw another house, but it was on the left. A small painted sign was hammered into a fir tree at the end of their driveway. *Bailey*. The house was white also, bigger than the last one, and it looked like a hundred people lived there, judging by the sheds, barn, garden, fence, clothes on the line, bikes, toys, truck and front loader in the yard. At that moment she wanted to turn in. It was welcoming, despite the chaos.

It had to be soon, surely. She was becoming very nervous, and then just around the corner there was the red cloth. "We're here, Pippy!" She turned into the short laneway and drove up to the house.

Pip picked up on her enthusiasm and danced circles on the seat before she put her paws up to the window and looked out.

Kitty looked out too, her hands still on the steering wheel. This was it?

She started to laugh. A retreat? She'd driven a thousand miles to park in front of a small, weathered, unpainted, shingled dwelling. Basically, a rectangle with a door in the middle and two paned windows on either side, with a stoop that ran along the front. Now, if someone had put flower boxes under the windows and painted the door a bright yellow or blue, and had a stone walkway leading up to it, it wouldn't be so bad, but it had none of those things.

It was obvious that recently, by the look and the smell, someone had had a heck of a time mowing the mighty long grass surrounding the place. When was the last time someone had lived here? Why hadn't she asked for more details? Did Gaynor even know?

Then it occurred to her that she didn't have a key. If she were a character in her own novel, she'd be disgusted.

Once out of the car she had a good long stretch. Pip seemed overwhelmed by the grass. Her little nose was twitching and she smelled ten things all at once. This was no city sidewalk. When she looked up at Kitty there was excitement in her eyes. That made all the difference. Someone liked this place already.

Kitty grabbed what she could and made her way up the stairs to the front door. "Please be unlocked. There can't possibly be anything worth stealing in here."

She was lucky. The door opened into a small kitchen. It smelled clean. Someone at least knew she was arriving, and that loosened the tightness in her chest. It also helped that there was a ceramic pitcher with wildflowers in the middle of a small round oak table, with a note, *Welcome*, and a key beside it. Also, a plate of something under a tea towel.

Kitty put her belongings on a white wooden chair, leaned over to smell the fragrant flowers, and peeked under the tea towel. Molasses cookies. She took a big bite. "So good!" She broke off a piece for Pip and ate two more as she walked around.

There was a counter along part of the back wall. A flowered piece of cloth hung from a rod under the farmhouse sink to hide what was underneath, with open shelves flanking the window above. She loved this look, and always hated the closed kitchen cupboards of her apartment. Just a blank boring space, but here you saw the plates, bowls, glasses, and mugs. She laughed at the size of the rounded fridge. Hopefully she'd get something in it. A narrow door was ajar beside it. She peeked in and there was a pokey pantry with more open shelves and a wooden counter that ran along three sides of the space. There was a cut piece of linoleum that served as a baking surface. Under that were mixing bowls, frying pans, pots, and cookie sheets. The shelves above held tin canisters for flour and sugar and the like. There were even some canned goods. She wasn't touching those.

Beyond the kitchen was a living room with a boxy, shallow fireplace. Whoever lived here loved flowers, but the wallpaper was old, stained, and faded to the colour of dried mud. There was a worn ladder leading to an open loft up above. It was too dark to see what was up there. The floral wallpaper in the bedroom had fared better, and the pattern was pretty. The white wrought-iron headboard indicated a three-quarter bed at best, a painted bureau and chair on one side, but there was an itty-bitty dressing table under the far window that was rather charming. A small bathroom with a pull chain for the light completed the quick perusal.

Why had she laughed when she first saw this place? Because she'd imagined something much more elaborate, but this was what she needed. When was the last time she'd felt cozy?

She was on her last trip out to the car, reaching into the trunk with Pip by her side, when she heard someone clear their throat and lots of giggling. She whipped around in a panic and then really panicked.

Behind her was the world's largest Viking and two enormous black dogs. He also appeared to be followed by a gaggle of children. Pip yipped and jumped into her arms.

The red-haired giant held out his hands. "I'm so sorry. We didn't mean to frighten you. Just wanted to welcome you to the neighbourhood. We saw an unfamiliar car drive by and knew you were expected soon. I'm Wallace Bailey, and these are a few monkeys I found in the ditch. I live only a little way back up the road. If you ever need anything, feel free to ask. If I'm not home, my mother is."

"Why...th-thank you. I'm sorry..."

"No need to apologize. We must be a frightening sight."

"Not at all. But those dogs are so big."

"Argus and Pride are Newfoundland dogs. Brilliant, loyal, lazy slobs. They'd never bother with..." He pointed to her pet.

"Oh, this is Pip."

"Well, Pip might not have anything to fear from these two galoots, but she'd make a mighty tasty morsel for our local coyotes and eagles. I wouldn't let her wander around the yard by herself."

"Oh, thank you. That's good to know."

They looked at each other, and it seemed like he was waiting for her to say something. That's when she remembered she hadn't introduced herself. "Oh, I'm Kitty Wagner."

"Nice to meet you," Wallace said. "You and your family are from Montreal, I hear."

"My husband isn't here. Just me."

This good-hearted Wallace looked momentarily alarmed. She knew he wasn't expecting that. But really, how many people would fit in this space?

"By the way, when was the last time someone lived here?"

"That would be a year ago. Old man Campbell. He was a nice fella."

"A bachelor?"

"Oh, no. He and his wife and four kids lived here."

"Six people in this house?!"

"Sure. You really only sleep and eat inside. The rest of the day you're out in the sunshine."

"It must never rain here."

"Oh, it does. That's when you'd get wet."

The kids started tittering again. "Time to get these little ones home. Do you need any more help with your luggage?"

"No, no, I'm fine. Thank you anyway."

"My mother wondered if you'd like to come to supper tomorrow night. Five sharp. She always says sharp. No idea why."

"That would be very kind. Would you mind if I brought Pip along? She'll be afraid to be alone in a new place."

"That goes without saying. Tomorrow, then."

And off the Pied Piper sauntered with his kids, his dogs, and she had to look twice, but she thought she saw a couple of chickens by the road.

She went back in the little house, and made sure the screen door was locked with the small hook to prevent Pip from venturing outside, but she seemed content to sit by it and drink in all the heavenly smells.

When Kitty was fiddling with a few boxes in the main room, Pip began to bark. Oh dear. Maybe a coyote was outside. Kitty picked up a broom she saw in the corner and approached the kitchen door. A scrawny, elderly woman with sharp features was on the other side of the screen, looking leery of the dog.

And Kitty had been worried there would be no one to hear her scream. People were crawling out of the woodwork.

"Yes? Hello?"

"Oh good! You speak English. Being from Montreal and that, I thought maybe you were French."

"Umm...does everyone here know where I'm from?"

"Oh, yes, dear. You're big news. I brought you something."

Kitty released the hook and opened the door. "Don't worry about Pip. She won't hurt you. I'm Kitty."

The lady came through and dumped her shopping bag on the table. "Titty? That's a funny name."

"Kitty!"

"Oh, Kitty. That makes more sense. I'm Ethel. I live in the first house on this road, and when I saw that there baby blue car go by, I knew it had to be the city folk. No one around here would have that odd colour."

"I see. Well, it's nice of you to drop by. I'm just trying to unpack."

"Whatcha doin' in this neck of the woods, anyway? Some kind of retreat, I hear?"

"I'm sorry, but I don't see how that's relevant."

"Just curious, that's all. Look, I brought you something." She pointed at the bag, so Kitty had no choice but to open it. Inside were half a dozen fluffy tea biscuits and a jar of delicious-looking marmalade. Then she realized that some of the marmalade was missing.

"Well, thank you, Ethel. That's very kind. I appreciate it."

"Oh, no trouble. Just being neighbourly. Where's your husband?"

"He's not with me."

"Not with you? You came here alone?"

"I'm not alone. I have the dog."

"That little hairball? That's not going to protect you if a bear happens by."

"A bear?!"

"It could happen. I saw one once. That's why I don't go out of the yard. Fools who walk up and down this roadway are just asking for trouble."

"Ethel, thank you for the tea biscuits and marmalade, but I really have to unpack before it gets dark."

Ethel tsked and turned around to flip on the light switch. "We do have electricity, you know. It was our Homeville Women's Institute who convinced the Nova Scotia Power Commission to change their mind after they told us we couldn't get electricity in South Head and Waddens Cove because of the Rural Electrification Act. We didn't have the required number of houses per mile. Well, that didn't sit right with us, and it took a while but we made it happen. Amazing what a group of country women can do when we put our minds to it."

"That's very impressive. Thank you for telling me. I'm sure we'll meet again." Kitty took a few steps towards the woman to give her the hint that she needed to leave. Ethel took a step backward and then pointed at the other room. "If you need to call me, I'm one long two short."

"Excuse me?"

"The telephone. We're on a party line. If you want to call me, you crank the handle one long ring and then two short ones. I'll pick up. You do know how a party line works, don't ya?"

"I've never used one, but I have a basic idea."

"You'll hear everyone's ring on this line."

"Everyone's? Even in the middle of the night?"

"No, child. Everyone's asleep then. The only time someone would call at night is if it was a real emergency, and luckily, we don't get many of those."

"What is my ring?"

"One long four short. I'll go home and call you, and if it doesn't go through, I'll tell Tootsie. She's the operator, but they probably didn't bother taking the line down."

"All right. Thanks again." This time Kitty pushed past her and opened the door. Pip took the opportunity to scurry outside.

"Oh no!" Kitty hurried down the steps, Ethel chasing her. "Pippy! Come here this instant!"

"That little rat might get caught in a trap! You have to be more careful."

Kitty grabbed Pip, and in her heightened state turned on the woman. "I'll thank you not to call my little dog a rat. Now goodbye."

She marched past Ethel and stomped up the stairs, closing not only the screen door but the inside door as well. Kitty watched her from the window, still standing in the yard. What on earth was wrong with that woman? It looked like she was coming back up the stairs but thought the better of it. Good thing. Kitty had no intention of opening the door.

She kissed Pippy's head. "What have I done? You're in mortal danger here. You're going to have to stay on a leash, Pip. If anything happened to you..."

Kitty went back to unpacking her suitcase when a sudden shrill noise made her jump. One long ring and four short. Oh damn. Ethel. She didn't want to answer, but Ethel seemed the sort who would keep ringing until she picked up.

"H-hello?"

"Kitty, it's Ethel. Turns out the line is still open, so you can use the phone."

"Thank you for letting me know."

"We're friends now. I'll be over tomorrow to—"

"NO! I'm sorry, I'm busy tomorrow. I have to go to the nearest town and get stocked up on essential items. Goodnight."

She put the mouthpiece back in the cradle and shuddered. The phone started ringing again. Oh no.

Fortunately, it was one long three short.

Chapter Four

It wasn't so much Dolly Wadden's plumbing that needed fixing but her marriage, as far as Wallace could tell. Not that he was interested, but while he replaced her sink and vanity for a more up-to-date model and installed the new toilet over a three-day period, she sat on a stool in the hallway to keep him company, and didn't have one nice thing to say about her poor husband. It was irritating. He was sorry he'd agreed to this project and needed it to be over and done with. He'd said as much to his mother the night before.

"I'm determined to finish it tomorrow. She's wasting her money anyway. There was nothing wrong with that sink or toilet."

"Of course there wasn't. She changes the fixtures in that house like she changes her outfits. That's what women do when they're unhappy."

He took the cover off the dented pot of turkey soup and gave it an appreciative sniff. "You must be the happiest woman alive."

"It's shameful to get rid of something that's still working."

Wallace thought about his mother's words when Dolly pointed at the old sink and surround. "That can go in the yard with the toilet. Larry will take it to the dump. It's about time he did something around here."

"I'm going to the dump myself after I finish here. I don't mind dropping it off."

"Well, that's very kind, Wallace. It's hard for me to understand why a nice man like yourself hasn't been snatched up by some pretty girl? Why, if I was five years younger..." She winked at him.

If you were five years younger, you'd still be ten years older than I am. He couldn't understand women like Dolly. His female compass was his mother. The thought of her chatting up some young man while he did a job for her was so ludicrous, he couldn't wrap his head around it. He was done with this lady.

"That should do it. I'll take this downstairs and be on my way." He grabbed the entire unit and walked out the bathroom door. Dolly had to scramble to get out of the way. "I'll get you a cheque. Meet me in the kitchen."

He went out into the yard and placed the sink and vanity in the back of his truck. Then he lifted the toilet in as well, wiping his hands on an old rag as he walked back into the house. She tore the cheque from her chequebook on the kitchen table and stood there, holding it out. He had to approach her, since she didn't move.

"I hope this is enough."

Wallace glanced at it. "Very generous, Mrs. Wadden. Thank you."

"For the last time, Wallace, it's Dolly." Then she threw up her arms and jumped on him, reaching for his mouth. He was so startled, she had time to plant a big kiss on his lips before he was able to push her away.

"Mrs.—"

"Kiss me back," she whispered. "Don't you get lonely, Wallace?"

"No ma'am, I don't."

"Ma'am? *Ma'am?!*"

"I'm sorry, I have to go."

He left her sputtering in the kitchen as he hurried to the truck and reversed out of the driveway like a shot. He vowed to be more careful with the jobs he selected, because drama was something he avoided. It reminded him of his father.

Wallace didn't go to the dump. He dropped off the sink and toilet to Skipper, an old fella on the outskirts of the village he knew could use it. Skipper insisted on taking a handful of onions out of his garden to give him as payment. Wallace thanked him and said his mother would appreciate it.

❦

Kitty opened her eyes. Pip licked her face and whined. Where was she? She rolled over in the lumpy bed and groaned. She hurt everywhere. Not only that, she was damp and cold. The sun was shining through the window but it felt like an icebox in this small bedroom. That's when she realized the curtains were blowing but the window wasn't open.

She gave a big sigh. "What fresh hell is this?"

Pip let her know she had to get up as quickly as possible. Kitty couldn't find her bathrobe, so she threw an old sweater over her flannel pajama set, grabbed Pip's leash hanging by the kitchen door, and took her outside.

It was so much warmer out here. How was that even possible?

Kitty kept an eye out for all manner of wildlife. She herself would've loved to see a rabbit or a deer, but she was now spooked about anything with fur or feathers. Pip kept sniffing and dragged her along to the side of the road. She wasn't going to go any further when she realized there was a vehicle barrelling up behind her. *Damn!* She tried to hide in the bushes until it went by, but it didn't. It stopped dead.

Two men in a truck wearing grungy ballcaps gave her a wave. "Hey now! You must be with the bunch from Montreal."

Kitty was acutely aware she wasn't wearing a bra, so she kept her arms across her chest and nodded. It didn't seem to register with them that she had her pajamas on.

"Goin' be a large day! The water's flat calm. Afraid you missed lobster season, but if you go down to the wharf in Morien, someone will toss you a fish or two."

She had to ask. "Is Morien far?"

"No, my dear. Fifteen minutes, maybe more depending on the potholes. At the top of this road, turn right and keep going until you get there."

"Are there shops?"

They both laughed. "Well, my love, it would be sad day if a village had no store. Have a good one!" And off they went.

So far in the last twenty-four hours she'd talked to more people here than she usually did in a month in crowded Montreal. So much for solitude.

After giving Pip her breakfast, Kitty sat at the kitchen table and ate two delicious tea biscuits with heavenly marmalade. Maybe Ethel wasn't a complete disaster. She made a list of things she needed at the store. That's when she noticed something she hadn't the night before. Was that a wood cook stove? She walked over to it and lifted one of the circular lids with the iron handle. Inside the narrow, blackened space were wood halves, sticks, paper, kindling, and twigs, all ready to go. She noticed the box of wooden matches and a bucket of chopped wood beside it. If she wanted to cook something, she'd have to keep this fire going.

"Wonderful! Thanks, Gaynor. A city girl completely helpless and at the mercy of a wood stove. I'll burn this drafty shack down trying to boil water."

And as soon as she said it, a wee part of her writer brain fired, in spite of herself.

A completely useless city girl finds herself in the country and hilarity ensues. It could be a comedy. That's what she needed after ten years of killing everyone in sight: a lighthearted story about a spoiled rich girl whose father has cut her off. She leaves in a huff and finds herself marooned in some backwater and everything goes wrong. There could be a whole range of characters. Ethel was perfect.

And then she lost it. It drained away. A stupid story that had already been done to death. And who was she kidding? She hadn't laughed in a very long time; wouldn't know funny if it hit her in the face.

She'd worry about the ridiculous stove later. Pip followed her into the tiny bathroom. Something else had just dawned on her.

There was no shower in here. An old claw-foot tub, but that was it. As she didn't normally soak in a bath, this sent her blood pressure soaring. She was so quick to jump at Gaynor's foolish suggestion that she never demanded the details. The woman said "retreat" and a modern country inn sprang to mind. She had come here on blind faith. The fact of the matter was, she was oblivious, and it was no one's fault but her own.

But that didn't mean she wasn't going to call Gaynor the first chance she got.

When she turned on both taps of the tub and rusty water came out, she shrieked, startling poor Pip. She sat on the edge of the tub and waited to see if it cleared. It did eventually, but it wasn't very hot. Nevertheless, she put in the plug and gathered about an inch or two at the bottom before grabbing a wash cloth and soap. She got in but didn't sit down. Just a hurried splashing around before it got too chilly to continue. Fortunately, she'd brought her own towels, but she had to remove Pip from the one she'd thrown on the mat beside the tub. "Sorry, baby, Mama needs this more that you at the moment."

As she brushed her teeth, Kitty looked at her reflection in the small oval mirror above the sink. She traced the dark circles under her eyes. She'd never noticed them before. Maybe because there was natural light coming through the bathroom window. There was no window in her bathroom at home. She looked worn down. Worn out.

This was exactly how she always felt inside. It came as a complete shock to see it manifested on her face. When she couldn't look anymore, she put her hair up in a ponytail, got dressed, and did a little more unpacking to stop from brooding.

That's when she remembered she had to call people to tell them she'd arrived. How did this dratted phone work? How did you get the operator? There was no other solution than to call Ethel. She said she was one long crank of this handle and two short. Ethel picked up after only one ring, so she must have been right by the phone.

"Hello?"

"Ethel, it's Kitty."

"Titty? OH, Kitty. Well, this a nice surprise. I was wondering if—"

"Ethel, how do you get the operator on this phone? I need to make some long-distance calls."

"Just crank the phone once and the operator will answer."

"Thank you."

"If you need—"

"Thanks again, I have to go." After placing the phone firmly in its cradle, Kitty took a small address book out of her purse. She'd written down the New York number Kurt left for her. Time to see if she could make this work. She cranked. What a great word.

"Operator," a pleasant voice said.

"Hello. I'd like to make some long-distance phones calls, please. I imagine I'll have to reverse the charges, is that correct? Fine. I'll call New York first, and when I finish, do I ring you back and ask for the next one? Yes, I'm at the old Campbell place. Oh, you knew that. I'm not sure how this works. Here's the number. Tell them it's Kitty Wagner calling. Thank you."

It was a few minutes before the operator came back on the line. "You're connected. Go ahead, please."

"Kurt? I mean, Robert?"

A female voice said, "I'm sorry, Mr. Chandler is busy. May I take a message?"

"And you are?"

"I work with the movie studio."

"When will Robert be available? This is his wife."

"That's hard to say. He's busy on set and the days can be very long."

"I know how it works. Could you please tell him I arrived

safely and I'll let him know what the number is as soon as I figure it out?"

"You don't know your phone number?"

"It's one long and four short, as it happens. I just don't know how to translate it so the rest of the civilized world can understand. Tell him to call me."

"He can't, remember? You don't know your number."

"Never mind!" She banged the ear piece back on the cradle. Was everything this difficult outside of an urban area?

By the time the operator connected Gaynor, she knew her number was Morien 10-14. She'd send her father a postcard with the number and see if he called her. She had no intention of wasting time talking to Martha. She probably wouldn't give him the message.

"You're connected. Go ahead, please."

"Gaynor?"

"Well, hallelujah! I was afraid you'd driven into the Atlantic. How long did it take to get there?"

"Three days of driving, and then guess what?"

"What?"

"I found myself in front of a rustic shed from the set of *Gunsmoke*. The wind blows in through the closed windows. There's a stove that needs burning wood before I can cook an egg. There is no shower and the water dribbles rust before it turns lukewarm at best. The bed is a lumpy old thing, there are predators ready to eat my dog, and people who seem to know my personal business. You can tell Mel Bloom thanks for nothing. This generous gift must have cost him all of twenty bucks for the whole two months."

"Dear God! That's terrible! I didn't know. I'm so sorry! Why don't you find yourself a nice hotel nearby and book yourself in there until we can find something decent?"

"A nice hotel nearby? Fat chance."

"Kitty, I'm so sorry. I didn't want this to add to your stress."

Kitty could tell Gaynor was very upset, and that made her pause. "Look, it's not a complete disaster. It is snug, despite the gaps in the walls, but it wasn't what I expected and I'm anxious about this cooker and it would help if the water had more pressure. I don't like baths at the best of times, but two-inch baths are even worse."

"Ain't that a bite! Find somewhere else to stay. You pick this time. I don't want you to be disappointed, although Simon said the Keltic Lodge was nice. We should've sent you there in the first place."

"I've already unpacked a lot of stuff and I'm about to go grocery shopping and I've been invited out to dinner. I did have homemade cookies on the table when I got here and someone came over with tea biscuits and marmalade."

There was a pause before Gaynor said, "So, not an outright catastrophe?"

"I suppose not."

"Look, feel free to go somewhere else or stay where you are. Just let me know. Any ideas brewing yet?"

"Hardly, unless I decide a manual on building fires might be popular. I better go to the village. Some guy in a truck said they'd throw a fish at me if I went to the wharf."

"Excuse me? What kind of place is this?"

"I'll let you know. Talk later."

As she and Pip headed out the door to the car, the phone rang. She held her breath, knowing she had cut Ethel off abruptly, but it wasn't for her.

The men in the truck were correct. She turned right at the top of the road and drove until she got to a fishing village. *This must be it*. There was the wharf. Was this the actual ocean? How did one get down to it? She pulled in front of what looked like a store. There was something hanging by a piece of twine at the side of the door. She couldn't make out what it was. Holding Pip in her arms, she approached warily. *Good lord!* Two dead rabbits. She wanted to see a rabbit hopping around like Thumper. She closed her eyes, opened the door, and heard a bell tinkle. There was an older man behind the counter sitting on a stool, smoking.

"How do."

Kitty nodded. "Hello. Did you know there are dead rabbits out here?"

"Yes, girlie. They'll be someone's dinner before too long."

"Oh. Right."

"Just so you know, people from around here don't bring their dogs into a store. You can tie it up outside."

"Oh. I'm sorry. It's just that she's very nervous and I've been told that bears eat little dogs."

This caused the old fella to laugh so much he started to cough. He wiped his eyes. "Oh my. Now in all my years sitting here, I have yet to see a bear walk by. And if it did, those rabbits would be long gone."

"I suppose I could put her back in the car, but she's new around here and will probably yip non-stop. If I keep her in my arms and off the floor, would that be all right? I do need a lot of things."

"Oh, go on, then. I haven't laughed that hard in ages."

She couldn't see any wire baskets, so as Kitty went around the store bringing back the items to place on the counter in front of the man, he tallied up the total on a small receipt pad. Several people came in and out, all of them giving her an odd look when they realized she was holding a dog, but nodding and smiling when she caught their eye.

At some point she was going to have to deal with that stove, so she'd better have something to cook on it. He wrapped up individual packages of bacon, a chicken breast, two pork chops, and a couple of pieces of cod. That should do her for a week, which made her realize she wasn't going to a nice hotel, despite growling to Gaynor. That reminded her. She nodded at the shelves behind the counter. "May I have two packs of du Maurier, please? And a bottle of aspirin?"

The accommodating store owner helped her out to the car with three boxes of groceries.

"You've been very kind. Thank you." She held out two quarters.

He shook his head. "No need, my girl. Just doing my job. How long do you plan on being here?"

"Who's to say? It depends on my mastery of the blasted kitchen appliances."

He gave a quick snort of laughter before disappearing into the store. She put the money back in her pocket.

⟶❧⟵

Wallace arrived mid-afternoon and dumped an armful of onions in a crate by the front porch as Bertha came in from the clothesline.

"Those are fine specimens."

"Yep. A gift from a grateful recipient of someone else's trash."

She gave him a sideways glance. "Good for you. You finished at Dolly's?"

"Don't mention that woman's name."

Argus and Pride came bounding from behind the house to greet him when they heard his voice. He ruffled the fur between their ears and walked off with them. His mother shook her head as she entered the kitchen, where her daughter Jean was peeling carrots while Jean's girls, Barbara and Linda, dusted furniture for Nanna, since company was coming for supper.

"It's not very often I see Wallace upset," Bertha said, "so God only knows what Dolly Wadden was up to this afternoon."

"It doesn't take a genius to figure it out. The woman is pathetic."

"Don't be unkind, Jean. The woman is unhappy in her marriage. It doesn't excuse her, but some people aren't as fortunate as we are."

Jean, who was the spitting image of her mother, turned at the sink. "Mom, you didn't have a completely happy marriage either, but you never went around throwing yourself at men."

"That's because I was bone-weary chasing you brats around all day. Dolly doesn't have anything to distract her."

"Nonsense. She's in every production from here to Sydney Mines. You're just too polite to say she's a floozy."

"What's a floozy, Mom?" Linda was in the doorway with a cloth in her hand.

"Never you mind, missy. Go upstairs and give the bureaus a dust too."

"That lady from Montreal isn't going up there, is she?" Linda whined.

"Do as you're told."

Linda stomped her foot and left. Jean and Bertha exchanged grins.

"I hated dusting too," Jean said. "Almost as much as I hate peeling vegetables."

"I remember. You used to stick your tongue out, but you'd run too fast for me to give you a swat."

Bertha opened the oven door to check her roast, sticking a fork in it to see how tender it was. The blast of heat brought a flush to her face. "I hope this woman likes pot roast."

Ethel had called Bertha that morning. "It's about this Kitty."

"You already called me last night to tell me you met her."

"And I told you she was a bit cranky."

Bertha knew how cranky people could get around Ethel, so didn't put much stock in it. "Yes."

"Well, so far she hates everything about this place! The house, windows, the wood stove, her bed, the fact that there's no shower, the low water pressure, the outdoors, and her nosy neighbours. Can you believe that?"

Bertha sighed. "Did she tell you this to your face?"

There was a long silence.

"If this poor soul expected something different, which considering that property is more than likely, and she was pouring her heart out to a friend, do you think it was a charitable thing to listen in on her private conversation and now report it back to me?"

More silence.

"Ethel, for the last time, if you can't stop listening in, then please do not repeat what you hear on other people's phone calls. It makes me guilty by association and I don't condone this behaviour. I don't want to feel awkward sitting across from her at dinner tonight."

"You invited her to dinner? You never invite me to dinner."

"That's not true."

"Not often."

"I have to go."

"I think her husband is a movie star!"

"Goodbye, Ethel."

⯌

At five sharp Kitty pulled into the Baileys' yard. Her hair was brushed with her waves behind her ears. They probably weren't a dinner-party crowd, so she wore plaid trousers with a wide belt and a white shirt upturned at the collar. Her red sweater was draped over her shoulders. Fingers crossed she wasn't underdressed. Pip was under one arm, and she held a box of chocolates in the other. One of only two left in the general store.

Wallace emerged from the front porch with another gaggle of children, but they seemed a bit older. How many kids did this man have? The giant dogs ambled over to sniff Pip, whose tail thumped rapidly, much to Kitty's amazement.

"Hello!" Wallace waved. "Had no trouble finding the place, then?"

She quickly realized he was pulling her leg. "It was a breeze."

He grinned. "Please come in, if you can get through this mob."

Five children rushed in ahead of her as Wallace held the door open. She stepped through the porch into the kitchen. A very pretty older woman stood by her cooktop. Her younger double was at the sink. A much smaller Wallace with blond hair was already seated at the table.

Wallace introduced her. "Everyone, this is Kitty Wagner. Kitty, this is my mother, Bertha, my sister Jean, and my brother Charlie. And here are some pirates who washed up on shore this morning."

"Hello, everyone." Kitty held out the chocolates. "Mrs. Bailey, thank you so much for inviting me. You already have so many mouths to feed."

Bertha took them. "Nonsense. There's hardly anyone here."

"Will I get to meet your wife, Wallace?"

Everyone laughed when a little boy shouted, "Walrus don't have no wife!"

"Walrus?" Kitty looked around. "But all these children? And the ones with you last night?"

"I have thirty nieces and nephews. And eleven greats, as I call them."

Her shocked expression brought on more giggling. "I never knew anyone with thirty grandchildren and eleven great-grandchildren. I know a woman who would be positively green with envy."

"I'm very lucky," Bertha said.

Linda approached Kitty. "Would you mind if I played with your dog?"

"Sure. Just don't let her outside. I don't want a bear to eat her."

This caused more laughing. Kitty made a face. "I'm starting to think that Ethel steered me wrong when she cautioned me about bears roaming up and down this area."

"Technically, you can never say they aren't, but the likelihood is small," Wallace informed her. "Bears can be found in the highlands. They don't like to be around people."

"And yet you have two black bears just outside your kitchen door begging to get in." She pointed to Argus and Pride.

"Pathetic, isn't it?"

All of them eventually sat at the kitchen table and polished off a magnificent pot roast with gravy, roasted potatoes, carrots, turnips, onions, and parsnips. There were also baskets of tea biscuits and fresh homemade rolls. When Kitty took a bite of the tea biscuit, she was amazed.

"Is everyone around here a fabulous baker? These are exactly like the tea biscuits Ethel brought over, along with her divine marmalade."

Jean looked puzzled. "I thought you said she didn't bake anymore, Mom? If that's the case, stop with the constant care packages. You have your hands full."

Bertha wiped her mouth with a napkin. "I'm sure she bakes from time to time."

"I should've said earlier how much I enjoyed those molasses cookies, Mrs. Bailey. It was such a treat to walk in after a very long drive and see that plate of goodies."

"I'm glad you enjoyed them." She winked at Wallace. They were his cookies.

As Bertha and Jean put bowls of freshly cut up strawberries and cream in front of everyone, Kitty reached down to pet Pip's head by her chair, but she wasn't there. She swivelled around to see Pip lying on the floor with her nose against the screen door, tail still wagging as Pride and Argus stared mournfully at her from the outside.

"After dinner, I'll let the dogs in and we can see how they get along," Wallace said. Kitty nodded.

"So how was your first night at the old Campbell place?" Charlie asked while wiping a drippy strawberry off his son's shirt. "Everyone around here was mighty surprised when his son was able to rent it. Not the first place you'd think of for a holiday destination."

Kitty sipped her tea. Should she say something? She didn't want to come across as some pampered princess. "Um, it was a bit unexpected. I didn't make the arrangements myself, which in hindsight was foolish on my part. It's a little drafty and damp. There's not much pressure in the water and it's not hot. But my biggest worry is the old stove. I've never used one before and I'm afraid to start a fire in it. I might burn the place down."

"I'll come over and show you how to use it," Wallace offered. "I'll check the water and make sure the oil heater is working, too. I'm sorry, I should've thought of that when I was over mowing."

"Thank you. I'd appreciate it."

Jean folded her elbows on the table. "Do you have family connections in this part of Cape Breton? Most tourists head to Baddeck or Ingonish. Not many of them find their way to South Head."

"No, I don't. I've never been here. But the scenery is spectacular, the food is amazing, and the neighbours are lovely. Ethel's quite a character, isn't she?"

Her dinner companions exchanged glances and smiled, but said nothing. Kitty's first impression was correct.

"And it amazes me that everyone knows I'm from Montreal."

"That happens in a small place, dear," Bertha said. "Once someone hears something new, it's repeated constantly, not to be malicious. It just passes the time for some folk."

Jean's daughter Barbara had her mouth full when she asked, "Do you have kids?"

Jean gave her an annoyed look. "Barbara! You don't ask adults questions like that. It's not your place."

Barbara looked at her lap. "Sorry."

As ever, Kitty's heart gave a little tug. "That's okay. No. I don't have any children."

"That's too bad. You're so pretty."

"Thank you." Kitty smiled. "You're very pretty too. You look like your mother and grandmother."

Barbara broke out in a grin.

Kitty felt a sudden wave of weariness sweep over her. She touched her forehead to ease the dizziness.

"Are you all right, dear?" Bertha asked.

"Yes. I'm a little tired."

Bertha got up from the table and walked around to Kitty's chair. She took her sweater off the back of it and held it out for her. "You look worn out, my love. We shouldn't have kept you talking for so long. Now, you go get a good night's sleep and Wallace will be over in the morning to sort out the stove and everything else."

Kitty stood and put her arms in her sweater like a little kid. "Thank you, Mrs. Bailey."

"Call me Bertha." Bertha squeezed Kitty's upper arms before letting her go. "Now, shoo!"

Kitty waved to everyone and they wished her goodnight. She picked up Pip, and Wallace held the door open for her. Poor Argus and Pride rushed in thinking they were going to finally get a good sniff of the little dog, but she was on the way to the car. Kitty started the engine and was backing out when she spotted Wallace coming towards her. She rolled down the window.

"Here's a flashlight, in case you need it. You don't want to stumble up those old crooked stairs at dusk."

"Thank you, Walrus."

He gave her a big grin.

The flashlight was handy. It was different coming up to the place in the evening. The woods looked darker and more mysterious. She kept it on while Pip sniffed around the yard, looking for the perfect spot to water the grass. It hadn't occurred to her to bring a flashlight. She would definitely buy one tomorrow and return this one to Wallace.

When the two of them finally crawled into the lumpy bed, Kitty was wearing her bathrobe over her pajamas and a pair of socks on her feet, and she pulled the wool blanket she kept in the car on top of her.

"You know what, Pip? There are still good people in this world. I'd forgotten that."

Chapter Five

To Kitty's utter astonishment, she had a great sleep. It had to be the pure country air that was knocking her out, even with this bumpy bed. She looked at her wristwatch on the side table. It was nine in the morning. That's when she remembered Wallace said he'd come by. *Oh dear.* She hustled Pip out the door and stood in the dewy grass keeping watch. Another lovely morning, but there were grey skies on the horizon. She must get a radio. It would be helpful to know the forecast. At that moment she heard a strange thumping in the woods.

"What was that?"

Pip raised her head and stared into the trees.

"Yikes! Let's get out of here!" Kitty raced up the stairs with Pip on her heels and she locked the screen door behind them. She fed Pip and automatically filled the kettle to make tea. Putting it on the cold stove reminded her it would have to wait for Wallace.

Then she hurried into the bathroom and put up with the lukewarm trickle of water to wash her face. Anything else would have to wait for Wallace.

Since eggs and bacon were a no-go until he arrived, she poured herself a bowl of Special K with milk and sliced a banana on top. As she ate, she marvelled at the silence. No radio, no television, no traffic, no sirens, no tuba, no *Magic Flute*, no footsteps above her head or voices in the hallway. Only the wind rustling the leaves on the trees, twittering birds, and the far-off roar of the ocean. She could get used to this.

As she gulped the last of the milk out of the bowl, a shadow filled the entire screen door. Wallace knocked quietly.

"Good morning!" Kitty jumped up to let him in.

He had to bend down so as not to bump his head against the door jamb. "Good day." He looked even more enormous in this small space. She looked behind him. "No kids? Dogs? Pip will be disappointed."

He smiled shyly. "Didn't think you needed the aggravation."

Without the kids and dogs, it felt like a part of him was missing. "Just so you know, I love both. I'm grateful that you're here so early."

"I was here at seven."

"You were?"

"Silly, I know. When you get up before five, seven seems mid-morning."

"I'm surprised Pip didn't hear you knock."

"I didn't knock. I couldn't hear anything, so I went home. That's when Mom told me to show up at a civilized hour."

"I'm ready for my lesson. I don't want to be known as someone who doesn't know how to boil water."

It was complicated. She tried to keep up with the words: *cooktop, open damper, flue, chimney, kindling, wood halves, ash box, under air.*

"When you clean out the ash box, your hands will get dirty. Sooty. There will be smoke when you open the lids. You aren't doing anything wrong if that happens. You might want to wear an apron or an old shirt when you first start. You don't want to ruin your lovely clothes."

He immediately blushed. She'd never seen a man do that before. He quickly cleared his throat. "I'll go check the water," and he disappeared outside. Why he had to go outside, she didn't know. She stood by the stove and looked down at Pip, who had spent the entire time stuck to Wallace's side.

"He thinks my clothes are lovely." Robert said her clothes were a bore and nagged her to wear something sexy. That was his only criteria. Which was enough to keep her away from exactly that.

She wanted to impress Wallace, so she struck a wooden match

and leaned in to light the crinkled newspaper shoved amongst the kindling. She replaced the lid with the iron handle and waited. For what, she didn't know, but just in case, she put the kettle on the cooktop to see if it worked.

By the time Wallace reappeared in the kitchen, she had two mugs of tea on the table and had put in more wood.

"I'm delighted! A roaring success!" She clapped her hands and pointed at the mugs.

Wallace looked at the stove and cocked his ear. "It's roaring, all right. Did you put more wood in this?"

Her blip of euphoria vanished. "Was that wrong?"

"A tad premature." He reached up to show her. "I'm shutting the flue and the vents on the side to prevent air from getting in. That feeds a fire. We'll have to wait for this to calm down. When you start a fire, you have to build it slowly. A slow burn as opposed to a bonfire right off the bat."

"Sorry. I wanted to surprise you. When the kettle boiled, I felt victorious."

"No harm done. That's how you learn." Wallace walked over to the sink and turned on the taps. The water gushed out, to the point it splashed up and got him wet. "Oops! Slight adjustment."

Out the door he went. Kitty turned off the taps, and when he reappeared and tried them again, they were better.

"Why do you keep going outside?"

"I'm going down in the cellar from the outside access. The water tank is down there. The water was rusty because it hasn't been used in a while, but I turned up the thermostat so the water will be hotter. And out here in the living room is the space heater. Once you know how to use this and the wood stove, you'll be warm despite the drafts. This place needs fixing up, obviously. Mr. Campbell let things go because he was elderly, and his kids lived away. It happens."

"Well, you've solved my issues, so please sit and have your tea. You've earned it."

"Much obliged."

"Will you stay with me until that beast is no longer breathing fire?"

"I'll stay until you put in another log so you can see what it should look like. Don't be afraid. You won't burn this place down. That stove has seen a lot of cooking in its time."

"Thank you for not making me feel foolish."

"You've never done this before. It will be old hat by the time you leave here."

Pip pawed at Wallace's overalls. He patted his thigh and she jumped up and settled in.

Kitty almost did a double-take before she broke into a big smile.

"She's never done that with anyone but me."

"No?"

"My husband steers clear of her."

Wallace put his big hand on Pip's head. "He's missing out."

Kitty held the mug up to her face. She watched him gaze at the dog. Neither of them spoke. Then she remembered.

"There was a really strange noise in the woods this morning. It was like a fast-thumping sound."

He nodded. "That would be a male ruffed grouse. Looks like a partridge. He beats his wings to attract a female in the spring and marks his territory closer to the fall. It's called drumming." He looked out the window, as if hoping to catch sight of one. "I love that sound. People think they aren't very smart, but I don't agree. Every animal has their own life to live."

She pointed at the door. "Speaking of living their own lives."

Wallace turned around and there were Argus and Pride behind the screen, big pink tongues hanging out.

"They must have been bugging Mom. I shut them in when I left."

"Let them come in. Look at Pip's tail wagging."

Kitty was not prepared for the sight of two giant dogs standing in the kitchen while Pippy zoomed around and underneath the table and chairs, too quick for either of them. They followed her with their massive heads and she led them on a merry chase without them moving an inch. Wallace slapped his knee with delight.

Kitty hadn't laughed this hard in years. She wiped tears from her eyes. "Oh, my. This will tucker her out. Look how excited she is. I've never seen her this joyful. Most days she sits under my desk, no doubt bored out of her mind."

Wallace swallowed his tea. "Your desk? You must be a teacher, although I don't suppose teachers bring their pets to school."

She hesitated.

"I'm sorry, it's none of my business."

"That's okay. I write. Fiction."

"Wonderful! I love to read."

"What sorts of books?"

"Mostly texts on philosophy, the natural world, or astronomy. I want to understand everything around me. It's such a privilege to be alive."

He was bursting with life, with curiosity and wonder. Everything she lacked. "I can't imagine being as happy as Pip."

"Animals live in the moment. We can learn a lot from them. I don't generally take to people who dislike other species. I don't trust them."

"I'm a kitty and you're a walrus."

"We're good then." They laughed together.

"I shouldn't keep you, Wallace. I'm sure you have plenty to do."

"Not much, as it happens. Going to take a quick trip into Glace Bay to pick up some things for Mom and take a run to the hardware store."

"Oh! That's where I have to go. I need a flashlight and a radio."

"I'd be happy to give you the directions, or if you'd like, you can tag along with me and I can show you where these stores are, so you can get the lay of the land."

She smiled at him. "Do you always make things so easy?"

"It's not hard."

He showed her how to use the oil heater so she could turn it on later, then had her bank the fire. He said it would probably last until he brought her home. He'd check it again then. Kitty grabbed her purse, and a rain jacket, as the clouds were getting greyer by the minute. She went to put Pip on the leash, but Wallace shook his head.

"She's not going to get into any trouble with Argus and Pride walking beside her."

So, the two of them strolled along the gravel road, the dogs running around with their noses to the ground.

"As soon as I get home, I'm going to get another little dog so Pip can have a friend to play with. How selfish to keep her alone in an apartment."

Wallace pulled up a long stalk of grass growing at the side of the road and chewed the end of it. "I've never been to Montreal. Do you live downtown?"

"Almost. It's a beautiful city, but like all cities, noisy and dirty. The complete opposite of this. Do you think you'll ever travel up that way?"

"I tend to stick close to home, but if I were to travel, I should do it in the next ten years, because once mom is in her eighties, she'll need me more than ever."

"You do have nine siblings."

"That's true, but they have families to tend to. My mother loves her home and I'll make sure she can stay in it for the rest of her life."

"You don't plan on ever settling down? Having a family of your own?"

"I'm as settled as I'm ever going to be and my family is already bursting at the seams."

"You are so fortunate."

"I'm very aware of that."

Bertha was in the kitchen wearing her floury apron when they piled in. She was in the middle of making bread and rolls with another daughter, who looked exactly like her daughter Jean. "I was beginning to wonder where you'd got to. Good morning, Kitty. This is Helen."

"Hello, Helen."

"Good to meet you, Kitty."

"Feeling better today?" Bertha asked.

"Much better, thank you."

Just then three little boys ran in from outside, one of them holding a plastic shortening container. "Walrus! Guess what? We found two snakes!"

Kitty's immediate reaction was alarm, but no one else thought it was a problem. They looked in the container, which was filled with grass. Wallace nodded. "Very good for these two little grass snakes. And what do we do when we're finished looking at them?"

"We put them back where we found them."

"Excellent. You'll make biologists yet."

They ran back out the door.

"Mom, Kitty and I are going to town. She wants to buy a radio and a flashlight and I said I'd show her Glace Bay so she can figure out where she's going next time."

"Great idea. The list is on the table, but bring me three boxes of lard instead of two. And I need more dish soap." Bertha went back to her dough.

"Need anything, Helen?"

"A new man."

"You say that every time."

"So stop asking."

"See you later."

Kitty picked up Pip. "Is it okay if she comes?"

"Sure."

The two of them waved and walked to the truck together. Wallace held the door open for her.

-⟡-

Bertha and Helen, their hands full of dough, ran to the kitchen window to watch in amazement.

"Well, I'll be."

"I'm seein' things." Helen whispered. "There is no way that boy would take a female stranger to a hardware store."

"He's not a boy, remember."

"That's how I think of him. He still lives with his mom. When was the last time you saw him open a truck door for a woman?"

"Last time he took Ethel home."

"They kind of look good together."

"She's married."

"Oh."

-⟡-

The embers were still burning when Wallace brought Kitty home and he watched her put more wood in the stove before he left. He also replenished her supply. She thanked him very much for helping her out before bidding him goodnight. Then she fried a piece of fish and had boiled potatoes with tinned peas for supper.

After spending the day laughing and chatting with Wallace, this place was suddenly much too quiet and so empty. She turned on the new radio and spent five minutes trying to tune into a local channel. Then she sat in the faded and worn red velour chesterfield and was almost swallowed up in the soft cushions. The springs had died long ago. She placed her mug of tea on the high, thick armrest with a claw-shaped wooden insert. There was a brass stand with a round glass ashtray at the perfect height just in front her, so she lit a cigarette while country music played in the background. Pip was out cold on the matching armchair.

She thought about her life in Montreal, and it seemed to be in black and white with shades of grey. Muted. Suddenly she was here, and everything about it was in blazing colour. The red-hot flames of the stove, the grey-blue of the waves in Morien, the kids in their colourful shirts, Bertha's towels on the line, the deep green of the fir and spruce trees.

If she ever did write again, this was the kind of place to write about. These were the people who should populate her book. Everywhere they went today, Wallace ran into someone he knew. How were they all connected? Everyone seemed to belong to everyone else. She needed to find out more about it. Become involved in the community. Just keep looking around and absorb it like a sponge. The thought of writing about another murder was unappealing. She'd pickled herself in death and sadness. No more dark night of the soul in the soulless city. The image that kept playing in her head was of Wallace coming to greet her with his kids and dogs and chickens.

She needed to surround herself with life, because hers was passing her by. She was a married woman who never saw her husband. When had that become okay with her? *Uh-oh*. She was a married woman who'd forgotten to call her husband back with her phone number.

When Kurt got on the phone, he seemed very jolly. "Great, you arrived? How was the trip?"

"I got here three days ago. Didn't you get my message?"

"What message?"

"I asked the woman who picked up the phone at the studio to tell you I got here in one piece."

"No one said anything to me."

"That's just great."

"Oh wait? Something about someone not knowing their phone number. Was that you?"

"Here I'm thinking you'd be frantic not hearing from me."

"You're a cool customer, Kitty. I knew you'd be all right."

She would, but it would be comforting to know that someone might worry if she never called again. "How's the movie going?"

"Oh, a complete ball up. The director quit in a snit and then changed his mind. We've gone through two script editors already. People keep waffling about the sets. The usual malarkey."

"What's your role?"

"A priest having a crisis of faith."

"That's a stretch."

"It's called acting, darling. Oops, have to run. Everyone's coming through the door. We're going for cocktails. Speak soon."

"Don't you want my phone number?"

"Oh, right."

When she hung up, the awful malaise that was so familiar washed over her. She was sorry she'd called him. After such a pleasant day, it was like a sour taste in her mouth. Kitty decided to have a bath, since that was her only option. She needed to unwind. Her fingers were crossed as she ran the water. Full blast, hot, non-rusty. As she eased herself into the heavenly water and leaned back against the lovely curved porcelain watching the steam rise, she decided she was a nitwit for never liking baths. But then, she'd never been in this kind of tub. Something else she should fix, but that would mean moving out of the apartment.

And require energy she didn't have.

It was only 8:00 P.M. as she crawled in bed. And 8:05 when she crawled out, thanks to the phone. She stubbed her toe on the way to pick it up.

"Hello?"

"Hello, Mrs. Wagner? This is Donna Smith. My husband's cousin is the man you rented the house from. He lives in Toronto, so we seem to be his go-between. We heard you arrived from Bertha and Ethel, and I tried to call you today, but you were out gallivanting with Wallace, I hear. No better tour guide. Just wanted you to know if you need anything, you can always call us. We're one long one short."

"Thank you, Donna. Can I just ask, is everyone on this

particular line one long? I'm sensing a pattern here. And if I find someone who is two long, do I call the operator to get her to connect me?"

"Yes, that's exactly how it works. There are about ten people on this line, and we can call each other directly without the operator. Of course, human nature being what it is, you always get someone who talks too much, so if you try and get through and they've been on for a while it's perfectly fine to ask them to move it along. Or you always have someone who listens in...isn't that right, Ethel?"

There was a quiet click on the other end. "This is what I wanted to warn you about," Donna said. "Ethel Macdonald listens in on phone calls, so if you have a big secret, do not talk about it on the phone."

"I'm grateful to you, Donna. Thanks for letting me know."

"I also wanted to invite you to a tea and sale we're having at the United Church next Saturday. It's always a good way to meet some of your neighbours, if you're going to be here for a while. But feel free to ignore it too. No pressure."

Kitty liked this woman, even if she had gotten her out of bed. "That sounds nice, actually."

"Just tag along with Bertha. She'll be baking for it. Everyone always wants Bertha's offerings."

"I don't bake often, but should I try and make something? I'm still getting the hang of this stove."

"No need. We always have plenty of goodies. You can stock up."

They heard someone pick up their line.

"That's my cue to cut this short. Once again, welcome to Cape Breton."

"Thank you. Goodnight."

As she snuggled back to bed, she rubbed Pippy's head. "An elderly Nosy Parker who listens in on people's phone calls. What if she gets the wrong end of the stick about something and creates complete havoc in a small town? A fictional epic disaster. But a spoof. I'm tired of real disasters. So tired."

That's as far as she got before her eyes closed.

-❀❀-

When her eyes opened, she realized why she dreamt about being on Noah's Ark all night. There were four steady drips from the ceiling landing on her bed. She reached for Pip and her fur was damp. She put her hand on the blanket. Damp. She touched her hair. Damp.

"What on earth? How long have I slept through this?"

There was a huge crack of thunder, as if God was trying to tell her. Then lightning lit up the room, with an accompanying crack. She and Pip jumped and scrambled out of the wet bed. Once she had on her bathrobe and slippers, she pulled the bed away from the drips, which hardly left any space to open a bureau drawer. She ripped off the blankets and sheets and knew she needed to dry everything as best she could. Which meant making a fire, not turning on a dryer. She balled everything up and was on the way to the kitchen when she spied another drip in the middle of the living room. "Okay, this is ridiculous. The entire roof must be leaking."

Pip scratched at the door to be let out. "Why didn't I bring an umbrella?!"

She stood in the pouring rain with her rain jacket like a tent over her head. Pippy wasn't making it easy, as she insisted on sniffing around even as it pelted down. "Hurry up, you foolish creature."

Pip gave her a filthy look, and that made Kitty smile. "Are you telling me you're wet anyway? Okay, I'll be quiet." But another rumble of thunder shortly after that sent them up the stairs in a hurry.

Once back inside, Pip shook all over her and the floor. "Oh well, what difference does it make?" she said to no one. Then she gathered pots and containers to collect the drips, which were multiplying like mushrooms. There was no way she was going to call Wallace for help. Not yet, anyway. She got the fire going, put on some clothes, and hung the sheets and blankets all over the kitchen, waiting for the warmth to do its job.

She washed down toast and peanut butter with a cup of hot cocoa as she tallied the drip locations. Now that she looked like she was in control, it was time to call Wallace, because this storm was not letting up, and the more water that accumulated, the worse it would be for all concerned.

Bertha answered.

"Hi, Bertha. It's Kitty."

"Hello, dear. Fine morning, what? No clothes on the line today!"

"It's actually raining inside my cabin. The roof is leaking everywhere. Would Wallace be around? He should probably take a look at this. I could call Donna. She got in touch last night, but seeing as how the owner is in Toronto, there isn't much he can do."

"That's awful! I'll send him right over. And then you and Pip come here for the day. You can't sightsee in this weather and you can't sit in that place catching your death. Gather your things, he'll be there in a jiffy."

As she hung up the phone, Kitty wondered how she'd ever managed life without the Baileys.

Wallace arrived two minutes later. He took in the sheets and blankets draped over the table and counters. "Grab this stuff. We'll dry it at our house. Let's see how bad this is."

They walked through the space. "The worst is in the bedroom," she told him.

"Right. The wind is howling from that direction, that's why. Noticed a few shingles in the yard. We'll empty the containers and put them down again. I'll get a tarp on this roof when the wind dies down a little and once I'm up there I can assess the damage."

"This man in Toronto had no business renting this place. I don't mind rustic, but this is a shame. Fixing his roof shouldn't be your problem. I can always go somewhere else."

"No need! It's no trouble at all. It's not that difficult to repair a roof this size. They're steady drips, but still only drips. If it was cascading in, then you'd have a problem."

The three of them ran to the truck and drove back to his place. The thunder and lightning weren't letting up. Pip hid under her coat. "This reminds me of storms at home."

"We always walk on the shore after a gale. You never know what's washed up."

"I need to get into the ocean. I've never been."

"Now that's a darn shame."

Bertha, Argus, and Pride were happy to see them.

"No kiddies today?"

"Not usually this early, and my crowd know it's a little harder for me to have them underfoot when they can't play outside because of the weather. No doubt we'll see a few before the day is out. Their parents are gearing up for the start of the school year, anyway. I'm going to miss the older ones something awful when they go back. Now sit yourself down by the fire and Wallace will bring us a cup of hot tea. And how about some of those tasty macaroons fresh out of the oven last night?"

It felt very strange to sit there while Wallace delivered the mugs of tea and cookies and then puttered in the kitchen hanging up sheets and blankets over drying racks. When he brought out a plate of zucchini loaf, she whispered to him, "Are you sure I can't help?"

"You are by just sitting here. That way Mom will put her feet up while she entertains you."

"What are you two muttering about?"

Wallace reached over by the chesterfield and took a soft tapestry bag with a wooden handle off the floor. "Here, Mom. Drink your tea and knit."

"You're some bossy, now." Bertha furrowed her brow at Kitty. "Always tellin' me what to do."

All three dogs followed Wallace out to the kitchen. Bertha took a big gulp of tea and popped a macaroon in her mouth. "Nothing like dessert for breakfast. Try one."

Kitty reached over and took one herself. "These are fantastic. I don't know how you do it."

Bertha leaned over. "Not mine." She pointed at the kitchen.

Kitty made a face and mouthed, "Wallace?"

His mother nodded and put her finger up to her lips. Then she took out a big ball of blue wool with two knitting needles sticking out of it and unfolded a half a sweater. "I must finish this for poor Benji. He's two months old already. Benjamin James George Bailey. His name is longer than he is. Our Georgie's wife is a sweet little thing, but with three kiddies under three, she's a bit overwhelmed at the moment."

"I can imagine. What I can't imagine is you raising ten children. How on earth did you do it?"

"You depend on the older ones to help out after a while. That's why all the kids say their sisters Mary and Annie are tyrants. They are more like mothers than sisters to them. Helen as well, but she has a sweeter nature. Do you have siblings?"

Kitty shook her head.

"Well, it's not the size that makes a family. I'm sure your parents are as proud as punch."

"My mom died when I was seven. In childbirth. My brother died too. His name was Benjamin."

Bertha dropped her knitting in her lap. "Oh, my sweet girl. That's so unbearably sad."

"My father never got over it."

"Of course he didn't. Thank God he had you."

Kitty reached over for a slice of loaf and took a big bite so she didn't have to respond.

"I lost three babies. Miscarriages. My mother always said it was God's way. That there must have been something wrong and it was nature's way of dealing with it. She was probably right, but it didn't feel like it at the time."

"I was always afraid to have a baby." (Why was it so easy to talk to this woman?)

"Is it any wonder?"

"Turned out I couldn't anyway."

Kitty drank her tea and Bertha picked up her knitting. "Well, dear heart, there are lots of ways to bring children into your life. They don't have to be yours to love them. Just ask Wallace."

"He's so good with them."

"Oh my, yes. He's a mother hen. You can be too. Just find a youngster who looks like they could use some affection and give it away. No sense keeping it to yourself."

"I knew a little girl who needed that."

"What happened to her?"

"She still needs it."

Chapter Six

Kitty spent that week purposely staying away from the Baileys. She didn't want to wear out her welcome, and she felt her own neediness when she was around them. Her problems were her own to sort out, and as much as she would've loved to crawl into Bertha's lap and suck her thumb, she needed space.

Of course, Wallace fixed her roof. He even battened down more shingles to the outside of her bedroom window to stop the draft. When she offered him money, he looked insulted, so she'd never do that again. Something else to scribble down about the way things worked in the country. No one seemed to want tips. They were being neighbourly.

In the spirit of doing things for herself, she went to the hardware store and bought a length of rope, clothespins, a galvanized wash pail, and a scrub board. She tied the rope between two maple trees and she and Pip rooted around for a good half hour before finding the perfect clothes prop in amongst the leaves and debris on the ground. She even fashioned a V-shaped notch at the top, ruining a perfectly good breadknife in the process. That would take care of drying bigger items like sheets and towels, blouses and slacks. She also bought a clothes rack like Bertha had, to put in front of the oil stove. The idea of Ethel mentioning her unmentionables swaying in the breeze made it a necessity.

After that bit of housekeeping she made day trips with Pip to see the sights. She found her way to the fortress in Louisburg and to St. Anns and Baddeck. She didn't realize how far it was. It made for a long day. People told her about the Cabot Trail, and maybe at some point she would get there, but that was definitely an overnight trip, so she was content to putter around the towns of Glace Bay and Dominion, and to drive along the coast to Donkin and Long Beach on her way back home. She sat with sandwiches at the sand bar and marvelled at the eagles and herons, ducks and seagulls, and then went to Mira Gut and looked out over Mira Bay while wading in the water for hours, picking up rocks, shells, and sea glass, even pieces of driftwood that caught her eye. She did swim a little, but it was chilly. She was aware she was by herself, so she stayed close to the beach. Pippy would get anxious and yip if she went too far, but otherwise her little dog was in absolute heaven. She leapt on the curls of waves as they broke on shore, and chased small sandpipers across the sand. Or picked up pieces of dry seaweed and shook them senseless. More than once they nodded off while lying on the Cape Breton tartan wool blanket she bought at the Gaelic College in St. Anns. There was nothing more delicious than smelling the salt air and hearing the gulls circle overhead. Or reading for hours in the lovely September sunshine.

She called Gaynor.

"I've been here for almost two weeks and I can't imagine ever coming home. How crazy is that? Even after the roof leaked."

"The roof leaked? This adventure belongs in a book, I hope you realize."

"Exactly."

"What about that woman detective? Is she still skulking around?"

"No, I've had it with—wait...would it be funny to have a detective who didn't want to be a detective? Someone who reluctantly has to solve a case? A case that doesn't really exist?"

"What do you mean?"

"I have no idea. I'm just pitching things around."

"The fact that you're pitching is brilliant!"

"Don't get excited. I haven't even unpacked my Underwood."

"But you sound so much better. You must like it there."

"It's beautiful. But I could do without the hanging dead rabbits."

"Hanging dead rabbits? Tossing fish? I hope they make it into the script!"

"Don't jinx this, Gaynor."

"My mouth is already shut. Goodbye." And she hung up.

It was later that same day, a foggy, drizzly afternoon, that Kitty made sure the fire was going and sat at the oak table so she could hear the wood crackling in the stove. Pip was in her now favourite spot, a hooked rug in front of the oven door. There were no water leaks, which was good news. She was supposed to be making a list of things she needed in the big metropolis of Sydney, but she kept doodling chickens and dogs instead.

There was a sudden rapping at the door, which gave her a start.

"Kitty! You in there?"

Who on earth?

She opened the door to find Ethel the Benedictine monk with a rain hood so large you could hardly see her face. "What are you doing out on a day like this? You'll get a chill. Come in quick."

Pip opened one sleepy eye and at the sight of Ethel tore off into the next room.

"I was just passing and thought you might like some company. Bertha told me to visit the elderly, or was it Beverly?"

"Probably Beverly, since I'm not exactly elderly. Let me hang up your...coat."

Ethel took it off and shook it before handing it over. Now the floor and their clothes were dappled with moisture.

Something else to store away for the story.

She couldn't believe that thought crossed her mind. And that she was looking forward to talking to Ethel one on one, so she set about making her a cup of tea.

Ethel sat at the table and passed her a rather damp paper bag. "Brought you something."

"You're too kind." She opened it up to find four macaroons, and the light bulb finally went on. "These look delicious, Ethel. You must enjoy baking."

"No, I hate raking. Don't see the point."

Kitty leaned closer as she poured the milk in their teacups. "You must enjoy baking!"

"Oh yes. I bake all the time. My husband, God rest his soul, couldn't get enough."

"I'm sorry you lost him."

"Don't be. I'd had enough of that man."

Kitty hid her smile behind her cup of tea and offered Ethel a macaroon. She waved it away.

"I'm not like those widows who cry crocodile tears when their man dies. The ones who bellyache about them all their lives, but the minute their husbands are six feet under they wail about how they were saints. Everyone knows the truth."

"I suppose in a small community they would."

"That's why I admire Bertha. She had a hard time with that Donald, but you'd never know it from her. And now that he's gone, she keeps just as quiet. Her business is her own."

"She's such a lovely person. I can't imagine her with someone who wasn't just as nice."

"Donald was nice and charming and very good looking, but he started drinking more than he should and had a nasty temper when that happened. Like a lot of drinkers."

"And then you get the drinkers who stay quiet and withdraw. Funny how that works."

"Who's that now?"

"No one. Just saying. So, do you like living here, Ethel?"

"Not really. People can be very judgmental. Do one thing wrong and they never forget. Like they're so perfect."

Kitty nodded to encourage her to keep talking.

"And they talk about you behind your back. Need to know all your business. People like that give me gas. But then you have people like Bertha, so it's not all bad. And that Walrus. Now there's a good lad. Always willing to help. I can't for the life of me figure out why he wasn't snapped up long ago. The girls who used to call when he first got home, you wouldn't believe. Eventually, they stopped embarrassing themselves."

"It seems to me he likes his life just the way it is. *Content* is the first word I think of when I see him."

"Nice for some. Now, tell me about Montreal. What's it like being a housewife in the big city?"

"The same as here. You know, cooking, cleaning."

"Do you have kids?"

"No."

"That's odd. Why not?"

"That's my business, Ethel."

"What does your husband do?"

"He works in an office."

Ethel nodded knowingly, as if she didn't believe her. That's when she remembered Donna's warning. She had to assume that all her conversations thus far were now in Ethel's memory bank. *Drat.* She tried to remember what she'd said to whom.

"And what do you do in your spare time if you don't have children to take care of? Life of luxury, I imagine."

That annoyed her. "I'm a writer."

"What kind of writer?"

"Um...a gossip column for a local newspaper."

"Really? How exciting!" Ethel's eyes lit up and she grabbed a macaroon and took a bite. "Tell me more!"

"There's nothing to it, really. I hear about what goes on around town and then I tell our subscribers about it. It's about keeping your ears open. Anyone can do it."

"And you get *paid*?!"

"Every two weeks."

"Imagine that. I think I have to move to Montreal."

Kitty laughed. "Your neighbours would miss you, Ethel."

She waved her hand in disgust. "No, they wouldn't. Not that Donna Smith. I wish she'd mind her own business. She's making life difficult for me."

"How so?"

"She just thinks she knows everything. Very bossy. Telling me what to do all the time."

"That must be rough."

"Tough? Oh, you have no idea. She's an old boot, just like her mother."

⁂

Wallace saw Ethel coming through the rain first. His sisters Mary and Annie were over for a visit with four of their grandchildren, as many as they could fit in the car.

"Ethel's here," he said. "She looks like the grim reaper with that coat on."

Bertha put the meatloaf on the table, while Mary doled out the mashed potatoes. "What is that poor soul doing, wandering around in weather like this?"

Ethel opened the door and hollered. "Anyone home?"

"Come in, dear. Pull up a chair. Can you stay for supper?"

"Well, that's not why I came over, but if you're asking, don't mind if I do. Here, Wallace." She took off her coat, shook it over the dogs, and passed it to him. He hung it up in the porch.

They gave her a plate with a thick slice of meatloaf, fluffy potatoes, peas, and carrots. "Oh, this looks delicious. Thank you." She took one small bite and dropped her fork. "So, I have news."

Wallace made sure not to make eye contact with his mother or sisters, just stared at his plate as he buttered his vegetables.

"And what's that, dear?" his mother replied.

"I just spent the whole afternoon with Kitty."

This made his head pop up.

"How is she?" Bertha asked. "We haven't seen her this week. She said she'd be sightseeing."

"No sense going anywhere today with the fog. She wouldn't see much, so I took a chance and sure enough, she was home. I told her I was just passing, but of course I don't usually go any farther than your place. She didn't know the difference, what with not being from here."

"Well, we won't tell her, will we, Mom?" Mary said before putting a forkful in her mouth.

Annie was busy trying to stop her grandsons from flinging peas at each other. "Your secret is safe with us."

"You'll never believe it. She's a writer!"

Wallace was mildly surprised that Kitty had told Ethel, perhaps because she'd seemed hesitant to tell him.

"She's a gossip columnist for a local paper!"

Okay. Now this made sense. He grinned at his meatloaf. But his mother and sisters didn't know the difference. Wallace kept what Kitty had told him to himself.

"Can you imagine being paid for that?" Ethel looked amazed.

Mary pointed her fork at her. "Perfect job for you."

Bertha gave her daughter a look, but she needn't have worried. It went right over Ethel's head. "Oh no. I can't write. I even hate writing Christmas cards. I never know what to say."

"A gossip columnist is the last thing I thought she'd be," Bertha said. "She doesn't strike me as the type."

"Did you happen to notice if there were any leaks while you were there?" Wallace piped up.

"Not that I could see. Do you know she doesn't have any children? Wouldn't say why."

Mary stared at her. "Ethel, that's very private. Why would she tell you?"

"No harm in it. I asked about her husband too, and she said he works in an office, but rumour has it he's an actor in New York. Or maybe he's a priest."

"A priest?! I doubt that," Bertha said, laughing.

"Odd that he didn't come with her. Maybe he's busy at church."

One of the little greats on his left tapped Wallace on the arm. "Walrus? Walrus?"

"Yes, bud?"

"What's a pries?"

"A priest is someone who kneels and prays, just like you do when you say your prayers at bedtime."

"I says God bless Ma and Da, but not my brudder."

"Try to include him next time."

Ethel took one more tiny bite and her fork clattered to the plate again. "And you're not going to believe this. She might be wanted by the police."

Everyone stopped what they were doing, including the kids.

Wallace cleared his throat. "I'm sure you're mistaken, Ethel."

"Then why is there a detective skulking around?"

"A detective?"

"And I almost forgot. Kitty said she was so excited to be here she forgot to unpack her underwear!"

❧❦

After Ethel left, Kitty sat in her saggy davenport and lit a cigarette. She wasn't thinking about anything in particular, but when she took the last drag and stubbed it out, she went straight into the bedroom and lifted her Underwood typewriter out from under the bed.

She took it to the kitchen table, and removed it from the case. She loved the teal blue colour with the grey keys, and this Universal 1955 model had a particularly satisfying clicking noise. Something she learned was important after writing seven novels. When you bang away at a typewriter for long enough, the sound it makes has to be pleasing to the ear.

It wasn't necessary to put paper in it just yet. It was enough that she even wanted to look at it. This little machine was a source of great comfort and even greater frustration. She had once thrown a typewriter across the room. Not her proudest moment.

Did she want this to sit here if she wasn't going to use it? Part of her did, because it felt like home. It was literally her best friend. On the other hand, all she could think of was Harry Gunn, and the whole point of leaving Montreal was to get away from him.

She tapped her fingers on the table while she mulled it over. And then the phone rang. She jumped every time it happened and always forgot that it might not be for her. But this time it was.

"Hello?"

"Catriona?"

"Dad?"

"Where are you?"

"You know where I am. You called me, so that means you got my letter and my information."

"A better question, why are you there? And why so long? You never even told me you were going."

"I tried, Dad. I called you at the office and you were in Quebec City, so I went over and told Martha before I left. Didn't she tell you?"

"It must have slipped her mind. Are you and Kurt having problems? Is that why you've left?"

"If I left every time Kurt and I had a problem, I'd never be home. This has nothing to do with him. I'm on a retreat. To try and kick-start my desire to write."

"You never told me you had writer's block."

"I never told you, Dad, because I never see you. You're always too busy."

"That's the nature of my job, as you know."

"Oh, I know. It's been ever thus."

She heard him sigh. "Look Cat, I'm sorry I'm not around, but you're a married woman with a career of your own. It's not like you're a kid."

"You weren't there when I was a kid either."

"Okay. I'm sure I deserve this. I just called to make sure you were all right. There's a big difference in knowing that at least you're in the same city if we need to see each other. But you're far from home. I do worry about you."

"Could have fooled me."

"Cat—"

"It's Kitty."

"Catriona, you sound like a petulant child."

"Martha thinks I'm a spoiled brat, so it must be true."

There was silence on the other end. She finally said, "Dad?"

Kitty thought she heard a catch in his voice. "Take care of yourself, Kitty. Let me know if you need anything."

And he hung up.

Kitty curled into the nearest chair with her arms around her knees and lowered her head. Pip jumped up and nuzzled under her chin.

Chapter Seven

That weekend Kitty offered to drive Bertha to the tea and sale at the United Church. It was Bertha who suggested they pick up Ethel on the way. "Her heart would be broken if we didn't."

Wallace put his mother's baked goods in the trunk. "This is my mother. She watches out for everyone, especially the ignored." He shut the trunk and helped her into the car. "Have fun, ladies...indoors in a church basement on a glorious afternoon."

"Thank you for babysitting Pip!"

He waved as Pip ran towards her best friends.

As they set off, Bertha turned to Kitty and grunted. "What do men know? As if you can ignore a tea and sale in this neck of the woods. Or a church supper, a strawberry festival, a penny sale, or a pancake breakfast. I mean, you could, but what kind of life would that be? Churches and organizations need to be supported, and who's going to do it if not the people in the community?"

"That's very true."

"Mind you, it's always the same people who organize these things, and they get worn out after a while. Is it any wonder? I'm not as active as I used to be, and I feel guilty about it."

"So, this support system is an integral part of how a small community works? Is this why everyone seems to know everyone else? They've worked together for years?"

"That's a big part of it, but the older generation remembers your kin, too. Ask any of the old-timers and they'll tell you who was related to who. And when you know that your neighbour's great-grandfather and your grandmother were siblings, you take more of an interest. People who come from away don't have that knowledge."

"That's the trouble with living in a big city. I don't even know my neighbours, let alone who they belong to. But then I live in an apartment building. There are wonderful communities within the city with their own social networks, I imagine."

"You need to find some. Get out of that apartment and buy a little house with a garden. I can't even imagine having to take an elevator to get to bed."

They laughed as they drove into Ethel's yard. Kitty had to stop abruptly. A black cat was daring her to play Chicken with the car. "Sorry! I hope the baking is okay back there."

"That darn cat! He's got a death wish, I swear."

"Maybe it's his only entertainment," Kitty said. "I'll go get her. You stay here."

"Thank you, dear."

The cat had the attitude of an outlaw, just about to draw his claw pistols. She skirted around him and knocked on Ethel's door. And then did it again, remembering she was a little hard of hearing. She finally opened the door. "ETHEL?"

"Who's there?"

"It's me, Kitty."

"Who?" Finally, she showed up in the kitchen. "Oh? What are you doing here?"

"Bertha and I are going to the United Church tea and sale, if you'd like to come along."

Her face lit up. "Why, thank you!" She grabbed her hat and sweater off a hook at the back of the door. "I'm ready." She turned her head and shouted, "I'm going out!"

No one answered.

"Deaf as a post, that one."

"Who?"

"My sister. She hates people. Let's go."

As they headed out, Bertha turned her head to include Ethel in the conversation. "Speaking of community, Ethel and I are members of the Homeville Women's Institute. I'm hosting the meeting later this month. You can be our guest."

"I look forward to it. Ethel mentioned the Institute the other day, saying it was instrumental in supplying power to the homes out here. But what is a Women's Institute? I've never heard of it."

"A woman named Adelaide Hoodless lost her little boy after he drank unpasteurized milk. She knew rural women needed to be educated about such things, so in 1919 she started this organization, for women, their families and communities. Knowledge is a powerful tool, especially when coupled with a woman's determination to protect and demand more for her loved ones."

"Sound impressive."

"And we have a lot of fun!" Ethel added. "It's nice to get together with the women who live around here. We're so isolated most of the time. A lot of our members don't even drive, so those who do, pick up the others or their husbands take them. Everyone takes a turn hosting the monthly meetings."

Bertha turned her head. "Except you. I wish you'd rethink that."

"My god, Bertha, remember the time we had the meeting further along South Head Road at Mary's house, and that particular night it was very rough and muddy over Grunts Hill. A whole carload of women and we had to back down and take another run before we topped the crest. I took out my dentures and told Mary that the road was so bad I lost my teeth!"

When they got to St. John's United, Ethel leapt out of the car and took off before Bertha shouted for her to come back and help bring in the sweets. All three of them had an armload. Ethel took credit for her share, telling the church women that she had baked all morning.

Kitty saw first-hand how intimate knowledge of fellow citizens worked. Bertha winked at the ladies and they smirked back. No one was fooled by Ethel's declaration and no one pointed out her delusion. It was a win-win.

Bertha introduced Kitty to the women who ran the tables, poured cups of tea, and watched over sandwich trays, and also made it her business to introduce her friends, most of whom sat at long tables enjoying a pleasant time together. If these ladies were anything like Bertha, they probably didn't get to sit and enjoy each other too often.

A pleasant lady came towards her with a smile. "Hello! I'm Donna Smith. We talked on the phone."

This was the old boot Ethel had mentioned.

They shook hands. "Nice to meet you, Donna."

"Wallace told me about the leaky roof. I'm mortified. I called Junior to tell him and he said it never leaked before, but I told him that counted for nothing and he should give you back some of your money."

"Please don't worry about it. Nothing was ruined and Wallace fixed it."

"That boy is a godsend."

Kitty couldn't help herself. "Wallace a boy? He's the biggest man I've ever seen."

Donna nodded. "You're right, but he has such a gentle way about him. However, you don't want to see him mad. I remember the year we had a parade at the fall fair, and a man riding a horse kept kicking it in the haunches to get it moving. Wallace reached up and threw the guy right out of the saddle into the dirt. Then he dropped some money on the ground and said the horse was coming home with him. The guy never said a word. He looked scared to death."

Kitty couldn't help grinning. What a great scene. She filed it away. That's when she noticed Ethel wave at her, dragging a very polished woman with her. Donna took one look and put her hand on Kitty's arm. "This is my cue to leave. I don't have the stomach for Ethel today. Lovely to meet you."

"Yes, you too."

"Kitty!" Ethel was almost out of breath. "You have to meet

Dolly Wadden. She's the councillor's wife who sings and acts in all the theatrical productions around here."

"Hello," Kitty said.

Dolly looked delighted to meet her. "Kitty, it's a pleasure. Ethel tells me your husband is a famous Hollywood actor?! How marvellous! Who is he? Will he be visiting while you're here? You must introduce me! Are you interested in the theatre? You're a striking woman!"

This came out as one long sentence without pause. Kitty stood there, unsure of how to react. Bertha reached over from her seat at the table and grabbed her hand. "Why don't you sit, dear? Have a cup of tea. Ethel and Dolly, take a chair on the other side. You're blocking the aisle standing here."

As the two ladies hurried around the table, Bertha whispered, "You don't have to say anything about your life. Ethel gets wild ideas and Dolly is the first to believe everything she hears."

Kitty nodded and took a sip from the cup Bertha passed her, but she also noticed that everyone else around the table looked mighty interested in the goings on. Why was she so afraid to tell the truth about her life? She'd already made up one lie about being a gossip columnist. The only reason she didn't want everyone to know she wrote novels was because people always asked what she was writing next and she didn't know the answer to that. But if she lied about everything, she'd be a cheat, and that was ridiculous.

Dolly looked positively giddy. "Please! You must tell us who your husband is!"

"He's a priest!" Ethel shouted.

All the ladies looked at Ethel, so she made a face. "What? Isn't he? I thought he was. Oh, I know! A detective!"

"He's a famous Hollywood actor." Dolly frowned. "That's what you told me."

Kitty glanced at Bertha. "No. He's not a famous Hollywood actor, but he is an actor. Robert Chandler."

All of them seemed shocked. Even Bertha. Dolly looked like she was going to pass out. "Your husband is Robert Chandler? The leading man on *Days of Summer? April in Paris?* The hero in *Westward Ho?*"

Kitty nodded. The ladies began to buzz and the news went around the room in about a minute and a half. Bertha leaned over. "Is this true?"

"Yes. But in case Ethel told you, I'm not a gossip columnist. I made that up on the spur of the moment to get her to stop asking questions."

"I knew darn well you weren't. Ethel told us the other night when she came for supper."

Dolly was definitely in a daze. She'd even smeared her perfectly applied red lipstick somehow. "What is it like to be married to Robert Chandler? Do you go to movie premieres?"

"A few. It's not that much fun, actually. Everyone wants to talk to him, not me. I'm usually left in the corner, so I don't go anymore."

"He doesn't mind?"

"No. He doesn't need me. There are plenty of women to keep him company."

The ladies glanced at each other and Kitty realized she'd said too much. She didn't want them to think badly of him. "It's fine, because he comes home to me."

They nodded and seemed satisfied with that. Not that it was always true, but she needed to save a dab of dignity for herself. That's when it occurred to her that she never talked about her marriage, so she didn't even know what she thought about it. Or how it sounded to others. She'd better get her story straight.

"How long are you going to be here, Kitty?" Dolly asked. "In November we put on a play at the Orange Hall across the street, and this year it's called *The Glorified Brat*. We are always looking for new blood, because let's face it, seeing the same faces year after year gets a bit tedious."

"Don't we know it," said a woman three seats down. "You're always in them."

"The leads have to be experienced. I'm talking about the extra characters. I'm sure Robert Chandler's wife would know a bit more about it than you, Myrna."

Kitty realized this was her chance to become more involved with people in the village. "I was in the drama society at school. I'd be happy to help out."

Dolly clapped her hands. "How marvellous! And will your husband be coming at some point?"

"He's in New York for four more weeks doing a movie, but he did say he'd like to visit, so maybe we can arrange it so he can be here for the play."

She might as well have thrown a firecracker into the middle of the proceedings, that's how much of a kerfuffle she created. Even Bertha was all atwitter. Kitty knew that Kurt wasn't exactly reliable, but if she told him that an entire community was overjoyed at the thought of him showing up, he'd come, just so he could bask in his own glory. It would mean staying here longer than she'd originally planned, but what did she have at home waiting for her? She'd have to ask Gaynor, of course.

When they dropped Ethel off, she looked pooped. She waved and headed inside. The cat hissed as she went by.

"Ethel didn't buy anything."

"She never does. Always says she forgot her wallet. That woman's memory comes and goes when it suits her. I really should warn you that Ethel likes to listen in on phone calls."

"Yes, Donna Smith told me."

"Did she, now? I've told Ethel to stop, that it's inconsiderate, but I don't like Donna giving her holy hell about it all the time. The poor soul has no one. What difference does it make if she repeats a little gossip? I know people are fed up with her, but if you can extend charity to someone, do it."

"You say she has no one, but her sister lives with her."

"Yes, but they're hot and cold with each other. Winnie is basically a hermit, because Ethel drives her around the bend at times. Winnie loves painting and that's how she steers clear of the daily drama. Wallace picks up supplies for her. That's the only way we know she's still alive. I keep waiting for Ethel to tell me Winnie's been dead in her bedroom for three days."

They pulled into the yard. Wallace was by the shed, chopping wood. The dogs and chickens formed a circle around him, and two little girls played nearby with a large cardboard box.

"Would you like to stay for supper? Nothing fancy. Corn chowder."

"That would be lovely."

"Go take the dogs for a walk. You did miss a beautiful day."

Pip ran over to Kitty wagging her tail so fast it was a propeller. "Did you miss me, puppy dog? I hope she didn't give you any trouble."

Wallace put his hands on his hips and shook his head sadly. "It was a complete disaster. She got into the chicken coop, smashed all the eggs, rolled around in horse dung, bit these two mermaids, and ate a dead crow. Isn't that right, girls?"

They put their hands over their mouths and giggled.

"How distressing!" Kitty smiled. "We must have a chat, Pippy. Your mother told me to take the dogs for a walk before supper, if you'd like to join me."

Everyone but the chickens walked through the field towards the water, the girls racing ahead, their fine blond hair blowing in the wind behind them.

"It's so good to breathe in the sea air."

Wallace chuckled. "Church basements are not the place to be when you could be looking at this."

This was perfection. A dark coastline, sparkling green-blue water against the dark fir trees, with billowy white clouds moving sedately across the indigo horizon. It didn't seem real to her. This belonged in a painting. She could see Argus and Pride in the long grass by the edge of the shore, and every so often Pip would jump up to try and see her way along. They were lucky this was low-lying land; Kitty could see the rugged, high cliffs farther along.

The girls perched on a large rock, marking it up with smaller rocks they used like pieces of chalk. Wallace and Kitty sat on a dried-out log that had washed up a long time ago. She tried not to keep looking at him, but his auburn hair was even more spectacular in the sun. There were glints of gold in those loose curls.

"I'm sorry, but your hair is glorious. It's such a shame it's not on my scalp."

Wallace looked down at the piece of stick in his hand. "Aw, shucks."

"People must tell you that all the time."

"No, I can't say I've ever had a woman tell me my hair is glorious. You are obviously a writer."

"I told your mom today that I'm not a gossip columnist. I'm sorry I said it to Ethel, but she was being nosy and I didn't want to get into my work."

"I figured that. I also knew that you didn't forget to unpack your underwear."

Kitty gave him a startled look. "What?!"

"Is your typewriter an Underwood?"

"Yes! Now tell me what's worse. A woman who eavesdrops, or a deaf woman who eavesdrops? How about a woman who talks about my underwear at the supper table?"

They laughed and laughed and one of the girls looked over. "What's so funny, Uncle Walrus?"

"Kitty's underwear."

The girls' mouths dropped open and snickering commenced.

"You are so bad," Kitty said.

"I know."

❧❦

Wallace locked up when the last family members left. His mom was crunching on Chicken Bones in her favourite chair by the fireplace, a book in her hand. She wore glasses most of the time but always took them off to read. He liked seeing her with her feet on the ottoman at the end of the long day, and she was more apt to stay put if he sat in the opposite chair and read too, so he picked up his book and settled in.

The mantel clock ticked, the dogs snored, and rain tapped on the window.

Bertha gasped and nearly choked on her candy. "Ohhh...how awful! I didn't see that coming!"

He was used to his mother jumping up in her seat. "What now?"

"An opera singer was just killed by a tuba!"

Wallace put his book down. "Honestly? Did the tuba suddenly sprout arms? This is the nonsense you read?"

"Why not? What are you reading?"

He looked at the cover. "*A Defense of Common Sense* by G. E. Moore."

"Fascinating. I'll start it the minute I finish this."

"I believe you need to, desperately."

"Oh, I forgot to tell you. Kitty caused a near riot at the tea and sale when Dolly Wadden asked her who her husband was."

"Why would Dolly ask her that?"

"Because Ethel told her that Kitty's husband was a movie star and she wanted to know who. And it turns out he is an actor. Robert Chandler!"

"*Westward Ho* Robert Chandler?"

"The very same! And then she asked if Kitty wanted to be in the play and Kitty said sure, and even said that maybe she could get her husband to come and visit when the play is on. That's when the place went nuts. And I know Dolly. She'll milk this for all it's worth. Probably tell everyone Kitty is her new best friend, and Robert Chandler is too."

"I wouldn't put it past her," Wallace said. "The woman is shameless."

"Imagine Kitty married to someone like that. She's a dark horse, that one. And I was right about her not being a gossip columnist. She told me. I wonder why she's here? Why would you run away by yourself to a place you don't know?"

"Common sense would say she's in trouble."

"Mmm."

"I'm going to bed." He dropped his book on the chair. "Goodnight, Mom."

She looked at her watch. "It's so early."

He didn't answer her. And she didn't read much after that.

⁂

Kitty was at the kitchen table listening to the rain, munching on pink sweets called Chicken Bones. Bertha had given her a package before she left. They were hard candy with a spicy cinnamon flavour, elongated like a bone. Inside was semi-sweet chocolate. She'd never had anything like it and wasn't sure at first if she liked them, but after she'd finished half a bag, the verdict was in. Then she looked at the baked goods she'd bought that afternoon. Everything here was so delicious. Food had never interested her before; she was never allowed in the kitchen after her mother died, and Martha had a boring repertoire of meals. Kurt was always gone, or wanted to eat out when he was home, so she didn't make the effort to put an elaborate meal together. Something else she should do when she got home.

The thought of going home made her stuff more candy into her mouth.

She looked at her forlorn typewriter but unzipped her red leather portfolio instead and took out a couple of sheets of writing paper, an envelope, and a favourite pen.

Dear Gaynor...

95

❧❧

There was a knock at her office door. "Come in."

Dolores entered, looking terribly efficient in her ironed blouse, clutching the morning mail, a cup of coffee, and a folded-up copy of the *Montreal Gazette*, which she proceeded to place on the blotter in front of Gaynor. "Mr. Bloom would like to see you at ten o'clock. Something about advance reading copies?"

"Great. Thanks."

Dolores left as efficiently as she'd arrived. She was giving Iris a run for her money.

She saw Kitty's handwriting, so she tore open that envelope first.

Dear Gaynor,

This may well be one of the main characters for my next book...a lonely widow who's hard of hearing and listens in on her telephone party line, only to get a story completely messed up, which leads to someone innocent being investigated for a crime that was never committed. Or maybe was, I'm not sure yet. A disgruntled woman detective who hates her life and job is put in charge of the mess.

What do you think?

Don't call me on the phone to talk about it. That lonely widow is a neighbour and I don't want her to know I write books. I'm trying to figure out how I'm going to say anything to anyone over the phone, knowing that she's listening in all the time. So, if I do call you and say something outrageous, it's for her benefit.

Actually, I don't really have to worry about that, since no one from home ever calls me.

I'm realizing how lonely I've been in Montreal, and I'm trying not to let it take over, because I don't want to ruin my time here. I've never laughed so much in my life, and that's why I think I can write this story as a satire perhaps. I'm still not sure, but I do feel more lighthearted thanks to the friends I've made and the families who live in this place.

It's only when you get away from your life and look at it from a distance that you see things that were always staring you in the face but you didn't have the energy to address.

When the thought of going home makes you want to cry, that's not a good thing, is it? But I can't worry about that now. It's enough that I see a small glint of hope about a new story, and that's more than I've had in a long time. I'm going to try to get out of my own way and hope for the best.

Kit xo

Gaynor stared at the letter and didn't mention it to Mel. She thought about it all day and when she walked in the door after work, the aroma of lasagna and the sight of Jersey May's velvet ears lifted her spirits, but not by much.

Simon was setting the table. "What's wrong?"

"I need your opinion, but it can wait until after dinner. Smells wonderful."

Their plates were empty and they were on their second glass of red wine when Simon read the letter.

"Oh dear."

"I know. I feel terrible that I was irritated that day she came to see me at the hairdressers. I haven't been a very good friend."

"I beg to differ. She came to you and you helped her. She wrote to tell you what's on her mind, that means she trusts you. It sounds like you're the only one she can talk to, since her family appears to be absent."

"She's writing to tell me she might have an idea for a story, which she knows I want. She's there because a publishing company sent her away and she's feeling the weight of obligation to deliver a manuscript. And that was the only thing I was worried about. I pooh-poohed her, thinking she was bored. It sounds like she's depressed, and how can you do anything when you feel like that? I was dwelling on our bottom line and, I'm ashamed to say, our trip to Florida if the Harry Gunn novels ever dried up. How callous can you get?"

"Okay, I understand you feel guilty, but you didn't know how unhappy she was. Sounds like she didn't know either, so don't beat yourself up. And you've sent her somewhere that seems to be making her more hopeful. She's even talking about making this novel funny."

Gaynor reached for a cigarette and Simon lit it for her with his lighter. She inhaled a few times to calm down. "I just want her to know that she doesn't have to write this damn story."

"Let her write it. That's what was driving her crazy, the fact that she didn't enjoy it anymore, not that she didn't want to do it ever again. Don't let her second-guess herself by saying you don't need her stories. You do. And so does she. And so do her readers."

Chapter Eight

As always, writing things out cleared the hazy muck sloshing around in Kitty's brain. But it came at a price.

Acknowledging to Gaynor that she was a very lonely woman had depressed her utterly. It surprised her to realize it, and the fact that she'd confessed it to someone else shocked her. The intention was to let Gaynor know she had a few story ideas brewing; that she wasn't a total failure on that score. But to lay herself bare like that was deflating.

Kitty wasn't used to being vulnerable. She kept herself in check at all times. Maybe that's where the discomfort was coming from. She spent two days moping about, doing not much of anything. Even Pip was annoyed with her. And then she made the mistake of trying to call Kurt, to allay her fear. Perhaps she was mistaken about the whole lonely business, but not being able to reach him confirmed it beautifully.

"I need to get a grip, Pip."

Just then she heard a vehicle pull up. She looked outside and saw Wallace get out of his truck holding something colourful. She looked closer. It was an enormous bouquet. She felt her spirits climb up out of the canyon they'd fallen into, leaping towards that fantastic array of flowers and the man carrying them. As Wallace walked up the steps, Kitty yanked open the door and hopped up and down.

"Oh, my word, thank you so much!" She threw her arms around his middle and hugged him tight. "What a thoughtful thing to do. You are the best. How did you know I needed cheering up?"

He didn't respond immediately. She tilted her chin and looked up into his face, then saw his cheeks redden. Oh no. She peeled herself off that solid, warm torso.

"They're not from you, are they?"

"I'm sorry. They came to our house instead, so I said I'd bring them over. Probably from your husband."

"Oh god. I'm mortified. And I can tell you right now they aren't from my husband." She took the flowers and opened the card. *Book or no book, you'll always be number one to us. Gaynor, Simon, and Mel (even though he didn't pay for this)*. "My publisher." She showed the card to Wallace.

"They must really think you're special."

"I'm glad someone does."

"I do."

The strange disappointment she felt knowing the beautiful arrangement wasn't from Wallace or her husband broke her in that moment. She put down the flowers and covered her face with her hands. Wallace reached over and put his arms around her, so she clung to his soft flannel shirt and cried her heart out. The tears wouldn't stop, and she had no idea how long they stood there, but it didn't seem awkward. Only when she eventually let him go.

"I'm sorry."

"Let me make you a cup of tea."

He puttered around and Kitty went to the bathroom to wash her face. She looked terrible, her eyes red and her skin mottled, but when she took a deep breath it seemed to come more easily.

She drank her hot tea. The steam made her stuffy nose feel better. Wallace didn't say anything, just sat and sipped his tea as well, like he had all the time in the world.

"I have to confess something," she said.

"You don't owe me any explanation about anything."

"I've never cried in front of anyone before."

"Not even as a little girl?"

"I stopped crying when my mother died. I didn't want to make my father even sadder."

He gave her such a sympathetic look. "What a terrible burden. I'm so sorry."

"You are exactly right, but I never realized it until this moment." She gazed out the window at the red leaves on the maple tree in the front yard. "You know why I'm grateful to be your friend? You absolutely know who you are. You know what you love and how to be. At the age of thirty-three, I know nothing. I don't know who I am, who I love or how to act. But these past weeks, you have inspired me to try and find out. I came here to write a book, not realizing the pages of my own life have nothing written on them."

"You're not giving yourself enough credit, Kitty. And you're giving me too much. Our public faces tend to hide the real story. Nothing is simple below the surface."

"But you're so sure of yourself."

"Not always."

"And what do you do when you're not?"

"I talk to my animals. They are incredible listeners. I've never had a chicken blab my secrets."

"How I envy you. Surrounded by your large family."

He took a sip of his tea and stared at the table. "A person can be in a room full of relatives and still be alone."

"How do you cope with that?"

"You become your own best friend. That way you always have someone on your side."

Kitty made a face. "Easier said than done."

"Stop putting up roadblocks."

She stuck her tongue out at him.

"For what it's worth, I do think you're special. Perhaps you should write this down so you'll believe it, too."

Her grocery list was in front of her. She picked up a pen. "Shoot."

"You write popular novels. Not everyone does that. You drove a thousand miles with your little dog to come to a place you'd never been. To live alone in an old leaky house in the woods. You learned how to keep a fire going despite being afraid of it. You took yourself sightseeing all over the island. You are friendly and intelligent and you smell like vanilla. That's always a big plus for me."

Kitty's cheeks flushed like a schoolgirl's, and her pen was still poised in the air. She quickly started doodling so she didn't have to look him in the eye. "Trust you to bring food into the conversation."

"Seriously, Kitty. Nothing you're doing right now is easy. Not every day will be good, but not every day will be bad."

"Okay, fine. Now you're being annoying."

"My cue to leave." When he got off the chair she immediately went over and hugged him. He patted her back before he went down the stairs. He was just about to get in the truck when she shouted out the door, "Tell your mother I'll be over tomorrow at five sharp with dinner for everyone. To give her a break."

❧

Kitty wiped her brow. "Not every day is good." The culinary disaster in front of her was a brilliant case in point.

But she didn't let it defeat her. She scraped the crunchy, underdone rice, the overcooked chicken, the burnt onions, and lumpy sauce into the garbage can, took off her apron, and gathered Pip and her purse. She had no choice but to drive into Glace Bay and go to Bernadette's diner for ten orders of fried chicken and fries. The smell of smoke, grease, and charred onions came along for the ride. Pip kept her nose out the window in protest. Even the waitress at Bernadette's guessed what had happened.

"Your dinner didn't go as planned?"

"You could say that."

When she arrived back at the Baileys' at five thirty and plunked down multiple brown paper bags, she held up her hands. "I don't want anyone to ask me about the total calamity that happened in my kitchen this afternoon. Just pretend I made this."

Everyone made a huge deal about how delicious everything was, saying they'd never had such fabulous cooking and could she give them the recipe? Her sides ached from laughing.

⊸✷⊶

Kitty helped Wallace do the dishes. She was over because Bertha was hosting their monthly Institute meeting, and had asked her to come a little early. It was just the three of them for a quick supper, and Bertha was now arranging the cutlery on the dining room table, making sure the cups and saucers matched and the dessert forks were lined up by the side plates and napkins. Kitty noticed there were two large teapots ready to go and a couple of plates of sweets beside them.

"She's not supposed to bake anything. Every month it's decided beforehand who brings the sandwiches and who brings the sweets, but that never stops her."

"I'm sure the other members are delighted she does. Oh, this batch looks like macaroons. Maybe they aren't hers after all."

Wallace pulled the plug in the sink to drain the soapy water. "She told you."

"Don't be cross with her. She's proud of you. I wish I could bake like that."

"Come help with the chairs."

They placed the dining room chairs and even some kitchen chairs into available spaces next to the chesterfield, wing chairs, and in front of the fireplace. It made a large circle.

"I can't believe there are this many women in a rural area. When you're driving by these small communities you don't see that many houses. Not until you get to Morien."

"Most of the houses are at the end of laneways, so you drive right by and don't notice them. These women live in Round Island, Homeville, and Black Brook for the most part."

The ladies arrived in groups of two or three with great shouts of laughter and merriment. Wallace made himself scarce and took the dogs with him. Kitty stood by Bertha as she introduced them coming through the door. Such a variety of shapes and sizes, but one thing they had in common was a wonderful camaraderie. Imagine having this many friends?

They quickly sat in every chair available, and Bertha presided over the meeting, since she was the president. Kitty watched with big eyes, wishing she'd brought a notebook and pen. Bertha called the meeting to order and they went through opening exercises. Then roll call.

Kitty tried to keep up with all the names as Bertha said them. Alice Holmes, Edie Phillips, Mary Ferguson, Effie Ferguson, Ruth Shepard, Mary Shepard, Mae Ferguson, Anne Lloyd, Margaret MacQueen, Madeline Dillon, Helen Peach, Bertha Peach, Annie MacQueen, Marion Dillon, Annie Peach, Ted Ferguson, Ina MacQueen. When each lady's name was called, she responded with a helpful household hint.

Ethel held up her hand. "You forgot me."

Bertha looked down at her book. "Oh yes, sorry Ethel. Ethel Macdonald."

Ethel kept her hand in the air. "My helpful hint is putting a piece of bread in a canister of brown sugar to soften it up."

"Thank you, Ethel."

"Don't forget yourself," she said.

"Fine. Bertha Bailey. Vinegar and baking soda are my best friends. May we have the minutes of the last meeting?"

The secretary, Edie, read the minutes. Once that was done, the treasurer, Marion, gave her report and then bills and correspondence. Helen had a bill for $1.10 for a projector and film. It was moved and seconded that this bill be paid, along with five dollars for the Scholarship Fund. They received an answer to a letter they'd sent to Simpson-Sears concerning a request for remnant cloth donations.

It seemed there were none available. Annie MacQueen, the convenor for Agriculture, had an article on how to produce eggs of quality from the *Maritime Farmer*. The convenor for Health and Welfare, Effie, read an article on appendicitis and another on tonsils. The gal in charge of Home Economics, Margaret, distributed a leaflet on milk with her favourite milk recipe, and Alice, the convenor of Legislation and Citizenship, read a letter from the provincial convener asking the branch to take up, as a study period, the immigration problem. Mary had the Red Cross convenorship, and didn't have a report as such but mentioned that cod liver oil pills had been distributed to the schools in South Head and Homeville. The card committee reported sending two cards, a sympathy card to a bereaved neighbour, Mrs. Erna Spencer, and a get-well card for Joe Turnbull, who was in hospital with a burst appendix.

The unfinished business was discussing the program for the coming year, and it was noted that the Christmas card book was being looked after and orders filled.

New business had Edie authorized to send away for official stationery, and the treasurer asked to pay fifteen dollars to Ted Ferguson for convention expenses, while five dollars would be used to send flowers to Hazel Murphy, an elderly shut-in, on the occasion of her eightieth birthday.

"Hey!" Ethel said. "I'm a shut-in."

"You're not eighty," Bertha said. "Hang around for another ten years."

Friday night meetings didn't suit everyone, so Madeline proposed that the meeting should be changed to the second Wednesday of the month. Motion carried. Ruth announced she had collected $28.75 for the Children's Aid Program, which was very gratifying. There had been two offers to buy the quilt they had made for twenty dollars. Mae gave seven dollars to the treasurer for the aprons she'd made and sold. Ina had an article about a girl's hope chest. Then Ann introduced a short film about the lobster-fishing industry.

Was there nothing this group didn't do? It sounded daunting to Kitty's ears. She doubted she'd last a minute with this bunch. And then Annie brought up a contest form to be filled in if any of them wanted to apply for "Miss Farmerette" at the Farmer picnic. None of them were keen.

They had a contest—how many other words can you make with the letters in *Home Economics* in five minutes. Kitty won that one easily. She took home a prize of toilet soap. A booby prize was given to the one who had the least. Ethel got a clear bag with three kernels of corn in it. "What's this?"

"It's a three-piece chicken dinner. It took me all day to make." Bertha hooted and slapped her knee.

After that they had a game. Since there were so many of them, they divided into two teams, put their shoes in the middle of the floor, and had everyone try to find their own while blindfolded. Kitty was in stitches. She was definitely going to use this.

The meeting was adjourned, motion carried, and ended with all of them standing, singing "God Save the Queen." Then it was on to the tea and plates of lobster sandwiches and egg salad sandwiches to tie in with the night's programs. For dessert, Queen's Lunch squares with chocolate icing, a date loaf, macaroons, brown sugar cookies, and a plate of creamy maple fudge.

It was almost ten thirty when the last of them hollered good-night as they went out the door. Bertha collapsed in her chair, and even though Kitty was only a bystander, she collapsed in the chair next to her. Wallace and the dogs showed up to sniff around the leftovers.

"How on earth do you ladies manage it?" Kitty marvelled. "So many topics, so many different projects? The Bertha who sat next to me makes doll clothes to sell at the fall fair to raise money for good causes. It's unbelievable. I'm so impressed. I thought I was in the middle of nowhere when I came here. I've learned more this evening than I have since leaving university. And had the best time of my life doing it."

⟡

The very next day, Kitty phoned Gaynor.

"Why are you calling me?" Gaynor panicked.

"To talk to you?"

"What's wrong? Have you hit a wall? Creative juices stop bubbling?"

"You might want to call Mitzi and schedule an appointment to get your hair done."

"No kidding. What a morning. Okay, I'll calm down. So spill it."

"Any chance Empire and Bloom will keep subsidizing me to be here? You said two months and it's the middle of October already, so it's almost over."

"Yes! If this means what I think it means."

"Perhaps. I just don't want to run out of time. Something has come up that might be fun if I can persuade hubby to join me."

"That's odd, but okay."

"My life is odd, Gaynor. You must know that by now."

"I only know what you tell me, and that's slim pickings."

"It's got to stay that way, if you catch my drift."

"Right. You keep your mouth shut and I'll keep my mouth shut. Therefore, there's no need to be on this phone." She slammed down the receiver. Kitty waited until she heard the soft click of Ethel's earpiece being replaced before she hung up.

⟡

It was now a habit that if Kitty was going somewhere, she dropped Pippy off in Bertha's kitchen. "She's here!" Bertha would shout back from wherever she was. "Come in and see your Nan, sweetheart." And Pip would run towards her voice without a backward glance.

Kitty hurried back outside to her car while leaves flew off the trees in this late October gale. She was late for rehearsal, and Dolly was a tyrant as far as that went. She turned the key and nothing. She turned it again. No sound, just a funny click. "Great! This is a brand-new car!" She hit the steering wheel with the palms of her hands as if that would help matters. Wallace's head poked out from the barn and she rolled down her window. "It won't start!!"

Naturally, he said he'd take a look at it, it probably wasn't anything serious, but in the meantime, he'd drive her to the hall and pick her up when she was ready to come home.

"You have a God-given talent for making things so easy for everyone else. You must practice."

He started up the truck and put it in gear. "No need. I watched my mother. I was a placid kid. Helen said they often forgot I was around. I'd sit at the kitchen table with a cookie in each hand and not say a thing. Over the years I saw Mom deal with every kind of problem you could imagine. She raised us kids around that table. We were fed, counselled, and listened to, and given old heck when we deserved it. We'd gather there after school doing our homework while she kneaded dough. All of us came to her and she always made things easier, even when it was still a disaster. It didn't seem as bad once you shared the worry with her. I have no idea how she did it then or continues to do it with people like Ethel, but I know a good thing when I see it and I can pay her no better compliment than to try and be just like her."

"Well, you are. I don't have a clue what would've happened to me if your family wasn't here."

"You'd be a cold, damp, dirty, hungry city slicker with no wheels. And only Ethel for company."

"I think I'd still want to be here."

Wallace dropped her off and she went through the double doors on the ground floor, which opened into a small foyer, and then through a set of swinging doors that exposed the main hall. A raised stage at the end was flanked by short stairways leading to the wings of the stage. That's where Dolly and the other cast members milled about, some with scripts in their hands, while others moved scenery around.

Dolly spied her. "Kitty! Finally."

"I'm sorry. My car wouldn't start." She took off her blue camel-hair topper coat with the big buttons, pockets, and collar. She noticed Wallace had given it an extra glance when she'd climbed in the truck.

She jumped up on the stage with her rolled-up script. "I don't think I have any lines in this scene."

"No, but you do open and close the door five times. Stand over there and look bossy."

"Bossy? Or bored. It might be funny if I was bored."

"I suppose you could try it both ways, since you are immersed in the theatre world, unlike some here," Dolly said. "By the way, did you speak with Robert about coming to the show?"

Kitty got a kick out of Dolly calling her husband Robert, as if they were fast friends. "I'm calling him tonight. He should be back by now."

"Make sure you tell him we get a wonderful write-up in the *Post Record* every year."

"Will do."

It was so entertaining to stand there and wait for her cue to open and close the door, because she got to see how this small group of neighbours made their own fun.

Dolly was the star, naturally, and Donna Smith was playing her partner in crime.

A tall, lanky fellow named Ken was also in the play, and it seemed to Kitty that he lived to make other people laugh, and he did a darn good job at it. He was behind Kitty waiting for his cue when Dolly spoke her first line. He said in a stage whisper, "Dolly was born to play a glorified brat's mother."

Dolly twirled around. "*Ken.* Stop horsing around."

"I'm completely serious," he muttered in Kitty's ear. She closed the door on him so she wouldn't laugh.

"Kitty! You have only one thing to do. Open and close the door. You do not close the door in Ken's face at this moment."

So, she opened it and Ken was standing there with his arms folded across his chest, looking very put out. "Yeah, missy. Don't close the door in my face, or I might say something I shouldn't."

There was no way she was going to get through this play with that man. And he knew it.

She'd never joked around with men before. It had never occurred to her. It was so incredibly easy to laugh with Wallace and Ken. She had a husband, but he didn't feel like her friend anymore. All these bombshells kept going off in her head as the days passed. She was almost afraid to think because she continued to stumble over deeply buried truths; her personal landmines.

Kitty opened and closed the door all afternoon, and in the end, everyone thought that when she looked bored it was much funnier. Even Dolly conceded as much.

"She's such a good little actress!" Dolly almost shouted. "Robert must have taught her well!"

"Robert who?" Ken shouted back. "Not Robert Chandler of *Westward Ho* fame? *That* Robert Chandler? The Robert Chandler who's married to this little lady right here? Is this Mrs. Robert Chandler? Well, I'll be. I never knew that."

Dolly gave him a dirty look and walked off the stage. Kitty had to bite her lip to keep her big grin hidden. The cast left in dribs and drabs, and she and Ken were still chatting when she looked at her watch. "Oh, gosh. I better call Wallace."

"You don't have to. He's at the back of the hall and has been hijacked by our esteemed director. Looks really happy about it too."

"Oh dear. This is my fault."

"Dolly makes a habit of ambushing Wallace. He's too nice for his own good."

They said goodbye and Kitty got into her coat and walked over to Wallace. "I was supposed to call you. I hope you haven't been waiting long."

"Nope."

Dolly put her hand on his arm and squeezed. "I kept him company. Trying to talk him into joining our little troupe. One day he might change his mind."

Wallace gave her a pained smile. "Goodbye, Dolly." He looked at Kitty. "Ready to go?"

Kitty put her arm through his very deliberately. "Can't wait." She'd never sashayed in her life, but she tried to until Dolly was out of sight.

He opened the truck door for her and she hopped in. When he started the engine, he turned to her. "Your car is fine, by the way."

"I knew it would be."

"Can I ask you something?"

"Sure."

"Did you have to go to theatre school to learn how to open and close doors like that?"

❧

That evening Kitty smoked three cigarettes, one after the other, before she called the operator. She was guessing Kurt was home; six weeks were up and she hadn't heard from him to tell her the shoot was extended. She could have called him, she supposed, but what was the point?

The operator came on the phone. "I'm sorry, there's no answer at that number."

"Okay, thank you anyway. Oh wait! Could I call another number?"

This time she got through. "Hello, Martha?" She knew her father never answered the phone.

"Yes?"

"It's Kitty."

There was silence.

"I'm calling to see if you've heard from Kurt?"

"Of course I've heard from Kurt. He calls me every night."

"Is he home?"

"Don't you know? He doesn't call you?"

"Is he home or not?"

"If he wanted you to know, he would phone and tell you."

She put her hand on her head to keep it from spinning. And suddenly she heard her father's voice. "Catriona?"

"Oh. Hi, Dad."

"Kurt got home earlier in the week. He's already been over three times for dinner. Are you all right?"

"I was wondering where my husband was, since he hasn't bothered to get in touch."

"I don't think the shoot went well. He's in a bad mood."

"That always happens. You've never seen it because I'm usually there to pick up the pieces. He hates returning to real life."

"I see. Everything else is okay? The writ—"

"Everything is fine. How about you?"

"Busy."

"Good. Well, I'll say goodbye. I'll try calling him again. If you happen to see him, tell him to call me. I want to ask him something. It's important."

"Okay, Kitty."

"Bye, Dad. And thanks for answering my question."

"Sure."

She took the flashlight and hooked up Pip to her leash. Then she put on the coat she now liked a whole lot and stood outside in the dark listening to the night sounds in the woods. An owl who lived nearby always let her know it was there. It was comforting, not lonely. The stars twinkled and a sliver of moon kept peeking out from behind the moving clouds. Leaves were dropping silently all around her, their life cycle almost complete. All that was left for them to do was to become a home for little critters living close to the ground.

It was hard to believe the play was happening in two weeks.

Not that she wanted Kurt to come here, but it felt like a test. To see if he would let her down.

Did she want him to pass or fail?

They went inside and did their nightly ritual, locked up, banked the fire, had what Bertha called a lunch: cookies or a bowl of cereal, Pip with her doggie treats. Then Kitty climbed into the greatest invention in modern history, the claw tub, and had a heavenly soak before putting on her pajamas, robe, and slippers. She sat at the kitchen table and grabbed her smokes. She put a stack of new paper on one side and inserted one sheet in her Underwood.

She typed CHAPTER NINE.

On the other side was her story thus far, face down. *One Long Ring Around the Rosy.*

She typed until four in the morning, Pip asleep on the mat at her feet.

Chapter Nine

Kate was called by her superior to explain herself.

"Is there a problem with this investigation, Higgins?"

"Other than there may or may not have been a murder? No one is quite sure now. But we seem to have twenty suspects anyway, and four hundred different motives. Every time I speak to someone in this small town, I get a different version of what happened, but no one wants to go into detail because I'm from the big city, so they don't trust me. Apparently, they want their local cop, Big Dan, to solve the case. Or not solve it, depending on who you talk to."

"What do you mean, there's no murder?"

"According to the know-it-all on the party line, the victim was strangled in her sleep. That's why she called Big Dan. But when he gets to the victim's home, they have no idea what he's talking about. The victim is eating oat cakes at her kitchen table. But they say maybe he has the wrong house and it could be the hermit up the road. People have wanted to kill her for years."

"Why would they want to kill her if she's a hermit?"

"Beats me. So, he goes there and the sister says that's nonsense, but Dan finds the hermit up in her bedroom, stone dead. He asks the woman if she knew her sister was dead and she said no, she hasn't seen her for three days. 'How's that possible?' Dan asks. 'I never check on her. She's a hermit, remember?' Then the woman starts throwing blame around, saying someone on her party line wants her dead and maybe they killed the wrong sister. Why doesn't Big Dan do his job and catch the real criminals in the neighbourhood?"

Kate ran out of breath.

"Are you having a breakdown, Higgins?"

"Yes."

The phone rang. Naturally. These were two things that did not go together: someone trying to write a novel while sitting in a house with a party line. The minute Kitty got to a good part, the loud ring took her out of the story, and sometimes it was a hard scramble to get back into it. And irritating because it was usually not for her. Until now.

"Hello?"

"I hear you're annoyed I didn't call. You didn't call me either. Did you notice that?"

"I did. You weren't home."

"I mean in New York."

"Didn't want to disturb you. How did it go?"

"Horrible. A stupid movie that won't see the light of day, I'm sure. Don't know why I wasted my time. When are you coming back?"

"I'm fine, thank you. Writing again, enjoying my time here. Meeting lovely people."

"Bully for you. So, what am I supposed to do? Eat at my mother's every day?"

"I'm sure she'd be delighted."

"What is up with your old man?"

Kitty stood straighter. "What do you mean?"

"He's even more of a sourpuss than usual."

"Probably because you're eating him out of house and home. Listen, I want to ask you something."

"What?"

"Don't sound so enthusiastic. I want you to come and visit me."

"No. It's too bloody far and I'm tired."

"The local village is putting on a play. When they found out who you were, they nearly lost their minds."

"Oh yeah?"

"They'd dearly love it if you could visit while the play is going on. I'm in it too."

"You?"

"I open and close a lot of doors and not much else, don't worry."

"When is it?"

"In two weeks. You could fly from Montreal to Sydney and I'll pick you up. We can visit and the locals would love to meet you. It will be fun."

"I don't know..."

"They might just give you a cameo. And my neighbour's cooking is to die for."

"At this point I'll do anything for food."

"So, you'll come?"

"Why not. I do miss you. It's weird not having that little mutt around."

"You mean me or the dog?"

⁂

One of the little ones wanted a grilled cheese sandwich, so Wallace buttered the bread and sliced the cheese, putting the frying pan on the warm part of the stove.

"Walrus?"

"That's my name."

"How come Kittycat isn't here?"

"I don't know, bud. Probably busy."

"I like it when she's here."

Wallace looked down at his little face. "And why's that?"

"Because you're even more happy."

"Out of the mouths of babes." His sister Helen gave him an elbow and snickered.

Bertha was folding clothes on the table. "Leave him be."

"Ma, Wallace is not ten. I'm only teasing."

"Yeah, Helen. Leave me be. I'm a fragile flower." He stood with a metal spatula in his hand waiting for the cheese to melt.

"She has been missing in action," Bertha mused. "I think I'll call and invite her for supper. Find out what she's been up to."

Wallace shook his head. "You're worse than Ethel."

The phone rang.

"Speak of the devil." Bertha put the dishtowel she was folding over her shoulder and stepped into the dining room. "Hel—"

"BERTHA? He's coming!"

"Who's coming?"

"That movie priest...*Western Ho* guy. Kitty's husband! He's coming to see the play! At first he said no, he was too tired and it was too bloody far—his words, not mine—but then he changed his mutt...I mean, mind. He must miss the dog."

"I have to go, Ethel."

"I have people to call, anyway." She hung up.

Bertha hated this feeling. She was invading Kitty's privacy just by picking up the phone and listening to Ethel. She was going to have to do something about this. Charity only went so far. But she'd said that before.

She called Kitty.

"Hello?" She sounded rushed.

"Hi, Kitty. Just me. Wondered if you'd like to come for supper. We haven't seen you in a while."

"Umm..."

"If you're busy, don't worry."

"No. I should eat. I have no food here. I'd love to come. Five sharp?"

"Five sharp."

"See you then!" She hung up.

No food? She should eat? What was that girl doing? Bertha went back into the kitchen. Wallace was cutting up the sandwich for the little fella, while Helen added the turnips and carrots to the corned beef simmering on the stove.

"Kitty is coming for supper."

"Hurrah!" Mr. Grilled Cheese grinned before taking his sandwich into the sunroom to play with his dinkies.

"Who was on the phone?" Helen asked.

"Ethel. To tell me Kitty's husband is coming for the play."

Helen's mouth gaped open. "I don't believe it! That play is going to be sold out and sold out again when this news makes the rounds."

"Ethel is busy making sure it does that now."

Wallace kept his back to them, washing up the pan in the sink, before he wiped his hands and grabbed his truck keys. "I'll be back in time for supper."

Argus and Pride stared out the window to watch him go.

"Is he okay?" Helen said.

"I hope so."

❀❀

Kitty was desperate for fresh air. She'd been holed up for days, trying to get as much written as she could. As always, the fear of losing the story and having it drain away if she wasn't completely focused on it kept her going. To the point that she really did need to get groceries. The next time she had rehearsal she'd pop over to the store and stock up. And although she wanted to keep typing, she also knew that sometimes a break was the best way to get a fresh take on a scene.

She decided to walk over to the Baileys', with Pip on her leash, and damn the bears, eagles, and coyotes. She'd hit them over the head with her flashlight if she had to. The crisp, cold air was a tonic. And she wasn't afraid of this place. It was familiar to her now. There was comfort here. Everything that had been so foreign was now welcome in her eyes. How could she go home? But she immediately stopped that thought because panic started to crawl up her throat.

Kitty loved knocking on the Baileys' door, because a chorus of voices yelled "Come in!" before she removed her coat or took Pip off the leash. Then the inner door opened and kids and dogs rushed to greet her, with the adults telling them to give her some space.

There were ten at the table that night. Helen and her grandson, and for the first time she met George and his wife, Rita, with their three tykes, Georgie, Elizabeth, and Benji.

She immediately found herself drawn to the baby. He was a little pudding. Rita was very obliging when Kitty offered to take him, and as he grasped his tiny fingers around her thumb she was in love. "Hello Benji."

He was content to stay with her, even as she sat at the table. Pippy looked mildly concerned and pressed her nose against Kitty's leg, but after being reassured with a loving pat she snuggled between her enormous furry friends.

"May I keep him? I'll hold him to the side while I eat, if Wallace wouldn't mind cutting up my meat."

Wallace did as he was told.

Kitty looked around the table. "How can someone this small be a real human being? I've never had the chance to be around babies, so this is amazing to me. You are so fortunate, Rita."

"I confess I don't always appreciate it when Benji cries all night and the other two have the flu."

Bertha passed over a pot of homemade mustard to George. "You've been busy, Kitty. We haven't seen you as much. I hope Dolly hasn't kept you completely monopolized with the play."

"I've got a small project I'm working on but rehearsals are going well. It should be a good time, especially for Dolly. I just found out my husband will be here to see the play, so that will put her in a good mood."

"Is he? How nice."

"He wasn't going to come, but when he found out the whole community wanted to meet him, he changed his tune. I knew he would. It also helped when I said he had to taste your delicious cooking, Bertha, so I hope we'll be invited for dinner at least once."

"Of course. How long will he be here?"

"I never thought to ask."

Kitty didn't relinquish Benji even after supper. Rita let her change him and she sat by the fireplace and rocked him while the others laughed and talked about nothing in particular. Just feeling this warm little bundle against her heart was a soothing balm. She found herself humming and realized it was the melody her mother used to sing to her when she brushed her hair.

A memory she had forgotten, and this little Benji had given it back to her. She swallowed hard.

Helen and her grandson were the first to go, and the family left when it was obvious the older two were fading fast. Kitty reluctantly handed the baby to his mother. "Thank you. He was exactly what I needed."

Wallace poured more tea for the three of them and then settled on the chesterfield. Pip was back in Kitty's lap.

"Did you like those Chicken Bones I gave you?" Bertha said.

"Yes! They were great, but I think I love the name even more. Words can make anything better."

"I love to read." Bertha picked up her book. "Mostly murder mysteries."

Bertha and detective stories? Kitty cleared her throat into her fist to buy her a fraction of a second to process this. That's when she noticed the cover and coughed outright. "Gosh, so you do. I believe that's a Harry Gunn novel. I recognize it."

"Well, whoever C. J. Faulkner is, he's a great writer. I never guess what's coming next."

"Did the tuba kill anyone else?" Wallace asked. "Did it go on a rampage and wipe out the entire opera company?"

His mother pointed at him. "Just because you don't read normal books like the rest of us doesn't mean you're superior, mister."

"Yeah," Kitty said, laughing. "Don't be a snob. There's plenty of room for all types of books and readers."

"What do you like to read?"

"Everything, but I often reread the children's books my mother read to me at bedtime. The only things I'd grab if we had a fire. Along with some of her belongings that my absent-minded father remembered to save for me. They are my prized possessions. And Pip of course." She kissed the top of her head.

She was weary. It was time to go. "Thank you again for dinner. I'd better head back." She got up and walked to the kitchen, the other two behind her.

Bertha passed her a bundle of goodies. "You said you didn't have groceries, so I made you a care package."

"Bertha! I have to be careful what I say around you. You're too kind." She reached over and gave the woman a kiss, and then opened the door. "Oops, I forgot I walked here."

"I'll take you back in the truck," Wallace said.

"I'm happy to walk, though I wouldn't mind help carrying this. I can kill two birds with one stone by giving Pip her nightly airing before bed. I have my flashlight. Bye, Bertha. Thanks again."

"Goodnight, honey."

They headed out. It was pitch black.

"You should've brought your flashlight," she said.

"No need. I've walked this road every day of my life. And if you look, you can see the light from our place through the trees."

"I love it here, Wallace. And that is so dangerous."

"Why? Here, let me hold that bag."

She passed it over to him as Pip trotted beside her. Argus and Pride slowly followed, not that she could see either of them, only their eyes when the flashlight hit them.

"Every day I find something I've been missing. The love of a mother, the joy of children, happy conversation, people gathered together around the supper table, having neighbours. The day I arrived I was so afraid. This road looked remote and isolated. I thought I would be alone, that no one would hear me if I was in trouble. Now I realize that was my life in Montreal."

"You had no one to talk to there?"

"No. Well, Gaynor to a point, she's my editor, but my father has been a remote figure. I love him, but over the years we've become more and more estranged without even realizing it. He's as damaged as I am over my mother's death."

"Your husband?"

"He never hears me. Even when I'm in the same room. Which isn't often."

Walking in the dark not looking at each other made it easier for her to talk. "We have a strange past. I've known him since I was a kid. It's very complicated. And his mother has made my life hell. I know one thing; I'm not going to take any more of her bullshit."

It was that exact moment when Wallace shouted, "Look out!" He grabbed her and almost pushed her to the ground, trying to cover her head. With the dogs barking and her letting out a screech, she didn't know what was going on, so she clung to him for dear life.

"What happened?!"

"A big old owl decided to swoop at us. You don't want to mess with those claws. It's gone now."

She continued to hold on. "Can I stay right here?"

He tightened his grip. "Sure."

"Walrus?"

"Yes?"

"Would you mind kissing me?"

⊰⊱

When Kitty jumped into bed that night with Pip, she covered her head and kicked her feet like a little kid. She'd never been kissed before. Not like that. Not ever. She didn't even know what kissing was. No wonder she'd never written romance novels. She could now, because that kiss would live in her memory forever.

Unfortunately, the guilt about it started the moment she opened her eyes in the bright morning sunshine. All had been perfect in the dark. There were only two people in the whole world last night on South Head Road. Now all she saw were her husband and mother-in-law. And the worst part? Martha was right. What a terrible wife.

She'd always been the injured party in their marriage, and she was proud that she had never stooped to Kurt's level with his open displays of affection for other women. Now that was gone. And what would Wallace think of her? She was married. He wasn't. What would Bertha say if she knew? And how was she supposed to act around his family? She couldn't tell anyone about this.

"Pip! I'm an idiot."

Pip looked like she agreed, because she wanted out. Kitty threw on her coat and grabbed the leash. When she opened the door, there was Wallace.

"I'm an idiot," he said.

"What have we done?" She went right past him and watched Pip crouch in the grass. "I can't go over to your house ever again!"

"And I shouldn't even be talking to you. Your husband is coming here soon, and how am I supposed to sit at the table with him? It's all my fault. I knew you were married. You were vulnerable and lonely and I took advantage of you."

"No. I told you to kiss me. And you know what's worse?"

"What?"

"I want you to do it again. That's not good, is it?"

"No. That's bad."

Kitty looked at the ground. "Is it, though?"

"Only one way to find out."

Chapter Ten

Gaynor was back under the hair-dryer, but this time instead of relaxing in Maui, she was snickering as she read the mimeograph of the first twelve chapters of Kitty's new book. She'd received it that morning by registered mail. Dolores had put it on top of the pile.

"An envelope from C. J. Faulkner, marked *Urgent.*"

"Hot damn!! Who can believe it! I don't want to be disturbed."

"Of course, Mrs. Ledbetter."

"At this point, Dolores, call me Gaynor. I'd marry you if I didn't already have a husband."

When she hadn't heard back from Kitty, she thought it might be because of the phone bandit. It never occurred to her that she'd be writing already. But she should've known. Once Kitty started, she didn't stop.

Gaynor ripped open the envelope. *One Long Ring Around the Rosy.*

"I love it already!! Oh Kit, you fabulous girl."

Even her hairdresser, Mitzi, wanted to know what was so funny. "My next bestseller, that's what. A whodunit. This writer has never written satire before, but this is astonishing. She should've been doing it all along. Kate Higgins is going to be famous!"

"Who's Kate Higgins?"

"The female detective in the book."

Mitzi took the can of hairspray and circled Gaynor's head ten times. "Now, that I would read. A woman detective is a nice change."

Which is exactly what Mel said when he jumped up and did a little jig when Gaynor showed him the script. She had Dolores mimeograph it and he assured her he would read it that night. She took home the original to show Simon. She did the dishes while he sat with his glass of wine in the living room, Jersey May curled up beside him on their davenport. Every time he laughed, Gaynor giggled. Detective Kate Higgins would be bigger than Harry Gunn. She felt it in her bones.

"Come here!" Simon shouted. She dried her hands on a dish-towel and hurried out to him. He pointed at the page. "This part!"

Kate tried to keep up. "So you're telling me you didn't actually speak to anyone to gather this information?"

"Yes, I did. I listened while they talked. That's speaking, isn't it?"

Myrtle Lovett, who reminded Kate of an elderly, scrawny chicken, was quite huffy about her line of questioning. "This is preposterous. Am I being charged with murder?"

"Did I say you were?"

"You city types don't fool me. One minute you come for tea and the next I'm being carted off to the clink. If anyone should be charged with murder, it's you!"

Kate looked around and then pointed at herself. "Me?"

"When I fall down dead in the next five minutes thanks to a stroke brought on by my skyrocketing blood pressure, who else should I blame?"

"Well, if you're dead, you can't blame anyone. Dead men don't talk, remember."

"I think you'll find women still do."

"This is priceless," Simon chuckled. "And so completely different from anything she's done before."

"I know, right? And you started the ball rolling."

Simon drained the last of the wine. "You can thank me later."

Mel was waiting for her when she got to work the next morning. He beckoned her from his office door, closing it behind them. He hit the script with the back of his hand.

"This is pure gold!"

"That's what I thought!"

"This part!" He turned to a page near the end.

Kate asked to use the phone, which was a foolish idea to begin with, seeing as how the place was crawling with kids and dogs, but she had no choice. She held her hand over her ear while the operator connected her.

"Stu?"

"Did you talk to that old woman, Myrtle Lovett? The one who listens in on phone calls?"

"Ugh. What a nightmare she is," Kate confessed.

"I am not!" Myrtle yelled over the phone.

Mel looked at her with a big grin. "When can she have this finished?"

Gaynor put up her hands. "Now, wait. This is only the first twelve chapters, and that's more than I could have hoped for at this point. The last thing I want to do is railroad her into finishing it. She puts too much pressure on herself as it is. Just let this unfold. Whatever she's doing there, it's working. I don't want to jinx it."

"All right. Send her something, will ya? Flowers? Chocolates? Just to let her know we love her."

"You big marshmallow."

"And the money she's going to make for us."

⊰❦⊱

Dolly wasn't home the first time Ethel called her, so she phoned everyone she could think of to tell them about Robert Chandler coming to the play, and by the time she called her again, Dolly knew.

That annoyed Ethel. "I wanted to tell you!"

"You did, essentially. You told Flora, Flora told Esther, Esther told Rose, Rose told Lottie, and Lottie told me. I can't wait to ask Kitty about it tonight at rehearsal."

"Let her tell you first."

"Why? She obviously told you. She must want people to know."

"She's aware it means a lot to you, so maybe she'd like to tell you herself."

"That's true. I can't believe he's coming!"

"And I can't believe you're giving him a cameo!"

"What? A cameo? Who said that?"

"Oh. Isn't it common knowledge?"

"No! The last thing I need is to be upstaged by Robert Chandler. No one will notice me if that happens. I want him in the audience so he can see me perform. Did Kitty make this suggestion? I wouldn't put it past her. She's not quite as innocent as she looks. Always making eyes at Wallace."

"Is that so?"

"Thanks a lot, Ethel. I felt great two minutes ago, and now I have to worry about this." She slammed the phone down.

�֍⚬

Kitty typed like a fiend all day, completely forgetting she had to drop Pip off at Bertha's and then get groceries before rehearsal. That meant showing up just as the Baileys were sitting down for supper, which wasn't her intention. This was not the time to face Wallace across the dinner table. Today her guilt had nothing to do with them feeding her so often.

"Come in and have a quick bite before you go," Bertha insisted. "You have lots of time for groceries before you get on stage."

She and Wallace looked at each other and then didn't. "That's okay…"

"Nonsense! You told me you have no groceries, so I insist."

Kitty had no choice but to sit down. Wallace's sisters Jean and Ruth were over with their girls, Linda, Barbara, Ruby, and Polly. Pip made the rounds of the table, waiting to be patted on the head. The two Newfoundland dogs didn't bat an eye and continued to snore at the entrance to the back porch.

Bertha put a delicious plate of home-baked beans and brown bread in front of her, and Kitty realized she was ravenous. She asked for seconds, which pleased Bertha to no end. Wallace kept his head down and concentrated on his plate as well.

"Walrus?" Ruby said.

He kept eating.

"Walrus?" When he didn't answer her, she looked at her mother. Ruth snapped her fingers under his nose.

He jumped back. "What? What is it?"

"Ruby's talking to you."

"Sorry." He looked at her.

"If I bring my bike over next time, will you pump the tires up for me? Dad says you can do it because you have an air pump."

"So does he."

He went back to eating. All the women at the table looked at him. Kitty cleared her throat and rose quickly. "I'm so sorry. I'd better go. That was delicious."

And she scurried out the door. Wallace wiped his mouth on a napkin and got up as well. "Excuse me. I forgot I have a job in the barn." He disappeared outside as the lights from Kitty's car made their way up the road.

Ruby looked crestfallen. Her mother patted her back. "Don't mind Walrus. He's just grumpy."

"He's never grumpy. I didn't think he knew what grumpy was."

"Girls, why don't I give you each an ice cream cone. You can eat it in the living room," their Nanna said.

Once they were sorted, Bertha, Jean, and Ruth sipped their tea and ate gingerbread cake heaped with whipped cream.

Ruth pointed her fork at her mother. "Something is going on with that fella. I've never heard him talk like that to the girls."

"Did you notice how the two of them were quite obvious about not looking at each other?" Jean said, nodding. "Something happened."

Bertha took a big bite of gingerbread instead of answering.

"Don't you think, Mom?"

"I think we should keep our big noses out of it. It's impossible to have any privacy in this house, and Wallace deserves to live his life without constant speculation from his family."

"We're only interested," Ruth said. "And he didn't have to take it out on Ruby."

Bertha put down her fork and crossed her arms. "And that's another thing. We're so used to Wallace being a big teddy bear, we expect him to be that way constantly. It takes a lot of effort to be as kind as he is. And if he has a bad moment now and then, he's allowed to without apologizing for it. God knows you girls are no saints!"

❧❧

When Kitty ran around the store shelves picking up essential food items, she was stopped by everyone she came across.

"Hear your actor husband is coming to the play."

"Someone told me that fella from *Wagon Train* is coming here. Is he your husband?"

"Are you the lady from Hollywood?"

Even as Hopper licked his pencil to write down her order, he glanced up. "You've caused a right stir. I think we'll have lots of people come by when they're here to see your mister."

"I'm happy for you."

When she arrived at the Orange Hall, all of the actors were on stage. Everyone knew what they were doing now. Ken waved as she climbed the stairs.

"So, I hear hubby is coming to give us a few pointers. I need all the help I can get."

Dolly whipped around. Her face was a thundercloud. "Truer words were never spoken."

"I'll take my leave." Ken tiptoed away.

"Hi, Dolly. Are you happy to hear that Robert is coming for the play?"

"I was, until I found out you offered him a cameo."

Kitty was going to wring Ethel's neck. "I said maybe, jokingly."

"You had no business saying anything. You're not the one working her fingers to the bone putting this production together. How about I give him your role if he wants a cameo so badly? He can open and close doors and yell 'Brat!' He might get an Academy Award."

"I'm sure you'll be able to teach him all he needs to know about acting, Dolly. How about we start now? I'd like an early night."

❦

Wallace was busy building a garage for a guy in Birch Grove all week. When he got home for supper his mother told him that Ethel's sister Winnie called about getting more art supplies. "She wants you to collect the money and the list. Here, you might as well take this with you." She handed him a casserole dish of beef stew.

He wanted to sit, but he didn't want Winnie to fret, and she always did until he showed up. He pulled in their yard and took the casserole dish in one hand, then reached down with the other to pat the friendly black cat who was always there to greet him and who rolled over on the ground now. Wallace rubbed his belly. "You're getting fat, Blackie." Blackie purred.

He knocked on the door and opened it slightly. Ethel was hard of hearing and Winnie was always in the back. "Ethel? Ethel?"

"Yes?!"

"It's me, Wallace." He stepped over the threshold. There was nothing cooking on the stove. They lived on eggs, bread, cheese, and sweets. "Mom sent over some beef stew."

"Oh, that blessed woman. Thank you."

"I'm here to get Winnie's list."

"Go on through. You know the drill. She wouldn't be caught dead in the kitchen."

Wallace did know the drill, and knew that Winnie couldn't take Ethel's constant bellyaching.

He knocked on the door to her room, which had been an old sun porch, with a separate door to the backyard so she could paint outside if the mood struck her. "Winnie? It's Wallace."

"Come in, dear."

Winnie was a lovely old lady. She was small like her sister but her features were softer. Wallace knew she'd never married. She'd been a bank teller all her life. When Ethel became a widow, it had made sense for the two sisters to live together to save money. Winnie had always lived in an upstairs apartment over a store in Dominion, so to be in the country and see flowers and trees out the sun porch windows delighted her. She'd begun to paint, and Wallace knew it was her only solace.

"I see you have a new roommate. I wondered where Tweety bird was. Didn't see him in his usual spot. Hello, little guy." He waggled his finger at the cage.

The blue budgie ruffled his feathers at the attention.

"Ethel wants him in here with me for some reason. I don't mind. He's charming company."

They got straight down to business. Wallace put out his hand and Winnie counted the bills individually, as she had done all her life. "Two and two and one. Five altogether. That will be enough for the two canvases, and this list of oil paints. I'm running out of the basics, green, white, and black. Thank you, dear."

"If you'd ever like a drive to town, Winnie, just say the word, and I can take you."

"No, child. Thank you anyway. I'm quite content to stay here out of the way. You forget, I dealt with the public all my life. I've had enough of human beings. Give me a flower any day."

He laughed. "I know what you mean. I'll get this tomorrow before work and drop it off at lunchtime."

"You're the best, Wallace. Your mother did a fine job raising you."

"Thank you. See you tomorrow."

Ethel was eating a bowl of stew when Wallace was on his way out. "Can you sit and chat?"

"Just for a few minutes. Mom likes dinner at five sharp."

"That woman and her five-sharp business. We'll have to put that on her gravestone."

Poor Ethel. She was always saying something inappropriate. But it was getting worse with age. Like his mother, Wallace had a soft spot for Ethel, despite her nonsense. She'd been a good friend to his mother when his father made life difficult at times. He remembered the day when he was little, sitting on a chair in the kitchen, and his father was drunk. His mother told his father to get out and sleep it off in the barn. He'd slapped her. But he didn't know Ethel was in the other room. She came flying in and slapped him right back, as small as she was. Told him to never touch Bertha again or she'd set the dog on him. She meant her husband. Everyone tended to stay away from that man.

"Is Kitty excited her husband is coming to town?"

"I suppose so."

"She didn't tell you?"

"No. I didn't ask."

"Are you going to meet him?"

"I imagine. Why?"

"Just making conversation."

Wallace stood up. "Sorry Ethel, I have to go. Make sure Winnie gets some of that stew."

"What are you implying, cheeky monkey?"

"Nothing. It's been a long day. I'll be back tomorrow."

Wallace patted Blackie once more and backed out of the yard.

He pulled over and stopped the truck just out of sight of the house. He rested his head on the steering wheel. This was going to be one godawful mess if Ethel caught wind of anything. But Ethel wasn't to blame. This was on him.

For the first time in his life, he was up to no good.

Chapter Eleven

Kitty took a quick trip over to Bertha's in the morning, knowing Wallace was at work.

"Just me," she said.

Bertha was alone, knitting. "Come in, my dear. Hello, Pip! What on earth is that?"

"The biggest box of chocolates in the world. My publisher sent them to me. I'll have a few here with you, and then please keep them and dole them out to the kids."

"Don't mind if I do."

They picked two each and chewed away. "Oh my. These are to die for," Bertha said, sighing.

"Unlike the chocolates I brought over the first night we met."

Bertha smiled. "I can't seem to remember a time when I didn't know you."

"My sentiments exactly. I love this place. I even love that drafty little house."

"I remember when I was a bride and Donald brought me here for the first time. I lived in Sydney, so I thought I was very sophisticated. All I saw was the scrub in the woods, fallen trees, and dirt roads. Everything looked messy. No uniform garden or fence. I know my mother thought I'd married beneath me when she first set eyes on the place. But she never saw the moments when the sun would rise up over the water in the stillness of the morning and the mist would roll in over the fields, with birdsong and surf the only sounds breaking the silence. It was heaven and I was grateful to be a part of it."

"Did your mother change her mind?"

"Probably not, but we didn't talk about it. People just carried on back then, and I had lots of babies so I was too busy to worry about what other people thought." Bertha popped another chocolate in her mouth. "That's a miserable way to live, anyway."

Kitty nodded. "I wish it was that simple."

"It is and it isn't. Life is like a recipe. What do you want in your life cake? What ingredients do you need to make it rise and taste wonderful? Sometimes the simplest recipe is the best, because the more you add to the mix, the more things can go wrong. You like to write. Go home and write your own recipe. See if that helps."

"How did you get so wise?" Kitty said, smiling.

"By making a lot of foolish mistakes over the course of my life. And I'm so grateful for them. It means I lived."

Kitty went home, and thought about pouring herself a glass of wine despite the fact that it was still morning. It seemed the obvious choice for this missive, but common sense prevailed and she had a glass of apple juice instead.

She tried to write her life recipe. After twenty minutes, she walked the blank sheet of paper over to the stove and dropped it in the flames. That's when she poured the wine.

⊛⊛

The week leading up to Kurt's arrival went by in a blur because Kitty did nothing but write. She knew where she was headed; the story was unfolding without effort. When that happened, it was a mad scramble to get it all down. Gaynor knew her process. Things didn't have to be completely neat. All that could be fixed up later. But the germ had to be there, and so far, so good.

The trouble was, the minute Kurt showed up it would disappear into the back of her mind. She needed it to be securely fastened before that happened. It was a precarious time. She was constantly fretting about her main character, Kate Higgins, and her unhappy life, Wallace and his warm neck, and her first foolish mistake, who would arrive the next day. Layered thinking was stressful.

Which was why, by nine o'clock that night, she laid her head down on the kitchen table and shivered. There was a soft knock.

"If that's you, come in. Everyone else, go away."

He did come in. She went to get up.

"Sit," Wallace said. "Just sit over there and stay put." He pulled out a chair and Pip jumped in his lap. "I shouldn't have come, but we need to be on the same page before your husband gets here."

"I'm sorry. I've been writing and trying not to think about it."

"I understand. Our woodpile has never been so neat. Let's look at this logically."

Kitty sat up straight. "Okay. Let's."

"We've become great friends and we like each other."

"Right."

"We've only kissed."

"Right. The first time was after an owl attack, so naturally we were emotional."

"And the kiss the next day was just confirming we were wrong and it was bad."

"Right."

"And that behaviour is not going to happen again, because you are married."

"Right."

"If you are unhappily married, you need to fix that problem before we can even examine what this is. Just to be completely fair to everyone involved."

She waved her hand between them. "And what exactly is this?"

"We can't discuss that now, because there is no *this*. Is there?"

Kitty frowned. "There isn't?"

"No!" Now he waved his hand back and forth. "*This never happened*. Remember?"

"Right."

"So now we can carry on like two carefree people who haven't done anything wrong, even though we have. But we are putting that out of our minds."

"Right. I agree. We're out of our minds."

"No kidding."

※ ※

Kurt came down the stairs of the plane, chatting with an attractive woman, naturally. Kitty actually grinned at the sight because it was so him. He couldn't help himself. He knew he was a big scoop of ice cream with a cherry on top. And she also knew what would happen next.

He came through the doors of the airport, aware that a few people had noticed who he was, and raised his arms with glee. "There she is! My darling little wifey!" He grabbed her in a big hug and twirled her around before planting a kiss on her lips. She was surprised he didn't bend her backwards, as he was known to do in bigger crowds.

"How are you, sweetheart?! You look...amazing, actually. This place must agree with you." Then he tapped her on the behind. "Don't get too fat, babe."

"Stop being rude."

Kurt gave her a quizzical look. "I'm joking. Lighten up!" He looked around, searching for people who might want his autograph, but it seemed no one did.

"There's only one gate here. Talk about depressing."

"This isn't New York."

"I'll say."

Once his suitcase arrived, they walked outside into a bitterly cold, wet, foggy day. The one he hadn't noticed while he chatted up the pretty lady. He gestured to the sky. "Even more depressing!"

"Good lord, we do have miserable days in Montreal and New York, if I'm not mistaken."

"Stop biting my head off. I just got here."

Kitty quickly realized that she now looked at everything through a new filter. Instead of ignoring him or agreeing with everything he said to shut him up, she was on edge. Becoming old Kitty might be in order for the time being, but acting wasn't her forte, despite her declaration to Dolly Wadden.

She saw Pip jump up and down in the driver's seat of the car at their approach. She hadn't dared drop her off with Bertha, because she'd have to pick her up, and that would be too dangerous today. "Look! Pip is happy to see you."

Kurt put his suitcase in the back seat and crawled into the front passenger side. "Hey, you."

Pip jumped on him when Kitty got behind the wheel and he tousled her ears for a moment. "Did you miss me?"

Pip licked his face.

"Okay, enough of that." He picked her up and tossed her in the back seat.

"Hey! Don't do that."

"Don't do what?"

"Put her in the back. Come here, Pippy."

Pip jumped over the seat again and snuggled next to Kitty. "She doesn't like the back. It makes her car sick."

"What is it with you and this dog? You treat it like a baby."

"She *is* my baby. You know, I never noticed that you call her *it*. So does your mother. And I don't appreciate that."

As she drove away, out of the corner of her eye she saw him look at her like she was a stranger. And she was. He didn't know this woman. The acting thing wasn't going well.

"And I don't appreciate you being so snarky. Boy, the apple doesn't fall far from the tree. You're exactly like your father, do you know that? How come I never noticed it before?"

"And what is he doing to you? You never go out of your way to see him."

"I'm allowed to go over to see my mother when my wife is not home to cook my meals. When my wife disappears for months on end for no good reason."

"I had a reason."

"And has it been sorted? After this goddamn play, are you allowed to go home?"

"The play is this Friday and Saturday night."

"And I'll be on the plane home on Monday."

She pulled over to the side of the road in a hurry. The car behind her honked at them for the abrupt manoeuvre.

"What the hell are you doing, Kitty?"

She gripped the wheel. "You came all this way just to go to the play?"

"I'm not just going to the play. I'm supposed to have a cameo, aren't I? And I need to get ready for another movie in Montreal, as it happens, but you weren't home to hear about it, so I can't help it if this is news to you."

She looked behind her shoulder and pulled back out onto the road. "Just as well, I guess."

"What is that supposed to mean?"

"We never seem to be able to talk to each other anyway. I thought being together for a few weeks would help us with that."

He reached over and massaged her neck. "Being together will help. No talking required."

When she didn't respond, Kurt looked out the window for most of the drive. "God. Nothing but trees."

Being quiet for a spell gave Kitty a chance to regroup. She needed the acrimony to deescalate if she had any chance of not blowing everything. "This is Port Morien, where I get my groceries. I know it's gloomy today, but most days the water is a lovely blue. And here is the Orange Hall, where the play will be."

"You're joking. That old building?"

"It's larger than it looks inside."

"And this is where you're staying? It's nothing but dirt roads!"

"This is the urban centre. We haven't hit rural yet."

"Christ."

They turned down South Head Road.

"You're not even on this so-called highway?"

"Nope. That's Ethel Macdonald's house."

"And this is interesting because...?"

"She has a grumpy black cat."

They chugged along and Kurt put out his hand to hold the dash. "My teeth are rattling! This is ridiculous."

Kitty smiled and thought of Ethel. When they neared the Baileys' driveway, she steeled herself. "And this is the Baileys' place. Bertha is the wonderful cook I told you about."

"Looks like a dump."

She resisted the urge to smack him, but not by much. They pulled into her yard. Kurt gave the property a long hard stare. "I stand corrected. This is the dump. You're not serious, are you?"

"It's wonderful. Wait and see."

She showed him everything.

"I still don't see the wonderful part."

"I thought that too when I first arrived, but now I have hot water, a glorious tub, a wood fire, and a place that doesn't leak. And Pippy is as happy as a clam, sniffing around outside. And best of all, I'm writing and enjoying it."

"Great. Glad to hear it. But get real, Kitty. You can't possibly expect me to stay here."

"Where else are you going to stay?"

"A hotel? You honestly thought I'd be happy in this place?"

"Your happiness never occurred to me. This is called visiting your wife, wherever she might be. Pretend it's a movie set if you have to. Act happy."

He walked over and grabbed her around the waist with both hands. "What has gotten into you? You're so saucy. I think I like it. Dour Catriona has been vanquished and this spitfire kitten has turned up. Me*ow*."

Oh, brother.

⇄

He complained about the bed. He complained about the tub. He complained about the stove, the phone, the lack of noise, the lumpy furniture, the cold drafts, and the fact that she'd forgotten to buy him a case of beer. And the pan-fried haddock.

"Unless it's fish and chips, I hate fish."

"Thank God you're only staying for a few days. Now I remember what a complete toddler you are."

"Why do you like this place so much? There's nothing here. We're in the middle of a forest."

"Not quite a forest. More like the woods. Think of *Goldilocks and the Three Bears*."

He sat at the kitchen table and rubbed his hands over his face. "Ugh. I think this solitude has unhinged you."

She poured him a cup of tea. "No, it's given me time to think. Something I haven't done in years."

"No coffee?"

"No. I don't drink coffee, remember?"

"Since when?" He poured a bit of milk in the teacup and added a spoonful of sugar. "You always drink coffee."

"YOU always drink coffee." She put her hands over her eyes. "What colour are my eyes?"

"Don't be stupid. Hazel."

"Brown, actually."

"Close enough. What are we doing today? I need to get out of here. The walls are closing in."

"We can go for a walk."

"No thanks. Don't want to be eaten by those three bears."

"We'll go to town and buy you some beer and coffee. I'll take you the long way around to show you the scenery."

"Wow, sounds like a blast. What's for breakfast?"

"I made porridge. Bertha showed me. It's really good."

"No bacon and eggs?"

Kitty had the pot of porridge in her hand. "No. I made it especially."

"Sorry. That stuff is wallpaper paste."

"This does not taste like your mother's. Believe me." She scooped up two servings, covered the porridge with brown sugar and cream, and sat down. "This is manna from heaven."

Kurt begrudgingly took a bite. And polished it off in a matter of minutes. "Now I know why you're so pudgy. Any more?"

She scraped the rest of the pot into his bowl instead of onto his head.

"Did this Bertha woman teach you how to make dinner too?"

"I do cook dinner."

"Not lately."

Had he always been such a jerk?

❧❧

Bertha was having a hard time concentrating on anything. It was obvious Wallace was not himself. And she thought she knew why, but didn't feel she could ask him about it. Or maybe she should? If he had no one to confide in, would that make it worse? It wasn't often she was in a dither about what to do in any given situation. She'd told her girls to keep their noses out of it, but maybe that didn't apply to her. She was his mother, after all. But he was a grown man. Why was it so difficult to know what to do? If this was John or Charlie or George, she'd keep quiet because they already had a woman in their life to talk to, but she and Wallace were best friends. If she wasn't talking to him, and Kitty couldn't talk to him, he was alone.

She seized the opportunity at lunch, which was homemade tomato soup and crispy crackers just out of the oven. She cut up old cheese on a plate and placed it beside the butter dish. The dogs let her know when his truck pulled up. Watching him through the window as he walked to the house, she saw the weight of the world on his shoulders.

"Hi, Mom. Smells good."

He greeted his pups. Put them each in a headlock and pounded their hindquarters with loving thumps. They lapped it up and didn't want him to stop, but after a few minutes he headed for the sink to wash his hands before sitting at the table.

Bertha spooned the soup into his bowl. "Get this down ya. It's mighty cold out today. Your hands looked red and chapped. Wear your work gloves."

"Stop fussing."

"Why? I'm so good at it." She sat opposite him and reached for a cracker.

"No soup?"

"Not that hungry. So, any gossip?"

"I'm building a garage. The only thing old Alex and his cronies talk about while I work are the Toronto Maple Leafs, so I have nothing to report."

"Pity." She cleared her throat. "While I have you here..."

"Uh-oh."

"What?" She put her head down and buttered another cracker.

"Let me help you out." He also took a cracker and added the cheese. "You're worried because Kitty's husband is down the road."

"Yes."

"And you think that she and I like each other."

"Who wouldn't like Kitty? She's adorable."

"Exactly. We're friends, Mom, so there's nothing to worry about."

Bertha nodded. "Okay. Just know..."

"You're here for me."

"Always."

"And, might I add, everyone else who's alive and breathing on this planet."

"Maybe not everyone, but you certainly. If you need to talk..."

"That's what the chickens are for."

❧

Ethel was at a loose end. No one was on the phone today. And because it was another grey and dreary afternoon, with the ground a mess of dead grass and wet mud, her mood was low. It didn't help that Blackie flattened his ears and growled when she walked by.

"Even my cat doesn't like me."

She wandered over to Winnie's bedroom door and knocked on it but then barged straight in and stood in the middle of the room.

Winnie looked up from her canvas. "Oh, it's you, Ethel. Come on in."

"Is that supposed to be funny?"

"Yes."

"Well, it's not." Ethel sat on the edge of Winnie's bed. "What are you doing?"

"I'm painting."

"What? Fog?"

"I'm painting Tweety, as it happens. He's being a great sport." Ethel pointed at him. "That's my bird."

"Yes, he told me. And you're welcome to him anytime, but I'd like to finish this portrait. Maybe you could hang it in your bedroom when it's done. It's rather good. See?" Winnie held it up and Ethel glanced at it.

"No, thanks. Only one picture goes over my bed, and that's Jesus."

"Suit yourself."

Winnie went back to her painting while Ethel stewed in her own juice. "Don't you ever get lonesome?"

"I suppose so, but when I do, I find something to occupy my

mind. You should try it. Draw a picture or write down your memories or do a little baking. You used to like crossword puzzles. I have lots of books you can borrow. You're making your world smaller than it needs to be."

Ethel jumped up. "What would you know about it? You live in this room. At least I have friends."

"That's something you can do. Go and visit Bertha. That will cheer you up."

"Maybe I will, because you sure don't." She didn't close the door after her.

She went to Kitty's first to try and get a glimpse of her husband, but the car wasn't in the yard, so she got out and tiptoed over to the kitchen window anyway and peered in. It looked a bit of a shambles, with dishes still on the table and a couple of men's shirts hanging from a chair. Too bad they weren't home. She turned to leave and stumbled on the last step of the stairs and had to save herself by banging into the hood of her car. It gave her an awful fright and she hurt her wrist. It crossed her mind that she was old now, and at this moment no one knew where she was. If she'd fallen and broken her hip, she'd be a bear's dinner. And no one would care.

Ethel knocked on Bertha's door with her good wrist and pushed the door open. "Bertha? You home?"

"I'm in the kitchen."

She took off her raincoat and hung it on a hook in the porch. When she opened the inner door, the giant dogs got in her way. "Shoo! Shoo, now! Bertha? I'm in the kitchen and you're not here."

"I am. Look down."

Ethel looked down and still couldn't see anything. "Where the blazes are you?"

"I'm on my knees scrubbing the floor on the other side of the table. Walk on the newspapers, please."

"Oh! There you are. Never scrub a floor on a rainy day. It's futile."

Bertha threw her scrub brush in the bucket of hot soapy water and used her arms on a chair seat to put one foot on the floor before she groaned and lifted herself up onto her other foot. She had to steady herself after she did. "Whew. It's not easy to get up at our age. I keep forgetting that."

"Another reason to never scrub a floor. Use a mop. Or get Wallace to do it."

"He does, and gets annoyed when I do this, but I like it. It helps me think. Want some tea?"

"Have I ever said no?"

"Not that I can recall."

While Ethel drank her tea, she polished off the last of the crackers and cheese on the table. "I've never been able to make crackers. You're the only person I know who still does."

"Wallace likes them."

"It must be nice to have a son you like."

"I know you, Ethel. You love your son. Stop saying shocking things to get sympathy. We've been friends too long for that to work anymore."

"Although you must be a little perturbed about what's been going on with Wallace and Kitty?"

Just the look on Bertha's face confirmed her suspicions. So, Wallace wasn't a complete angel. As much as Ethel loved Bertha, it was nice to know her family wasn't perfect.

"What on earth do you mean, Ethel Macdonald? And don't you dare say it's common knowledge."

"Dolly Wadden said that Kitty had designs on Wallace. She said she's not as innocent as she looks. That's all I know."

"Did she now? Says the woman who can't keep her hands off Wallace. The woman who chases everything in pants. And you believed her?"

"Well, I—"

"Know this, Ethel. Kitty and Wallace are friends. And for you to repeat anything Dolly Wadden says is beneath you. And you're my friend. How do you think it makes me feel when you blurt out something like that? It hurts."

To Ethel's dismay, Bertha began to tear up and took a tissue she had up her sleeve to wipe her nose. Ethel immediately got up and went over to put her arm around her friend. "I'm sorry, Bertha. You're right. I had no business saying that to you. Especially since I know it's not true. Wallace would never have anything to do with a married woman and I should've known better than to listen to that tarted-up tart. Please forgive me."

Bertha nodded and blew her nose. "Sorry. I'm having an off day."

Chapter Twelve

Kitty was exhausted. She'd never realized how much energy she expended making Kurt happy, or at least satisfied. Of course, her guilt was a heavy burden, but even so. She tried to remember what it was like to have him home. Was it always this fraught with anxiety?

And then it occurred to her. She disappeared into her writing when he prowled around. Is that how her books had started? As a way to avoid him? And did he constantly go out because she had spent the last decade in her study? The two of them were so disconnected it wasn't funny.

After a very long day trying to show him around to get more than a grunt out of him, Kitty made cheeseburgers for supper.

"That's it?"

"We have to be at dress rehearsal for six. I don't have time to make a standing rib roast."

"So why aren't we having dinner with this Bertha woman? I thought you said we would."

"Maybe tomorrow."

Kurt lit a cigarette and put his feet up on the kitchen table. "The effort you've made to organize this amazing vacation is astonishing. You should be a cruise director with your skills."

She flipped the burgers. "You don't have an audience. You can stop being clever."

He laughed. "You're right. Sorry. I get carried away."

Kitty leaned over and grabbed the cigarette from him. "Do you ever miss me when you're on set?"

He shook his head. "No. Not if I'm being honest. I'm too busy to think about anything. Maybe that's why I like acting. I don't have to be myself."

She took the frying pan off the hottest part of the stove, so it wouldn't burn. "Do you ever think of our childhood? How weird it was?"

"I couldn't wait to get out of there because of your dad. He didn't like me very much."

She took a drag and blew the smoke in his face. "Because you were spoiled rotten. And I couldn't wait to get out of there because of your mother. You know she always hated me."

"Because you hated her! I remember her crying over it. You never warmed up to her, no matter what she did. It wasn't her fault your mother died. But it's like you blamed her for it. You're right, our childhood was a complete disaster."

She'd made Martha cry? Could a seven-year-old have that kind of power? Kitty had never considered this before. She was always the victim in the story. And so was her father.

"Do you think we married each other to get out of the house?" she asked.

"Definitely."

"And why are we still together?"

"Isn't it obvious?" He grabbed her hand and pulled her onto his lap. "Me Tarzan, you Jane."

"Oh, please." Kitty struggled to get up but Kurt reached over and stroked her cheek with his thumb. "I love ya, babe."

She hadn't expected that.

❦

When Robert Chandler walked into the Orange Hall for the dress rehearsal, the complete cast and the multitudes of hangers-on broke out in applause. Dolly, seemingly forgetting her fury, rushed over and grabbed his hands to lean in for a kiss on both cheeks.

"Robert Chandler! How wonderful to meet you! I'm Dolly Wadden, the producer, director, and lead actress of this delightful escapade."

Robert wasn't an actor for nothing. "My dear Dolly. What an asset you are to this community. The arts need people like yourself in these remote outposts. I hear you're giving me a teensy little cameo to include me on this visit, which is very generous and thoughtful. You never know when I might be able to repay the favour."

Kitty had to stop herself from rolling her eyes. Surely the woman knew nonsense when she heard it—but apparently not. Dolly grabbed her throat and swooned a little. "How marvellous!"

Robert took her by the arm. "Now, fill me in on my tiny little role. I'm a very quick study." He pulled her away to the stage. The entire cast followed except Ken.

"He certainly is a handsome fella."

"Yes."

"He's a lot taller on television."

Kitty looked up at him. "Actors can grow and shrink at will. Didn't you know that?"

"Ingenious creatures, wha'?"

They joined the others on stage. Robert rubbed his hands together. "So, what would you like me to do, Madame Director? As this is called *The Glorified Brat*, I take it you're the brat?"

"I'm the brat's mother," Dolly said.

"Nonsense!" Robert exclaimed. "You're far too young to be a mother."

Dolly tittered. Ken and Kitty made darn sure their eyes didn't meet.

After fifteen minutes of trying to figure out what Robert could do, with the entire cast making unhelpful suggestions about tweaking this and that, it was obvious to Kitty that Robert was bored. She wouldn't put it past him to walk out without a word.

"I know! How about Robert play my role? All I do is open and close the door five times and yell, 'Brat!' and then I fall down the stairs in the last scene. I know there's not much dialogue, but—"

"It's perfect!" Robert shouted. "That's just what we'll do."

"Are you sure?" Ken asked her. "You've become an expert at slamming doors."

"Ken!" Dolly frowned. "It's been decided. And by none other than a fabulous actor. You know nothing about the theatre!"

Kitty hoped Dolly was enjoying tonight. Because by this time tomorrow Robert would blow her right off her own stage and she'd never see it coming.

❧

The actor was gone. Kurt moped through the next day and kept asking if they were going to Bertha's. Damn it all. Why had she ever mentioned her? Kitty finally picked up the phone and called. "Is it too late to book a table at Chez Bertha for tonight? If we eat at five sharp, we should have time to make it to the show. Kurt is looking forward to it."

"Of course. I'm making a big mess of spare ribs because it seems some of my kids want to go to the play. I'll be babysitting only a few of the grandchildren. Everyone made their own arrangements."

Once that was sorted, Kitty insisted Kurt come with her for a walk down to the shore. "We need to talk."

"Oooh. You sound like a character in one of your novels."

"How would you know? You've never read them."

Kurt wrapped a scarf around his throat after he buttoned up his jacket. "I read the first two. After that there was no point. They were almost identical. Someone gets killed and that Harry fella figures out who did it."

Kitty crammed her hat on her head and put on that favourite blue coat before she attached Pip to her leash. "You have to like reading murder mysteries. Or books, for that matter."

"Reading isn't my thing. That doesn't make me stupid."

"Doesn't make you smart, either."

As they stepped outside into the cold November afternoon, Kurt put his arm through Kitty's and squeezed it. "Where did all this piss and vinegar come from?"

"I've changed. This place has transformed me. It's what I want to talk about. Wait till we get to the water."

"That sounds ominous. Are you planning to drown me?"

"Don't give me any ideas."

They walked in unison as Pip hurried by Kitty's side. The sun peeked out for the first time since Kurt had arrived and it made everything look a lot cheerier. The warmth felt good on Kitty's face and it calmed her breathing. It was odd that they'd always been able to walk together almost as one, with the same stride and pace. As long as they were arm in arm. It completely fell apart when they tried to hold hands, but they hadn't done that in years.

When they got to the shoreline, after tramping over uneven dirt road, fields, fallen trees, mossy undergrowth, and lots of birch twigs, they were a bit winded, but in a good way. Salty gusts came at them from across the water. Kurt took a deep breath and exhaled. "I have to admit, it smells..."

"...clean? Fresh?"

"It's not even the smell. It *feels* different. Filling. Like I'm actually breathing air and not air mucked up with dirt."

She took a deep breath too. "You're right. It's very filling."

They sat on a flat rock and looked out over the water. Kitty pointed. "There's the eagle!"

"How do you know?"

"Do you see its white head? And the way it glides in circles around and around? That's why I keep Pip on a leash when she's outside. Eagles will eat a little dog."

"No way! A dog?"

"I don't know about a big dog, but they are scavengers, remember."

"So when you kill me, they'll feast on my bones?"

"That's the plan."

Kurt picked up a few twigs and broke them into small pieces. "Remember that time we tried camping? What a disaster."

"When you bring the wrong tent poles, there's bound to be a hiccup."

"The monsoon didn't help."

They glanced at each other and smiled. Kitty was the first to speak. "Why did we stop doing things like that?"

"Shivering in soggy sleeping bags isn't a great hobby."

"We stopped hanging out with each other," Kitty said, sighing. "I think that's why you don't miss me when you're working and I haven't missed you while I've been here. We've become so accustomed to passing each other like ships in the night that we think it's normal. But is it?"

He put his hands back in his pockets. "No two marriages are the same. Whatever works should be the rule. Not what someone else says it should be."

"And does our marriage work for you?"

Kurt looked at her in puzzlement. "Yes. Are you implying it doesn't for you?"

"I'm starting to wonder."

"Gee, thanks."

"Look, Kurt, I told you I've done a lot of thinking since I've been here, and I suddenly realized how lonely I've been. I wasn't even aware of it until everything became too much and I stopped writing. Something was wrong, and it wasn't until I stepped out of my own life and looked at it from afar that I've come to see that you and I are..."

"Are what?"

"Are you in love with me?"

Kurt stood abruptly and marched towards the water over the uneven rocks. He threw his hands in the air before he turned around and glared at her. "What a stupid question!" he shouted. "Of course I'm in love with you. Do you honestly think I'd still be here if I wasn't?"

She hadn't expected that.

❦

Though Kitty wouldn't be acting on stage tonight, she knew she had to give the performance of her life at the Bailey supper table.

When they pulled up in the yard, Wallace came out of the barn right away, with the dogs. Kitty assumed that he didn't want an audience when he first met Kurt. It was safer outdoors.

"My god! What a massive specimen he is. Are those dogs? Never mind the eagle. Pip is as good as dead."

Kitty opened her car door and Pip sailed out and ran to her three best friends. "She's good. She loves them."

Kurt trailed after her as she walked over to Wallace. "Wallace, this is my husband, Kurt Wagner. Better known as Robert Chandler."

Wallace extended his hand. "Nice to meet you, Robert. I've seen you in *Westward Ho*. A great show."

"Hello, Wallace. My goodness. If you're ever in the mood to make a little money, you could always be my stunt double!"

Wallace and Kitty laughed politely. Then Wallace extended his arm towards the house. "You'd better get inside. There's a room full of very excited people who can't wait to meet a famous actor. I've got a bit of a job with the tractor, so I'll be in when supper is on the table."

"I'll leave Pip with you then," Kitty said as she steered Kurt towards the house. Wallace walked away but put up his hand to indicate he'd heard her.

"Seems like a nice fella," said Kurt.

"The whole family is nice."

Everyone had the usual reaction when meeting her husband for the first time. It never failed. Either people were very nervous and said nothing or they talked over each other. Robert turned on the charm and they were smitten. He was very comfortable in this type of situation.

Wallace showed up just as the platters of ribs made an appearance. As they sat around the dining room table, Robert entertained them with stories from behind the scenes of their favourite shows.

"I told the producers of *Westward Ho* that I knew how to ride a horse. I'd never been on one in my life. Remember that, Kitty?"

She smiled and nodded. How many times had she heard this story? She tuned him out and nibbled on the ribs in front of her, which were fantastic, but she had no appetite. Wallace didn't either. The few times she glanced at him from under her eyelashes, he was moving his dinner around but not actually eating. It was only towards the end of the meal that she became aware that Bertha wasn't her usual smiley self. She appeared nervous and edgy. Had Wallace said something to her? Were they all looking at her? Did they know?

A wave of dizziness made her pitch forward, and it was only Wallace's brother Charlie who kept her from landing face-first on her plate. Everyone stopped and made sympathetic noises. Wallace started to rise from his chair, and then thought better of it, thank goodness.

She held out her hands. "I'm sorry, everyone. Don't be alarmed. I'm fine."

Robert tore the meat off his rib with his teeth. "She's okay," he said with his mouth full. "She does this all the time. She used to faint a lot when she was a kid."

Bertha poured a glass of water from the pitcher on the table and brought it to her. "You knew each other when you were young?" She kept her hand on Kitty's back as she drank it.

"I can hardly remember a time when I didn't know her. Isn't that so, Kitty?" He wiped his mouth on a napkin.

She finished the water and put down the glass. "Yes, but it's a long and boring story and I think we'd better get going, or Dolly will have our heads."

"That, Mrs. Bailey, was the best serving of ribs I've ever had in my life, and I've been to a lot of very fancy restaurants. Kitty, get this recipe and try not to make a hash of it...there's a good girl."

When Kitty thanked Bertha for the lovely meal, Bertha grabbed her in a hug and squeezed her for longer than normal.

Everyone shouted good luck as they made their way to the car, and that they'd see them at the play. Pip disappeared back into the house with her pals.

As they drove up the road in the dark, the headlights the only illumination around, Kurt patted his belly. "That was incredible. You were right about that woman. She'd make a fortune cooking like that in a swanky New York eatery."

"That's the last place she'd want to be."

"So all those people at the table were her kids?"

"A few were missing. She has ten altogether, and thirty grandchildren and eleven great-grandchildren. Your mother would give her right arm to be so lucky."

"You think that's lucky? A screaming pack of kids? I'm glad I was an only child. Aren't you?"

"I wasn't an only child."

"Okay, split hairs."

"Can you stop talking?"

"Are you mad at me? What for? You told me to take your part in the play."

"No, Kurt. I'm not mad about that. I think you'll do it brilliantly."

Boy, did he ever.

The entire audience was convulsing from beginning to end. Dolly had a giant hit on her hands, thanks to the excitement caused by having Robert Chandler be the doorman. The play was funny anyway, but the biggest laughs were when Robert ad libbed his part every single time. He jammed his own fingers in the door, purposely forgot to open it on cue, slammed it shut over and over again, made faces when Dolly marched through, mimicking her walk. Anything he could think of to take all the attention. He even made yelling the word "Brat!" sound like rapid machine-gun fire. And watching from the audience, Kitty knew that her castmates loved it. She thought Ken would bust trying not to laugh out loud right on stage. The only one getting increasingly flustered was Dolly. And Kitty felt sorry for her. She knew exactly how it felt to be one-upped by the dazzling Robert Chandler.

When Robert managed to make his fall down the stairs thirty seconds long, as he flailed and bounced in slow-motion off the walls and steps in an elaborate dance of body parts, it was so astonishing the audience leapt to their feet and gave him a standing ovation before the play was even over.

When the play finally did end, Robert made sure that he himself was at the front of the stage clapping for Dolly, encouraging the audience to yell "Bravo!" when it was her turn to be highlighted. He bowed to her and kissed her hand as if she were a fair maiden. In that moment, he won her over all over again.

Kitty suddenly realized that's how he did it. He got what he wanted and then made a great big fuss over you, so you'd forget about what he did five minutes ago.

She had to wait an hour for Robert to stop lapping up the adoration from his many fans. Dolly stood next to him the entire time, grinning. By the time the tenth person said how lucky Kitty was to be married to him, she had a splitting headache. She must have looked peaky, because he suddenly stopped signing autographs and announced to the remaining crowd, "I'm so sorry. My poor wife has waited here for too long. It's time to take her to bed."

A few ladies fanned themselves with their programs, including Dolly.

"That line is old," she whispered as he held out her coat.

"But it always works." He slipped it up over her shoulders

as he kissed her back of her head. Then he returned to Dolly and grabbed both her hands. "A wonderful job, madame. We will see you tomorrow."

"Oh yes," she breathed and held out her cheek. He managed to stumble a little and caught the edge of her mouth as he kissed her.

That was an old trick, too, and it certainly made Dolly's night, if not her year. Kitty was so over it all, she headed straight out the door without waiting for him. She started the car and watched as he shook a few hands with the departing crowd before he ran over and jumped in.

"Man, it's cold out."

"Yep." It wasn't often there were more than a couple of cars at this time of night on the main street of Morien, but tonight there were headlights everywhere. She had to wait to pull out.

"So how do you think it went?" He lit a cigarette and cracked the window open a tad.

"You know how it went. It was amazing. So much better than if I'd done it."

"Hey! Don't sell yourself short. You can ham it up when you want to. You used to be very funny."

"Was I? I wonder what happened."

"Damned if I know."

She pulled into the Baileys' yard. "I'll run in and get Pip."

"Uh-huh." He sounded half asleep.

Kitty knocked on their door and opened it right away. "Just me." She went into the kitchen, but only the lamp by the shelf of cookbooks was on, so she stepped into the living room. Bertha had nodded off while reading. The three dogs were by the fire. Pip ran over to her, and Wallace turned around in his chair before standing up. They returned to the kitchen.

"You okay?" he asked quietly, so as not to wake his mother.

She nodded.

"I was worried."

"Don't be. He's right. I swoon like that all the time for some reason."

"Charlie and his wife came back to get the kids and they were still laughing. Said it was the best thing they'd ever seen."

"He can pull out all the stops when he wants to."

"I have a ticket for tomorrow."

"Why?"

He shrugged. "I'll stay away. I won't even speak to you."

She picked up Pip. "I wish you hadn't done that. We're trying to steer clear of each other. It's safer."

"I won't go if you really don't want me to."

"Never mind. I don't know what I want. Except for this nightmare to be over. Thanks for looking after Pip." She was careful not to make a noise as she left.

⚜

Saturday was surprisingly relaxing. Kurt slept in despite his moaning about the bed, and Kitty knew it was the filling air that did it. She was able to get a good three hours done on her script before he even showed his face. He asked for porridge and made his own coffee. Then he had some calls to make, and after Kitty showed him how the phone worked, he talked to the director of the new movie about his schedule. She never bothered to tell him that Ethel listened in. It's not like anything he said would make sense to anyone else, although it would keep Ethel amused for weeks. A few times he tried to make more calls but had to wait his turn, so he sat quietly playing solitaire at the kitchen table.

He even put more wood on the fire when she asked him to. There wasn't a sarcastic remark, or a play for attention. It was almost spooky. He made them peanut butter sandwiches for lunch. When she asked him if he wanted to go sightseeing, he declined.

"I like listening to the fire in this stove. If we ever move, we should get a fireplace."

As he read his script, it dawned on her that he was quiet because his surroundings were quiet. He fed off other people's energy, and when there was no one around that he could get easy access to, he fell into a stupor. Life was so much easier like this.

She put another sheet of paper in her typewriter. "Would you like to live in the country? I think it would be a good idea."

He chewed his thumbnail as he stared at his screenplay. "Hell no. Nice air and all, but I'd go mad if I had to do this all day."

"What? Spend time with your wife?"

"Well, there is that, but waiting to use this phone is a nightmare." He got up again and checked. "Yippee! It's free. I have to call Doug."

"Who's Doug?"

"The casting director. He had trouble deciding between two actresses and wants me to do a screen test with both of them to see which one has more chemistry with me. We have to meet on Tuesday."

He looked through his pockets trying to find Doug's number. Kitty leaned on the kitchen door frame. "It's a romantic flick?"

"Yeah. A woman has the hots for this guy but she's married and the guilt is driving her crazy. I play the guy, naturally, not the husband."

"I can't believe I've never asked you before, but what's it like to kiss someone you don't even know?"

"I won't lie, it can be great, but if they have bad breath they can't pay me enough. Sorry, I have to grab this while it's free."

Kitty wandered back over to her favourite kitchen chair and Pip made a beeline for her lap. She rubbed her soft fur. "Guilt does drive you crazy, Pip. As well as not knowing what you want. Or who you are. Or who you used to be. Why don't we trade places? I'd love to be a dog."

She thought exactly the same thing when she dropped Pip off before the play. If only she could stay and eat chocolates with Bertha.

She hollered through the door and said she had to go. "No worries!" Bertha cried back. "Hope it goes well."

❀

The place was packed and the buzz around the room was electric. Wallace had never seen this many people in the building. He made sure he stayed at the back; people got annoyed when he sat in front of them.

Kitty was near the stage. She kept looking around until she saw him. His face didn't move a muscle. She, however, gave him a quick wave and a little smile, as if to apologize for saying he shouldn't have come, so he nodded his head and smiled back.

All he ever wanted to do was smile when he saw her. She was beautiful. He'd love to be able to tell her, but it wasn't likely to happen. He needed to keep a lid on thoughts like that.

The play was very funny, but he only pretended to laugh, so he wouldn't stand out. From the moment he met this Kurt/Robert character, he couldn't stand him. A smarmy little know-it-all who loved to hear himself talk and be the centre of attention. Who wasn't the least concerned when Kitty had a spell at the dinner table? And a joke at her expense about not making a hash of the rib recipe? Saying, "There's a good girl." Wallace had almost reached over and clocked him in the face.

And watching him now make a spectacle of himself to prove he was better than the entire amateur cast on stage was sickening. Wallace even pitied Dolly, who was trying desperately not to have her performance go completely unnoticed by the audience.

The only time Wallace genuinely laughed was when Kurt/Robert fell down the stairs, because he could pretend that's exactly how the jerk would look if he had knocked him out.

He left the building while people were still clapping and hollering. After all that time with the raucous crowd, the silence in the truck as he drove home was welcome. If yesterday was anything to go by, Mr. Man would accept accolades for at least another hour. Poor Kitty. He knew she'd want to go home. At least he'd see her for a minute when she picked up Pip.

All three dogs were by the door when he arrived. They always heard the truck. He took them out into the yard to give them a piddle, since he'd ordered his mother to never go out with the dogs at night anymore. She could stumble and fall on anything, most likely a kid's toy. She promised she wouldn't.

Back inside, after giving the gang some dog treats, he joined his mom in front of the fire. Tonight, she was wide awake.

"Want a cup of tea?" he asked.

"No, dear. But could you bring me that enormous box of chocolates Kitty gave me? I hid it in the sideboard. I told her I'd share it with the kids, but they're so good I've kept them for myself. Don't let her know I'm a greedy old woman."

"She wouldn't believe that anyway." He bent down and pulled them out of the crammed shelf. "The size of this!"

"I know. That publishing company of hers must really love her. Everything they send her is massive."

"She deserves it."

He handed it to her and she opened the lid. "Take one or two or five."

She laughed when he took five and sat in his chair. "So how did it go? Was it as funny as the kids said?"

"Oh, it was funny, all right. He made sure of that by upstaging everyone and everything."

"Well, he is a professional actor."

"He's an unruly child. A glorified brat."

"Isn't that the name of the play?"

"Yes. Perfect, don't you think?"

Bertha chewed on her caramel before commenting. "I have to say, I wasn't too keen on him myself. How did Kitty ever end up with someone like that? She never calls attention to herself."

Wallace threw his hands in the air. "It's a mystery to me."

"Well, my love. I know you. You weren't going to like him even if he was the nicest guy around, were you?"

"Just leave it."

"Okay." She popped another chocolate in her mouth.

Bertha was asleep in her chair by the time the car headlights approached the house. Wallace picked up Pip and stood in the kitchen waiting for Kitty. There was a soft knock and the inner door opened.

Robert Chandler entered the room. "Hey, Wallace!"

"Sorry, my mother is asleep in the next room."

Robert put his index finger up to his mouth and then whispered, "Right, apologies. Just saving Kitty from having to get out of the car. She's pretty tired."

Wallace handed Pip to him. "I'm sure she is."

"So, how did you enjoy the show? I noticed you left abruptly."

"Wanted to get out before the crowd."

"Good thinking. And here's something else to think about, big guy. You'd better leave my wife alone. I know her, and she's a goody-two-shoes. Always afraid to upset Daddy. She's not built for an affair or even a dalliance, unlike myself. If you care for her, and it's spectacularly obvious that you do, you'll leave her be. Got that, chum?"

And out the door he went.

Chapter Thirteen

Kitty dreamt that the whole village of Morien was laughing at her, pointing their fingers and holding their bellies. Why wouldn't they stop? She tried to shout at them, but she had no voice. And then she saw Kurt up on a stage. He was egging them on.

She sat up in bed with her heart pounding, in a daze. She was alone. Not even Pip was with her. It took her a few moments to remember where she was.

"Hello?"

"Oh!" Kurt called out. "She's awake! Stay right there. Let's go surprise Mommy!"

He came into the bedroom carrying a tray with a glass of orange juice, a cup of tea, and six pieces of toast already spread with jam. "Good morning, my love. Breakfast in bed, served with a smile." Kurt kissed her astonished face, placed the tray in front of her, and sat on the edge of the bed. He even patted the mattress, inviting Pip to join them.

"Goodness," Kitty squeaked. "That's a lot."

"I'll take one." He grabbed a slice and took a bite.

She put her hand to her forehead and he took it away. "Stop fretting. The dog has been walked..."

"What?! Did you put her on a leash?"

"Yes. Even though there didn't seem to be any eagles in the area. Then I started the fire..."

"What?! Is it roaring?"

"No. I'm not a complete idiot. I do know how to make a fire, thanks to—"

"Your cowboy days. I remember. Well, thank you, but I have to visit the ladies'."

He removed the tray. "Come right back."

After she was finished, she looked in the mirror as she washed her hands. That had been a nightmare, not a dream. The worst part was not being able to speak. She supposed she knew what that meant, but she didn't want to think about it.

Kitty crawled back under the covers. She'd never had breakfast in bed, so she wasn't going to miss it. Kurt put the tray back in front of her. She looked at it. Now there were only three pieces of toast left.

"What's the matter? The dog ate one too."

"No, she didn't. She'd never be able to eat a slice that fast. Do you always lie this easily?"

He shrugged.

"That's a yes." She took a sip of tea and a big bite of what remained of her breakfast.

"So, I was thinking," he said. "Since today is our last full day, why don't we go for a nice walk, and then dinner and a movie? You said you couldn't remember the last time we had a date."

She smiled. "That sounds nice, but I don't want to leave Pip with the Baileys three nights in a row. I feel like I'm taking advantage of them."

"Can this dog not spend any time alone?"

"I'd really rather she didn't. It's so isolated out here. At least at home if something happened, someone would hear her barking."

He looked like he was going to argue but suddenly changed his mind. "Fine."

"We can go for a walk, though, and then venture to Glace Bay and pick up a couple of steaks and a bottle of wine? How does that sound?"

"If you say so. I need more toast, because you've hogged it all." He slapped her thigh through the covers before he got up.

"Hey, you! I've had one bite. Although I do plan to eat the rest.

And share some with my baby, unlike you."

"You spoil that dog!" he shouted from the kitchen.

All in all, they had a pleasant day together. Kurt was more animated and pointed out the scenery as they drove through Glace Bay and then Sydney. They even went as far as Louisbourg to look at the lighthouse there, and took a couple of pictures of the impressive structure jutting out on the outcrop of rock by the coast, but they didn't stay long as the fog rolled in and the temperature dropped.

They got home just before the fire went out, and while Kitty made a salad and put potatoes in the oven to bake, Kurt went over his lines by pacing in the living room and reciting them out loud.

"Leave the son-of-a-bitch! He's done nothing but make your life a living hell. You know I'm right, darling. Let me hold you and kiss you like a real man. Smooch, smooch, smooch, etc."

"A real man must have written that drivel," she said, laughing. "You should write screenplays."

"No, thank you."

The potatoes were crispy, the salad fresh, and the steaks medium-rare, the way he liked them. They sat at the kitchen table and finished off the bottle of red wine. They had a cigarette for dessert.

Kurt reached out his hand and took hers. "I have to say, my love, I've had a really wonderful time here. I know I bitched about it when I first came..."

"To be fair, so did I."

"But I can see why you like this place. It is very cozy. The quiet takes some getting used to, but it's rather pleasant."

"It's made it so much easier for me to write. Maybe we should think about moving to the country. Or get a little house with a garden."

"We could certainly look into it. I want you to know that I've heard you. Your loneliness. And it's true. I'm not sure how we ended up taking each other for granted, but I'd like that to change. And I don't think we got married just to get out of the house. I did love you and still do. I know I can be a pain in the ass, and what I do for a living is insane, but we were happy once upon a time and I know we can be again. I'm certainly willing to try if you are."

Kitty felt tears in her eyes but wasn't sure why they were there.

"Hey now, hey now! You never cry! Come here, you old softie."

And he took her to bed.

※

On her way home from the airport, Kitty stopped off at the store in Morien. She waved hello to the rabbits on the way in.

"I'll take a carton of du Maurier and three huge bags of penny candy. Also, eight boxes of Cherry Blossoms."

Hopper chuckled. "Sounds like someone is having a bad day. Or a good day."

"I can't decide."

She spent the next three days writing. She had a moment when she thought she'd lost it, but pushed herself to remember the way forward. It was much easier dealing with Kate Higgins's life than her own.

In the back of her mind, she expected Wallace to show up, but then she couldn't remember if she'd told him when Kurt was leaving. And she wasn't sure how she'd feel when she did see him, so it was safer to stay put and focus her attention on the typewriter.

※

Bertha was anxious.

Wallace was unusually quiet. But it wasn't even that. Ethel had told her that Robert Chandler had to be in Montreal on Tuesday to meet with two actresses, so that meant he had to leave on Monday at the very latest. It was now Thursday, and they still hadn't heard a peep from Kitty. Even the dogs looked confused, moping on the front porch.

That evening, for the first time in a long time, no one was

coming for supper. As Wallace washed his hands after his last day of building that garage, she broached the subject.

"Should we invite Kitty to join us for supper? There's lots of shepherd's pie."

"If she wanted to be here, she would. She's not shy about inviting herself over."

"I wonder what she's doing."

"She's writing."

"Oh. Is that the project she mentioned?"

"I suppose so. I don't exactly know. I've been busy, haven't I?"

Bertha's big scoop paused in mid-air, but she didn't turn around. "Yes, I suppose you have." She dropped the spoonful of dinner on his plate and added another one before taking it over to him.

"Thanks," he muttered.

She got her own dinner and sat with him, but she never said another word. And he didn't notice.

⁂

Okay, this was ridiculous. Wallace still hadn't shown up and Bertha hadn't called. What was going on? It was now Friday. If he was giving her space, it was too much space. She wrote the same paragraph over and over again before she ripped the page from the typewriter, balled it up, and threw it across the room. No, she didn't know how she'd feel when she saw Wallace, but it had to be better than not seeing him at all.

She grabbed Pip and her flashlight and stalked up the road. She knocked on the door and waited to be invited in. Wallace's oldest sister, Mary, opened the door. "Well, hello, Kitty. We were just talking about you. Come on in. Dinner's almost on the table."

The dogs rushed from the back porch and almost knocked her over. Pip struggled to get out of her arms and down with her buddies.

Bertha came forward. "It's so good to see you, dear! I was worried, but I didn't want to disturb you. Wallace said you were writing."

"Yes, I've been busy, but I miss everyone. I didn't even look at the time. I don't expect you to feed me."

"Nonsense, come on in. There's only Mary and Ethel and me tonight. Wallace had to go to a meeting."

Her heart sank. She hadn't noticed his truck was gone. Still, all that quiet was beginning to bug her, so it would be good to talk to someone.

Tonight's menu was tuna noodle casserole with warm biscuits. She held out her plate before Bertha even got to her. Oh, she'd missed this.

"What did your husband think of the play?" Ethel asked. "Was he pleased with all the attention?"

"Yes, he thought the audience here was so welcoming and appreciative. It's a treat for him to play in front of a live crowd."

"Well, Dolly got her wish and I think she's been kicking herself ever since."

Mary took a biscuit from the basket in front of her. "Why's that?"

Ethel leaned forward. "A little birdie told me that she's been crying her eyes out since reading the article in the *Post Record* about the play. They never even mentioned her. Just her name along with the other cast members in the photo. It was all about Robert Chandler and how he came to town and knocked it out of the park."

"Oh dear," Kitty said. "I knew that would happen."

"Serves her right," Ethel sniffed. "She's a tarted-up tart who spreads rumours about good people, like you and Wallace."

Kitty's fork stopped on the way to her mouth.

"Ethel." Bertha looked grim.

"Well, I'm sorry, but I think she should know that Dolly thinks Kitty spends all her time trying to weasel her way around Wallace. But don't you worry, my girl. Bertha and me don't believe a word of it, do we, Bertha? You can count on us."

Bertha sighed. "Don't give it another thought, Kitty. Dolly is a sad woman who would love nothing better than to have Wallace to herself."

It seemed wise to put the forkful of noodles in her mouth so she had to chew it instead of answer. Then she drank a sip of water before she spoke. "I'm not worried about the Dollys of this world, but it bothers me that she'd bring Wallace into it. I really don't understand people who gossip."

Mary coughed and Bertha covered her mouth with her napkin. Kitty patted Ethel's hand. "Thanks for having my back, Ethel."

Ethel looked very self-important. "That's no trouble, my dear. We look after our own here in this neck of the woods."

They had a great old laugh at the table while they munched on carrot cake with cream cheese icing. And then Wallace arrived home. He took one look at Kitty and practically froze at the door.

"Are you coming in?" Mary grumbled. "You're letting in all that cold air from the porch."

He shut the door. "Hi, Kitty. Nice to see you."

"Hi, Wallace. I couldn't stand it anymore and invited myself over. You must have been busy this week."

"Yep, yep. Lots to do." He took off his jacket and put it on the hook by the door. Then he fumbled around with a bunch of papers he had in his hand.

"Do you want something to eat?" asked his mother.

"No, thanks. Mrs. Murrant made us sandwiches."

"What was the meeting about?" Kitty asked.

"Maybe building an outdoor rink for the kids in Morien this winter and how to come up with the funds for the project."

Bertha looked at Mary and Ethel. "You know what, Ethel? Why don't Mary and I drive you home and I'll bring a plate of supper and some cake for Winnie. We can have our tea with her. I'm sure she could use the company. You'd be doing me a favour. I need to get out of this kitchen from time to time."

And as simple as that, Kitty and Wallace were alone.

"Your mother missed her calling. She should've been a diplomat."

Wallace seemed tired. He brushed his hair back off his face. "My mother should stop trying to orchestrate everyone's life." He stood at the sink and poured himself a glass of water, drinking it down in one go.

"Are you okay?" she asked.

"Me? I'm peachy." He turned the kitchen chair around in front of him and straddled it, folding his arms across the back. "So, how was your visit?"

"It was fine. Did you like the play?"

"Can't say I did."

"I knew you wouldn't. The original, yes, but Robert is an acquired taste."

"You were much better at slamming doors. He made a spectacle of himself."

Kitty looked down at her hands. "He was showing off, that's all. Probably for my benefit."

"I don't think he does anything for anyone else's benefit. Only his own."

She crossed her arms. "You met him for what, thirty minutes? And you know all about him?"

"Two minutes was all I needed to figure out that particular fellow."

"Okay. Let's talk about something else."

"Like what?"

She slammed her hand on the table. "Like why you're being such an asshole."

"*He's* the asshole!" Wallace got up from the chair and paced around the table. "I cannot for the life of me figure out how you—YOU—of all people ended up with a self-important nitwit like that. Are you out of your mind?"

She stood up as well. And so did the dogs. They didn't like this energy zipping around the table. "You are talking about my husband, Wallace. Be careful what you say."

"I don't feel like being careful. I'm always careful. But the thought of that man being with you is enough to make my skin crawl."

She stamped her foot. "And you're just...just...augh! Are you going to kiss me or not?!"

All three dogs wagged their tails.

⁂

It was like having a hangover. What was wrong with her? She didn't want to get out of bed because that would mean she'd have to think. And she was worn out dealing with the conversations going on inside her head. There were already too many characters buzzing around in there, and trying to swim through it all while dealing with her own life was weighing her down.

She threw off the covers anyway, took Pip outside, and then went straight back into the house to turn on the oil stove. The place was chilly and needed to heat up if she wanted a soak in her tub. The satisfying whoosh up the chimney from the oil when she threw in the lighted paper was a sound she'd become fond of. It meant the floor wasn't as cold.

She took a box of Cheerios into the bathroom and filled the tub with hot water. After lowering herself in, she spilled some on the floor for Pip, who lapped them up. After chowing down on a couple of mouthfuls herself, she addressed her puppy.

"I came here, Pip, thinking I didn't like writing anymore. But I discovered it was my life I didn't like. I do love to write, and I love this story. It might be my best work, but instead of celebrating I'm in this tub brooding. I tell Kurt that we have to make our marriage better and when he finally agrees with me, I keep kissing another man. What kind of lunatic does that? If Dad were here, he'd tell me to look at the facts. I *know* the facts. But how do you decide which facts are the most important ones?"

Pippy put her paws up on the tub to beg for extra Cheerios, so Kitty poured more out on the bath mat.

"There's need versus want. There's fidelity versus disloyalty. There's good versus bad. Oh my god, I sound like Wallace. *Wallace*. The best kisser in the world. That has to be at the top of any list I ever make." She sighed dreamily. "Don't get me wrong, Pip. He's not perfect. He has no sense of style. He wears plaid shirts and overalls most of the time. His hair is too long. Oh, that hair. And he is definitely a mama's boy like Kurt. Aren't they lucky? People with moms."

Kitty shoved another handful of cereal in her mouth. A few pieces fell in the water and she tried to scoop them up but failed misterably.

"Pip, did you know I made Martha cry? I wasn't aware she was capable of that. Now that I think about it, I wouldn't talk to her for about a year, but then I hardly said a word to anyone." She shook the box. "I miss my mom. She was so nice, and Dad was really happy. And then he wasn't. Why am I talking about my father?" She held the box up to her mouth and was about to pour more in when she stopped. "There's one person I love, and that's Bertha. You feel the same way, Pippy. That woman is a huge ball of love. How am I going to leave her? That's who I've fallen in love with!"

She dropped the Cheerios box on the floor, much to Pip's delight, and big tears sprang from her eyes. She basically howled for ten minutes and splashed water on her face to wipe away the tears, drool, and mucus that dripped down her face.

But after that, when she got out of the tub, grabbed the cereal box from piggy Pip, and got dressed, she felt much better. This was definitely a behaviour she'd rely on in the future. No more being afraid of tears.

Her manuscript was on the table. Probably another couple of chapters or so left to complete the story. But she needed to clear her head after that episode, so she bundled up and took Pip for a walk down to the shoreline. She had to cross the Bailey property to do it, but she didn't go near the house.

It was a cold, grey day. The water looked like softly rippled iron. There was no real wind to speak of, which made it pleasant for sitting. Across the bay, Port Morien looked like a muted postcard, the village houses perched along the cliffs and further up the hill, with the wharf and grey buildings of the fish plant below it. Looking over to the right, she saw the jut of land known as South Head leading out into the Atlantic, and little Flint Island with its lighthouse that Wallace told her about. Just further down the rocky edge of the water, she watched a seagull float upward and drop its clam from a height onto the rocks below to crack it open. So incredibly smart.

There was much more to the world than just her and her ridiculous dilemma. There was an entire universe out there that was billions of years old. What did she matter in the scheme of things? She was a blip in time. Not worth remembering.

"Except by you, Pippy." She held the leash as Pip dug some rocks out of the sand, and then the dog looked up and started to yip excitedly. Pride and Argus were on them in seconds. An excited dance commenced around her. "Hey, guys! What are you doing here?"

"You can't sneak off with those noses around," Wallace said. He sat down next to her and smiled. "Hey, you."

"Hey."

"What are you up to?"

She looked around. "This is it. Trying to make sense of things."

"I've been thinking about that. Do you remember before your husband showed up how we vowed our behaviour would not be repeated, because you are married, and if you decide you're unhappily married, you need to fix that problem before we can even examine what this is?"

"And I said, 'What exactly is this?' and you said there is no *this* because *this* never happened."

"Exactly. Last night never happened either, and we'll start again from there."

Sighing, Kitty looked out over the water. "Kurt wants to work on our marriage."

"Go home and work on it."

She turned to him and fluttered her hand between them. "You want to give up on *this*? The *this* that never happened?"

He clasped his hands together in front of him and took a deep breath. "Just bear with me for a minute. You've heard of the golden mean?"

"I guess so, but don't ask me what it is."

"Aristotle believed that every situation has two extremes of action, the vice of defect and the vice of excess. The ethical action is the mean between these two extremes."

"For the love of Pete. You think I can figure out what you just said in my current state of mind?"

"If you leave your husband now and stay with me, that is the vice of excess. If you give up and go back to your old life, that is the vice of defect. The medium between these extremes is moderation. You can't know what you want until you go home and try to fix your marriage. You'll never figure it out here."

"You keep telling me to go home and work on my relationship with Kurt. Repeating that there is no *this*! I think you want to get rid of me, that's what I think." She looked back at her seagull.

He took her chin in his hand and brought her around so he could see her face. "Are you pouting?"

"Yes! I haven't had a good pout in years."

"Do you honestly think I want you to leave this place?"

She eventually shook her head.

"I have no right to ask you anything. Or to expect anything. We can't go any further with *this*." He flapped his hand around frantically and made her laugh. "What I'm suggesting is only common sense."

"Oh, right. You love reading about common sense, instead of your mom's books about murdering tubas."

Now he laughed and they bumped shoulders playfully, but that's as far as it went.

"Would you do me a favour?" she asked.

"Sure."

"I know it's not your cup of tea, but would you read my new book and tell me what you think? It's not my usual fare...well, it is and it isn't. I respect your opinion and would love to have your take on it."

"I'd be happy to. Is it finished? That's awfully quick."

"I have about three more days to finish the story. As it is now, there's a foundation and walls and a roof. Like your garage. I still have to fix up the inside, but I do that back and forth with my editor. She never steers me wrong and always makes the story so much better."

"I never realized the work that goes into writing a book."

"It really helps me when I use my underwear."

Chapter Fourteen

She finished four days later. She never wrote *The End* at the end. Because this was just the beginning. Now the fiddly part started, but the first thing Kitty did was go to the print shop in Sydney and had them make two copies of the original manuscript: one for Wallace and one for Gaynor. She'd paid to copy the first twelve chapters she'd sent to Gaynor, but this expense was on Empire & Bloom's tab.

While she waited, she sat on an uncomfortable chair and looked at the calendar stuck on the wall with a thumbtack. It was December 1. She'd arrived in Cape Breton the last week of August. Basically, three months and she'd achieved what she set out to do. That and a lot of other stuff she hadn't bargained for. Three months ago, she hadn't known Wallace or Bertha, Argus and Pride, Ethel and Dolly, or Wallace's gang of pirate mermaid monkeys. That filled her with dismay. She'd had such fun here, when she wasn't agonizing over her past, constantly fretting about her future, and creating a world for Kate Higgins. No wonder she felt loopy.

She mailed the manuscript to Gaynor with a note: *Mission Accomplished. Hope you like it. Kit. xo*

Then she called Bertha from town to say she would bring supper for the gang because she was in the mood to celebrate. She was delighted to hear Benji would be there. She added, "And you're invited too, Ethel," before she hung up.

As she arrived at the house, Wallace was pulling in with Ethel in the front seat of his truck. "I had a flat tire," Ethel shouted the minute she got out of the cab. "Wallace will fix it later. Thanks for inviting me." She proceeded into the house with Pip right behind her.

Kitty gestured to Wallace. "Could you help me with this?" She popped open the trunk.

"Did you really tell her over the phone to come for supper when you called Mom?"

"Why not? It saved time."

He looked in the back of her car. "Lobsters? How many are there?"

"Three dozen. All cooked. We need a treat."

"Lord have mercy."

"And I have this for you." She reached into the front and took out a fat manila envelope. "Here's the book."

He took it in his hands. "Wow. You really did this, didn't you?"

"Yep. And I can't believe it, which is why I'm going to eat two lobsters tonight."

"I'll be right in with them. Gonna put this in a safe place first."

"Please. I don't want anyone else to see it."

Wallace walked towards the barn. That was the best place for it. Their two cows didn't read.

The family gathered that night did a darn good job getting rid of most of the lobsters, but Bertha saved four for Ethel to take back to Winnie for a couple of meals, and Wallace shucked the last eight so his mother could can the meat for her seafood chowders.

Benji was plunked in Kitty's arms almost immediately upon her arrival, and she was still bouncing him up and down when his mother, Rita, got him dressed to go. Kitty kissed his fat cheeks. "See ya, little man, although you're not so little anymore. Does that sweater you knit even fit him anymore, Bertha?"

"Barely. No problem. I found out today we're expecting a twelfth grand! Let's hope it's a boy so Rita can pass it along."

Everyone left and Wallace drove Ethel home. He'd be a little while because he had to fix her flat tire, so the two ladies sat on opposite ends of the fireplace with the three dogs at their feet.

"That was such a treat," Bertha said, sighing.

"I'm glad. I owe you so much more than that. I've eaten you out of house and home for the last three months."

The older woman put her hands up to adjust a hairpin back into her bun. "Nonsense. There's always enough for one more plate."

"Bertha? I know this is none of my business, but I have no one else to ask. Were you happy in your marriage?"

"Yes and no. There were a hundred reasons to stay and a hundred reasons to leave."

"Do you think spending more time together helps?"

"Sometimes the only helpful thing is to spend time apart!" She laughed but then got serious. "Never measure your relationship with someone else's ruler. No one knows all the facts. It's usually clear what you should do if you keep your eyes open. That said, my husband died before I had to make that call, and I was probably a decade too late anyway. It's not easy when you have kids. And Donald was always so sorry. He didn't like the way he was either. So, do you give up on a person when you have a history together? When you have lovely memories of who they used to be? I have no idea if I did the right thing or the wrong thing by staying with him."

Kitty nodded.

"Listen to that little voice in your head."

Kitty groaned. "I usually have thirty people up there at any given time. I can't hear myself think."

"What's it like, writing a story?"

She put her head back and stared at the ceiling while she thought about it.

"It's fun when it's just you and the words. But then it gets scary. Is it good? Is it bad? Sometimes I wonder why we do it. Why make up this other world and then show it to everyone and wait for them to judge it?" She looked at Bertha. "Ya know?"

"Why do you write?"

Kitty shrugged. "I can pretend to be someone else. I can be rude and slam the door in someone's face, which I've always wanted to do but never had the courage. I can pretend I still have a mother, or a little brother. Lots of reasons."

"Well, I think it's a wonderful accomplishment."

"Thanks, Bertha." She glanced down at Pip. "I think it's time to head home, little girl, and sleep for two days straight. I feel myself fading."

They both rose from their chairs at the same time. Bertha reached over and hugged her. Kitty put her head on Bertha's shoulder and snuggled into that soft bosom.

"Kitty, you are such a ladybug."

A shock went right through Kitty's skull. She stood up straight. "My mother used to call me ladybug!"

Bertha held her shoulders. "Your mother is always with you, child. Wherever you are, you're not without her."

⁂

Kitty sat up in bed. "And on the third day, she rose again."

Pip cocked her head and whined.

"I know, that was blasphemy. Sue me."

Feeling a thousand percent better about everything now that she had a marathon of sleep to make up for the long nights at the typewriter, she set about her morning routine. When they went outside for a tinkle, a light dusting of snow covered the ground. "Oh, look Pip! This does look magical."

They chased each other around, and she tried to make a snowball but it wouldn't stick. Still, by the time they went inside to start the fire, they were panting.

Kitty was on her second cup of tea after her plate of scrambled eggs when the phone rang, and it was her number. "Hello?"

"Kitty!! You incredibly fabulous girl!!"

"Hi, Gaynor. You got it, then?"

"I've been up all night because I couldn't put it down! Oh, Kit, it's perfect. It's so you and yet so not you. There's humour and fun and hope all mixed in with the usual nonsense. I absolutely adore all the characters, and that Kate Higgins, I could just eat her! I want to be her mother, and I don't want to be anyone's mother. How she doesn't end up strangling Stu is beyond me. And Myrtle Lovett? A shrine will be erected to that woman for snooping! I'm simply amazed that you managed to pull this out of your hat. And you told me you never wanted to write again. You see! This is why I hate writers and love writers all at the same time. You give me more grey hairs than I can count and then turn around and totally enchant me all over again. This is big, kiddo. This is going to be so big! I can't wait to show it to Mel. He'll have a heart attack. A good one."

"Thanks, Gaynor. I'm so happy you like it."

"I don't like it. I LOVE it. I adore it!"

"Trying to make me feel good?"

"Yes, I am because you deserve it. Look, I'm heading to the office but I'll call when Mel reads it. A big kiss from me. Talk soon!"

Well, that was nice. Gaynor always made a fuss, but never quite to this extent. Maybe it really was a good story.

It felt mighty odd not writing. Kitty wasn't sure what to do with her hands, so she found the old deck of cards Kurt had rescued from a side table drawer and played solitaire, which she used to do as a kid in her room. To avoid Martha. Memories continued to bubble to the surface. Bertha's ladybug comment was still giving her chills.

There was a familiar knock at the door. "Come in, Wallace."

He stamped his feet on the mat. "Finally, snow."

She noticed he had the manuscript with him. "Come and have tea. This is my lucky morning. Gaynor called and she absolutely loves the book. I can't tell you how relieved I am."

"Great. Hey Pip, did you see the snow?" He sat down and Pip was all over him. He put the manuscript on the table and reached for the mug of tea. "Thanks." He continued to rub Pip's head and not look at Kitty.

"Well? I'm assuming you read it?"

"Yes."

"Since you don't read fiction, I understand if you found it trivial, but I'm hoping it was entertaining."

He still didn't look at her.

"What's wrong? You hated it?"

"You can't publish this."

If he'd slapped her, she wouldn't have been as dumbstruck. "*What?*"

"You literally took everyone in my life and made fun of them. You made us look ridiculous. I can't understand it. I thought you liked us."

She shoved the chair out from beneath her as she stood. "Okay, this must be a joke. But it's not funny. I love all of you. I'm not making fun of real people. I used them for inspiration to tell a fictional story that has no connection with the real world. How do you think writers get their ideas? A person like Dolly walks in the room and you use her mannerisms, but you'd never use her name or mention her love of theatre. No one would realize it was Dolly I was thinking of."

"And you're telling me no one would figure out that Myrtle Lovett is Ethel? Not only does she listen in on phone calls, she actually looks like a scrawny chicken, which is exactly how you describe her, so don't tell me no one will recognize her."

"Wait—"

"But the one that really got to me was killing off poor Winnie. You call her a hermit and said people wanted to kill her. You've never even met that sweet woman, and yet you describe her lying lifeless on the bed. That really bothered me. Not to mention the fact that the place where Kate is rooming drives her mad with all the kids and dogs, noise and clutter. An obvious reference to our house, which you charitably describe as 'disorganized bedlam.' One of the suspects is a great big fella who looks like 'an unmade bed.' I'm surprised you didn't give him red hair."

"Enough! I've heard enough! I'm sorry you didn't like it, but it was never my intention to make fun of anyone. I used all the wonderful people I've met here to create a funny and heartfelt story about a woman who was completely lost when she arrived in a small town and ends up realizing that life can be good again if she surrounds herself with the right people. The so-called murder aspect of it is a device to talk about the characters. You have to have a story about something. And believe it or not, most people have never heard of South Head or your family and friends. And they would never link me with the book. I write under C. J. Faulkner. Catriona Jane Faulkner, my maiden name. Not Kitty Wagner. Your mother wasn't aware that the tuba murder was written by me. She thought I was a man. That's why we use initials. Publishers sell more books if the writer is male."

"*You* wrote the killer tuba?"

"The tuba wasn't the actual killer! It was the instrument of death, used by the real killer to bash in the brains of a woman who wouldn't stop warbling! And at this moment, if I had a tuba, that's what I'd be doing to you!"

Wallace put Pip down and rubbed his hands across his face. "Look, I didn't come here to make you angry—"

"I thought I'd never write again, and then I come up with perhaps my best work and you tell me I can't publish it. How was that not going to make me angry?"

"Okay, but you must see that it was upsetting. It felt wrong—"

"With your one-track, analytical mind, you jumped to the conclusion that I had bad intentions, not good ones. I wasn't writing about Ethel personally! Or Winnie! Or your house! I used the wonderful energy around me to bring my story to life, that's all. To kick-start that spark I get when a story starts to take shape out of nothing."

"Obviously, I know nothing about this process."

"You should've started with that, Wallace. Now, get out."

He stood up. "Kitty—"

"OUT!"

He left, the manuscript still on the table. Kitty reached over and threw it in the fire in the stove, which she realized was stupid when she heard the roaring sound. She shut the flue and the valves and waited for it to pass.

She sat there for an hour and then got up and called Gaynor's office. Dolores said she was in a meeting.

"It's Mrs. Kurt Wagner, otherwise known as the great C. J. Faulkner."

"Yes, Mrs. Wagner?"

"Please give Gaynor a message from me. Tell her the book *One Long Ring Around the Rosy* is no longer for sale. Thank you."

⁂

This was a red-letter day for Ethel on the phone. First there was the woman who called Kitty very excited about something, talking about people she'd never heard of. There was mention of a heart attack, which didn't upset either of them. Then another call where Kitty said her name was Mrs. Bert Wagner. Wasn't she married to Robert Chandler? And she called herself Falcon. The girl had too many names. Maybe she was hiding something. This was news. And she had no idea what "ring around the nosy" meant, but it wasn't for sale anymore. Interesting.

Just then she thought she heard a thud from Winnie's room. "Winnie? Are you okay?" She hurried to the door and opened it. Winnie was on the floor and looked like she was in pain.

"Oh dear. What happened?" Ethel got down on her knees and stroked her sister's head.

"It was my own fault. I tripped over my paint case. It's my ankle, I can't move it."

"You're lucky it's not your hip."

"I don't feel lucky at the moment. Would you call Wallace? He can take me to the hospital. It might be broken."

"Of course."

Ethel had a bit of a time getting back up on her feet, but eventually she made it to the phone. She was surprised when Wallace answered it. "Winnie's fallen, and I think she's broken her ankle!"

"I'll be right there."

Thank God for that boy. It never occurred to either of them to call Ethel's son. Of course, Wallace was closer, but that's how important the Baileys were to them. Like family.

When Wallace arrived, he had Winnie bundled up and in Ethel's car in a matter of minutes. He placed Winnie in the back and put pillows against the door so she could lean against it with her feet up. Ethel got in the front.

Wallace had to adjust the seat so he could fit in behind the steering wheel. And off they went.

"I'm so grateful for this," Winnie said in a small voice. "Thank goodness you were home."

"I'm glad I was in the house to hear the phone."

"I'm surprised your mother didn't answer," Ethel said.

"Jean came out and got Mom yesterday. The girls had a piano recital last evening and she stayed overnight."

"I feel like such a silly old woman," Winnie said, grumbling.

"You are a silly old woman! You gave me quite a fright. When we go home, I'll take that clutter in your room and give it a good going over."

Winnie's voice got stronger. "You'll do no such thing, Ethel Macdonald. That is my room, and I'll thank you to keep out."

"How about I build you some shelves?" Wallace suggested. "That way you can keep your art supplies off the floor and out of harm's way."

"You are an angel. Ooh...this is so painful."

They got her into the emergency department at Glace Bay General, and when the nurse wheeled Winnie away for an X-ray, Wallace and Ethel sat in the waiting room together.

"I'm so grateful it wasn't her hip," Ethel said. "You hear that all the time. Old people break their hip and it's downhill from there. That's my one fear. Breaking my hip. I almost did, on Kitty's stairs. I could've been lying there and had a bear wander by. You can't run away from a bear with a broken hip..."

Wallace noticed a man two seats down glance at Ethel and then give him a sympathetic look. But Wallace had tuned poor Ethel out. He felt sick about what had transpired at Kitty's that morning.

What had he been thinking? He never should've gone over there having just finished reading it. Why didn't he reflect on it first? He did with everything else. It was such a shock to read about people he knew, or thought he knew. And it did seem like she'd made fun of them. Or got a laugh at their expense. He didn't judge the book on whether it was comical or clever or had the right pacing, or kept his interest. He never noticed the storyline of a young woman who was adrift but managed to find herself because of the people she met.

Oh my God. The character's name was Kate. Kat. Kitty.

Where did he get off, on his moral high ground, telling her not to publish the book? Who was he to walk in there and dismiss her efforts? She came here because she was afraid of writing, but she managed it even though she was unhappy and he completely complicated her life with his attention. And not only that, he said the thought of her with her husband made his skin crawl. At that moment he was so ashamed he had to get up.

"Sorry, Ethel. I'm going to step outside."

"I didn't mean to be gossiping about Kitty."

He shook his head. "What?"

"It was an accident that I listened in on her this morning. I tried to call someone and wanted to see if the line was free and only overheard a minute. I have no idea what ring around the nosy means. Do you?"

He sat down again.

"She told this woman that ring around the nosy wasn't for sale."

He put his hand up to his mouth.

"Are you okay?" Ethel asked.

"I need some air. I'll be right back."

He lurched out of the emergency doors and walked away from the entrance before doubling over with his hands on his knees. "You fucking idiot."

It was absolute torture to sit in that waiting room. Even Ethel had realized something was up with him because she'd remained quiet. That was the only thing he was grateful for.

Eventually Winnie appeared with the nurse pushing her in the wheelchair. Her ankle was wrapped in a bandage.

"Good news," Winnie said. "It's not broken, just a lot of torn ligaments."

"Which is very painful," said the nurse. "Stay off that foot as much as you can."

"I'll bring the car around."

Wallace didn't register a thing the sisters said to each other on the way back. Didn't even know if they'd talked to him. He drove as fast as he dared and couldn't wait to be released from this mercy mission. Thankfully, they pulled up and Wallace carried Winnie to her bed, with Ethel fussing behind him.

"I'm sorry, ladies. I have to run."

Winnie grabbed his hand. "We've kept you too long. Thank you, my dear, for being so kind to me. I don't know what we would have done."

"Feel better."

And he rushed out of the house and ignored poor Blackie, who was waiting with his belly up, jumped in his truck, and tore up the road to get to Kitty's, his heart pounding.

Oh no. Her car wasn't there. Now he'd have to wait until she got home to apologize for being such an insensitive holier-then-thou bastard.

She'd forgotten to close the outside door properly and Wallace didn't want it to bang in the wind. He went up the stairs to shut it and looked in the window out of habit. Something didn't look right. His mouth went dry as he pushed the door open. He looked around.

Everything was gone.

He went from room to room and it was like she'd never been there. No little Pip, no clothes thrown everywhere, no overflowing ashtray or slippers. No underwear.

There was only one thing on the kitchen table. The house key.

Chapter Fifteen

Gaynor tried very hard to keep her upper and lower teeth from touching. The dentist said she was grinding them down to dust. And it was thanks to guys like Gavin Haddock, the writer of popular fish-and-tackle field guides, who was on the phone giving her a spiel about his next book.

"I'm branching into beavers and their dams. Get it? Branching."

"How droll. Do any of us need to know about beaver dams?"

"My readers are interested in the great outdoors, as you know. I think it's a natural progression. The next step in my nature series. And this *is* Canada, after all."

"Call me when you have a book about a moose being ridden by a Mountie."

"Excuse me?"

"Sorry, Gavin. This isn't a good time. Can we talk about it over lunch next Tuesday at Schwartz's? Say 12:30?"

"I guess so."

"Thanks so much. Have to run. Bye-bye."

She put down the phone and rubbed her temples. It would be one of those days. And it had started out so spectacularly. It's too bad all her writers weren't Kitty.

There was a quick knock on her door. Dolores would have seen the phone line disconnect.

"Enter!"

Dolores struggled to open the door while she held a very large coffee and a pastry treat.

"What have we here?"

"Coffee, cream, two sugars, and a mille feuille from the pastry shop down the street."

Gaynor rubbed her hands together and Dolores placed both in front of her. "You eat this and I'll be back with your messages."

Dolores tiptoed out and Gaynor savoured her lovely snack. She bet even Iris didn't deliver mille feuille to Mel. With still a couple of gulps of coffee left, she buzzed for Dolores, who appeared instantly.

"That was wonderful. Thank you. I'm sure we don't pay you enough."

"You'll fire me when you hear this."

"I knew it. It's one of those days." Gaynor drained the coffee. "What?"

"C. J. Faulkner called."

"Oh? I talked to her this morning."

"She wanted me to give you a message. She said *One Long Ring Around the Rosy* is no longer for sale."

Gaynor collapsed back into her chair. She felt like someone had kicked her in the stomach. "What?"

"I'm afraid that's all she said. She hung up after that."

"Was she crying? In distress? She was delighted when I talked to her."

"She sounded a bit mechanical. Like she had no feelings, or was trying to hold them in."

"Get her on the phone this instant!"

Dolores ran to her desk and Gaynor charged after her. She waited like a hawk over the phone as Dolores called the operator.

"What's taking so long?!"

Her poor secretary shook her head. "There doesn't seem to be any answer. The operator has tried a few times."

Gaynor clenched her fist in the air. "Damn. We'll have to wait until she gets back. What the hell happened?"

Iris looked over at them. "Everything all right?"

Gaynor swivelled her head. "Fine. No worries." Then she turned back and leaned close to Dolores. "Not a word about this to anyone. I gave that script to Mel and he's reading it now. I don't want him to know anything until I talk to Kitty."

They both heard the peals of laughter coming from Mel's office.

❧

Bertha couldn't understand it. She came home in the afternoon and the phone rang three times for Kitty, but she didn't answer. And Wallace was nowhere to be found. Ethel did call at one point to tell her what had happened to Winnie.

"I'd come over with a casserole, but I don't have the truck. Wallace isn't here and it's after five. Did he say anything about going somewhere? He usually leaves a note."

"To tell you the truth, he didn't look too happy when he left. Could hardly get two words out of him on the way home."

Bertha hung up the phone, sat in a chair, and absentmindedly rubbed Pride's head. Maybe the two of them had gone somewhere together? But why all the phone calls? It gave her an uneasy feeling.

Bertha ate alone, a very rare occurrence. All the kids were busy with one thing and another. When December hit, their households began to gear up for Christmas, with baking, gift buying, and cleaning. There were Christmas concerts to attend, and church nativity plays to make costumes for, which she completely understood, having done it herself. But it wasn't like Wallace not to let her know where he was.

She took out the chocolate box and munched one after the other. There was only one layer left. She'd eaten almost all of them herself. Someday she might confess her foul deed to Kitty, who would no doubt have a great chuckle about it. She was always quick to laugh, despite her sad eyes.

Thankfully, she heard the truck pull up. "Praise the Lord. I thought he was in a ditch."

She and the dogs were ready to give him what for. He held the door open to let the dogs out and shut the door as his mother stood with her hands on her hips, just like she used to when he was fourteen and didn't come home until midnight.

"Where have you been?"

"Out."

"You could've let me know."

"Sorry."

"What's the matter? Something is very wrong. I hope you had Kitty with you, because someone has tried to get ahold of her but she hasn't answered. I'm worried it might be a family member. It's been persistent."

"Kitty isn't here. She's gone back to Montreal."

Bertha stumbled backwards and grabbed the back of a chair. "She left without saying goodbye? Why? I can't believe she'd do that."

"She had no choice. I made it impossible for her to stay."

"What does that mean, Wallace?"

He took a deep breath and was obviously trying to stay calm. "Mom, I cannot talk about this right now. I would've stayed out in the woods if I could, but it's too damn cold and I'm not dressed for it. I'll be in my room and I'll come out when I'm good and ready. Okay? Let the dogs in, please."

And he walked away.

Bertha wanted to cry, but she was too concerned about both of them. It wasn't any of her business and she knew it, but still. Kitty had become another child to her; a child who now faced a very long journey alone and was no doubt upset about whatever had happened with Wallace. She was concerned that Kitty wouldn't have the sense to pull over before dark. She'd be in no condition to drive for hours, especially at night.

Honestly, she wanted to wring both their necks, making her fret like this. She couldn't believe she might never see Kitty again.

Kitty's ring once more. Bertha did everyone on the line a favour and picked it up because she couldn't stand it. "Hello?"

"KITTY?!"

"I'm sorry, this isn't Kitty. I'm her neighbour, Bertha Bailey. This is a party line, and I can hear how many times you've tried to call and I'm worried you might have an urgent message for her."

"I've been frantic! This is Gaynor Ledbetter, her editor. I talked to her this morning and she sounded fine. And then I got this terrible message pertaining to her new book and she's not answering the phone. I think something might have happened to her."

"She's fine. Physically, at least. I don't exactly know what happened, but my son just told me that she's gone back to Montreal, which is very unexpected. She didn't even say goodbye, and that's not like her."

"She's gone back to Montreal?!" Ethel shouted.

"Ethel! Get off the phone!"

There was a click.

"Let me guess. Myrtle?"

"Who?"

"Never mind," Gaynor said. "Look, I really appreciate you picking up the phone. I was very anxious thinking something had happened to her. Hopefully I'll see her in a few days."

Bertha's voice quivered. "Could you tell her that we love her and will miss her very much? And if she ever needs anything, I'm always here."

"I will, Bertha. I definitely will. Thanks again."

❧❦

Kitty got as far as Antigonish before she had to stop. It was late afternoon, but her eyes throbbed with unshed tears, and she was seeing double on the highway. There was little Pip, who didn't know she'd never see Argus and Pride again, innocently curled up on the front seat. If she got in an accident and anything happened to this precious little being, it would be the end of Kitty, so she pulled into a motel and got them settled for the night, which meant finding a corner store to pick up more dog food and water. She bought two packs of cigarettes, a couple of bottles of Coke, and a large bag of chips.

She fed the dog, took her for a walk around the parking lot several times, and then locked them in for the night. Throwing her clothes on the floor of the bathroom, she shivered and scowled at the square, hard-edged tub. She turned on the shower, then stood under it and let everything go. Pippy whimpered behind the shower curtain.

Only when she ran out of hot water did she get out and dry off. She put on her pajamas and crawled under the slippery, ugly bedspread, completely ignoring the Coke, chips, and cigarettes. All she could do was lie there and count the water marks on the ceiling. Pip crawled up and tucked her head into Kitty's shoulder.

"Hey, sweetheart. I hate to tell you this, but you know Argus and Pride? Their daddy is a virtuous, incorruptible cutthroat. And I mean that in the nicest possible way."

⊰⊱

Bertha didn't sleep most of the night. When Ethel knocked on the front door at eight o'clock in the morning, she wasn't best pleased.

"Ethel, it's too early to be here. Go home and come back later. You should be with your sister, anyway. Since you're here, take her some of these blueberry muffins." She scurried around to get the muffins into a tin.

"I tossed and turned until dawn," Ethel said. "What happened to Kitty? Why did she leave without saying goodbye? Something dreadful must have happened."

"Your guess is as good as mine. I can't add any information on that score."

"But Wallace must know. That's probably why he looked so upset yesterday. And there he was, trying to help us at the same time."

Bertha firmly put the muffins in Ethel's hands. "Wallace has said nothing to me, and even if he did, I would not be telling you. Now go home and take care of Winnie. It looks like a miserable day out there, and I'm tired. I'm going back to bed."

"That's a first. Okay, but if you need me..."

"I know where to find you."

"I'm going to miss Kitty," Ethel said sadly.

Bertha could only nod her head as she closed the door. She ended up in her chair and started to knit mittens for her grandchildren's Christmas stockings. She woke herself up with a snore. Great, now she had a kink in her neck. The mantel clock indicated it was after ten. No wonder her neck was sore.

Yawning, she put her wool away and went to the bathroom before she headed to the kitchen to make a cup of tea. Wallace was at the table with mug in hand, eating the last of a muffin.

She decided to be nonchalant. "Good morning. Is there still tea in the pot?"

He nodded.

She busied herself making a poached egg on toast. Wallace was silent. Two could play that game. She gathered her breakfast together and even squeezed herself some fresh orange juice. Then she sat at the table, opened the paper, and read it as she ate, completely ignoring the large, gloomy presence on the other side.

She was halfway through a crossword puzzle when he finally spoke.

"Mom?"

Her eyes never left the puzzle. "Yeah?"

"What do you do when you've made the biggest mistake of your life?"

She looked up. "She was never yours to begin with."

"That's not the problem. I took something from her. The one thing that meant the most."

Bertha put down her pencil. "What are you talking about?"

He rubbed his eyes. "She asked me to read her new book,

because she valued my opinion. I read it and promptly went over and told her she shouldn't publish it. Of course, she was furious and told me to get out. Then Winnie happened and I realized what a self-righteous fool I was and rushed home to tell her that, but she was gone."

"I talked to her editor last night. She was desperate to get ahold of her."

"That's because the editor called her yesterday to say she loved the book and Kitty was really happy about it. After I left, she apparently called them to tell them not to publish it. Because of me."

Bertha's mouth dropped open. "Why in heaven's name would you tell her not to publish it? What do you know about fiction, anyway?"

"I recognized the people and places in the story and thought she was making fun of us."

"That is absolute nonsense! You should've known better. Why would you think that?"

"There's a woman in it who listens in on party lines and looks like a scrawny chicken."

Bertha laughed right out loud. "Ethel! Fabulous! Is it a comedy?"

"Yes. A humourous whodunit, or who-didn't-do-it."

"Oh my god, I can't wait to read it!" Then she slapped her hand on the table. "Or I would have, if you hadn't opened your big mouth!"

He looked so woebegone that she regretted the remark instantly. "I'm sorry. I shouldn't have said that."

"It's true."

Wallace put his folded arms on the table and laid his head down. His mother got up and stood beside him, stroking that beautiful hair she loved so much. "We all make mistakes. It means you're living. And you've lived more in the last three months than in your entire life. You have Kitty to thank for that, even if you never see her again."

※

No doubt thanks to Kitty's current mood, driving in Montreal traffic was ten times more aggravating than it used to be. Outside, despite the closed windows of the car, everything was deafening. Horns blared, sirens wailed, buses rumbled by spewing exhaust fumes. And she'd forgotten how people tried to cross the street despite the red lights. You needed eyes in the back of your head to manoeuvre in this chaos.

Their apartment was in Mile End, a thirty-minute walk from her father in Milton Park, which made it seem worse when she didn't see him for weeks on end. Near McGill University, it was a quaint quarter of the city with lots of nationalities, and plenty of cafes, bars, restaurants, specialty grocery stores, and consignment and bookshops. Most of which Kitty had never frequented, unlike her husband.

When she pulled up outside the apartment building and turned off the key, she put her head back and stared at the red bricks. Everywhere she looked there were bricks. Her cozy little nest made of wood seemed like a dream. The trees that lined the street were in a row, reaching their branches out to each other but not quite touching. Everything was straight and symmetrical, unlike the curves of South Head Road. And pavement. No bounce or give when you step on pavement.

Pip brought her out of her reverie. She smelled home and was anxious to see it. The thought of unpacking the car was daunting, and then she remembered that Kurt was here in the city and not away. Hopefully he'd be home. Not that he knew she was coming. None of them knew.

She put Pip on her leash, grabbed her purse and as many bags in the front seat as she could, and stepped out, locking the door behind her. Pip made a dash to her favourite tree and crouched beside it. It was a long pee, poor thing. Kitty needed to get her upstairs and into the apartment to unpack properly.

She went into the lobby and up to the mailbox out of habit, but there was nothing in it. Then she turned around, and standing in front of the narrow elevator was a hefty man carrying a tuba. Of all people to see. Immediately in her mind the tuba grew arms and ran over to attack her, and that made her grin a little. The man thought she was smiling at him.

"Hello. That's a very nice dog you have there."

"Thank you. That's a very nice tuba."

He chuckled. "Most people in this building hate me and this tuba. And not just because they don't like getting in the elevator with me. It's a bit of a squeeze, to be truthful."

"I don't mind."

The elevator opened and he gallantly let her in first. He followed and tried to make himself as small as possible. "What floor?"

"Second. Thanks."

He pushed the round 2 and 3. "I'll have to get out to let you by."

It was hardly a long ride. Kitty was ashamed when she used the elevator, but it did come in handy when bringing home groceries, or unpacking the car.

The bell dinged, the doors opened, and the man and his tuba got out. She thanked him as she went by. He nodded.

Their apartment was at the corner end of the building, which gave them a great view of two streets. Pippy ran down the carpeted hall to the end with her leash trailing behind her and jumped up at their door. Number 27. Kitty struggled to get the keys out of her purse without dropping everything.

When they did go through, there was Kurt across the room on the sofa with his arm draped over the shoulders of a very pretty woman. It looked like they were talking, but he leapt to his feet in a panic.

"Kitty! What are you doing here?"

"I live here." She looked at the woman. "Hello. I'm Kitty."

The pretty lady got up as well, and seem flustered. "Hello, it's nice to meet you. I'm Janette."

"Janette and I were rehearsing. She's my new lead in the movie."

"Great. Congratulations on getting the part."

"Thank you. I'm very excited. It's my first big role, and Robert has been very generous with his time."

Kitty stood there with the stuff in her hands. She held out the packages as a not-too-subtle hint for him to help her with it. He hurried over and whispered, "Why didn't you let me know you were coming?"

"It was a last-minute decision. I need help unpacking the car."

"I have to drive Janette home."

"Now?"

"What's she going to do while I schlep up and down the stairs bringing in your stuff?"

"How about I make her a cup of tea?" Kitty said through gritted teeth.

"Don't worry, I'll do it when I come back."

He hustled Janette out the door and the two women had a hasty goodbye. Kitty put some water and food down for the dog and stood there. She had no idea when he'd be back. God knows where Janette lived, and she needed her stuff inside before it got dark. Bloody hell.

She ran down the stairs and went back to the car. As she leaned into the trunk, it was deja-vu.

"Would you like some help?"

Tuba man was behind her, carrying a bag from their local corner store.

"Are you sure you don't mind?"

"Not at all. Here, give me some of the heavier stuff. I'm Dimitri, by the way."

"Kitty. I'm afraid I have a lot of stuff. I've been away for three months."

He smiled at her. "I have no plans this evening."

On their third trip in the elevator, she asked him about the tuba. "The super told me you play for the Montreal Symphony. That must be quite something. I hear you practicing. I believe you live in the apartment above us."

"Yes. I love what I do, but I apologize for the noise. Most of my practicing is done elsewhere, but occasionally I have to check things out at home."

He placed the final load next to the other suitcases and boxes in the entranceway. Pip wagged her tail and was happy to see him every time he showed up. "I believe you remind her of someone we know."

Dimitri patted Pip's head. "I'll say goodnight."

"I can't thank you enough."

"Happy to help. Au revoir."

When Kurt walked in an hour later, she had cleared her bits and pieces into the rooms they belonged in. "I'll go get your stuff. Where are the car keys?"

She was in the bedroom. "I already did it." Should she tell him about tuba man or let him think she suffered through it herself?

He showed up at the door. "I told you to leave all that. You're so impatient."

"A nice man helped me."

"Oh, well then." He came forward and took her in his arms. "So, bonjour, madame." He kissed her and gave her a hug. "This was very unexpected. You led me to believe you wouldn't be home for another couple of weeks at least."

"We got snow a few days ago and suddenly it felt like winter. It seemed wise to hit the road while the going was good."

"Very sensible." He stretched out on the bed and when Pip tried to snuggle up to him, he moved her away. "Hey, now. You belong on that side of the bed. I have to say, I didn't miss this one taking up all the space."

"She curls into a ball about the size of a dinner plate."

He put his hands behind his head and watched her take a jumble of clothes out of the suitcase. "I can see you left in a hurry. You're usually more careful packing your things."

"Everything was dirty anyway."

"So how are the Baileys? I'm sure they're going to miss you."

"They're good."

"Did you get that spare rib recipe, by any chance? I told the girls at the craft service table about it yesterday."

"No, sorry."

"Make sure you call Bertha and ask her."

That's when the phone rang. It sounded so odd, just one ring. Kurt quickly picked it up from his bedside table. "Hello? Oh hi, Gaynor. Yes, she's right here. She got in an hour ago. Did she tell you she was coming home? Because she didn't tell me. Oh. Right. How are you and Simon, anyway? Good, good. Well, I'll pass her over."

He held out the phone receiver. "When she tried calling you at the cabin and you didn't answer for a few days, she hoped you were here. I'm going down to the corner for some cigarettes."

Kitty waited until he was gone before she put the phone to her ear. "Hi."

"Are you all right?"

"Not really."

"This isn't the time to talk about anything. I just wanted to make sure that you made it home safely."

"Thanks."

"But when you're up to it, I hope you'll let me take you out to dinner, just the two of us, and we'll talk things through. No pressure. Just friend to friend."

"I think I need one."

"I'm always here for you. Oh, that reminds me. Bertha said they love you and will miss you very much and if you ever need anything, she's always there."

Kitty's face crumpled. "You talked to Bertha?"

"I tried to call you all day and you weren't answering. She picked up the phone and said she was worried that it was a relative trying to get ahold of you, and she told me you left for Montreal. She asked me to make sure to give you that message."

"Thank you. I have to go."

"Okay, dear. Get some rest."

Kitty ran to the bathroom and slammed the door shut, and then opened it and let Pip in and slammed it again. She ran the water in the tub and jumped in before it had a chance to fill. It was uncomfortable against the hard edges, but it was a safe place for her to flush her eyes and hide the sound of her weeping.

Kurt knocked on the door. "Want some company?"

"NO."

"Didn't think so."

❧

It was a bit of a slushy mess when Gaynor parked her car on Mansfield Street to get to her office. The rain was becoming snow in a hurry and made for a miserable walk in her chunky leather T-straps. Time to get out the winter boots.

Because Kitty was on her mind, she walked up the stairs instead of taking the elevator to the third floor. Gaynor needed more exercise thanks to Dolores and her constant treats.

As she took off her coat and gave it a little shake, Dolores was already out of her chair with her morning coffee and mail. "Good morning," she said brightly. "Mr. Bloom asked to see you as soon as you arrived." She followed Gaynor into her office.

"Thanks. I'm dreading this." Gaynor hung up her coat, scarf, hat, and purse.

"Have you spoken to C. J. Faulkner yet? Did she change her mind?"

"Call her Kitty. I always think of a fat old man when I say C. J. Faulkner. And yes, I did speak to her for a minute last night, but she just got home after a very long drive and now is not the time to badger her. That's what I have to tell Mel. Wish me luck."

"Good luck."

Gaynor grabbed her coffee, then went out the door and right by Iris, who didn't look up from her typewriter. "Go on in, he's waiting for you."

She knocked on the door and opened it. As usual, Mel's feet were up on his desk and he was leaning back in his chair with the phone cradled next to his neck, a stack of papers in his hand.

"Look, I'll have to call you back. My favourite editor just walked through the door. Thanks." He put down the phone, stood up and held out his arms. "There she is! How soon can you get this fabulous book ready? We need to get it into the hands of not only her readers but the totally new audience she'll win over with this change of style. I know she's not your only client, but I swear, Gaynor, this Detective Kate Higgins will be bigger than Harry Gunn. I don't know how that girl did it, but I like this book best of all. Why wasn't she writing satire before? Who knew she was so funny? And where the hell did she come up with these characters? And how did she think up that scene with the mêlée of women and their shoes?!"

Gaynor sat in the chair in front of his desk and took a big sip of coffee.

When he finally noticed she wasn't smiling, Mel slowly lowered himself back into his chair. "Goddammit. Why is it always the good ones? Spill it."

"She says she doesn't want to publish it."

He put his hands on his head as if to keep it from exploding. "Are you joking right now? Why the hell not?"

"I really don't know. She got back from Cape Breton last night and sounded very tired and discouraged for some reason. I told her I was here, and we'd talk when she was ready. I invited her to dinner."

"But..."

She pointed at him. "She needs to rest and calm down. She wrote a novel in three months when she didn't think she ever would again. I'm sure she's emotionally drained, and if we harangue her to tell us what's going on, she might clam up and never give it to us. Let me handle it. I know you want this book. So do I. But let's be patient. Otherwise, it might disappear in a puff of smoke."

Mel leaned back in his chair and stared at the ceiling. "Why the hell did I ever become a publisher? Writers drive me nuts."

"You and me both."

Chapter Sixteen

Kitty's first few days home were spent mostly in bed sleeping. Not being awake was preferable at the moment. Robert came home late at night and was usually gone before she woke up. He might as well have been in New York. But a few things had changed. He'd leave a Cornflakes box on the counter, with a bowl, spoon, and banana out for her, or a loaf of bread by the toaster, something he'd never done before. She knew he was trying and she appreciated it.

The only non-filling air she got was when she took a dispirited Pip out for a walk about the neighbourhood. Other than that, they snuggled together under the covers, both of them trying to forget their lovely friends and one giant wet blanket far away.

Kitty sat up in bed one morning and took a notepad and held it against her knees. *My Life Recipe: family, friends, a little house, and a second dog. Writing, when I get the courage to do it again.*

She needed to send a letter to Bertha, because Bertha should know her address and phone number. Not that they'd be able to call about anything private, but maybe they could become pen pals. Kitty needed and wanted to keep the connection.

The doorbell rang and she slipped on her robe and went to the door. A delivery man handed her a bouquet of flowers in a glass vase. She thanked him and put them on the hall table to unwrap the cellophane. There was a card.

"The time has come," the Walrus said, "to talk of many things." I betrayed you. I'm so sorry.

Her hand covered her mouth and she knew she had to sit down as her head felt woozy. He was sorry. He used the word *betrayed*, which was exactly how she felt. Wait. How did Wallace know where she lived? This was crazy. She was relieved, upset, and lonesome all at the same time. Grateful, but still smarting about the way it had played out. He'd driven her out of the one place she felt safe. And that hurt. He was sorry, but did it matter?

And then the phone rang. She waited to see if it was her number and then remembered she didn't have to. She got it on the third ring. "Hello?"

"Kitty?"

"Hi, Dad."

"All I ever do these days is try and figure out where you are. Why didn't you tell me you were coming home? I called the number in Cape Breton a couple of times, but there was no answer, so I phoned Gaynor this morning to ask if she knew anything, only to find out you'd arrived home three days ago."

"I'm sorry. It was spur of the moment and I've been unpacking and sleeping ever since. It's a very long drive. I'm surprised Kurt didn't tell his mother, but he's been busy."

"He called her last night. She never mentioned anything."

"She wouldn't, would she?"

"Sorry?"

Damn it. Kitty swore she wouldn't do this again. That was her old life, and she wanted nothing to do with it, no matter how upset she was. "Dad, why don't we get together?"

"Fine. Tonight? I'll ask Martha to put on another chop."

"I don't want to go to your house. I'd like it to be the two of us. Is there any way we can meet for dinner, or lunch?"

"Today? I'm busy today but I could find time for a quick bite at noon tomorrow."

"How about that little dive we used to go to? Just up the street?"

"Okay. I'll meet you there. I look forward to it."

"Me too."

Kitty was finally going on a date. With her dad. And that gave her some solace on this unsettled morning. She kept peeking at the card. "That moment really did hurt, Wallace. I'm not going to pretend otherwise."

She didn't realize she'd said it out loud until Pip put her front paws up on her leg and gave her an inquiring look.

Kitty cast an eye over the apartment, wanting comfort, but there was none to be found. The leather sofa and chairs were sleek, the coffee and end tables glass and metal. The radio was another stream-lined piece of teak. Only the giant starburst clock that hung above it had a circle in the middle, but you never noticed it with the shiny spikes glinting in every direction. Heavy drapes flanked the windows and the two lamps on either side of the sofa were enormous. She'd never noticed how large they were. Kurt said they were modern. As were the paintings on the wall. The biggest one had various-sized boxes of different colours all held together with straight lines ver-tically and horizontally. It reminded her of...nothing.

Where was *she* in this room? In this apartment? She opened her study door, which she always kept closed. To keep the rest of this space from encroaching in on her?

There was the mess, the roundness of things. Everything jum-bled and chaotic. The happy times in her childhood were here. The books she and her mom had read together, her stuffed toys, the few pictures of the three of them. The secretary desk that sometimes held her typewriter was her mother's. Kitty remembered she'd loved to sit at her mom's feet when she put the leaf down to write letters, because it felt like a cubbyhole, and her mom would stroke her hair as Kitty leaned against her legs.

Her mother's jewellery box was at the top of one of her book-cases. She took it down and it was covered with dust. How shameful. Why had it been so long since she'd opened it? Pip jumped up on the daybed and made a nest with the tartan throw they'd sat on at the beach in Mira Gut. Kitty joined her and unclasped the lock.

Here were round things. A lot of costume jewellery, earrings, brooches, and bracelets, but there were two pieces inside that mattered. Her mom's platinum Art Deco wedding band and a pearl necklace. Kitty had always loved the lustrous pearls, because they were quite small, even dainty, unlike the bigger ones you saw on necklaces today. The necklace and red, velvet-lined case that held them seemed to belonged to a long-ago princess. She touched the pearls, knowing her mother would have done the same. And then she placed the wedding band on the ring finger of her right hand. It fit perfectly. Why had she never worn this before? *My god*. She was a princess. Sleeping Beauty. Everything hidden under dust. That would have horrified Mrs. Mary Jane Faulkner. *Get out and live, my little kitten*, she heard her say. Kitty held her hand up in the air to look at the ring.

"I promise, Mama."

⊷⊱⊰⊶

That night Kurt stumbled home at one in the morning. He woke her up when he hit the end of the bed, tiptoeing through, saying, "SHHH! SHHHH!"

She sat up and turned on the bedside lamp. "I hope you didn't drive home like that."

"Kitty! You're awake! What a wondrous surprise." He weaved as he tried to stand straight. "You've been either snoring or crying in the bathtub to avoid me since you got home."

"I don't ignore you. You get home at midnight and leave before six. Did you and the cast have a party of some sort?"

"No. A few drinks with dinner. Why weren't you there?"

"You never asked me."

"Because you never come."

"Okay. The next time your cast goes out for dinner together, let me know and I'll be there."

He waved her away. "Nah! You wouldn't like it. All we do is talk shop."

"And drink yourselves senseless. It's been a while since I did that. It might be a good idea."

Kurt almost strangled himself taking off his tie. "Nah! That's what I love about you. You're classy. You don't guzzle wine and make the rounds sitting on men's laps like some women I know. I'm always proud to take you anywhere."

"Sweet of you to say, but you never take me anywhere."

He pointed at her and almost unbalanced himself. "That changes now! We'll do everything differently. Ozzie and Harriet! What do ya say?"

He fell across the bed with a whoomph, startling poor Pip.

"Timber."

❦

He was gone the next morning. Kitty had lept in her study because she couldn't get Sleeping Beauty to move no matter what she did, so she had thrown one end of the bedspread over Kurt and left, fully expecting to shake him awake. But it appeared he'd managed on his own. Kurt never did need much sleep, and he was tenacious when he wanted to be. *He must be having a good time on this set*, she thought. He was doing everything he could to show up on time in the morning, no matter how late he got home, or in what condition.

She had her breakfast listening to the transistor radio she bought in Glace Bay. It didn't look the same on the counter in a windowless kitchen, but she was glad for its company.

There were still things to be put away, and that reminded her of Dimitri, who'd helped her unpack the car. He was nice, despite the tuba. What would Bertha do if he had helped her? She'd bake him cookies and send a plate up to him. That's what Kitty would do. She even had a bag of chocolate chips in the pantry.

The cookies looked nothing like Bertha's and didn't taste as good, but that wasn't the point. The point was to thank the man. This was community. This was connection. The W. I. members would be proud of her. This is what she needed to do to make herself whole again.

Kitty and Pip headed out for their walk but took the stairs to the third floor first and knocked on Dimitri's door. It took a while, but he opened it. He might have been sleeping. He'd probably had a concert the night before. She hadn't considered that.

"Oh! Hello. Kitty, isn't it?"

"I'm sorry for waking you."

"Not at all."

She passed over the plate of cookies. "This is to thank you for your help the other day. I hope you enjoy them."

He gave her such a lovely smile. "Well, thank you, what a surprise. This is what my mother does at home in Olympos. Always taking food over to the neighbours. You miss that when you live in an apartment."

"Don't worry about the plate. I'll get it another time. I need to take Pip out for her walk. Enjoy." She and Pip headed down the hallway.

He leaned out the door. "Thanks again."

Gosh, that felt good.

They walked over to the McGill campus, always a lovely jaunt. To be surrounded by so many trees, even if they had no leaves, and the large assortment of heritage buildings at the edge of a modern metropolis, made you realize what a gem it was. She had enjoyed her time here. She watched the women students walk with their friends and was surprised at how young they looked. She had been that young, but certainly not carefree, as she'd been a married woman attending classes here. What a shame.

Kitty looked at the time and realized she'd better hurry if she wanted to meet her father for lunch. She'd almost forgotten about it. A muddled frame of mind seemed to be her permanent state.

Once Pip was settled, curled up on the daybed in her study, already zonked out because of the long walk, Kitty left the apartment feeling less guilty. How did she manage before? She barely went out. Always too busy writing to agonize about having no friends. There, she'd said it. She had no companions to speak of here. But there were plenty in another part of the world, and she missed them.

Her father, Leo, short for Leonard, was already seated in the corner of the local sandwich shop. The menu was on a blackboard up on the wall behind the cash register, and the small round tables covered in red-checkered plastic tablecloths were supposed to be reminiscent of a Parisian Cafe, but the place was a little too grimy and rundown to make it believable. Still, they liked it here because it was never too crowded.

Dad was looking at his spiral notebook. He always seemed so lonely. His grey fedora was on the table beside him. His wavy hair was almost completely silver now. It was thinning, too; a small circle of scalp had appeared at the back of his crown. She'd never noticed that before, and it bothered her.

He was a six-foot barrel-chested man who usually wore a permanent scowl, someone you wouldn't want to cross. His full-length grey gabardine trench coat was a staple. He had two more in his closet. His craggy face was drawn, his skin sallow, but when he looked up with those light blue eyes of his, they seemed so out of place with his drab persona, it was startling.

The minute he saw her, those eyes sparkled for a moment. "Kitty!" He jumped to his feet and gave her a big hug. "Gosh, I've missed you. Knowing you weren't here really bothered me."

She hugged him back. "Hi, Dad. I've missed you too."

They sat down and Dad raised his hand to the owner. "I ordered our favourite."

They got themselves settled, shrugging out of their coats to let them fall on the back of the chairs. The man came over and put down two large soup bowls. "Deux soupes aux pois."

"Merci," Dad said.

Then the man rushed back with a bread basket. "Baguette."

They nodded their thanks.

"I haven't had pea soup in a long time," Kitty confessed, taking a sip. "As good as ever."

Her dad reached for the baguette, broke off a piece, and dipped it in his soup. "I'd completely forgotten about this place. Why did we stop coming here?"

"*Why* seems to be a word I've grappled with for the last three months."

"How so?" They continued to eat as they talked.

"Dad, have you ever lived anywhere else for months at a time?"

"Nope. What's it like? Did you enjoy yourself away?"

"I had the best time of my life. I met some delightful people and they live in a place that seems out of the way and remote, but scratch the surface and there's a busy beehive of activity going on, lots of work, cooperation, good deeds, and community fun. My closest neighbour, Bertha Bailey, has oodles of kids, grandkids, and great-grandkids, and they all adore her. Food is her language of love. She keeps filling you up, in more ways than one. Most people wouldn't give her a second glance, or think she's a rural housewife leading a sheltered life and how can she stand the monotony of it all? But she is blessed and knows it. I met the Homeville Women's Institute, a whole gaggle of rural women who have monthly meetings to make their community better. They realized that by joining together they had a stronger voice, and that is empowering. They were a real inspiration to me. Just what I needed to see. That you can advocate for yourself."

"I haven't heard you talk this much in years. It's lovely. Now tell me, did you get your writing inspiration back?"

"I did."

"Gaynor must be relieved."

She nodded and tore off a piece of bread for herself. "You know,

I keep saying this, but to move away from all you know gives you a unique perspective, and I'm grateful to have had it. And not just for the writing." She took a bite of bread to calm herself, and he waited for her to finish the thought. "It made me realize that all was not well with me for a very long time."

His head jutted forward, full of concern. "Are you sick?"

"No, Dad. I'm not physically sick, but I've been sick at heart for twenty-five years and so have you."

He got quiet. She'd known he would. He kept his head down.

"Dad. Look at me."

"Catriona, I can't have a conversation about your mother here in public. I wasn't prepared for this today. I have to go soon, so there's no sense getting into it."

"Okay," she said, sighing. He was right. This wasn't the place.

"I'm not saying we can never talk about this. Your being away made me realize how much I take you for granted. I was very unsettled, knowing I couldn't see you."

"But in the last few years, Dad, we haven't seen that much of each other. Why is that? It's like we drifted apart."

"I blame myself."

"I don't."

"What do you mean?"

She tapped her own cheek to remind herself this was the new Kitty. "Nothing. I mean we're both to blame. And I don't plan to let that happen again. Bertha's family reminded me that I have a special dad of my own, and I need to spend more time with you. I've taken you for granted as well."

She drank more of her soup and looked up. He was staring at her hand. "Is that…"

"Yes, it's Mom's. I hope you don't mind if I wear it. She feels near me when I have it on. I don't know why I didn't put it on before."

He looked stricken. "That's because you tried it on when you were a little girl and I told you to take it off and put it away. Not because it was too big for you or I was afraid you'd lose it, but because I didn't want to look at it. I was cross with you. And as I say that now, I realize how heartless that was."

They both put down their spoons and stared at the table.

"I think you're correct," he said. "*Heartsick* is the right word."

She reached over and touched the back of his hand. "It's okay, Dad. We don't have to talk about it. We have the rest of our lives to do that."

He nodded. "Okay." He took her hand in his own and squeezed.

"I'm glad we did this. Thank you for coming." She smiled. "Same time next week?"

She tried to pay for lunch, but he insisted. They kissed each other goodbye and he drove back to work while she walked the long way home, to digest what had happened. Kitty felt so much better after forty minutes with her dad. The key was to meet him alone. They never discussed anything in front of Martha. Martha always made sure of that.

Kitty wasn't looking forward to Christmas day, when the four of them sat around a dry turkey and waited for it to be over. She dreaded it every year. Her mother and brother had died on Christmas day. Her father had pretended to have a good time when she was little, and she had pretended it worked. Now that they were adults, that charade was over. After one particularly difficult year, Kurt stormed out. "They died twenty years ago! Why is this tradition of moping around with long faces still going on? Why can't we have a normal Christmas dinner like the rest of the world?"

Kitty remembered being hurt, but looking back she realized he was exactly right. She'd have to make more of an effort this year. With that in mind, she stopped in front of a small antique store and looked in the window. There was the prettiest tea set. Four round teacups and saucers sitting on top of square plates with rounded, indented corners. She'd never seen square plates with a set like this. The cups inside were white with a gold trim, but the wide rims on the cups, saucers, and plates were painted with an entwined vine border of green leaves and blue, orange, and brown berries, all of them visible when the plates were stacked. There was a creamer, a sugar bowl, and a rectangular biscuit plate. The colours popped even from behind the cloudy window pane.

She immediately went inside and asked about it. It was an Aynsley England tea set, circa 1925. It didn't matter what it cost. She had to have it, and asked if they could wrap it up properly and ship it for her. They could indeed.

"The address?"

"Please deliver this to Mrs. Donald Bailey, South Head Road, Homeville, Cape Breton, Nova Scotia."

"Of course. Is this a Christmas gift?"

"No. It's a thank-you, I-love-you-and-miss-you gift."

As she walked home, a bubble of happiness welled up. Only four days ago she'd been so upset and could scarcely see straight, and now she was absolutely delighted to think of Bertha opening her gift and displaying it for her Institute friends at their next meeting. She was actually humming when she walked into the apartment and sat down at her mother's desk, after a swift kiss to the top of Pippy's head. She took out her writing paper and pen.

Saturday, December 10, 1955

Dearest Bertha,

I am sending you a gift as an apology for my abrupt leaving. It was never my intention to depart in such a manner, especially not when you and your family were so incredibly kind to me. I had the happiest time of my life on South Head Road and you were a big reason for that. I'll never forget your friendship, your advice, your heavenly cooking, and our many laughs together. I do hope we can become pen pals, but I know you're busy. I'll call you from time to time, but we'll probably have to use code words to keep any secrets from Ethel. I miss her too! I miss Argus and Pride, all the kiddies and chickens. And yes, I miss Wallace...kind of. Please tell him I received his flowers and appreciated the message.

I'll put my personal details at the bottom of the page, along with my father's address and phone number, just in case. I want you to be able to contact me. Apparently, you know my current address already, but I can't for the life of me figure out how!

Thank you for everything. I love you and miss you.

Kitty xoxoxo

⁂

Gaynor was happily lying on a beach in Maui, the hot sun baking the back of her neck. The roar of the ocean filled her ears as she drifted off. A lovely calm overtook her frayed nerves. This was just the ticket.

And then some kind of hermit crab kept pinching her shoulder. Her eyes flew open and she sat up, hitting her forehead on the front of the hair dryer with a thwack. "OW!"

Gaynor pulled up the dryer and gave the young woman in front of her an astonished look. "Kitty? Is that really you? How did you know I was here? It's not my usual day."

"Your new secretary told me. She said you'd be thrilled by the interruption."

"Hot dang, I love that woman! Can you wait until I'm done? Do you have time?"

"I hoped you'd take me to lunch at the restaurant next door."

Gaynor clapped her hands together. "Done!"

"May I bum a smoke?"

Gaynor pointed at the purse at her feet. "Why do you never buy your own cigarettes?"

"You always have them."

As Mitzi took out her rollers, Gaynor watched Kitty read a

magazine. She jerked her head towards her. "Remember I told you about that writer? The one who wrote the funny female detective? That's her."

Mitzi took a sneak peek. "That striking girl is the writer? I thought she'd be an old lady like Agatha Christie. I'd love to get my hands on that head of hair."

When Gaynor was finished, she walked over to Kitty, who butt her cigarette out when she saw her coming and stood up. "I have no idea how you breathe with that chemical soup enveloping your head."

Gaynor put her arm through hers. "And I have no idea how you look so damn good."

"I've put on weight. Kurt calls me pudgy and tells me I better not get fat."

"Did Kurt ever read your book where the wife pushes the miserable husband out of the upstairs window, impaling him on a spiked wrought-iron fence?"

"I don't believe so."

They went to the bistro next door and Gaynor asked the hostess for a booth at the back. They settled in and Gaynor ordered two red wines.

"What would you like for lunch?" she asked. "It's on me."

"How about tourtière? It's cold out there."

They made chit-chat while they waited for their meal. Gaynor drank her first glass of wine rather quickly and asked for another when the waitress came back with their orders. They tucked in and it was the perfect choice for a wintery day.

"I can't believe it's December," Kitty said. "And a lifetime since I interrupted your last hair appointment."

"You'll hear no complaint from me about that. You know I've been waiting to hear from you. Honestly, I thought it would take longer."

"Me too."

"So how are you, my darling? What's been going on? You're obviously feeling better since the last time we talked."

"I am. I've slept, walked the dog to clear my head and actually had lunch with my dad, which was a lovely treat. I've missed him so much. Not just since I've been away, but long before that. It was nice to find out he really missed me too."

Gaynor cut the meat pie with the side of her fork. "That, I am very happy about. I was worried when you sent that first letter, but in a blink of an eye you had the first twelve chapters and then bingo, it was done. I'm used to your fast work, but to have it returned so quickly was rather astonishing when you consider the change in style."

"A person can write happy, funny thoughts when they're happy." Kitty drank from her wineglass. "What does Mel think of it?"

"I believe he sent you twenty pounds of very expensive chocolate, did he not? Is that why you're 'pudgy'?"

She shook her head. "I'm pudgy because Bertha baked, cooked, stewed, fried, roasted, and sautéed. The woman is a genius. I have no idea how I will live my life without her."

"I'm delighted you had a great time. Up until the last day." Gaynor downed her second glass of wine. "I called you in the morning to celebrate and by that night you'd left the island and told me not to publish."

"I know."

"Not to publish the best book you've ever written, mind you."

"Do you really think so?"

"The thought of this book not going to print tears my heart out. It's brilliant, Kitty. How did you come up with these characters? I mean, I understand Kate's journey, obviously. You might as well have called her Kitty. But the nonsense with everyone else! Real, flesh-and-blood, down-to-earth rare birds."

"That's the problem."

Gaynor put down her fork and crossed her arms. "I'm listening."

"My very good friend, Wallace, who is literally the nicest human I've ever met, is a very moral person. Someone who thinks seriously about what is good in this world. What has value. Doing the right thing. I asked him to read it and he was horrified when he recognized almost everyone in it as his family, friends, and neighbours. He thought I was making fun of them, because of how slapstick and broad all the comedy in the book is. But if he had taken the time to process it, he'd know that that makes no sense." She shook her head. "I professed every day how much I loved everyone there, I would never have made fun of them. However...now I'm worried that he might have a point. I jumped down his throat, saying all writers use characteristics of people they know, or a compilation of people they've met, but would never use a real person or their name. That's why the fine print declaring the book a work of fiction. But honestly, the first time I met Ethel Macdonald, I knew she was a perfect character for a book. And what did I do? I described her as a scrawny chicken and a party-line pooper, which is exactly what she is in real life. Now, I know she wouldn't recognize herself, because we never admit our own foibles and she doesn't read my books or would even know I wrote it since I use a pen name...but that's not the point, is it?"

Gaynor reached for her wineglass, but it was empty, so she took a gulp of water instead. "Myrtle Lovett is my favourite character in the book. She's priceless. There cannot possibly be only one scrawny lady in the Dominion of Canada who listens in on party lines. Are you not going to publish it in case they get offended?"

"I don't know them, do I?"

Gaynor nodded. "True enough. Has Wallace read your other books?'

"He doesn't read fiction."

"I hate him already."

"No, you'd love him."

"He doesn't read fiction, he doesn't read murder mysteries,

he's never read your work, he doesn't understand the process of how a story comes to be, doesn't understand the complexity of creating a fictional world while living in a real one. And yet he criticized you. Of course you're going to use what you've experienced, who made you laugh, what made you cry, the situations that pull at your heartstrings. That's what writers do. They lift life off the ground, put it on the page, and offer it for others to examine. To help them learn and know they're not alone. He's dead wrong about this."

"He knows that. He sent me flowers and apologized for betraying me."

"His words?"

"He quoted 'The Walrus and the Carpenter' by Lewis Carroll. A poem about betrayal. His nickname is Walrus."

"Okay, he's clever, but he has caused me a few grey hairs, and poor Mel has ripped out the few strands he had left."

Now Kitty finished her wine in one gulp. "I really threw you two in it, didn't I? I'm sorry. I was in such a state when I called."

The waitress came back and they ordered coffee and sugar pie to finish off a truly Québécois lunch.

"What I can't figure out is how he got my address."

Gaynor lit another cigarette. "Ah. That's my doing."

"You?"

"Remember I told you that I talked to Bertha the night you left? A day later she called me. Wallace knew your publishing company and she remembered my name, so they tracked me down. Bertha said he needed to apologize. I assumed it had something to do with the debacle, so I gave it to her. I hope I did the right thing."

"Of course. The flowers were lovely."

Their dessert and coffee were delivered and disappeared quite quickly. They sat back, stuffed to the gills.

"That was great. Thanks, Gaynor."

"My pleasure. So what do we do, Kitty? Obviously, this is your creative work, and your decision, no matter what Mel and I want. Did you discuss it with your dad?"

Kitty took a deep breath. "No, but he would say look at the facts. And the fact is that I wrote this book with only loving intentions."

"And?"

"I'm dedicating it to Bertha."

Chapter Seventeen

Bertha was a woman possessed, trying to get all her Christmas baking done. Not just for her family, but for the people who paid her to do it for them, like Dolly Wadden. It's how she made extra money. She even had customers come out from Glace Bay and Sydney to get her baking for their own Christmas parties. Everyone asked if she'd bake for them on other occasions, but she kept it to Christmas. If she baked all year for other people, her life wouldn't be her own. Everyone was awed by her endless energy, but what they didn't know was she had a very large elf who helped her in the evenings when visitors left.

The poor man had to do something to occupy his mind. Wallace was not the same person he'd been before Kitty left. His guilt plagued him. Bertha could see it, and when she tried to talk to him, he'd clam up. She had no one to discuss it with. It would kill him if anyone found out what he'd done; his shame was isolating as it was.

The only time he made an effort was with the kids. They could still make him smile.

The porch door opened and a gust of cold air came in with it, which was welcome since the kitchen was a blast furnace thanks to the wood stove. Bertha took the latest batch of shortbreads out of the oven and put them on cooling racks.

"Did you get the mail?"

Wallace nodded as he went through it. "Yeah. Mrs. Turner says hello." Mrs. Turner in Homeville ran the post office out of her house. "Four Christmas cards, a Credit Union statement, and…"

"And what?"

"A letter for you, postmarked Montreal. It's from Kitty. That's her return address."

"Oh my." Bertha wiped her hands on her apron and sat down at the kitchen table. Wallace handed it to her. "Do you want me to leave?"

"Don't be foolish." She tore open the envelope, took off her fogged-up glasses, and held the stationery at eye level so she could see it better. Her lips moved as she read and she had a big smile on her face. "Oh, that was lovely. What a dear girl."

"What did she say?"

"That there's a gift coming for me and she misses all of us. She said to thank you for the flowers and she appreciated the message."

"She said that?"

"Yes. So you see? She doesn't hate us. She sounds great."

"Did she mention if she's publishing the book?"

"No, she doesn't say one way or the other."

Wallace gave a big sigh. "I'm glad she got the flowers and liked the message."

Bertha put the letter back in its envelope and placed it in her apron pocket. "You see how nice it is to hear from someone? I'm glad you sent her flowers, but now that you know she still loves and misses us, why don't you write her a proper letter? I think she'd appreciate it."

"She still loves us?"

"Of course she does. She loves our whole family and we love her. That won't change, even if she never comes back. People come into your life and some of them snuggle into your heart forever."

She could see he looked a little better, and that was a Christmas present she desperately needed. Living with a happy Wallace was a joy. Living with a very sad Wallace was getting on her last nerve. None of her friends had thirty-five-year-old sons still at home—even poor Ethel, with her neediness, was on her own—their children were married. As much as she loved her boy, there were times when she wouldn't have minded being alone. With him here, she could never take off her bra until she crawled into bed. The sight of her big bobbling boobs under a nightgown would scar him for life. And passing wind without worrying about it would be pleasant. She was mortified the morning he caught her plucking her chin hairs. There were some things a son never needed to know about his mother.

⁂

Wednesday, December 14, 1955

Dear Kitty,

Mom was thrilled to get your letter. You made her very happy. We've been terribly worried about you and I was relieved to hear that you liked the flowers and my message. I feel I owe you a more formal letter of apology, which is why I'm writing this today.

I've thought of nothing else since I basically chased you away from here. You were rudely uprooted with no warning. On what should have been a very happy day for you with your editor's congratulatory phone call, I came stomping in with my skewed opinions. Just being asked to read it was a privilege. No matter what I thought at the time, I should have respected the incredible effort it took to write it and complimented you on that and that alone.

I knew I was completely out of line when I finally fessed up to Mom about what I said to you. She told me it was absolute nonsense that you were making fun of us and I should have known better.

And I do know better. But that won't erase the unpleasant memory of me pontificating about something I know nothing about. I am ashamed of my behavior. I am so very, very sorry. I hope you'll forgive me. You've brought me so much happiness with your friendship.

We all miss you and little Pip. I keep thinking Argus and Pride are giving me disgusted looks. And I deserve them.

I know when the book comes out, it will be a smash hit.

Always,
Wallace

❧

The next day Bertha's three eldest daughters, Mary, Annie, and Helen, were over without a single child or grandchild. This was a serious visit. To firm up plans on who was doing what for Christmas dinner. They sat around the kitchen table, each one with their own pad of paper and pen, because these master plans would have to be distributed to their own extended families. The younger daughters, Jean, Lizzie, and Ruth, gave the older ones their blessing to figure it out. They wanted no part in organizing it. Whatever they decided was fine with them. John, Charlie, and George were off the hook food-wise. Their wives and mothers-in-law did the dirty work. But they were in charge of setting up tables and would collect chairs from various households. Wallace had already made the plum pudding and fruitcake, but that was a secret.

"Okay. So as far as you know we'll only have about thirty to thirty-five for dinner this year?" Bertha asked. "I've invited Ethel and Winnie to come as well, since her son is off to Mabou with his wife's relatives."

"Give or take," said Mary. "Some of my bunch will be at the other grandmother's house. But they always whine about it, not because they want to be with me, but because I come here and they don't want to miss out."

"Should I cook a thirty-pound turkey and you cook a twenty-pound turkey, or should we divide it up and three of us cook a twenty-pound bird each? You know how everyone wants to divvy up the leftovers. You can never have enough turkey with this bunch."

"Let's do three twenty-pound birds," Annie suggested. "You don't want your oven tied up for six hours. So that's turkeys for Mom, Mary, and me."

They wrote that down.

"That means I'll be in charge of the potatoes and dressing," Helen said.

They wrote that down.

Bertha bit the end of her pencil. "Let's give the carrots, turnips, and Brussels sprouts to Jean. No, Lizzie. Jean hates cutting up veggies. Jean can do the peas, sweet-potato casserole, and cranberry sauce."

"That's not much," Annie said, frowning. "Give her dinner rolls too."

"What do you have to do but throw a turkey in the oven?" Mary said. "You do the rolls."

"You've only got a turkey too. If I do the rolls, then you're going to have to do a couple of desserts."

"Girls."

These middle-aged women kept bickering.

"Girls!"

The three of them looked at their mother.

"And what's Ruth going to do? Paint her nails?"

They looked at each other. "We forgot Ruth. Give her the rolls and a couple of desserts," Mary said. "Looking after a turkey all day is a job and a half. Especially when you have to carve it and make the gravy."

That seemed to satisfy everyone. They wrote it down.

"Obviously, I've already made the fruitcake and plum pudding," Bertha said. "Should I make a couple of pumpkin pies too?"

Why not?

Mary got up and poured everyone a cup of tea. She added the milk at the counter. "I'll bring my silver. It's the nicest. Yours isn't bad either, Helen, so bring it with you. Between that and Mom's we should have enough cutlery to go around."

When Mary handed a teacup to Annie, Annie pursed her lips. "Your silver belongs to your mother-in-law, and the poor soul isn't dead yet."

Bertha doodled on her paper, drank her tea, and suddenly held up her pencil. "Teacups! All of you girls bring four each. Six times four is twenty-four. With mine we'll have enough. The kids don't drink tea."

"You can't eat turkey in a teacup," Helen said. "Everyone brings four plates as well."

"What time are we having dinner this year?" Mary wanted to know.

"And we still have to figure out who's driving who out here," Annie added. "Hubby said he'd make a couple of runs if necessary."

Bertha kept tapping her pencil. "What about tablecloths? Mary, bring over those date squares. I'm peckish."

"Wallace is Santa Claus this year, as usual, so..." Helen said.

"Actually, about that," Bertha interrupted, "I think we should change it up. I don't know how the tradition started, but Wallace is too young to play Santa. I think your husbands would be better suited, since they're grandfathers. Your Ed should do it, Helen. He's a soft, squishy sort and even has a grey beard."

"That's a good idea. I think he'd love that."

There was a sharp rap at the door and Ethel yelled, "It's only me!"

"She should just live here," Mary tsked.

Ethel pushed open the kitchen door, her coat still on. "I need help."

Bertha jumped to her feet. "What's wrong?"

"Nothing. I just need one of you girls to bring in something from the car. I don't want to drop it."

"What is it?" Bertha said.

"I was at the post office and they told me there was a package for you from Montreal. I said I was going home and I'd take it. Mr. Turner put it in the trunk for me."

"OH! It's my gift from Kitty already! My goodness, she must have sent it by air."

"Kitty!" Ethel exclaimed. "Oh, how exciting."

Helen went out the door and came back in with a solid square package. "It's not as heavy as it looks."

Ethel was beside herself. "I wonder what it is?"

Grabbing a pair of scissors, Bertha started to cut away the packing tape. "Gosh, this is like Christmas. I thought she was sending a trinket of some sort."

"You knew this was coming, Mom?" Helen asked.

"Yes, Kitty wrote me a letter."

"You never told me that," Ethel complained. "You always tell me everything."

Bertha winked at her girls as she continued to cut away the brown paper wrapping. "It must have slipped my mind."

Once the box was opened, she had to contend with a copious amount of packing paper and wrapping. "What on earth is this? She had no business sending so much. It must have cost a fortune to mail it."

When the first plate was revealed, every one of them oohed and ahhed. "It's exquisite," Bertha exclaimed.

When they had the entire tea set on the table, they were stunned into silence. None of them had ever seen anything like it. Bertha had a huge smile on her face. "Can you believe it? This is the nicest gift I've ever received."

"Kitty obviously thinks a great deal of you. I saw it on her face every time she was over here," Mary said.

"But she spent too much."

"That was for her to decide, Mom." Annie patted her mother's back. "You deserve this and more."

"Oh, wait until my next Institute meeting."

Wallace happened to come in with the dogs and was startled when they shouted at him to keep the dogs outside. "Okay, okay!"

Poor old Argus and Pride were escorted back out and he came back in. "What was that all about?"

"The dogs might have knocked into the kitchen table," Bertha said, "and if any of this gets broken, there will be hell to pay."

Wallace looked at the vibrant fine china. "Wow. Who owns this?"

"It's mine. A gift from Kitty."

He stared at it for what seemed like a long time and whispered, "It's beautiful. Like her."

Ethel cocked her head. "What did he say?"

"He said it's very nice," Bertha sniffed.

Wallace left the room.

❧❦

Thursday, December 15, 1955

Dear Kitty,

Your beautiful gift arrived today, all of it in one piece, without so much as a chip or a crack anywhere. It's the loveliest tea set I've ever seen and I will treasure it always. Hopefully someday you and I can share a cup of tea and a biscuit over it. It's so pretty I want to look at it every day and planned to display it on the sideboard, but was fretful that the dogs or kids might bump into it. It was Wallace who suggested I keep it on my little table under the window in my bedroom, so I can see it. The children and dogs are not allowed in my sanctuary! A perfect solution.

And certainly, I will be your pen pal. I've never had one before. We miss you very much. I look back at the three months you were here as a very happy time for all of us. The kids still ask when you're coming home. I know that the dogs and Wallace and I really miss Pip. Remember, you and your family are always welcome here, Kitty.

Please look after yourself. Make sure you're eating properly and always wear a hat and a scarf on cold winter mornings when you take Pip for a walk. You have a tendency to daydream, so be careful of traffic.

I love you. And I love my tea set.

Bertha xoxoxo

·❧·

It seemed to Wallace that his mother was keeping him constantly busy with real and imagined jobs. He barely had time to sit down before she'd ask him to run to the store, or the post office, or one of his siblings' houses to pick up something she needed for her huge Christmas dinner. He welcomed the distraction, but it was obvious that she felt he required looking after, and that annoyed him. He needed to get a grip.

He was exceedingly relieved not to have to play Santa Claus this year. The thought of trying to be that cheery was daunting. He assumed his mother had something to do with it, and he was grateful. Once again, she'd made things easy.

It was a cold, windy day. And damp. The kind of weather that went through you instead of around you. The sky looked like it was about to burst with snow that hadn't fallen yet, but it was coming, so he decided to take the dogs for a walk. He'd baked all morning. He and his mother made a killing with these Christmas orders. Maybe he should look into expanding her little business on other occasions. His mother wouldn't have to be involved, except to say that she'd baked the stuff, but at this point he was mighty good at popping out dozens of squares and cookies in one evening. As they came out of the wood stove, he saw dollar signs.

Just as he headed out, his brother John drove up. "Hey, Wally."

"You need anything?"

"No. Mom wanted me to drop off some chairs. I stopped in and got your mail on the way over. There's one here for you."

"Thanks."

His brother passed it to him and continued inside with the rest. A letter. For him. From Kitty.

His heart raced in spite of his attempt to stay calm. He shoved the envelope in his pocket and headed out across the soft fields to the shoreline. The dogs tried to keep up to him. The thought of being totally alone when he opened her letter was the only thing on his mind. That way he could snivel if he needed to, without his entire family breathing down his neck.

He sat on the same log the two of them had used the last time she was down by the shore. He spent a lengthy time looking out over the water, so long the dogs gave up on their trek and settled down beside him. In a way, he was almost reluctant to open the letter. Right now, he could imagine what it said without the reality of its contents. Perhaps disappointment was coming and at this moment he was still hopeful, so he wanted that to linger for a bit.

Eventually the chilly air made the decision for him and he opened the envelope carefully, not wanting to tear it.

Sunday, December 18, 1955

Dear Wallace,

Thank you for your letter of apology. Of course I forgive you. What I said to you and how I reacted was just one moment of the time we spent together. We've shared many, many wonderful hours laughing, making fires, going for walks, and frequenting the retailers of Glace Bay. Not to mention eating everything in sight. None of it will ever be erased from my memory. You will always be my dear friend. Please know that I do plan on publishing the book, and it was my fault that I called Gaynor and caused all of the upset with the publishers. Like you, I didn't think before I acted. Because everyone on South Head Road means so much to me, I panicked when I thought I'd overstepped the bounds of familiarity.

But I know why I wrote the book, and my new friends were my writing inspiration.

You never had the power to make that decision. It was always mine alone. So please release yourself from the guilt I know you feel.

You're a good man, Wallace Bailey. Merry Christmas.

Your friend,

Kitty xoxo

Wallace folded the letter into its envelope and placed it inside his jacket pocket next to his heart. He put his head down, held his hands over his face, and cried and cried. The anguish of the last two weeks left his body with his tears. He sensed the extreme tension leave his muscles and felt his lungs opening. He knew the mental torture he'd been under, but hadn't been aware of how his body had been gripped by the stress of it. Not until he felt it release did he realize how badly he'd needed to hear from her.

The dogs were anxious and whining when he finally lifted his face and wiped his eyes with the sleeve of his jacket. He reached over and hugged their huge furry bodies to reassure them.

"She's still our friend. She doesn't hate me. She's forgiven me. That's all I want. To know that we can still be friends."

He got up and took the dogs for their promised walk on their beautiful property, just to move his cold limbs. How grateful he was for all of it. To look out and see the ocean, to hear the wind through the fir trees. And then he saw the moving cloud of snow come his way over the water, so he whistled for the dogs and they headed back.

By the time Bertha heard them come in the porch, she was ready to brain him. He had no business being out in this weather. She opened the door to the porch. The three of them were completely covered with heavy snow, the dogs' black bodies now white. Wallace would make a perfect Santa Claus with that snowy beard.

"Stay there!" she shrieked, laughing. "I'll get some towels."

When everyone was finally dried off, she made Wallace sit down with a cup of hot cocoa and a plate of oatmeal raisin cookies. He sat there and smiled. "Thank you."

"That's the first genuine smile I've seen on your face in a long time. It must be because you're glad to be alive instead of wandering around lost in a snowstorm. I don't care how big you are. You come in when the weather gets nasty."

"Yes, Mother dear."

Her ears perked up. This sounded like old Wallace. "Did something happen?"

"Yes. Kitty wrote me a letter saying she's forgiven me and still wants to be my friend. And she's publishing the book."

Bertha raised her hands to the heavens. "Thank you, God! You see! I told you she still loved us. Do you feel better now?"

"I feel free."

⟡

Christmas morning arrived. There was still snow on the ground thanks to the storm. Wallace had cut down a balsam fir two days before and a mob of grandchildren had come over to help them decorate it that evening.

The crowd wasn't descending until mid-afternoon, to give everyone a chance to be in their own houses opening gifts under their trees. It also gave the women a chance to get their cooking done.

Mother and son slept in, then sat in the kitchen eating their breakfast of French toast, maple syrup, and bacon. They decided to use two of Kitty's teacups and saucers for their morning tea. They held them up in a toast.

"Merry Christmas, Mom."

"Merry Christmas, Wallace. And a very happy Christmas to Kitty!"

"Hear, hear."

They sipped from the teacups.

Wallace nodded. "Tea tastes ten times better in this cup."

"And the teacup handle is extremely comfortable. That matters, you know. Sometimes they're too skinny or an awkward shape. This is very pleasing," Bertha decided.

"Kitty would be in hysterics if she heard us," Wallace said, laughing.

"Now that she and I are pen pals, I'll have to write and tell her about this five-star rating."

Wallace cut into his French toast. "I suppose I can be a pen pal too."

Bertha put down her cup. "Be careful with that. I know she's your friend, but she's a married friend. If that husband of hers sees too many letters from you, he might give her a hard time, and you don't want that."

"No, you're right. Maybe I can sneak in an occasional letter with yours, so he doesn't know I've written to her."

"Once in a while, I suppose. I don't want to feel like I'm being underhanded. We'll find our own rhythm about this. We may not hear from her for quite a while. We keep thinking she's only across the road. But she does have her own life to lead."

Wallace got up from the table and grabbed another slice of French toast out of the frying pan. "We'll hear from her very shortly."

Bertha looked up from giving the dogs a piece of bacon. "What do you mean?"

"Kitty send another parcel. It came on Friday, but I hid it because she wrote on the outside, *Do not open until Christmas Day!*

"Oh, what fun! I hate to think what this postage costs."

"She doesn't seem to mind."

The phone rang. "Want to bet it's Ethel, asking me what time you're picking them up?"

"What time do you want them over?"

"It's Christmas. We'll give them lunch too."

She went into the dining room and picked up the phone, "Hel—"

"Bertha! That you?!"

"Yes, dear. Merry Christmas."

"Merry Christmas to you too! What time is Wallace picking us up?"

"He'll come and get you at noon. In four hours. You can have lunch with us."

"Oh! Splendid! Four hours, you say? Can't come soon enough."

"We'll have a great day."

At twelve sharp, Wallace was at Ethel and Winnie's door. When he knocked and walked in, the two women were sitting at the kitchen table with their coats and boots on. He hated to think how long they'd been there.

There was a very small tree sitting in the middle of the table with painted Christmas decorations hanging from ribbons.

"Merry Christmas, ladies!"

They both greeted him happily.

Blackie the cat ran in and rubbed herself all over his legs. "Merry Christmas, Blackie." He reached down to give his ears a scratch.

The sisters looked at each other.

"Can you believe that, Winnie? That cat almost tears the face off me when I feed her, and this one walks in and he's melted butter."

"I've always believed in miracles," Winnie chuckled. "Do you like our tree, Wallace? I know it's only eighteen inches high, but I think Ethel did a really good job. She found it and sawed it down."

"It's very pretty. How did you manage it?"

"I was determined we were going to have something," Ethel said, "so I went over to the edge of the woods and Winnie hobbled to the door to keep an eye out for bears and I took the old hacksaw and it was done in no time. Without me breaking my hip, I might add."

"Great job. We'd better go, Mom has lunch ready. Tomato soup, cheese, and she made those crackers you like, Ethel. Winnie, I'll carry you. Don't forget your walking stick. How's your ankle, anyway?"

She told him about it as he ferried her outside. Ethel closed the door behind them and scurried into the front seat of the truck from Wallace's side, so Winnie would be close to the door.

The four neighbours had a very jolly time around Kitty's full tea set. Winnie was quite smitten with every piece.

"These colours are incredible together. The cobalt blue, rust red, and amber of the berries on the lime green vine are offset by the crisp white interior, as well as the tiny black-and-white-checkered pattern around the edge."

"Golly," Bertha said. "They're even more beautiful now."

They exchanged small gifts. They had for years. The sisters gave Bertha two sets of pot holders, which she desperately needed, and Wallace received new socks, also desperately needed. In return, they acquired a large dark fruitcake, which they both loved and would keep them going for weeks. Wallace hoped the dried fruit and nuts would fatten them up.

Soon enough, the family arrived in increments, and with each addition there was much merriment, hugs, kisses, greetings, and eggnog poured. Winnie found her way out to the sun porch and played Christmas carols on the old untuned piano as they got dinner ready. She was much more comfortable out of the way. Ethel stuck to Bertha like glue, unfortunately, which was a bit trying, since Bertha was the general in charge of this major operation. When her girls wrangled over where to put all the casserole dishes and platters of turkey, she held up her hands.

"Ladies: my kitchen, my rules. And not another word."

The children were fed first at a card table and a piece of plywood placed on two sawhorses in the sunroom. With a tablecloth on it, it looked quite respectable. They loved being together, out of the way of the boring adult table and their parents' meddling eyes.

The only way they could get everyone a plate of food without the dining room table collapsing under the weight of casserole dishes was to put them out on the kitchen counters and on the kitchen table and have everyone go around and help themselves before heading back into the dining room. Bertha had the good sense to seat Winnie and Ethel first and give them each a plate, so they wouldn't hold up the line. They'd learned the hard way one year when Ethel couldn't decide what she wanted to eat and held everyone up for what seemed like eternity.

They sat down at five not-so-sharp and didn't get back up until six thirty, when the kids whined about wanting their stockings from Nanna and Walrus. But first they had to gather on the stairs, oldest to youngest, for the annual picture. Trying to figure out how old everyone was when half of them were missing was a trial. Wallace finally whistled to shut everyone up.

"Can we please put this mob of desperadoes in a bunch? Who cares how old they are? We still have gifts to unwrap, and Santa is making a not-so-surprise visit. I for one would like to be tucked up in bed before midnight."

Eventually, they got through it all and only had one mishap, when Argus knocked an entire plate of gingerbread men onto the floor and gobbled up most of them before Wallace grabbed him. Ruth was annoyed. "I made those!"

That's when Wallace came out with the parcel.

"We received this a couple of days ago from our friend Kitty. I have no idea what's in it."

What was in it were many children's books for the kids, including *The Night Before Christmas*, *Anne of Green Gables*, *Stuart Little*, *Little Women*, *Charlotte's Web*, *Robinson Crusoe*, *Goodnight Moon*, and *A Child's Garden of Verses*. With a note: *Merry Christmas, little ones! These are books to keep at Nanna's house. I will add to the collection every year. I miss you. Love Kitty xo*

There was a gift for Benji, who happened to be there just by luck. His mother held him in her lap while Georgie and Elizabeth opened it. It was a blue snowsuit. From Eaton's. *Merry Christmas, Benji! I miss you. Love Kitty xo*

Wallace passed a gift to his mother.

"Oh, she did not! I already have the tea set. Foolish girl." But she was smiling as she said it. Turned out it was a recipe book on Quebec cuisine. *Merry Christmas, Bertha! For your cookbook collection. I miss you. Love Kitty xo*

Next up was a gift for Ethel.

"For me?!" Ethel went pink with pleasure. "How kind! She remembered me."

"I don't think she'll ever forget you, Ethel," Wallace said.

She took her time opening it. "Oh! This is also from Eaton's. I've never had anything from Eaton's before." She took the lid off the box and unfolded the tissue paper. She held up a lilac cashmere sweater with flower buttons. "Oh my. Oh my! It's so soft."

"Try it on!" Bertha said. "Here, I'll help."

She had to because Ethel's hands shook. She tried it on, and it was obvious she was delighted. "It's the perfect weight. Not heavy at all."

The women agreed it was a lovely colour for her. Any colour would be perfect because she never wore any, but this definitely made her skin rosier.

Merry Christmas, Ethel! Thank you for your friendship. I miss you. Love Kitty xo

Wallace took out one more gift. "This is for Winnie."

Winnie looked surprised and pleased. "She never met me. This is awfully kind." She opened the gift and gasped. A box filled with squirrel-hair-and-bristle paintbrushes. "Oh look. Here's a large round, a flat tip, and a rigger. Gosh, and a filbert and a fan brush too. This is overwhelming!"

She read the note.

Merry Christmas, Winnie! Any friend of Wallace's is a friend of mine. Love Kitty xo

He reached in and took out one more gift. "Oh. This is for me. I'll open it later."

Those with younger children took them home, after Bertha divided up everyone's share of turkey to take with them. The rest stayed behind and helped with the clearing up and the dishes. Wallace took the very tired Macdonald sisters home, both of them declaring it was the best day they'd had in a very long time.

It was close to midnight when Wallace said goodnight to his weary mother and closed his bedroom door. He sat on the bed and opened his gift. It was a book. *The Second Sex* by Simone de Beauvoir.

Merry Christmas Wallace!

In my search for a book to send you, I remembered buying this when it first came out only a few years ago. I'm sure you've never read the philosophical point of view of a woman in all the tomes you've studied so far. It's enlightening.

I miss you. Love Kitty. xo

Chapter Eighteen

Kitty was determined to get into the Christmas spirit. To send the Baileys gifts in a big parcel gave her such pleasure. She'd never had anyone to send a parcel to before. All her grandparents had died before she was born. Her mother was an only child, and her dad's younger brother, Ben, was killed at the age of twenty-one during the First World War.

Kurt was almost impossible to pin down. His schedule was relentless, so she resorted to waking early. As he was always in a hurry, she had to stand in the steam of the bathroom while he showered.

"I thought I'd make Christmas dinner this year. What do you think?" She raised her voice to be heard over the fan.

"You mean have dinner here?"

"Yes. It might be a nice change."

"You know Mom. She hates change. You can ask her. I don't care one way or the other."

"Why can't you tell her that we'd like Christmas dinner at our own house this year? We're allowed to change things up. We're not kids."

He shut off the water, shoved the shower curtain aside, and wiped his face and hair on a towel before he wrapped it around his waist and stepped out. "Kitty, just handle it, will you? I don't have time to argue with my mother right now. I'll be lucky if I get Christmas day off at this point."

"But you'll stick up for me?"

He hugged her with his wet torso and kissed her forehead. "Yes.

I'm a changed man, remember?" He held her a little tighter. "Say, I might have five minutes if you're interested..."

"Five minutes doesn't do it for me."

He rolled his eyes and released her. "I thought we had to work at this marriage thing. Don't say I'm not trying."

Since she was up anyway, she made him a plate of scrambled eggs and toast, then threw on some clothes to take Pip for her morning walk. The two of them were at the door ready to leave when someone knocked on it.

"Who can that be? It's kind of early, isn't it?" Kurt opened the door.

Dimitri was standing there with her plate. "Good morning."

"Do I know you?"

Kitty brushed by Kurt and reached out to take it. "Oh, thank you, Dimitri."

"I know it's early, but I was on my way out and I thought I'd drop it off. They were delicious, by the way. I really enjoyed them. Thank you again."

"I'm glad."

Dimitri saw Kurt's confused face. "Your wife kindly made me cookies. You're a lucky man. Good day."

"Bye." Kitty shut the door, so Pip wouldn't follow him. Her tail was wagging.

Kurt gave her an incredulous look. "You bake cookies for complete strangers in our building but not me?"

She put the plate on the console. "Don't be a big baby. Dimitri helped me in with my luggage when you drove your co-star home because that was more important. I thought I'd thank him. If you'd helped me, I might have done the same for you." She finished her remarks with a flick on his nose.

"Well, you certainly have a type."

"Huh?"

"You seem to love big, brawny guys."

Kitty put her hand on her waist. "Care to explain yourself?"

"That fella looks like a Greek Wallace."

Kitty willed her face not to react. "And you, sir, are full of shit."

Kurt grinned. "Very true." He glanced at his watch. "Yikes, gotta run. I won't be home until late." He gave her a quick peck and fled out the door.

Kitty closed it and leaned against the wood. She thought she'd gotten away with it, but somehow, he knew that she and Wallace were attracted to each other. It was only natural that he would, since it was his field of specialty. Right now, she could use a big dose of Wallace. His calm energy and steadfast reliability were like ports in a storm. She was adrift without them. The only way to handle it if Kurt brought it up again was to feign ignorance. Act disdainful. That's what he did.

After their walk, Kitty tried to get ahold of her dad to ask him about Christmas dinner, but he wasn't available. She needed to know if she should go grocery shopping. She had never cooked a turkey before, but mashed potatoes and carrots were simple enough, as were gravy and stuffing. No Brussels sprouts because she didn't like them, and her dad preferred canned cranberry sauce. Maybe she'd bake an apple pie. That was his favourite. Her excitement grew at the thought of it, and then she remembered she had to ask permission.

There was no way she was going over there. Kitty called her on the phone.

"Hello?"

"Martha, it's Kate."

"Kate who?"

"It's Kitty."

"Why didn't you say that, then?"

"Sorry."

"As you know, your father works during the day."

"I called to talk to you."

She immediately sounded suspicious. "Why?"

"I'd like to cook Christmas dinner this year and have it in our apartment. It will be a nice change. I'll do all the cooking."

"No."

"No?"

"I've already bought the turkey and the fixings, not to mention the plum pudding. There's no point. And Kurt loves my cooking. He waits all year for it. So does your father."

Kitty knew that was a lie but was too discouraged to continue. "Fine."

"Is that all?"

"Goodbye, Martha."

Martha hung up on her.

Pip always knew when she was down. She jumped up and licked Kitty's face to try and cheer her up. "Oh, yes. Thank you for the kisses. I love you too." Kitty put her head back and groaned. "So much for not taking her bullshit anymore. It's like she knows exactly how to drain me. How did I put up with this for so long? What am I saying? I'm still putting up with it. I need so much help. Therapy. That's what I need, Pippy."

The phone rang and for a minute she thought it might be her dad calling back. But she wouldn't mention her idea to him. His Christmases were always hard enough. He didn't need to be embroiled in a battle between the two women in his life. She'd bake an apple pie for him and bring it over anyway. Stuff Martha's plum pudding.

The phone was still ringing. "Hello?"

"I almost hung up," Gaynor said. "It seems I'm always trying to get a hold of you."

"Nice to hear from you. You can't possibly be working on the story now? It's almost Christmas."

"No, plenty of time for that. Well, not really. Mel is determined we get this done sooner rather than later, just to warn you."

"That's fine. I need a distraction. I'm twiddling my thumbs. Kurt works every hour God sends, and so does my dad."

"I'm calling to invite you to a wine and cheese at our house tonight. I decided at the very last minute to have the gang from the office in. My dear Simon called me Ebenezer Scrooge the other day, so I've taken the hint and will be the perfect hostess for three hours. After which I will be back to bah-humbugging ad nauseum."

"That sounds wonderful. Kurt won't be able to make it."

"Hate to say it, but that's fine. It was you I wanted, not English Canada's heartthrob."

"Can't wait. What time?"

Kitty was at Gaynor's door at seven sharp. A red-brick duplex in Outremont only a short taxi ride away. This was an evening for wine. She told Pip not to wait up.

Under her coat she wore an emerald green polyester cocktail dress with a high neckline, Peter Pan collar, and belt with a full skirt. She only had two dresses, and this one was the most comfortable.

Simon answered the door. "Kitty! So good to see you, my dear." He kissed her cheek.

"Hi, Simon. Thank you for inviting me." She slipped her coat off and handed it to him.

"My, don't you look ravishing!"

"You always were an old flirt."

"No. I mean it. I've never seen you look so well."

"I've put on some weight."

He leaned over. "Don't tell Gaynor that. It will only depress her."

She greeted Jersey May, who sauntered down the hall wearing a big red bow. "Merry Christmas, you beautiful girl."

They walked into the living room, where there was already a crowd of people. The Christmas tree was spindly but thick with silver icicles on every other branch and red glass ornaments. A draped garland and candles decorated the fireplace mantel, and bookshelves lined the walls, this being the home of an English professor and a book editor. Kitty couldn't look away from the dancing fire and was immediately homesick for South Head. This space was cozy in another way, with large stuffed sofas and chairs, and artwork featuring English landscapes with horses and hounds. It could be a gentlemen's club, considering the glittering crystal on the mirrored bar that held an amazing assortment of wine. The coffee table was filled with a variety of crackers, sliced baguettes, wooden trays of cheese, and an assortment of nuts, olives, and small bunches of red and green grapes.

Gaynor spied her from across the room. "Kitty!" She came over and gave her a peck. "Why did I invite you? You make the rest of us old broads look decrepit." She turned around and raised her voice. "Everyone, the amazing C. J. Faulkner is here!"

The room of Empire & Bloom employees cheered, which made Kitty's cheeks grow warm. It was a nice moment. Mel Bloom hurried over with a glass of red wine and a glass of white. "For you, my dear. Which would you like?"

"Both."

He laughed and handed them to her, and then he bussed her as well. She put the red wine on an end table and took a big gulp of the white. "Oh, I needed this."

Mel puffed on his cigar while Simon passed her a cigarette and lit it for her. She inhaled and blew the smoke in the air. "I needed this, too."

"Before I let you talk to anyone else, I have to tell you something." Mel took the cigar out of his mouth. "To say I'm impressed with your new novel is a complete understatement. It's astonishingly good, Kitty. We obviously know what a great writer you are, but considering your difficulties this past fall, I wasn't prepared for what you delivered. Something completely new and fresh. Writing with a comic bent is truly your strength. I'm surprised you never did it before."

"I've never felt I could. The ink that spills onto the page has to be deep in your bones first, and if you don't have access to that sentiment, it will never show up."

Mel glanced at Simon. "Beauty *and* brains."

Gaynor snorted. "It's a good thing you don't write for a living, with chestnuts like that coming out of your mouth."

Mel ignored her. "Can I say that I've never seen you looking so well, Kitty. That Cape Breton adventure obviously agreed with you."

She smiled and nodded. "I'm incredibly grateful to the three of you for making it happen. Thank you from the bottom of my heart. It's changed my life already, and I know it will continue to. The lessons I learned there, the people I met..." Kitty had to stop. Now was not the time to wallow. She raised her glass. "Here's to Myrtle Lovett!"

"To Myrtle Lovett!" The three of them laughed.

Kitty had the best time. Of course, having more than a bottle of wine herself helped with that. She kicked off her shoes, which reminded her of the W. I., and she tipsily tried to tell her dance partner about the blindfolded ladies and their pile of shoes, and he had no idea what she was talking about, which made it even funnier.

It seemed as if she danced all night. This was supposed to be a wine and cheese and quickly turned into a free-for-all. Never trust book people. They love to drink and look for stories. Even in her inebriated state, she knew most of the men in the room were looking at her. She'd never had that happen before. Perhaps because she'd never danced and had a good time at a party. Kurt was always with her, and she knew better than to take the attention away from him.

She fell into the sofa beside Gaynor, whose cigarette was mostly ash. "I am one pathetic human being."

Gaynor raised her chin to look at her. "No. Right now you're two pathetic human beings. And you keep moving. Stop it."

"I need to stick up for myself. I need to like me."

Gaynor punched her shoulder. "Atta girl. You've always been Little Red Hiding Hood."

"Little Red Hiding Hood! I love it. That'll be my next story. Hiding Hood goes to Martha's house and says 'My, what big teeth you have!' And Martha says, 'The better to eat you and my Christmas dinner with.'"

"What the hell are you talking about?"

"I don't have a clue. Gaynor?"

"Yes, C. J.? Catriona? Kitty? Kit? How many names have you got?"

"Do I deserve to be happy?"

Gaynor stopped swaying and looked her dead in the eyes. "Yes. And don't you fucking forget it."

At the stroke of midnight, Gaynor stood up. "Jesus. I'm Cinderella. The hostess has turned into a bitch. Everyone get the hell out. I'm tired. Except you, Dolores. You have to promise to come and live with me. I don't care if you do have a husband and three kids."

Simon bundled Kitty into her coat and Mel and his wife took her in their taxi. Mel held her arm as he walked her into the building.

"Thanks, Mel," she giggled. "You're such a gentleman."

"Knock it off. I'm protecting my investment. Merry Christmas!"

"Merry Christmas."

She danced into the elevator, danced on the elevator, and danced out of the elevator again and continued to groove down the hallway singing "Rocking Around the Christmas Tree."

There was only a bit of trouble putting the key in the lock. "Pippy! Mommy's home. Do you need to pee?" Pip wiggled around her.

"I took her out."

Kitty nearly jumped out of her skin. "God!"

Kurt was sitting on the chesterfield with a drink in his hand. "What time do you call this?"

She looked at her watch. "I'm not sure. I can't see. Why don't you tell me?"

"Where were you? I called your father and now he's all upset."

She dropped her coat and sobered up instantly. "Great. Why did you do that?"

"Because I didn't know where the hell you were."

"You said you wouldn't be home so I went to a party. I have to call him."

"It's after midnight."

"Do you think he's sleeping?" She went to the phone and her dad picked up immediately. "Kitty?"

"I'm home. Sorry Kurt jumped the gun. I didn't leave a note because he said he'd be late and I assumed I'd be back in time. Gaynor had a wine and cheese at her house and it ran a little long. Mel escorted me home."

"Thanks, I got worried. You never go out."

"That might change. I'll come and pick you up Christmas morning."

"Righto. Goodnight, dear."

"Night."

Kurt took the last mouthful of his drink. "Looks like you had a good time."

"I did, thank you. Why are you home so early?' She flopped into one of the armchairs, or at least tried to, but it was too stiff to be comfortable. Naturally, Pip joined her.

"I came home to be with you. Stupidly, I thought you'd be here."

"I'm always here. The invitation was from my publishing company. I do work for a living, remember."

"We've been invited to a New Year's Eve party in Westmount. The executive producer's place. Janette says the house is quite something. Will you be able to make that, or will you be busy gallivanting?"

She was tired and sparring with him was a buzzkill. "Sounds fun."

"Are you going to wear that?" He pointed his cigarette at her.

Kitty glanced down at her dress. "What's wrong with this? Everyone said I looked great."

"You always look great, but that's buttoned up to your neck. You could be a fancy librarian. Please wear something off the shoulder, or at least tighter. Pip is all but lost in the folds of your shirt."

She laughed because it was true. "I'm going to bed."

Kurt extinguished his cigarette, stood up, and reached over to take her hand and pull her off the chair. He threw his arm over her shoulder and escorted her to the bedroom. "Great minds think alike, Mrs. Wagner."

"Just do it and get it over with."

Oops. Did she say that out loud?

-⊛⊛-

Her head hurt. But it was worth it.

She rolled over and Kurt was gone. It was 6:00 A.M. on Christmas Eve. Who knew when he'd show up? Pip did her dance on the bed. "Okay. Give me a second."

It was cold and still outside, too early for a lot of traffic. The quiet street reminded her of home. Of her little house, which wasn't her house at all. She wondered what kind of morning it was there. Could imagine the crackling of the fire as she brewed her tea, and Wallace's horses in the hoarfrost-covered field, their breath visible in the cold air.

A taxi driver slammed on his brakes and laid on the horn. Kitty jumped back onto the sidewalk, her heart pounding. She hadn't seen him. She had to stop daydreaming. That reminded her of Bertha. What was she doing this morning? She could almost smell the banana-walnut loaf.

When Kitty got back to the apartment, she knew something was off. It took a minute, and then she realized it wasn't decorated for Christmas like Gaynor's home. They had a small artificial tree in a closet somewhere and one box of decorations and that was it. As pathetic as that was, at least they'd put it up in Christmases past. She was supposed to make an effort, so once she fed Pip and had a bowl of cereal, Kitty rooted around and assembled the dreary little tree in the corner of the living room. She put a Nat King Cole Christmas album on to get her in the mood and hung the ornaments up. It took all of three minutes.

"Well, that was fun. Now what?"

She wrapped her few gifts, then spent the afternoon making two apple pies. The first one ended up in the garbage chute. She'd forgotten how fussy pastry could be. The second actually looked like a pie. The rest of the day was spent alone in her study, trying to figure out how she could use almost being run over by a taxi in her next Kate Higgins novel. Because there would be a next one. She liked Kate and enjoyed seeing the ridiculous in situations, instead of hard reality. If you can't have fun in real life, create it on the page.

Kitty took Pip for two more walks, just to enjoy the Christmas lights. It was bitterly cold, which made looking into other people's lit-up windows heartwarming. She imagined big families gathered there. What must that be like? The Baileys would be having a jolly old time. How she wished she was there. Her whole life she'd pushed Christmas away as a trial to be endured. Would that make her mother happy? She was doing her mother a terrible disservice by using the occasion of her death to keep joy at bay. Kitty didn't want to be sad anymore when she thought of her mom and baby brother.

That was a Christmas gift she could and would give herself.

Chapter Nineteen

Christmas morning Kitty turned over, half expecting Kurt to be missing, but he was on his side facing away from her, still sleeping. She hadn't heard him come in.

By the time he did wake up, she had walked Pip, taken her shower, dressed, and had a stack of pancakes made. She entered the bedroom with a cup of hot coffee. "Merry Christmas."

"What time is it?"

"It's nine. I'm leaving soon to pick up Dad." She put the coffee on the side table.

"Thank you. Merry Christmas." He held his face up and she kissed him.

"I have pancakes. Do you want them in bed?"

"Sure."

She put everything on a tray and they ate together on top of the messed-up sheets. "I put the tree up yesterday. I almost forgot. What does that say about us?"

He had a mouthful, so he took a big gulp of coffee to wash it down. "Are you serious? Christmas has always been miserable in this family. What are you doing after breakfast?"

"Going to the cemetery."

"I rest my case. Can we open our gifts now?"

"You're worse than a little kid. Okay."

He seemed really pleased with the new suitcase. She tried to be enthusiastic with the pink silk negligee. Pippy was very happy with her new chew toy and dog treats. Then he went back to bed with Pip and Kitty went to get her father.

Mount Royal Cemetery was quite a landmark in the city, a garden of a hundred and sixty-five acres. Its huge stone gate with the turrets had always reminded Kitty of a castle. It was a quiet oasis of hills and woodlands with large trees and meandering pathways, more like a terraced park. In a way it felt like home, too. It was the only place her entire family was together.

Kitty enjoyed this time with her father. At least they were alone. They walked along arm in arm at a leisurely pace, since there was no wind to make the frigid air unpleasant. Clouds were gathering, so perhaps there would be snow later, but for now there was enough on the ground to make it look like winter. It was at least a thirty-minute walk to their gravesite. They always parked the car at the entrance. Her dad carried a bag containing a winter arrangement, a wreath with holly berries, pine cones, evergreen, and silver bells with a red velvet bow.

They never said much as they made this pilgrimage. It was enough to be together.

They approached the grave. It was tucked away in a bit of a corner by a large pine tree. The granite headstone was grey and upright, almost delicate in comparison to some of the others nearby. They had planted a rose bush in behind it, which was always glorious in the summer but looked sparse and bare in winter, which is why they liked to put the wreath at the foot of it.

Mary Jane Faulkner
July 17, 1900–December 25, 1929
Benjamin Leonard Faulkner
Infant son, December 25, 1929
Sleep in Heavenly Peace

Her father took the wreath and placed it against the stone. "Hi, sweetheart. Hi, Ben. I love you." He never said any more. That covered it. He'd always had a hard time expressing himself, so Kitty did it for him.

"Hi, Mama. Merry Christmas. We miss you and Ben very much. Another year has gone by, but our memories never fade. I still love looking at pictures of us. The one Dad took of you and me on the merry-go-round and the one where Dad held me on a pony and I had a cowboy hat on. This year I met a baby named Ben and I had a lovely time holding him and thought of you, little brother. I feel you both with me and I want you to keep watching over us." She kissed her glove and placed her hand on top of the granite. She turned to her father. "Let's go sit."

They walked a few steps away and perched on the ornate cast iron bench under the pine tree. How many hours had they spent here over the years?

"Dad, I think you and I should make a pact."

He stared straight ahead. "All right. What am I getting myself into?"

"We can't let anything separate us again. You and I are a family. Mom is with Ben and you're with me. And I'm thankful for that. I blamed you for a long time. You didn't help me after Mom died, but now I'm aware that you couldn't come to your own rescue, let alone mine. I shouldn't hold that against you."

"Yes, you should. I was your parent and I abdicated that responsibility, lost in my own grief. That was no excuse."

"We've been operating in suspended animation for a very long time. We have to help each other. I think Mom would like that."

Her father turned his head and smiled at her. He put his arm around her shoulders and gave her a squeeze. "Your mother would be so proud of you. As am I. I don't say it enough. I realized that when you left the city. This place seemed incredibly empty without you. With you writing in your study for the last ten years, I always knew where you were. It was a lazy way out for me. You've never given me any trouble, except when you got married."

Kitty laughed. "You always did think I was too young. And then I find out you married Mom when she was a year younger, so that argument was blown out of the water."

"You're right, Kitty. I promise to never forsake you again."

"Nor I, you."

They shook on it.

※

The Wagners arrived for Christmas dinner in the late afternoon. There was never any point in going earlier, since it was hard enough to keep the conversation going after the first twenty minutes. Kitty made sure Pip's paws were wiped before she let her loose, then asked Martha if she needed help in the kitchen, which Martha never did. Dad and Kurt sat down on opposite sides of the room and drank a beer together. It was always a safe bet to talk about the Montreal Canadiens. And then her father would ask Kurt about his latest movie project and that would keep Kurt talking for the next half an hour. Martha would join them before dinner with a glass of sherry. That's when they opened the few gifts under the tree.

Kitty opened her present from Kurt's mother. It was a polyester blouse in Martha's favourite colour and size.

"Thank you. It's very pretty."

Kitty would leave it behind as she did every year, so Martha could put it in her closet. The men never noticed this game.

Her dad usually gave her a book or a journal or leather gloves and a scarf, but this year he passed her a small gift. A jewellery-sized box.

"Dad? This is a surprise."

He leaned forward in his chair and put his elbows on his knees, excited, it seemed. "Open it."

She didn't want to, wishing instead to linger over this moment, but he was eager so she unwrapped the paper and opened the velvet box. A pair of pearl earrings.

"To go with your mother's necklace."

Kitty held her hand to her cheek. "Oh, Dad. Thank you." She got up and hugged him and he gave her a big squeeze back. It was the first time she'd felt genuinely happy on Christmas day since she was a child, and from the shy smile on her father's face, she was sure he felt the same way.

She gave her father a new leather wallet, because when he'd paid for lunch, she'd seen that his was almost worn out. Kurt made sure Leo knew the money in it was from him. It was always a nightmare to figure out what to get Martha, so Kitty usually went with something for the kitchen. This year it was a new pressure cooker. Kurt gave his mother a watch, and she pointed out the small diamonds in the setting, making sure Kitty had a good look at it. Martha never asked to see the earrings. Dad gave Kurt tickets to the latest musical at Theatre St. Denis. Kurt received ten gifts from his mom, all very nice clothes from the best stores. She did have good taste in menswear.

While there seemed to be a change in her father's demeanour when they opened gifts, his old behaviour returned as they sat through dinner. Kitty knew he was remembering a time when her mother presided over this table, but what she had never noticed before was that Martha kept plying him with Scotch throughout the dreary, tasteless meal.

When her father got up at one point and left briefly, Kitty leaned forward and spoke to Martha in a lowered voice. "I think Dad's had enough to drink."

"Your father is a grown man who can do as he pleases. This is a difficult day for him. Stop interfering."

Kitty looked at Kurt. "Don't you think he's had enough?"

"Relax. Give the poor guy a break. He's easier to deal with when he's drinking."

"Thanks for the support," Kitty said, frowning.

"You are not always right," Martha pointed at her. "You have a bad habit of thinking you know everything, especially when it comes to your father. You don't own him."

"I'm his daughter. I'm allowed to worry."

He came back in the room and the matter was dropped. Kitty had to go out to the kitchen to bring in the pie, since Martha didn't offer it to anyone. It was obvious that Dad enjoyed it, and that's all that mattered. Kurt didn't make any comment and his mother said it was dry.

It wasn't long till they said goodnight. Her dad looked weary. When Kitty hugged him, she said, "Are you all right?"

He looked at her sadly. "I tried to be better today, but it's still hard. Maybe next year."

"You did really well. Thank you for my earrings. It was so thoughtful."

He swayed a little and gave her a silly grin. "I love you, Catriona."

She couldn't remember the last time he'd said that.

The next day was always such a relief. Christmas, with its loaded memories and unhappy rituals, was over for another year. She and her father had made real progress, but Kitty knew the holiday would never have the happy connotations it did for other families. That was just a fact, and instead of wishing it was different, she would hang on to the small moments, like their pact at the cemetery and her father's lovely gift. Her time away had seemed to affect him greatly, and that was something to hold on to.

Kurt warned her that he would be extremely busy for the next few weeks, so not to count on him for anything. She bit her tongue.

"Don't forget, we have that New Year's Eve party we have to go to. It's a big deal, so make sure you get dolled up."

All that week Kitty sat at her desk with Kate Higgins, willing her to say or do something funny, but there was nothing there. Not a single idea she tried worked. Sometimes writing was groping her way through a maze. One scene might be promising, but if it didn't flow into the next, the story came to a shuddering halt. Nothing but dead ends. And when that happened, the wisp of imagination was extinguished before it caught fire. Do it often enough and a blank page became a glaringly obvious sign that she was a fraud. She couldn't be a writer if she wasn't writing, and if she wasn't writing, what was she? Who was she?

Her heart began to thump in her chest as she tried not to panic. Her old friend was wrapping itself around her again. Melancholy. She loved the sound of the word, but hated its presence.

When the phone rang it was a welcome distraction. "Hello?"

"This is your miserable editor calling. I tried to leave you alone for a few days, but Mel is already bugging me about the script. Are you ready to do a few edits? I've been at this all week and still find it fabulous."

"That's nice. I need something to distract me from thinking I'm a hack."

"I'll pretend you didn't say that. Do you mind if I come over there? I've become soft in the head and gave Dolores a few days off to enjoy her family over the holidays. Strangely, people don't like to hear from me at this time of year, so I can afford to be generous."

"I'd love that. I'll make us a nice pot of tea."

"You really are Agatha Christie. Splash some vodka in it. I'll be there in a flash."

Something to keep the loneliness at bay. She quickly made a batch of tea biscuits, her version anyway, and had them in the oven when Gaynor arrived with her pricey purse, a large portfolio containing two copies of the manuscript, and a stack of sharpened pencils.

"Helloooo! I had to sweep off the car. It's snowing more than I thought. Hi, Pippy! Are you being a lovely girl?" She reached down to give Pip a pat and then straightened up and leaned over to give Kitty a quick half hug. The woman was not one for displays of affection. Kitty took her coat and put it in the hall closet. Gaynor walked into the living room.

"This place always reminds me of a hotel lobby, only there's not even a magazine to capture your interest."

"Thank you for saying that. My feelings exactly. Let's set up at the dining room table, so we can spread out."

When Kitty reappeared carrying a tray, Gaynor had everything ready. "What on earth is all this? High tea?"

"Ever since South Head, I feel the need to feed people when they show up in my space. These biscuits and jam are nothing like Bertha's, but we can pretend. You can also pretend there's vodka in this tea."

They got straight to it. Most of the editing was ordinary stuff, the usual. Too many filler words: *just*, *so*, *many*, *more*, *best*, etc. Kitty always had a hard time with tense; she tended to write too fast to check. Starting sentences with *I* or *she*, or *he*. Flip the sentence around. Don't use too many adjectives or adverbs. The show-don't-tell dilemma, which always irked her, because that wasn't an easy fix and sometimes not necessary in her mind, but it seemed to be a rule with editors.

Then the picky stuff. "The middle is a bit draggy. The timing is off. There are a few scenes where I know you're trying too hard, but it's not necessary. The reactions of the others will provide the clues of Kate's emotional state. And there are a few times when Myrtle's comebacks are a bit too slick. She's not sophisticated by a long shot, so would she use words like *preposterous* or *skyrocketing*?"

"You're right. I'll go over her dialogue and watch for that."

Gaynor turned to a page near the end. "This resolution comes too quickly and is much too neat for my liking. I know that loose ends are a bugaboo with murder mysteries, but this isn't about a real murder, so everything doesn't have to wrap up nicely."

"True."

"Especially if Kate Higgins is going to be a continuing character for subsequent novels. She needs to be complex and still hate aspects of her job, because you can't have a 'non-murder' in every book from now on. Yes, she was lost and now she's found a path, but it's still foggy out there and I want her to disappear from time to time, like the rest of us mere mortals."

Kitty sat back in her chair. "I'm not sure if there will be any more Kate Higgins novels. I'm spinning my wheels again. The light laughter that came so easily with this story has disappeared again. And my aversion to dealing with murders hasn't abated yet."

"What am I saying? You can have a non-murder in every book. Kate is a detective, but she doesn't have to be with homicide. She could decide to be a private detective, with missing persons cases, fraud, lost and stolen property, insurance claims. You name it. If you're sick of killing people, no problem. I'd much rather see Kate investigate the absurdity of human nature with that wit of hers than deal with gory crime scenes. That can be your focus. Ordinary people and their behaviour are a damn sight more intriguing than your average homicidal manic."

"You might be right."

"I'm always right. Any more of these tea biscuits? The diet starts January first."

Four hours later they decided they'd done enough for the day, and after polishing off the rest of the baking, they convened in the living room for more tea and cigarettes.

"I had so much fun at your wine and cheese. It was the highlight of my Christmas."

"You were on fire! It was lovely to witness."

"We're going to a New Year's Eve party in Westmount with the movie people. Kurt wants me to get dolled up, as he put it."

"Just walk in the room and that's all the dolling up you need. I wish you could see that."

"You're good for the ego, Gaynor."

"I never lie. Unless it proves necessary, which is almost always."

Kitty felt much better about everything by the time Gaynor said goodbye. She and Pip walked her to her car and continued on their way. The falling snow kept everything muted. The world always seemed softer when large white flakes took their time to reach the ground. She'd always had a vision of walking away on a day like this. Just disappearing into the whiteness, never to be seen again. It's rather how she imagined her mother leaving, with Ben in her arms. They left and never turned around. But it wasn't sad, it was always going to happen. Maybe they were exactly where they were meant to be. She and her father needed to stop struggling and accept the truth. Her mother and brother were at peace. They always had been.

❦

When Kitty emerged from the bedroom in her sleeveless sheath dress, she was pleased that her mother's pearls looked so lovely against the black fabric. She put her hair up as best she could to show off her earrings.

Kurt was waiting for her in a tux. "Kitty! I told you to wear something sexy."

"I think this looks nice."

"Sure, it's nice, but again, it's up to your neck, and only old ladies wear pearls. Don't you have some costume jewellery? A big gaudy pin or something flashy?"

"The only gaudy thing I can think of is you."

He tsked and passed over her coat. "Oh, it's going to be one of those evenings. Save the feistiness for the bedroom. Don't show me up."

"Do you want me to go at all? I'm happy to stay home and ring in 1956 with Pip. These huge parties are a bore."

"I can count on one hand how many times you've been to a huge party. People are beginning to think I made you up. Now let's go."

It was exactly as she imagined it. People with so much money they continued spending it until everything looked vulgar and over-done. It was almost a talent, and she made note of the objects that stood out to make her point, like the swan ice sculpture and choco-late fountain. The mansion itself was a gorgeous old gal, but they'd dressed her up to an absurd degree. The amount of draped red velvet

261

would cover a football field, and the various patterns of chintz on the wallpaper, upholstery, and linens clashed with everything. There was only one place for her eye to rest, and that was the fireplace. She longed to go over there and sit by it, but instead she was pulled about the room and introduced to so many people she didn't remember a single name. And all of them said the same thing: "We thought Robert was joking when he said he was married. Where has he been hiding you?"

Kurt didn't have any friends, not from childhood or from drama school. Every movie set was a new group of people he would get close to for a few months or so, but then he was on to the next bunch. There were a few well-known actors who were in multiple productions and he did run into them from time to time, but none of them seemed to be at the party. The only person Kitty had met before was Janette, who came over the minute she spied them. She and Kurt kissed each other's cheeks and Janette held out her hand to Kitty. "So nice to see you again."

"Hi, Janette. You're still talking to Robert, so that's a good sign."

She put her hand on his arm. "He's an absolute doll. Everything's going very well. The director thinks we have great chemistry, isn't that right, Robbie?"

Kurt winced. "It's Robert. How many gin and tonics have you had? There are eyes everywhere in this room. Don't give them an excuse to fire you."

Janette pouted and looked at Kitty. "Is he always a grumpy bear?"

"Pretty much."

He took Janette by the arm. "Excuse me, Kitty. I need a word with my co-star. Find yourself a drink." And he hauled Janette off, obviously giving her an earful as they left. Kitty looked around. How odd. If people didn't know better, they'd assume Janette was the wife and Kitty the guest. It struck her as rather funny, so she did wander to the bar and ask for a white wine. Then she made her way to the fireplace and sat in the nearest armchair, perfectly content. The crackling brought back nice memories. When her days were simple and satisfying.

"Mind if I join you?"

A tall, handsome fellow peered down at her. He was obviously an actor; after all these years, Kitty knew the look.

"Unless you sit in my lap, I'm not sure you can."

He seemed delighted with that response as he pulled over the ottoman and settled down before offering her a cigarette, which she took. He lit it for her and held out his hand. "Miles Jarvis."

She shook it. "Kitty Wagner. Let me guess. Your real name is Millhouse Gervais and you're the lead in this movie."

"Close. Milton Goldman, and I play the detective."

"The detective the husband hires to catch my husband in the act."

"Your husband?"

"Robert Chandler."

"Oh. I didn't know Robert was married."

"You are about the fifth person who's said that to me tonight. It's not his fault. I generally refuse to come to these things."

"A wise woman. I hate this sort of party. It's a tax write-off for the producers, but I promised myself I wouldn't talk about the job. It's a bore. Tell me about yourself. What are your interests?"

"I write novels."

She loved it when people did that double-take. No one expected her to say that, and it was the one perk of the job she enjoyed—when she wasn't trying to hide it from the Ethels of the world.

"I knew you were intriguing when I first laid eyes on you. What kind of novels?"

"Murder mysteries."

"Like the Harry Gunn series?"

"Exactly."

Miles took a drink from his glass. "Now, that C. J. Faulkner is a man's man. He knows how the underbelly of society works. Everything rings true when I read them."

"Why, thank you. Except she's a woman and you're talking to her."

His face lit up and he looked around to see if anyone else had heard this miraculous news. "You're joking, right? You have to be joking! I love those novels. You're C. J. Faulkner?"

Now she took a big gulp of wine and nodded. She was enjoying this. When was the last time she'd been able to brag about anything?

Miles was clearly delighted and wanted to know how she did it, and which were her favourites. He clearly had his, and he remembered most of the plots that she'd forgotten. They were having a great conversation until Kurt hurried over and interrupted. "Oh, hi, Miles. Kitty, you okay here on your own?"

"I'm not on my own."

"There's buzz about the next project and I want to meet with the backers who happen to be here. I'll be in the library."

"Fine."

"Hey Robert, how come you never told me your gifted wife was C. J. Faulkner? Who goes around keeping that under their hat?"

"She writes books when she's bored." And he dashed off.

Miles watched him leave and then turned to her. "You're married to him. No wonder you're bored."

She shouldn't have laughed, but she did.

"Kitty, would you mind meeting a couple of my business partners? We've been on the lookout for movie projects, and I think any of your Harry Gunn novels would adapt beautifully to the screen. I'm interested in hearing what they think, and the fact that the author is right here is a coup."

"Sure. Why not?"

Miles introduced her to Claude Racine and Pierre Levesque, both of them film producers in Montreal. They were charming and absolutely thrilled to meet her. Claude was like Miles. He'd read every one of the series.

What an evening. She'd never talked so much in her life. It had never occurred to her that Detective Harry Gunn could be a movie character. They wanted to know if she'd ever done screenplays but didn't seem deterred when she said no. They still wanted her to collaborate with the entire process. But they needed to know. "Do you own your film rights?"

"Why yes, I do."

All three men gave her their business cards, and that's when Miles suggested she get a business card for herself. "It gives you a polished edge. People know you're serious about your talent when you have one to hand out. And I think you're going to need it."

After two glasses of wine, she went looking for the powder room, which wasn't an easy task. She opened a few doors before she found it. While she washed her hands, she glanced in the mirror and saw her eyes shining. All the lovely chatter about the books and the possibility of a movie or television series had given her a tremendous lift. Wait until she told Gaynor. She could hear her screaming already.

She opened the bathroom door to find a very drunk Janette crying in the arms of another woman and blocking the way. "Oh! Sorry. Are you okay, Janette?"

Janette lurched at her and the friend had no choice but to follow her into the small powder room so she wouldn't tip over. Kitty backed up when Janette poked her in the shoulder. "Why don't you let him go? He doesn't love you. He loves me."

The friend looked mortified. "I'm sorry, she's drunk and doesn't know what she's saying."

Kitty gave her a small smile. "I think she does know what she's saying. Did Robert tell you that?"

"Yes! He says you don't love him but I do. We want to be together. He's my Robbie!"

"I'm sorry, Janette. He does this a lot. You're not the first young actress to fall under his spell. Please do yourself a favour and move on."

The minute it came out of her mouth, Kitty looked at herself in the mirror. "Please do yourself a favour, Kitty, and move on."

She reached for the door. "Excuse me, please."

Once out in the hall, she spied Miles near the living room entrance. "I'm sorry, Miles. I have to go. If you happen to see Robert, would you tell him I took a taxi home?"

"Of course. Would you like me to accompany you?"

"No, thank you. I'm a grown woman." She walked over to the coat check and waited for them to find hers. Miles followed her and took the coat, holding it open for her.

"Thank you. We'll speak soon," she said.

"I look forward to it."

She turned away.

"He doesn't deserve you."

Kitty looked over her shoulder. "I know."

Chapter Twenty

The minute Kitty got home she took off her finery and jumped into old walking clothes, bundled up in her winter coat, and took Pip for a long walk. Life was very strange. She had walked into that party still confused about her future, and walked out knowing exactly what she wanted to do. Miles and Janette had given her messages she'd needed to hear. How long had poor old Gaynor been trying to get her to look at herself clearly?

She had admired Wallace for knowing exactly who he was. That power had eluded her, but no more. Not that it would be easy, but she needed to make a start. No more hesitating.

And then as she rounded the corner, she saw Kurt get out of a taxi and immediately she felt nervous. It was still only eleven o'clock. Much too early for him. He was probably furious she'd left.

"Help me stay strong, Pip."

Pip looked up and barked. Kurt turned his head as the taxi drove off. "There you are! Why the hell did you leave?"

"I didn't see you all night. You were busy and I was tired."

He approached her, and for a second she thought he was going to strangle her, but he wrapped his arms around her instead, lifted her off the ground, and spun her around. "You brilliant girl! You have to tell me everything!"

"What are you talking about?"

"Don't be coy with me. You and Miles, Claude, and Pierre! Do you know who those guys are? They own their own film company here in Montreal. Let's go in, it's freezing out here."

Once they were in the apartment, he poured himself a stiff drink. "Sit! I want to hear all about it."

Kitty continued to hang up her coat and go into the kitchen to give Pip her nightly treats.

"Forget the damn dog!"

She re-emerged, sat in the nearest chair, and crossed her legs. "What do you want to know?"

"I came out of that library with those backers, who seem to be crooks if you ask me, and heard Miles talking to Claude and Pierre about you. Something about wanting to make one of the Harry Gunn books a movie, or television series?"

"Then you know as much as I do."

"It's fucking brilliant! Why didn't I think of that before? I'm perfect for the role!"

Kitty scoffed. "Harry Gunn is in his fifties and certainly no pretty boy."

"Don't you know anything? Movies are never the book. You take the idea and jazz it up so it's more appealing to a cinematic audience. You can make that a stipulation in your contract. You want your husband as the lead! What could be more perfect as far as advertising goes? Wife writes books, husband brings them to life. We can share the same agent. It's going to be gold! They were so impressed with you. You should have been coming to these things all along. Man, oh man, this is just what I need."

He downed his drink and started to take off his tux as he went into the bedroom. Kitty stayed where she was.

"Are you coming in here? I think we should celebrate, don't you?"

"No, thanks."

He showed up with his pajama bottoms on. "What now? Jesus, can't you be happy about anything?"

"This is just an idea. There are no guarantees it's going to happen, but if it does, then of course I'm happy about it. It will breathe new life into old Harry Gunn. But you will never be Harry Gunn. I won't let you. You won't be my husband, either. I won't let you."

It was out.

He blinked and blinked again. It was almost comical. "What did you say?"

"I want a divorce."

"I don't care what you want. You're never getting a divorce. I won't let you. It suits me to be married to you."

"Oh, I know," she said, sighing. "I'm a handy excuse as to why you don't have a family. Just tell your mother you don't want kids. What's she going to do? Kill you? Then she'll never be a grandmother, so your chances are pretty good that she'll let you live."

"How can you even bring up something like this? Tonight, of all nights. I was giddy about the thought of a Harry Gunn movie. Happy for you! To have everyone talking about my wife like she's something special. I was on cloud nine and now this. It's like you can't stand for me to get ahead. You bring me down at every opportunity."

"I'm sure Janette will make you feel better. She loves you and you love her, according to what she told me in the bathroom."

"You believed that little bitch? Did you see how much she was drinking? I have to put up with this shit all the time. Ingénues who think if they take you to bed you can put in a good word for them."

"Poor Janette. You took her to bed and the only word you have for her is *bitch*."

"She's not the only one! Sleep in the study, and don't think for one minute that anything changes around here." He left the room and came back. "And you keep your mouth shut about Janette! I don't need bad publicity at this point in my career." He stomped off and slammed the bedroom door. Pip instantly jumped up on Kitty and trembled. She always knew when things were bad.

"I think I did pretty well, Pip. Were you proud of me? Now I have to figure out tomorrow. Wouldn't it be nice to have a happy new year?"

❧❦

Kurt stayed away from her. She'd known he would. He was holed up in some hotel downtown as a way to punish her. She noticed he'd taken his new suitcase, so he couldn't hate her that much.

Once the city was open for business again, she went straight to the printer's to have business cards made, but realized her address and phone number might change in the near future, so there was no point in getting them done now. While she was downtown, she stopped in at Empire & Bloom, on the off-chance that Gaynor was in her office.

Dolores gave her a big smile when she came up the stairwell. "Hello, Kitty. Happy New Year."

"Happy New Year to you too. I hear Gaynor gave you a few days off."

"Can you believe it?" Iris yelled over. "She's becoming human in her old age."

"Iris!" Dolores laughed. "Don't be mean."

"Just ask the first Dolores if I'm right. Oh, sorry, you can't. She ran out of here in a flood of tears, never to be seen again."

Gaynor's office door opened. "There are voices out here! Why is mine not one of them?" She looked around. "Kitty! Come on in. And you two hooligans get back to work. Oh, but we'll have coffee, Dolores."

Kitty held up a finger. "I don't drink coffee, remember?"

"Why not?"

"It's bitter."

"Dolores, bring us coffee with two creams and two sugars. It's time this one grew up."

Instead of draping herself on the chaise lounge, Kitty sat straight up in the chair in front of Gaynor's desk. Gaynor took her usual seat and shoved over a pack of cigarettes and a lighter. "Before you even ask."

"Thank you."

"You can't possibly have finished those edits."

Kitty took a puff and shook the match out before passing them back. "No, I haven't even started. Thanks for reminding me."

"I won't tell Mel, but don't leave it too long."

Dolores came back with two mugs of steaming hot coffee and a sleeve of Arrowroots. "Sorry, this was the only thing left in the break room. Enjoy." She left as quietly as she came in.

"You see?" Gaynor said. "Always just a little bit extra. That's what she does. Of course, she knows my sweet tooth, so I'm easy to read. Take a sip."

Kitty did as she was told. The cream and sugar were comforting, warm, and smooth. "This is nice, thank you. I thought all coffee tasted like Martha's."

"Who's Martha?"

"Hopefully my soon-to-be-ex mother-in-law."

Gaynor nearly spit out her coffee. "Shut up. No, don't. Talk."

"I can't do it anymore. But he'll fight me tooth and nail. It's going to be ugly. I hope I have the stamina."

"Did you tell him?"

"Yes. He's disappeared for a while so he doesn't have to deal with it. I'm afraid that's how we've always handled things. Like we're still in high school."

"I don't know a lot about this relationship, but from what I've gleaned over the years, he's never been in your corner, and as someone who luckily has that, I know how essential it is."

Kitty tapped the ash off her cigarette. "I've always admired you and Simon. You're best friends."

"Best friends who often want to kill each other, but hey, that's marriage."

"It's only recently that I've come to know how lovely it is to have a man as a friend."

"Wallace?"

"I miss him, but I can't dwell on it just now. I also made friends with three other men on New Year's Eve."

In the outer office, Dolores and Iris were startled by Gaynor's screaming. It was only when they heard her laugh that they realized Kitty hadn't stabbed her.

❦

Kitty was neck deep in edits four days later when she heard the apartment door open in the middle of the day. It couldn't be Kurt; he was never home at this hour. Especially not when he was sulking.

"Hello?"

Pip jumped off the daybed and barked at the study door. Even when she was alone Kitty kept her door closed, so all the words stayed with her instead of roaming around the apartment. She got up from her desk and went to see what was going on.

It was Kurt. With his new suitcase. "I'm home."

"Well done, you."

He held out his hands. "Don't go into your condescending mode. You don't have to. I'm aware I'm an asshole. I'm here to apologize and beg your forgiveness."

"That's nice. But it's not going to work."

"I booked us a table at Antonio's for dinner. You used to love going there."

"Sorry, I'm up to my ears. Gaynor needs these edits immediately. It's only the first round."

He crossed over to her and put his hands on her shoulders. "Would you sit with me for a minute? Just a minute."

This tactic was always more effective than his temper tantrums, so Kitty made a note of it. She needed to be present instead of slipping into her usual fog.

They sat on the chesterfield together facing each other and he took her hands. "I am aware I don't make life easy for you. This career of mine is full of situations that most people don't have to deal with, like pretending to be in love with someone in front of a camera. It can lead to unfortunate situations that mean absolutely

272

nothing, and I've been guilty of that in the past. But I promise to never let that happen again. You don't deserve it and I apologize for my behaviour. You need to forgive me and we can start to rebuild our relationship. There are all kinds of opportunities coming for us, and it's thrilling that maybe we can work together. Don't throw us away just yet. I've already told Janette to stay away from me and that I didn't appreciate her accosting you like that. It makes it awkward on set at the moment, but it's something I had to do. For you. For us."

Gosh, he was a great actor. Anyone would think he meant every word.

"Kurt, I'm not upset about Janette. She is not the reason I want to end our marriage. We loved each other a very long time ago when we were kids. But we're grown-ups now, and it's time to start the next chapter. No hard feelings. I'll always care about what happens to you, but I need to create a life I'm excited about. I can't hide anymore."

"But I love you, Kitty!"

She smiled at him. "I know you do. As much as you can love anyone, I know you love me. But it's not enough. It will never be enough. I'm sorry."

He jumped up and paced the living room. "It's that Wallace, isn't it? You're in love with him!"

"This has nothing to do with Wallace."

"Bullshit. I told him. I told him to leave you alone. That you weren't cut out for an affair."

Now Kitty rose to her feet. "You said something to Wallace?"

"Why wouldn't I?" he yelled. "It was obvious he was sniffing around. Great big country bumpkin. Why did he think he had a chance when you're married to me?"

"You're talking about me like I'm a commodity. I will decide what happens in my life. You had no right saying anything to my friend."

He pointed at her. "I had every right! I'm your husband. And I will remain your husband. I'm not going to give up on us, Kitty. We belong together. I'm going to win you back! You just wait and see."

He picked up his suitcase and took it into the bedroom. Kitty and Pip went back to her study and shut the door. She sat in front of the typewriter and put her head in her hands. "Pippy, I think I might be ready to write about another murder. Something involving a suitcase."

⁂

The trouble with trying to dissolve a marriage is that people have to live in the real world in the meantime. Kitty wrote out a shopping list: *apples, eggs, milk, bread, lawyer.*

And what that lawyer had to say was startling. Kitty had never really thought about what a divorce would entail. But it turned out, in Quebec a divorce was granted by a Senate Divorce Committee and was three times more expensive than a divorce court in other provinces. Her lawyer suggested they meet with her local MP, who could introduce a Private Member's Bill in the House of Commons to declare the marriage ended, which seemed to Kitty ridiculous, but that's what was required. Luckily, she had the financial means, there were no children to worry about, or alimony, and she didn't care that it might take a year or more. Since adultery was the sole grounds for divorce, she was all set on that score too.

It was going to be complicated but not impossible. Her lawyer would be in charge of this mess. She had enough to do.

She and Gaynor had another meeting and Gaynor accepted Kitty's changes with glee. Off Kitty went with a few more suggestions to work on, and then it would go to Mel to have a quick peek, then back to Gaynor to have another go, and then over to Kitty for one more perusal before her part was over. That was always a happy day, because if she had to read the damn thing once more, she'd need a sedative. Kitty never read her novels in book form. She was usually onto the next story by the time they came out and it was like drinking cold tea to immerse herself in it again.

In the meantime, Kurt arrived home early every night around ten with a Chinese takeout, a bottle of perfume, a box of macarons, a new bone for Pip. It was endless.

"I'm not changing my mind, Kurt."

"Yes, you will my darling. This is just a hiccup. I hope you notice I'm not badgering you in the bedroom."

"I'm not in the bedroom."

"If you were, I'd leave you alone."

"How thoughtful."

This was the time she could use a girlfriend. Gaynor was extremely busy and Kitty didn't want to do anything to upset their relationship. It was great as it was, but not intimate. And she knew that Gaynor would have only one thing to say about it anyway. "Get rid of the bum. And don't be nice about it."

That's what she was trying to do, but Kitty couldn't stomach raving like a lunatic. She even thought of writing to Bertha, but what was the point? Bertha would only worry, and that wasn't fair. And Wallace? She'd love nothing better than to listen to his calm, rational thoughts about it, but he was too invested. And she was trying not to think about Wallace.

Walrus.

In an astonishing turn of events, it was Miles who became her confidante. He called and asked her to meet him for lunch downtown. She found herself taking a few extra minutes to brush her hair and put on a dab of lipstick. It was a business lunch, so she wore tailored slacks and a silk blouse. Miles took her seriously, and so would she.

He stood up at the table when she arrived. The maître d' took her coat. She and Miles shook hands and he held the back of her chair as she sat down. They each ordered a glass of white wine and Miles suggested their famous fish casserole, which was fine with her.

"I'm sorry Claude and Pierre couldn't be here. Claude is in Vancouver on business and Pierre's wife is about to give birth."

"How exciting."

"He's on pins and needles. They have four sons and he's desperate for a girl."

"Aren't they lucky?" She lifted her glass. "To Baby."

He smiled. "To Baby."

"Do you have children, Miles?"

"Yes. Timothé is ten, Adèle, eight. They have their beautiful mother's looks. Do you and Robert have…"

"No, one child in the family is enough." She took a big swig of her drink. "Sorry. I shouldn't have said that."

"I believe you are correct."

"What's he like on set? Does he drive everyone crazy? You're not talking out of turn. I'm trying to divorce the man, but he's not having it. It's like I'm not a part of the equation, and I need to know how to deal with him, but I have no one to ask. I'm sorry. I'm babbling here. I don't get out much." And she took another gulp. "Good lord, I need another drink, which is a terrible thing to say to someone who might want to do business with me. I've been living with this for a while, and I didn't realize how desperate I've become to talk to someone."

He put up his hand for the waiter, who brought Kitty another glass of wine. Then he sat back and reassured her. "I will answer truthfully. We've only just met, but I knew instantly that you and Robert have nothing in common, and if you are still married it's only because of your efforts, not his. Don't get me wrong. He's a very charming man. And an extremely talented actor, which is why everyone in the film industry wants him, despite his occasional ego flare-ups. But then, all actors have big egos, myself included. We have to. It's our craft. But some are not as mature about it, and that's Robert's problem. He's a little boy who never grew up."

"If you knew his mother, you'd know why."

"Unfortunately, he's also pitched as a romantic lead because he's a handsome guy, but sometimes actors in that position feel the need to project that image to every female on set."

"Which is a very polite way of saying he's a Lothario."

"Exactly."

"I'm aware of that, and I put up with it because I didn't care. He's not completely to blame. When you know deep down you don't matter to someone, you look elsewhere. He thinks if he apologizes enough for his behaviour with Janette, we'll be fine. I feel sorry for her."

"Don't. She knows exactly what she's doing. Robert just falls for it."

Their meal arrived and it was piping hot and delicious.

"I needed this. Something warm to thaw my frozen heart."

"How can I tell you're a writer? A writer we're very interested in."

They talked shop for the next hour. Miles told her that the company Un Film Bien was definitely interested in bringing the first Harry Gunn novel to the silver screen, and if successful, the others would follow. There were a lot of things to be sorted, obviously, like Kitty procuring a film agent to go over her contract. They were interested in her perhaps doing a screenplay for them, the first draft anyway, to see what she could come up with. The stipulation being that they would bring in a seasoned screenwriter for the subsequent drafts, someone who had experience working on sets, with budget constraints and production concerns, of which she knew nothing at this point.

"If everything falls into place, this can go very quickly depending on funding, or it can take years, so I'm warning you now, patience will be a virtue with a project like this. We're used to the nonsense that can go on, but people who aren't in the industry tend to want to pull their hair out."

"Kurt...Robert suggested that I use his agent. He was beyond excited when he got home that night. He thinks he'd be a perfect Harry Gunn. That I should put it in my contract."

"That's not going to happen. He's too young."

"I told him that. And I don't want to use his agent, obviously. Do you know of any female film agents? I'd prefer that. She'll look out for another woman."

"I do, as it happens, a very good one. Sophie Blanchette. I'll get her to call you."

They finished their coffee, which Kitty was drinking almost every day now, and were preparing to leave when she leaned over the table. "Please don't think badly of Robert. Just because I can't be married to him anymore doesn't mean I don't want the best for him. It's a difficult thing. Ending a marriage feels shameful. It's not something you ever want to happen. There's always great sorrow in leaving someone behind. What makes it harder are the nice memories you don't want to forget."

"You're not only a talented writer, but a good woman. I can understand why Robert wants to keep you in his life."

"My dear friend Bertha once said, 'If you can extend charity to someone, do it.'"

Chapter Twenty-One

When Kitty got up the next day, she opened the study door and found a note taped to it: *Roses are red, violets are blue, sugar is sweet and so are you to.*

You to? You too?

Pip didn't seem to be in a particular rush this morning so Kitty hopped in the shower, got dressed, and made a cup of coffee before taking Pip outside. There was a note on the fridge: *Look inside for a treat.*

She opened it. There was a giant heart cookie with livid red and blue icing piped all over it. She took it out and broke the heart in two. Then put it back for him to find.

As she bundled up for the cold morning and put Pip on her leash, there was another note taped to the front door: *You forgot something. Look behind you.*

She turned around and there was a present on the living room coffee table. "Oh no." She didn't want to open it, but curiosity got the better of her. It was a necklace with a heart pendant, engraved with two intertwined Ks and a note: *Remember this?*

There was an almost identical one in the back of her sock drawer that he'd given her in grade eleven. Instantly she wavered. She was back in high school by her locker, Kurt giving her a big, saucy grin when she opened the gift he'd handed her. Looking at the heart filled the lonely space that constantly cried out for someone to love her. She had put her arms around his neck, and when he asked her if she liked it, she couldn't speak. That made him laugh.

Damn. Damn. Damn. Now was not the time to become

sentimental. They had had lots of nice moments like that, but this was another world, and she was in a different place.

If there was one thing Kurt was good at, it was a dramatic gesture. She had to remember that. She could almost hear Gaynor say, "Don't get gooey."

She put it back in the box and left it on the end table. But it hurt to see it there.

They walked and walked, going a little further afield today, since her edits weren't dire and she was in desperate need of shaking off what just happened. She made plans to call her dad to make sure they were still on for lunch at the end of the week.

The weather turned and the wind began to blow snow around. She decided to take a shortcut down an alley. Wooden and chain-link fences faced each other. Some had none at all. Backyards full of things people didn't need every day, everything looking neglected under piles of snow. There were also garages or sheds with old tires, rusty bikes, and pipes leaning against them. This could be a beautiful pathway if everyone on two streets got together and worked on it.

This wasn't Pip's usual stomping grounds. She was smelling new and intoxicating odours, so they didn't make up any time after all. Finally, Kitty gave her a tug to get her moving, but she refused. She whined instead.

"What's wrong?" Kitty looked around but didn't see anything. Nothing put piles of snow.

"Let's go."

Pip wouldn't budge. That's when Kitty thought she saw something move and heard whimpering. She looked closer and what she'd thought was a pile of snow was a very small white puppy. She picked it up. "What are you doing here?"

Pip jumped up and yipped. She wanted to make sure the puppy was okay too, so Kitty bent down and let her sniff it all over. Then she quickly opened her jacket and put the shivering pup inside next to her heart.

"Okay, this is insane. Where did this dog come from? Pip, can you smell anything else?" She was afraid someone had thrown out a litter, as unbelievable as that sounded. The two of them searched high and low, and by the time they left, Kitty was sure they weren't leaving anyone behind. The dear little soul in her jacket must have fallen asleep with the sudden warmth.

They hurried home as fast as they could. Kitty got a cardboard box and lined it with towels and a hot water bottle. She called the vet, who said it was okay to give her a little warm milk but to bring her right in so he could assess the situation.

By noon, Kitty was the proud owner of a puppy named Pearl. Pearl was about seven weeks old and seemed to be in good health, despite being a little too young to be without her mother. Kitty had food and instructions on Pearl's dietary needs and a date for her rabies vaccine. The vet said to take her outside to do her business between five and twenty minutes after feeding her.

"This is a beautiful dog," he stroked her head. "I can't understand why she would be on her own. She's very lucky you came along."

"I don't want to think about what would've happened if I hadn't taken that shortcut."

"You were meant to have her. Or she was meant to have you, as I like to think of it."

"Will she get much bigger?"

The vet made a face. "Oh yeah."

"Like how big?"

"She's a female, so around a hundred pounds. Think small pony. She's a Great Pyrenees. If she was male, you're talking a hundred and fifty pounds."

"Oh my god. I live in an apartment."

"They're gentle giants who like having quiet time in the house and enjoy a predictable, orderly routine." He passed the dog over to her and Kitty held her under her chin.

"It doesn't matter how big you get, does it, Pearl?"

"Cute name."

"Snowball seemed too obvious. Besides, she has beautiful brown eyes like my mom."

Becoming a mother when you least expect it brings its own chaos. And when one of those mothers is a poodle frantically waiting at the door for you to come home, it's double the fun. It took all day for Kitty to prepare a space for Pearl, and the obvious place was in her study. She bought a smaller cage to begin with, for the times when she'd have to leave the two of them alone. No doubt Pippy would want to be in with Pearl, but in the meantime, she thought the little box would be more comforting. Pip brought over one of her stuffed toys and dropped it on Pearl's head and spent the entire afternoon staring at the new addition while she snored. Kitty laid newspapers all over the floor in case of accidents, but so far, after a full tummy and two quick runs to the front lawn, they remained bone dry.

Kitty picked her up after the second visit to the front lawn and cuddled her. "You absolute angel. You're so smart! Isn't she, Pip? Let's go in, it's too cold for babies."

While the dogs slept, Kitty did some editing, but her focus wasn't on her task. She kept looking around to take a peek at her little cotton ball. There was only one person she wanted to share this news with, and that was Wallace. Should she? They'd exchanged a few letters, but this would be her first time talking to him in person since that awful day. She was probably going to open a huge can of worms.

But she was lonesome.

She called their number, and hearing the one long and three

short rings brought a visceral reaction. Tears came unbidden. This was a big mistake. She was about to hang up when she heard Bertha's voice.

"Hello?"

"B-Bertha?"

"Yes?"

"It's...Kit..."

"Kitty? Is that you?"

"Yes," she whispered.

"God love your little heart! Are you okay? You sound upset. What do you need? I'll be right over...what am I saying? I still think you're just down the road. It's all right, my love. I'm here."

Kitty kept crying. Bertha waited patiently for her to stop, saying, "It's okay, honey," every so often. "I'm still here." Then she heard Bertha say, "Ethel, be quiet and go back in the kitchen. I'm on the phone with Kitty."

"TITTY?"

It was exactly what she needed. Kitty howled with laughter. "Oh my god, I miss you guys so much! Say hi to Ethel for me!"

"Oh, we miss you too, child. And dear little Pip. The place isn't the same without you."

"Is everyone okay? Are you okay? How are the kids and dogs and chickens? How's Wallace?"

"We're all fine, dear. You've only been gone for about six weeks, although it feels like six years."

"I don't know why I didn't call before. I guess I was afraid that I'd have that reaction."

"You call us anytime you like. I'm not as good as I thought I'd be about being a pen pal. I'd much rather hear your voice."

"Oh, me too."

"Now, are you all right?"

"There are a few things going on, but nothing I can't handle. I wanted to tell Wallace about my new puppy. I found her in a back alley today, although when I look at her, it's like she's always been here."

"Oh, he'll love to hear that. Let me go shout for him. He's outside somewhere. Here, talk to Ethel, since she refuses to stay in the kitchen. Here, Ethel, say something to Kitty."

There was a fumbling noise as the mouthpiece was passed between hands. "Like what? Hello, Kitty!! Is that you? I'm glad you called. You're not going to believe what happened to Dolly!"

"Oh, no. What?"

"There was a New Year's Dance at the Legion and someone rigged a contraption to drop down like the Time's Square New Year's Eve ball and she was on stage counting off the seconds, but it fell on her head and knocked her out! Luckily she came to a few minutes later, but she missed everyone shouting 'Happy New Year.'"

Kitty had to hold her fist to her mouth to keep quiet. "Oh, dear. That's terrible."

"She says she's suing Earl Butts because he's a fisherman and should know more about ropes. Oh, here's Wallace. That was quick."

Wallace sounded out of breath. "Kitty?"

Hearing his voice felt like he'd just put his arms around her. She was awash in a safe sea of calm, and then whoosh. Heat. How she missed him.

"Hi, Wallace. It's really nice to speak to you."

"Same here. This is a nice surprise. How was your Christmas? Everyone was thrilled with their gifts."

"It was fine. I'm so glad they liked them. Did the snowsuit fit Ben?"

"It was perfect. Just big enough to do him all winter."

"That makes me happy."

"Are you okay? Not that I'm not thrilled to hear from you, but I hope nothing is wrong."

Kitty turned her head to look at Pearl once more. "You were the one person I wanted to tell. I found a puppy today in a back alley. She's only seven weeks old and she's beautiful. You know I always wanted another dog, and it's like she dropped out of the sky to make that dream come true and I can't quite believe it. I've had her to the vet and he says she's healthy."

"I'm so pleased for you. What on earth was the little mite doing in a back alley? Was that the only one?"

"Pip was the one who found her, and she sniffed everywhere but we couldn't find anything else. You should see her. She's pure white."

"Not a mutt, then."

"You're not going to believe this. She's a Great Pyrenees. She'll be almost as big as Pride."

He started to laugh. "And there you are in the city with this huge dog. You better get that house you're always talking about. I can't see taking her up and down in an elevator."

"We do have stairs, believe it or not. And the vet says they like quiet time in the house and a predictable, orderly routine. His words."

"You better not bring her here!"

"Wouldn't that be fun?"

She was sorry she said it when she heard him clear his throat. "How's little Pip? Argus and Pride miss her."

"She's still mad at me for leaving. I hope Pearl will make her happy again."

"Pearl is very lucky. It means a lot that you wanted to tell me."

"I knew you'd understand how much these dogs mean to me. They're the only children I'll ever have. I'd better go. I've already been on this call for too long, but I'm so happy I got to talk to you today, Wallace. I really miss you."

"And I you. Take good care."

"Tell your mom I love her."

"I will. Bye."

"Bye."

She put down the receiver and curled up in a ball on her daybed, hauling the tartan wool blanket up and over her head.

⁕

Kurt came home at eight o'clock, unfortunately. Kitty was in the middle of cleaning up a piddle on the carpet. "I didn't expect you so soon."

"Obviously. Look, I brought you a box of fudge." He took off his coat and threw it over a chair. "What are you doing?"

"Cleaning dog pee."

"Does that damn dog pee all over the place when I'm not here?"

"We all do."

Pip ran into the living room, the puppy nipping at her paws. Pearl and Kurt looked at each other. She lowered her hind quarters and peed again.

Kurt blew his top. "What the hell is going on? What's this?"

Kitty put more paper towels down on the new spot. "This is Pearl. She lives here."

"Oh no, she doesn't!"

"Oh yes, she does."

"Is this some kind of plot to get me out of this house?"

Kitty straightened up. "I never thought of that, but now that you say it..."

"This is what I come home to? Another dog? I gave you a necklace this morning. And a cookie. Did you see it?" He rushed over to the fridge and took out the broken heart. "Oh, very clever." He threw it in the sink and put his hand on his forehead as if trying to believe the scene in front of him. "There are newspapers everywhere!"

"She's a puppy. She's going to have accidents."

"Why are you doing this? Why are you making it impossible for

286

me to try and make things up to you? You keep putting roadblocks in my way on purpose!"

She threw the paper towels at him. "Only you would think I'd use an abandoned pup to my own advantage. It hasn't even occurred to you to ask me about how this little one came into my life. How upsetting it was to find her alone, cold and shivering in the snow. You don't give a damn about that. Or me. Or anyone else. And for the last time, you are never making things up to me, because I have no interest in saving this marriage. It's over, Kurt. It's bloody over." She ripped off the rubber gloves and threw them to the floor.

He held up his hands in surrender. "Okay, okay, I overreacted. But I'm not cleaning up dog piss."

"You don't have to. I'm leaving."

She rushed out of the room and grabbed an overnight bag in the closet. There was no thought, she just had to run.

He followed her. "Okay, wait a minute! Wait a minute! I'm sorry! I didn't mean it. I'll clean up dog piss. I promise."

Kitty turned and looked him right in the face. "Piss off!"

He continued to chase after her as she went from room to room. At one point he put his hand on her arm to stop her, but when she stared at it and then back at him, he took it away. She gathered up a few clothes and toiletries, her manuscript and typewriter, all the dogs' belongings, toys and food, the crate, the box, the heating pad, leashes, blankets, her wool tartan throw, and her pillow and piled it all by the door.

Kurt was yammering the entire time.

"If you're going to follow me, at least be useful." She shoved a box in his arms and he went down the stairwell with her. She would take the dogs last.

They got to the car and she opened the trunk, putting her armful in, and grabbed the box from him.

"This is madness. Where are you going?"

"I don't know. It doesn't matter."

"Of course it matters."

She ran back inside and into the stairwell again. "So, you're the only person who gets to hide out in a hotel when you're unhappy? Two can play that game."

"Kitty, calm down. This isn't like you."

She spun around in the second-floor corridor. "This *is* me, Kurt. This has been me for as long as I can remember, and I'm tired of it. So very tired. I refuse to put up with it anymore."

Someone came out of their apartment at that moment, saw them, thought the better of it, and closed the door again.

Three more trips to the car and all that was left was her purse, one dog in a box, and one dog on a leash.

"When will you be back? I know you're not serious about this," he said. "This is just a little show to put me in my place, and God knows I deserve it."

Both dogs were whining now. "You keep saying you know you deserve this. What I've never deserved is that even now, when I tell you it's over, you dismiss me. I don't matter to you, Kurt. Can't you see that?" She opened the apartment door.

"You'll never be able to get a divorce!" he shouted. The door was closed in his face.

She knew exactly where she was going. Even used her own key to get in.

"Dad?!"

She heard his voice. "Kitty?" Thank God he was here.

He appeared in the hallway and looked shocked. "Catriona, are you okay? What's wrong?"

"Can I stay here for a few days?"

"Of course. What's going on?"

"I'm leaving Kurt. I want a divorce and he's against it. I had no choice but to leave since he won't budge."

"Is that...?"

"Another dog, yes. I'm sorry. I found her today and she's mine. I'd better take her out for another pee. I have some stuff in the car."

He shook off his slippers. "I'll help you."

They brought in her belongings. Kitty was surprised that Martha hadn't shown up to see what was going on. Not that Kitty wanted her to. She made a soft bed in the crate and put the dogs in her old bedroom while she got their things organized and food dishes sorted. Her father gathered old newspapers and towels just in case.

"Let's take a minute," he said. "Would you like a drink?"

She didn't like her dad drinking. "I wouldn't mind a coffee."

He brewed her a cup as she sat at the kitchen table and rubbed her weary eyes.

"I'm sorry it's come to this," he said.

"I'm not. I should've done it years ago."

"Yes, you should have."

She crossed her arms. "Then why didn't you say something?"

"I believe I told you not to do it before you got married, but you told me to mind my own business. So, I did."

"Well, that was a mistake. One of the many, many I've made."

He poured the coffee in a cup. "Cream? Sugar?"

"Yes, please."

He brought it over to her. "Advice about romance is best from a mother. Fathers don't know a girl's heart. I was afraid to make a mistake."

Martha suddenly loomed in the doorway. "What have you done to my Kurt? He was on the phone crying about your disgusting behaviour! How dare you leave him?"

"You've always wanted him to leave me."

"Exactly! Not the other way around! His heart is broken, you selfish, selfish girl. A minx, that's what you are. I never liked you, and now I know why."

Her father got up from the table. "What did you say to my daughter?"

It was almost as if Martha hadn't realized he was in the room. She became flustered. "I'm upset, Leo. My son is crying on the phone. And she's responsible. She doesn't give him children and then walks out on him. What kind of a woman does that? I have every right to be angry."

Dad didn't say anything, as usual. Why didn't he stand up to her?

And then he blurted, "You're fired!"

"I'm fired?" Martha screeched.

Kitty spilled coffee on the placemat. "She's fired? Did you just fire your girlfriend?"

Dad looked at her in horror. "My girlfriend? She's my housekeeper."

"But I thought...when she didn't move out...you were...you know..."

Now he was angry. "You thought *what*? That this woman took your mother's place? That I would have a relationship with her when I'd been married to the best woman in the world? Kitty, use your head."

"Why didn't you tell me?"

"Tell you what?! She was always the housekeeper. Wasn't it obvious?"

"No! And this goes to show you how long it's been since you and I had a heart-to-heart about anything, never mind our personal lives." Now Kitty stood and faced Martha. "You were aware I thought you and Dad were a couple all this time. It suited you to have me believe that. You've been able to treat me like dirt because you knew I didn't want my father to be unhappy. That I wouldn't say anything to him about the way you've treated me."

Martha lifted her chin. "Rubbish."

Her father looked confused. "What do you mean, the way she's treated you? What's been going on?"

"For God's sake, Dad! Open your eyes. She's a mean spirit. She made me afraid to come to my own house. Made me unwelcome in my mother's home, and I'll never forgive her for that." She was too upset to stay still. She went over to the sink and gripped the edge of it before she spun around and pointed at her father. "And you let it happen."

"Wait—" her father tried to interject, but she ignored him.

"You never paid attention to the fact that you and I were drifting further and further apart. She made me feel like an intruder. Didn't want Pip over here. Never giving you messages, like the fact that I was leaving for Cape Breton." She turned away, aware that her voice was slightly hysterical, but she was on a roll, so she faced them again.

"And this year I wanted to make Christmas dinner for you and have it at our house and she refused. Wouldn't even entertain the idea! Instead, she plied you with booze all day so you'd stay in your bubble of despair. She's a big part of the reason our relationship hasn't flourished. She wanted you all to herself." She threw up her hands and looked around. "Or maybe it was just this house she wanted. Who wouldn't want this situation? You pay her a salary and she gets to live in a beautiful house without paying rent or heat or insurance or groceries. You could have kept her as a housekeeper. She's good at it, but why did she keep living here after Kurt and I left? And you wonder why I thought you were an item?"

Her father was baffled. "I don't know. She'd been here for ten years by then and..."

"It's that suspended animation I talked about. You were never going to get better, Dad, because there's no happiness here. There's nothing here. This place is steeped in sadness. And she used that to her advantage."

Dad's shoulders slumped. "Martha, pack your things and go."

Martha glared at them. "I've lived here for twenty-five years. You think it's that easy?"

"It is that easy, because everything is mine. You haven't con-
tributed anything. I've been a fool."

"I kept the house clean."

"And I paid you well for that service. I'll give you two months'
severance and I want you gone."

"I have nowhere to go."

"You have a sister in Verdun and a son up the street. I'll call
you a cab."

Kitty couldn't help herself. When Martha marched out the door
with two suitcases, she held out the pressure cooker. "I believe this
is yours."

Chapter Twenty-Two

Being in her old bedroom made her shiver. She had a few memories of her mother standing at the door of her dark room, the hall light behind her, in a dress, going out for the evening. The full skirt swished as she walked over to the bed and kissed her cheek. "Goodnight, my little kittycat. Sweet dreams." Her perfume lingered and Kitty thought she was lucky to have a mother as pretty as a princess.

But most of her memories in here were sad ones. With everything that had happened today and dealing with a new puppy, she hadn't slept at all. She had to take Pearl outside again and Pip was right with her. When she went by the living room, she saw her dad in his easy chair in the dark, smoking.

As she put on her winter coat, hat, and gloves, she gave Pearl a kiss. Pearl wiggled and licked her nose. "It would've been so much easier if I'd found you in the summer."

Once back in the house she settled her two sweet Ps and went into the darkened living room and dropped into the chair next to her father.

"I can't sleep either," she said, sighing.

"How did I get this so wrong?"

"You're human. I should've confronted Martha long ago, but I've always been a little bit afraid of her."

"Me too."

"God, Dad. For two smart people we're laughably dull-witted."

"She was never a good cook."

"Exactly! Think of all the poor turkeys who gave up their lives so she could bake them bone dry."

"She did the same thing to ham. Now that I think of it, her specialty was cremated meat."

They both chuckled.

He knocked the tobacco out of his pipe. "I think I know why I let it happen. Her staying on, I mean."

"Oh yeah?"

"I liked pulling up to the house after work and having the lights on. I liked having dinner on the table, even if it was dry. It was nice to smell a clean house. It was great to go in my closet in the morning and have my shirts ironed. Have fresh underwear and socks in my drawers. It made me feel less lonely. Sometimes I would pretend it was your mother in the kitchen doing the dishes. Martha is not the only one to blame for this situation. It obviously served my purposes as well."

"Damn." Kitty rubbed her forehead. "You're right. I've been so cross with her, I never thought about how it might have helped you to have her here."

"That's how it started, but it needed to end. I'm not quite as pathetic as I was fifteen years ago when you and Kurt left. The house seemed too empty then. And you're right. I didn't pay attention to how she behaved with you. I honestly wasn't aware of it."

"I know, because I never said anything. I didn't want to rock the boat."

"How foolish, thinking I'd be with Martha. I'm still in love with your mother."

"Dad, aren't you tired of being alone? Wouldn't you like to have another woman in your life?"

"I had one up until a few hours ago. Ask me in a couple of months."

"Stop being cute. You know what I mean. A relationship."

He turned on the lamp beside him. "If we're going to sit here, we might as well see each other. And the answer is no. I don't want another relationship. Your mother was it for me. I'm not interested in replacing her. I'll happily live with my memories, as old-fashioned as that sounds."

She leaned her cheek against the side of the chair. "That's not old-fashioned, just very romantic."

He smiled at her. "Sitting there you look just like your mom. She was a beautiful woman. I have no idea why she wanted me. A bulldog from the wrong side of the tracks."

"A bulldog with gorgeous blue eyes. Paul Newman eyes."

"You have your mother's eyes, which makes me very happy."

"Me too."

He made a move to get up. It was still the middle of the night. "We should hit the hay."

"Dad?"

He turned around. "What?"

"I think we should leave this house."

"Why?"

"You have Mom's memory in your head, so you carry her wherever you go. You don't need this space anymore. After all these years, it's saturated in Martha. There are more bad memories here than good ones." She got up from the chair, went over and placed her hand on his arm. "Those first years struggling after Mom and Ben died. You drinking a lot or hiding away. Me alone in my room. I hate sleeping in there. I always have a knot in my stomach when I come up to the door. And it's much too big now. Let's find a small house with a garden and a fenced-in yard for the dogs. Let's make new memories."

He looked sad. "Catriona, I've had a hell of a day. I'm old and tired and can't think right now. I just got rid of my housekeeper and now you want me to get rid of my house. Enough is enough. Go to sleep."

She lay on her childhood bed, the dogs snoring beside her, her hand on Pearl's soft head.

It was worth a try.

-❦❦-

Three days later, on Saturday, she needed more clothes, and she kept looking for things that she'd forgotten to take. When her dad came in from taking the dogs to the corner and back, which was as far as Pearl could manage before she flopped on the sidewalk and refused to budge, she approached him.

"I need to get my things from the apartment."

"Okay. What are we talking about? Can we handle it ourselves?"

"I think so. I want all my clothes, obviously, more stuff from the bathroom drawers and everything in my study, furniture included, and my books, but that's it. I don't want anything else. Oh, and my teapot and mug, a few things from the kitchen. There are a couple of dishtowels I bought with the Eiffel Tower on them that I like. And a new set of sheets and towels I bought before I left for Cape Breton. I haven't even used them."

"Ted next door has a utility trailer. I'll ask if we can borrow it and we can do it in one trip. I'll buy him a case of beer."

It felt odd going up in the elevator with her father. He'd only been to their place a few times. Probably because whenever he was over, he looked uncomfortable. Maybe he'd had to sit too close to Kurt.

Kitty unlocked the door and went inside, her father behind her. The place was a mess, clothes and dishes everywhere. The paper towels were still on the floor where she'd thrown them.

"You start gathering things out of the study while I pack up my clothes. We'll assemble a big pile here in the living room before we start taking it downstairs."

"All right."

Her father went to her study and she carried two big suitcases into the bedroom. The bed was a mess. She plunked them down on the mattress.

"OW!" Kurt poked his head out from under the covers. "What are you doing?"

Her hand flew to her throat. "God! You startled me. I didn't know you were in here. I thought you'd be at work."

"Technical difficulties. I don't have to be there until this afternoon. What are you doing here?" He immediately sat up straight. "Have you reconsidered? Have you come back to me?"

"No. I'm here to get my things."

"What things? You can't have any of it."

"I'm taking my clothes and the belongings in my study. You're welcome to your huge lamps and uncomfortable furniture."

She opened the suitcases, which forced Kurt out of the bed. He wrapped his bathrobe around himself and lit a cigarette while he paced the room. Kitty opened her bureau drawers and took everything out at once, shoving it into the suitcases until they were full.

"You and your father have some nerve. First you leave me and then he throws my mother out of the house! That's gratitude for you."

"Where is your mother? I thought she'd be here with you. As you're her only child, I assumed you'd take the poor woman in."

"Don't be ridiculous. A movie star living with his mother? Do you want to ruin my career as well? Your old man had no business treating her like that! Ungrateful bastard!"

Dad showed up at the bedroom door. "Did you want to say something to me, son?"

Kurt shrank away and sat in the chair on his side of the room. "It wasn't very nice of you, was it?"

"It was unfortunate that it ended like that, but it was time for us to part ways."

"You left her without a penny to her name!"

"Untrue. I have the cheque stub to prove it. Now, get dressed and help me take Kitty's things out to the trailer."

"My wife is leaving me and you want me to help her pack? Go fuck yourself."

Her father's face suddenly did look like a bulldog from the wrong side of the tracks. He took two steps in Kurt's direction before Kurt jumped up with his hands in front of him. "Sorry! Didn't mean that. Just upset."

"Get moving, you little twerp."

They never said another word to each other. Kurt and her father dragged things out as Kitty packed them up. Boxes of books, bookcases, her desk, the jewellery box, all the pictures and posters off the wall. She hadn't realized how many toiletries she owned, but she was happy to see them again. There was more in the kitchen than she realized, but it was personal things, like her favourite egg cup. Nothing that would leave Kurt short. And funnily enough, she grabbed the picture on the fridge of the two of them when they were fourteen on a school trip to Niagara Falls. She'd always loved it because she looked so good in it. Kurt always took a great picture, so it was no big deal to him. But it was the first time she'd ever felt pretty. And it had been a happy day.

On the final load, her father stayed in the car. He'd paid two young boys who were hanging around to watch the trailer while they were upstairs getting more stuff. They were thrilled with the unexpected pocket money.

Kitty took one last look around. Her empty study gave her pause. This was where Harry Gunn began. The time she spent in here saved her life and then almost destroyed it. The exact scenario of her marriage.

She went into the living room for the last time. Kurt was looking out the window.

"Thank you for your help."

"I didn't want my face punched in."

"He wasn't going to hurt you."

"He's wanted to knock me out for years."

"Then it's a good thing you'll never have to see him again. Or me."

He turned to look at her. "It's not over, Kitty. I always get what I want."

"Bye, Kurt. Say hi to Janette."

She closed the door and by the sounds of it he threw his large ashtray at the door. Not a smart move. The super was super fussy.

As they drove away from the curb, she turned to her father. "Dad, I need you to do something for me."

❧❦

Gone were the days of nothing happening. The month of February was a whirlwind of meetings. Edits with Gaynor, meetings with her lawyer, negotiations with her agent, Sophie Blanchette, business discussions with the three amigos of Un Film Bien. The last one was with Pierre Levesque. Kitty brought a pink teddy bear for his newborn daughter and he was delighted with her thoughtfulness, proudly showing her a picture of the little pink bundle amid her four big brothers.

On top of that, Kitty was still dealing with a baby who needed a lot of attention. Pip was a wonderful babysitter, but Pearl could be very stubborn. Especially with Kitty's father. He was always happy to take them out for a walk after work, but the minute Pearl decided she'd had enough, she'd collapse onto the sidewalk and Dad would have to carry her home. At some point in the future that wouldn't be possible. She was becoming too big for such nonsense. But he soon solved the problem by putting Cheezies in his pocket to entice her off the pavement. He didn't seem to mind.

It might have been her imagination, but Kitty thought her father looked brighter these days. And he wasn't drinking like he used to; he would engage in conversation instead of disappearing into the den. If he noticed that Kitty was slowly but surely changing things around in the house, he never mentioned it. Martha had a fetish for throw rugs, and it gave Kitty great pleasure to throw those throw rugs in the bin. She asked him if she could re-wallpaper the kitchen and he said yes, but she couldn't find the time to go shopping.

Kurt showed up one night at two in the morning and scared her to death, banging on the front door, drunk and belligerent. She tried to talk sense into him, but that didn't work. Her father told her to go back to bed, that he'd handle it. She was afraid that meant throttle him, but it turned out her father took Kurt into the living room and listened to him moan about how his life was ruined. Her father held Kurt up as he took him to the car to drive him home.

Kitty met Gaynor at Schwartz's Deli so she could deliver the last of the edits. They both took huge bites of their smoked-meat sandwiches. It was a silly place to conduct business, because it was so crowded and loud, with strangers sitting next to them at one of the many tables, but that was part of the fun. Kitty got mustard on the manuscript. Gaynor put down her sandwich and opened her famous black hole of a purse. "Give me that. I'll stick it in here, otherwise I won't be able to read it what with the pickle juice, meat drippings, and spilled beer."

Kitty told Gaynor about Kurt pounding on the door and how her father had handled it.

"Do you think it was a performance?"

"That's the trouble. I'm so jaded by his behaviour, I can't tell if it's a tactic to make me feel guilty as hell or if he's really struggling."

"Probably both." She took another bite. "God, this is good."

Kitty licked her fingers. "He says I'm not going to win. That's what this is to him. A contest. He's so unbelievably immature. He has no idea how much better his life is going to be without me."

Gaynor wagged her finger at her. "I don't agree. His life was always much better with you in it. I think you're seeing panic."

"Oh, great. Now I feel bad."

More finger wagging. "Don't you dare! Don't go all girly and soft on me. He's put you through the wringer, and just because he's suffering now doesn't mean he didn't bring this on himself. You are not to blame. God, I hate women who do that. It's so bloody frustrating. He's been screwing his co-star. I don't feel one bit sorry for the little prick."

"You're right."

Gaynor leaned closer. "And is it?"

"Is it what?"

"Little?"

Kitty threw her balled-up napkin at her.

⊰❦⊱

A week after that, Kitty drove away from her father's house and parked in front of the apartment, her stomach twisting. It was almost midnight. She wanted to make sure Kurt was home, because she had no intention of letting this drama continue. All she wanted was for her life to move on. Kitty knew how it felt to start a fresh new story. She'd done it for her fictional characters. Now it was her turn.

She used the stairs and slowly walked down the corridor. It was very quiet, with most of the residents in bed. Until she got in front of her door. There was music blaring from inside, and at that very moment the man across the hall opened his door.

"Will you tell that idiot to knock it off with Hank Williams? If I hear 'I'm so Lonesome I Could Cry' one more time tonight I won't be held responsible for my actions!"

"I'm very sorry. I'll turn it off."

He shut the door and Kitty knocked, but there was no way Kurt would hear it over the record, so she opened the door with her key. Kurt lay on the chesterfield with his arm over his eyes, a drink in his hand. She crossed the floor and took the tone arm off the record. He jumped up.

"Christ, you scared me! How dare you barge in here. You don't live here anymore, remember. Give me that damn key!"

She put the key on the coffee table. "The man across the hall is going to call the superintendent if you don't stop playing that record at an ear-splitting level."

"Who cares." He looked at the clock on the wall. "It's midnight."

"I wanted to make sure you were home. To give you something."

She put a manila envelope on the coffee table next to the key.

"And what's this?"

"Open it."

He put down his drink and tore the flap with his thumb. Then slid eight-by-ten pictures out of the envelope. His face went grey as he shifted through them. "Where did you get these?"

"My father's a detective, remember."

"Goddamn it. You didn't. How could you do this to me?"

She sat down beside him. "I did it because my lawyer needed evidence to prove infidelity, and it's all there in blazing technicolor. You know it's the only way I can get a divorce."

"Publicity like this will ruin me."

"No, it won't."

"I'm a leading man! A romantic lead!"

"Doing what you do best. It will enhance your reputation, if anything. This is a man's world. Just say you fell in love with Janette. I won't mention your other affairs, and we both know you've had them. I'm not interested in making you suffer."

He reached over and gulped the last of his drink. "And what if I decide to accuse you and Wallace of an affair? You left me for three months! Not exactly adoring wife behaviour. I could make things very difficult for you too, ya know."

"You have no evidence that I had an affair. My publisher arranged a business trip. I was working and have a new novel to prove it. You can be very selfish, Kurt, but deep down you're not a nasty person, and I don't believe you want to be mean to someone you say you love."

He looked at the pictures again before turning them over so he wouldn't have to see them. "Okay. You win."

"Neither one of us is winning, Kurt."

A sob escaped his lips. "I'm losing you. I never wanted that to happen."

"You'll be okay."

He looked up at her and wiped his eyes. "I'm sorry."

"I know."

Chapter
Twenty-Three

Bertha looked out her kitchen window at the swirling snow. It looked cold, but she was nice and toasty, with the dogs lying like lumps on the floor around the wood stove. She took a broom and gave them a shove on the bum with the straw end.

"How am I supposed to take these rolls out of the oven if I have to step over you two? Never mind breaking my neck outside in the dark. I'll do it right here in the kitchen."

They reluctantly got up, walked into the living room, and plunked in the front of the fireplace.

"There. Was that so hard?"

Argus groaned and hid his face with his massive paw.

"Don't give me any lip."

She took three dozen rolls out of the stove and brushed melted butter on the tops of them as they cooled on wire racks. Her seafood chowder simmered on the stove. As she was making it, she thought of Kitty, because she used the first of her preserving jars stuffed with lobster to add to the mix.

Wallace's truck pulled into the yard and she watched as he helped Ethel and Winnie into the house. It wasn't for their sakes, but her own. Winter days were long without as much company. She was happy to have someone to feed and was delighted when Winnie had agreed to come, saying she loved seafood chowder.

They trooped in calling, "Hello, hello!"

"Come on in, girls. It's almost ready."

Wallace helped them off with their coats and put a chair in the porch for them to sit on so they could safely take off their boots without falling over. They had brought slippers to wear.

"Why did this year have to be a leap year?" Ethel said. "An extra day of snow? Who needs it?"

"Well, it wouldn't be Cape Breton in the winter if we didn't have snow," Bertha said. "It hasn't been too bad so far."

"Excuse me. You're not the one shovelling it," Wallace said.

"You're not either. You've got a tractor."

"How do you think I get to the tractor? It doesn't shovel itself out of the shed. And I can hardly bring it up to the front door, so I have to shovel that. And Ethel's—"

"You're right. Sorry I spoke." Bertha pointed at the dogs, who showed up in the kitchen the minute they heard Wallace's voice. "Go on! Get! Back to the fireplace."

They moped back to their spots, but Wallace went with them and gave them some love.

The ladies settled in at the kitchen table. "How's your ankle, Winnie?"

"So much better, thank you. I'm not limping at all."

"Yes, you are," Ethel said. "You limp all the time."

"I've always limped because of my hip. That hasn't changed. She asked about my ankle."

"A limp is a limp."

Winnie shook her head at Bertha. "I swear, she'd argue with the devil himself."

"I would not!"

"You see."

"See what?" Ethel asked.

Bertha patted her hand. "She's teasing you. That's what big sisters do."

Ethel scowled. "She's some good at that, let me tell ya."

"What on earth would you do if you didn't have Winnie with you?"

"She's never with me. She's always in her room painting those blasted flowers."

"I'm painting snowscapes at the moment."

"But at least she's in the house if anything happened," Bertha reminded her. "You'd be mighty sad if you had to live there by yourself. Especially on cold winter days like this."

"I know. That's why she'd better not die."

Winnie laughed. "I'll try not to."

"On that note, supper's ready. Wallace?"

They enjoyed the chowder and polished off a dozen rolls between them, the lion's share going to Wallace. He'd been out in the elements all day. Then Bertha brought out her prized tea set and they had buttermilk cake with their hot cups of tea.

Winnie sat back when she was finished. "How did we get so lucky, Ethel? We live next door to the world's best baker."

"Oh, that's not mine. Wallace made it."

Ethel was all over that. "You made this, Wallace?"

"Mom was busy. I just stirred it and shoved it in the oven for her. No big deal, right, Mom?"

"Right. He was doing me a favour."

Winnie picked up a teacup. "I still love this set. The colours fascinate me."

"I must ask Kitty where she bought it next time I talk to her."

Wallace jumped up and went to his coat pocket, then reached over and handed an envelope to his mother. "I almost forgot. There's a letter for you from Kitty. I went to the post office first."

"Open it," said Ethel.

"No. It's private."

Ethel winked. "Tell me later."

Bertha suggested they play tarabish, but Ethel wasn't keen.

"Them trumps and bids and bells drive me foolish. How about cribbage?"

They played a few rounds of cribbage at the kitchen table, but Winnie was having a hard time keeping her eyes open. "I'm sorry. All that rich food is putting me to sleep."

It took about ten minutes for them to get themselves sorted, taking off their slippers and putting on coats and hats, boots and gloves. Wallace was able to get the dishes done while he waited. Then they thanked their hostess and bade her farewell, and he led them back out to the truck to drive them home.

Bertha sat in her chair by the fireplace and took off her glasses. She opened the envelope.

Sunday, February 26, 1956

Dearest Bertha,

It was so wonderful to talk to you recently, but I'm not going to risk a phone call with this bit of news. Since you were my ear about my marriage, I want to tell you that Kurt and I are getting a divorce. Goodness knows when it will be finalized—it's a very complicated procedure in this province—but at least the process has started. I did try to work things out when I got home, but it was obvious rather quickly that our relationship was never going to change. I know it's the right thing to do, but it's a very sad and lonely journey trying to extricate yourself from someone who used to mean everything to you. Even after all the nonsense he put me through, I have fond memories. You are the only person I know who probably understands how it feels. We never had a conventional marriage, what with me not being able to have children. I've always felt like a failure on that score, and now it seems I've failed at this. Even though it has to be done, the little girl who dreamed of having a happy family with babies and a white picket fence will always be sad that it's come to this.

What I wouldn't give to be sitting with you right now in front of the fire while you knit a baby sweater. I am missing my friends. The good news is that I'm living with my father. I'll write the address and phone number below. I think I gave it to you but in case you misplaced it. My biggest fear is you not being able to reach me!

I'm going to be okay. Don't worry about me. I just wanted you to know the latest. A big hug and kiss from me. Love Kitty xoxo

"Well, well, well," Bertha said out loud.

Both dogs lifted their heads in her direction and then ran to the kitchen when Wallace returned. He came into the living room and saw his mother still holding the letter.

"How is she?"

"She's getting a divorce."

Wallace collapsed into the nearest chair and stared at nothing.

"It's upsetting for her, obviously, even if she knows it needs to be done. Poor dear."

He didn't say anything.

"She says she's missing her friends, meaning all of us. Funny, she never mentioned having any girlfriends when she was here. She talked about Gaynor, but that's it. She doesn't have a mother or a grandmother or an aunt, it seems. This is the time when you need a mother hen around you."

Wallace stood up. "I'm going."

Bertha wasn't sure what he was talking about. "Going where?"

"To Montreal."

"Are you crazy?! You've never been off this island except to go to war. I know how you feel about this girl, but she's in no state to pursue a romance! The last thing she needs in her life right now is a suitor."

Wallace gave her a look, and started pacing the room, the dogs watching him with worried faces. "I'm not that insensitive. And that's not why I'm going. We're good pals, and I think she needs that at the moment. I've been blessed my whole life with a big family who yes, drive me crazy at times, but I've never had a lack of people to talk to. Can you imagine how lonely it must be to look for comfort and no one is there? I know she has her father, but she's had her issues with him."

"Can't you talk to her on the phone?"

"Sure. Kitty, Ethel, and I will have it hashed out in no time."

"Oh lord. But how will you know how to get there? Will the truck make it that far? It's getting old."

"That's true."

"And it's the middle of winter. You could run into all kinds of trouble on the road."

"Damn." He sank back in his chair.

"Wait! Why don't you take the train? Donna did it last year when she went to Montreal to visit her sister. Central Station is in the middle of the city. You wouldn't have to worry about driving in traffic. You can even get a roomette."

"That's a great idea. But I'm not wasting money on a room. I'm fine with sitting up all night. But I'll have to make arrangements for someone to be here with you every night."

"I can look after myself."

"Mom. You can't look after the dogs at night, and if there's a snowstorm you can't deal with it yourself. Between all of your many kids, I'm sure we can come up with a schedule what only inconveniences one sibling per night. I'll be gone a week. I can't afford to take off more time than that. Two days to get there, three days in the city, two days back. Is she still in the apartment?"

"No, she's moved into her dad's place. Will you stay there?"

"I'm sure they have an old chesterfield I can use. If not, I can stay at the YMCA."

"I can't believe I'm letting you do this."

"Letting me? I'm a grown man and I decide where I'm going."

She took a wad of tissue from her sweater sleeve and blew her nose. "But you've never left home before. You're my last chick."

"Good gravy."

"Will you let her know you're coming?"

"No. She'll tell me not to."

"Oh, dear. When will you leave?"

"As soon as I make the arrangements."

"This is all so sudden. I'm in a flap."

"I know what you can do."

She put the letter back in the envelope. "Yes, give me something to do."

"Make a box of baked goods for her. That way you'll be on the trip with me."

She jumped up and ran to the kitchen. "Good idea!"

"Not now! It's late. Start tomorrow. It's going to take a couple of days to get this organized."

She turned around, hugged him, and ran to her bedroom. "Goodnight! I have to make a list."

❦

Three days later Wallace's brother Charlie arrived to drive him to the train station in Sydney, their mom waving from the porch with the two dogs by her side until they were out of sight. He had one suitcase, which held his clothes, a letter from his mother for Kitty, a small painting of summer flowers from Winnie, several crocheted dishcloths from Ethel, pictures of the kids with Argus and Pride, and a snapshot of Ben in his snowsuit. He also carried a box of baked goods, all wrapped and labelled.

If Kitty couldn't get to them, they were coming to her.

Charlie kept giving him a sly look as they drove to Sydney. "Going to the big city to see your girl. Will wonders never cease."

"She's not my girl. She's a friend."

"Keep telling yourself that."

"Knock it off."

"Hey, I'm just thrilled that you're finally making a break from Mom's apron strings. I was losing hope that you'd ever have a life of your own."

"Charlie, just because my life doesn't resemble yours, is it worth less? I'm with Mom by choice, not because I have no other option. I've had plenty of opportunities to create a different future, but this is the one I want. I'm content exactly where I am. In South Head."

"Well, I hope you and your beautiful *friend* have a great time."

"She's in the middle of a divorce. We're not going to be whooping it up. But you're right." He smiled. "She is beautiful."

"I knew it! Don't think you can fool me, baby brother. You're just as much a sucker for a pretty face as the rest of us."

When they stopped, he reached down and took a camera out of a shopping bag on the floor of the truck. "Here, take mine. I know you don't have one. There's film in it and a couple of extra rolls."

"Hey, thanks, Charlie. I never thought of that."

As the train left the station, Wallace was excited. He looked forward to seeing his own country. But he wasn't quite as confident as he'd made it seem to his mother. He worried about what Kitty's reaction would be. Maybe he was interfering. And his motives weren't entirely pure, no matter how he tried to convince himself otherwise. He was dying to see her again. But he pushed that aside. He truly was going because he knew she needed him. That little bastard had had her stitched up for so long, no wonder she was confused about absolutely everything. The man could play anyone he wanted whenever it suited him. A forlorn child, a loving husband, a heartbroken spouse. Wallace had met manipulators before. Dolly was one, but not quite in Robert Chandler's league. And somehow these characters always managed to insinuate themselves into people's big hearts. Probably because they had no hearts of their own.

There was another reason he wanted to go. To make sure Kitty didn't slide backwards. The fact that she'd started the process was impressive, but she needed support to make sure she kept the barricades up.

He'd brought a book with him to read, *The Old Man and the Sea* by Ernest Hemingway. That was something he'd promised himself after Kitty left. To read more fiction. It was expanding his mind in ways he'd not thought possible. But on this journey, the window kept calling to him. The beauty of the landscape, the ocean of trees. Pulling into the stations in small towns, watching cars stopped by the flashing lights at railway crossings as the train hurtled by. The mechanical rhythm of the tracks lulling him to sleep and the sound of the train whistle as it rushed past farms with cattle gathered around the warmth of the barn. At one point there was a group of children building a snow fort and they stopped to wave at the passengers. Wallace waved back. Kids were the same everywhere.

He slept on and off through the night and in the morning grabbed a tea and ham and cheese sandwich from the cart before he locked himself in the toilet to have a quick wash and brush his teeth. They weren't getting into Montreal yet, but seeing Quebec City from a distance was amazing to him. To catch sight of it was an explosion to his senses, and he was only looking through a plate-glass window.

When he debarked in Montreal it felt like an assault. He was confused and unfamiliar with everything. People were in such a hurry, walking around him impatiently as he wandered about the cavernous space. Some spoke French; some, languages he'd never heard before. The noise was incredible, with bells and announcements over speakers of incoming trains. He needed to get out of here, but when he went up the escalator and out onto the street, he immediately panicked. Cars everywhere, horns blaring, sirens going off, buses rumbling by. People were even more impatient on the street, as he stood in the middle of the sidewalk looking at the towering buildings. He'd never seen anything so high in his life. He wanted to cover his ears, but that was impossible with his suitcase and box. He wanted to cover his eyes and pretend to be in his fields. There was nothing here but concrete.

He took a deep breath to calm himself. What had he expected? It was a city. He focused and looked around. There was a taxi stand on the corner, which was handy, but then he realized that a lot of people getting off a train would need to be taken somewhere. He was only one of many.

And most of the cabs were gone. He hurried to the one left. The driver indicated he could take him. Wallace opened the back door, put in his suitcase and box, and then got in the front seat. Or tried to.

"Mon dieu, Monsieur. You big guy! Not enough room up here. I put your things in the trunk. You sit in the back, d'accord?" He pointed to the back.

"Oh, okay. Sorry."

They were ready. The last time Wallace was in the back seat of a car, he was a kid. It felt awkward and strange.

"Où?"

"I beg your pardon?"

"Where to?"

"Oh, right." When he showed the man a piece of paper, he barely glanced at it. "Okay, monsieur. Aucun problème."

"There's a problem?"

The taxi driver looked at him in the rear-view mirror, his cigarette dangling from his lips. "Non! No problème. I will get you there."

Wallace's heart was racing. "Oh good. Thank you. I'm sorry, I don't speak French."

"French is the language of love. Amour! You should learn."

"I'll do that."

"Your first time in Montreal?"

Charlie warned him not to tell a taxi driver he'd never been there before because they could take him all over the city and he wouldn't know it. "No, I've been here many times."

Wallace saw the guy smirk. He wasn't fooling him.

It took only fifteen minutes to get to Milton Park with traffic, so her father was obviously close to downtown. The architecture was unlike anything Wallace had seen before. Their street was mostly greystone row houses with balconies and stairs and elaborate dormer windows. He thanked the driver and gave him a dollar tip. The driver smirked again. He must be a yokel. Was that not enough or too much?

It was a cold day, but Wallace was in a lather of sweat. Maybe this was a huge mistake. It had sounded so reasonable at home, but now it felt invasive. What if her father told him to take a hike? What if *she* told him to take a hike?

There was nothing else to do but go up the stairs and ring the doorbell. He held his breath. No answer. He rang it again. No answer. In all his daydreams she'd opened the door and fallen into his arms with gratitude.

Life was never what you imagined.

He had no choice but to sit on the step. Maybe Kitty and her dad were out of town. Why hadn't he thought of that? What would he do? As the minutes ticked by, he had all kinds of time to think about what a fool he was.

And then he saw her coming around the corner with the dogs. He got up and went down the steps to stand on the sidewalk. Pip began to yip and jump around trying to get to him. Kitty looked up, her hand went to her mouth, and she let go of Pip's leash. Pip ran down the sidewalk as fast as she could and jumped into Wallace's arms. She wiggled so much he had a hard time holding on to her.

Kitty picked up her white puffball and slowly came towards him. He smiled at her. She walked right into his one free arm and sagged against him. He patted her back.

"This is Pearl," she said.

"Hello, Pearl."

And then Pearl went nuts.

❦

They sat at the kitchen together eating Fat Archies with their cups of tea. Both dogs were at Wallace's feet.

"It's like your mom is right here!" Kitty clapped with delight before she grabbed another cookie.

"She sent you a letter, and I have a few other things I'll give you later."

"Oh, I can't wait!"

"Will your dad be home soon? I'm nervous. A complete stranger showing up. He might not be too pleased. I don't have to stay if he doesn't want me to."

"If he doesn't, he'll put you in handcuffs and cart you off to jail."

"That's a bit drastic."

She gave him a big grin. "He's a police detective. But I don't think he'll bother. He gets enough of that at work."

Wallace nodded. "Okay. Now I understand the Harry Gunn fascination."

"He wasn't around enough in real life, so I spent time with him in my books."

"And is he exactly like the character in your novels?"

"Smartass! No, I had to make a few changes. Harry Gunn drinks port, mumbles, and scribbles on napkins. Dad doesn't. But now that I think about it, he does drive a Volvo. And smoke a pipe. Gosh, he wears slippers too, and nicks himself shaving, but I'm sure there are a million other men who do the same thing."

"And he didn't mind being the inspiration for Harry Gunn?"

She folded her arms across her chest. "You're going to make me say it, aren't you? He's very proud of my books. The guys at work call him Gunner."

"Interesting."

"Okay, okay! You've made your point."

They laughed together. The dogs started to bark and ran out

315

of the room. "Oh, he's home. I never know when he'll show up. It's not exactly a nine-to-five job. Dad?"

"Yeah?" It sounded like he threw his car keys in a glass bowl.

"Come in the kitchen. I want you to meet someone."

"It better not be a new housekeeper."

Wallace stood up as soon Kitty's father walked in the room. He looked exactly like Wallace imagined a detective would look, with a large overcoat and a fedora in his hand. He was the complete opposite of Kitty, with her smooth skin and fine features. This man looked like he'd seen it all. A gruff, no-nonsense kind of guy, with blue eyes that could pierce you with his stare.

"Dad, this is my friend Wallace Bailey. Wallace, this is my father, Leo Faulkner."

They shook hands. Leo was solid and strong. His handshake was a doozy.

"How do you do, sir? It's nice to meet you."

"Welcome."

"Dad, Wallace came on the train all the way from South Head. He lives on the farm that was next to my place. He's never been here before. I know this is a surprise, but would it be okay if he stayed downstairs for the three days he's here?"

"She didn't know you were coming, son?"

"No sir. I should've told her, but I knew she'd tell me not to."

"And do you always do the exact opposite of what she'd tell you?"

Wallace could see Kitty tense up. "In this case, yes. Kitty would tell me to stay home because she knew it would take some planning for me to get here. But I was aware that she needed a friend at this moment in her life, and she and I are friends. I thought that out-weighed her opinion on the matter. And from her reaction when she saw me, I know I made the right decision."

Leo nodded. "Okay, sounds reasonable. He can stay. What's for supper?

Chapter Twenty-Four

Kitty woke up in the middle of the night to take Pearl outside for a quick pee. Pip didn't join them on these midnight runs anymore. And Pearl only needed to go out once, instead of twice. Kitty could probably get away with not taking the puppy out at all, but she was still wakeful sleeping in her old bedroom, and whenever she tossed and turned, Pearl would start to whine.

Kitty stood on the sidewalk and let Pearl sniff around the tree that grew opposite their front door, between the sidewalk and the street itself. The street lamps glowed all the way down the street and in each circle of light, she saw a soft snow falling. She hugged herself. Inside Wallace was sleeping. Wallace was here! She had thought she was dreaming when she saw his large familiar shape waiting for her. She'd walked to him, not wanting to run because she needed the moment to last. The only thing she felt when he put his arm around her was gratitude.

Of course he'd come.

After Wallace went downstairs for the night, Kitty got ready for bed herself and walked out of the bathroom still rubbing cream on her face. Her dad was waiting to get in.

"Thanks for letting him stay, Dad."

"It's your house too."

"So, tell me, what was your first impression when you met him?"

"That he could kill me with one blow. I wonder if he's ever considered a career with the police. They'd love to get their hands on someone like him."

"No. Not in a million years."

"He likes you."

"I like him."

"Hmph. Goodnight."

"Goodnight."

Kitty made porridge in the morning and Wallace declared it was as good as his mother's. "Is your dad not eating?"

"He's gone already, and left a note saying he won't be home for supper, which means he's in the middle of something big. Some nights he doesn't get home at all, just sleeps on a settee in the coffee room at the police station. He's used to the odd hours. Can I get you a cup of coffee?"

"You're drinking coffee now?"

"Yes. It's delicious with cream and sugar."

"Okay, I'll have some."

She poured them both a cup and opened a package of Bertha's raisin tea biscuits. "Oh my god. Heaven." She slapped the table. "I know what we can do! I want to show you around the city and when we go downtown, I'll take you to my publisher and you can meet Gaynor. I've got to bring her some of these goodies. She'll love me even more than she already does."

"All right, but you should save most of it for yourself."

"Oh, don't worry. I'm not that generous."

"I'll eat plain toast if you have it. I can eat these any old time."

"Braggart."

She made him toast and while she waited for it to pop up, she turned to him. Both dogs were trying to get up onto his lap. Pip won.

"Wallace, I know you came here because you think I'm sad and need someone to talk to, and I definitely do, but the one thing I don't want to talk about is Kurt. I want us to have a great time while you're here, and not waste a minute of it. That's what I need. Just to be carefree and not think about it at all."

"Suits me fine. Although I'm not sure about going downtown. It scared the life out of me."

"It's much nicer to be with someone who knows what they're doing. Think about how I needed you when I first got to South Head. Now you need me to find your way around this beautiful city."

"It might be beautiful, but it's too damn loud."

They took the dogs for a walk around the neighbourhood first.

"There are no yards. Your front doors are so close to the sidewalks."

"It looks pretty bare at the moment, but people do plant flowers along their walkways or under their windows. And when there are leaves on the trees, the whole street turns green."

"I can't imagine having other people so close to me. What do you do if you don't get along?"

"Fortunately, the two families on either side of us have been here almost as long as Dad. Because of his job, he doesn't have a wide circle of friends, but I know both guys next door would do anything for him. I remember Ted telling me once he felt safe with Dad around. I was proud of that."

Pearl decided to do her "I can't walk another step" routine and Wallace was the one who carried her home.

Kitty wrapped up two of everything. Fat Archies, raisin tea biscuits, pineapple squares, date squares, yum yums, coconut cookies, chocolate squares, and porcupines. She didn't slice up the spice cake. She arranged everything in a cookie tin with waxed paper between them and they filled it.

"I can't wait to see her face. Let's go. We'll take the bus. Trying to find parking downtown is a chore."

As they left, they looked back and saw both dogs on the chesterfield in the window watching them go. "I always feel guilty, but not as much as when Pip didn't have anyone with her. They'll curl up together on my bed. That's where I always find them when I sneak into the house."

To see Wallace on the bus made Kitty feel sorry for him. He was nervous, and she'd only ever seen him calm. He didn't fit in the seat comfortably, so when an elderly lady walked on he quickly got up and offered it to her. She didn't acknowledge him but sat in it anyway. He looked out the window and hung on to the bar above his head, swaying with the rhythm of the bus. At one stop a lot of kids came aboard and spent the entire time calling back and forth in French.

Kitty reached up and pulled the cord along the side of the bus above the windows and got to her feet. She hung on to the seat handles as she lurched to the back door, Wallace at her heels like a little kid, afraid she'd leave him behind. When they disembarked, she put her arm through his. "So, how was that?"

"Unnerving. Why did you go out the back door?"

"People get on in the front. It's easier for all concerned to leave out the back, unless you're sitting in the first few seats."

"Those kids were talking so fast."

"They were impressed with the size of you."

"Do you speak French?"

"Un peu. A bit. Not as much as I should. I understand it more than speak it. Not everyone in Quebec is from a French family. Faulkner is English, Anglo-Saxon descent. Let me give you a bit of a tour before we see Gaynor."

She pointed around as they walked. They went down Peel Street and wandered through Dorchester Square with its green space now covered with snow, looked at the monuments, and then strolled along Dorchester to look at the iconic SunLife Building on Metcalfe. They continued up to Mansfield Street, passing Mary, Queen of the World Cathedral. The statues of the patron saints of the parishes of Montreal atop the cathedral's main entrance fascinated him.

"Can you imagine the work that went into that?"

"You should see the inside, but we're running a little late. Gaynor will probably be gone for lunch if we keep stopping. We're almost there. Empire and Bloom is on Metcalfe."

"Wait. Is that Central Station up the street?"

"Yes! You see? You're not completely lost."

They went into the office building and Kitty started for the stairs.

"Can we go up in the elevator? I've never been in one."

When the elevator doors opened, he hurried out. "I never want to be in another one."

She laughed as she pulled open the doors to Empire & Bloom. Iris saw her first.

"Hi, Kitty."

"Hello, Iris. This is my friend Wallace."

"Nice to meet you."

"And you," he said.

Kitty looked over in front of Gaynor's door. "Oh no. Where's Dolores? Is Gaynor not here today?"

"She's here, driving me crazy. Poor old Dolores has an impacted wisdom tooth. She's off for a few days. I don't think your editor will survive if she doesn't show up tomorrow."

Gaynor's door flew open. "Iris! Where are those sales figures for the last three years for C. J. Faulkner? Speak of the devil. Kitty!" She stopped in her tracks and gave Wallace an exaggerated up-and-down perusal. "And you, my dear, have got to be the famous Wallace."

Kitty grinned. "Yes, he surprised me with a visit. Wallace Bailey, this is my editor, Gaynor Ledbetter."

"Nice to meet you, Gaynor."

She approached him with her hand out and while she shook his, she looked him in the eye. "You are responsible for my ulcer; I hope you know that."

"My abject apologies. I was totally in the wrong and should never have opened my big mouth."

"You are completely correct."

"You'll forgive him." Kitty held out the cookie tin. "He brought his mother's baking."

"You have complete absolution."

"Hey! Can't I even get a peek?" Iris said.

"Are you insane? Get back to work."

"Sheesh. I can't wait for Dolores to come back."

"I wondered if you'd like to go to lunch at Dunn's. I want Wallace to try our favourite. Smoked meat."

Gaynor looked at her watch. "It's almost noon. We should hurry if we want to get a table. Let me get my coat."

She ran back in the office and came out with her coat on, carrying her purse. She still had the cookie tin in her hand.

"Are you taking that?" Kitty asked.

"Yes! I don't trust the people around here. Remember, I want those sales figures on my desk when I get back," she said as she passed Iris.

They went down the stairs and heard Iris reply, "I'm not your secretary, remember?"

Kitty tsked. "You can give her one, surely."

Gaynor stuck out her tongue. "Maybe one."

Dunn's was around the corner. They certainly knew Gaynor, and just their luck, the seat at the window was being vacated and the waiter took them right over. The ladies sat looking towards the counter and stools so Wallace could watch the parade of people down the sidewalk.

"I have to open this," Gaynor said, gripping the tin.

"Don't! You'll eat everything now," Kitty told her.

"Wallace, what do you think I should do?"

"I'd have one. The trouble is picking which one."

Gaynor's eyes lit up. "How many different goodies are in here?"

"Around eight. She didn't cut up the spice cake."

She put the cookie tin in her lap. "The anticipation is part of the fun. I'll wait."

The ladies got a sandwich and Wallace got the smoked-meat

plate. A half a pound, with rye bread on the side, homemade fries, coleslaw, and a dill pickle. He ate every bite.

"Oh, man. Wait until I tell my brothers."

As they drank coffee, Gaynor and Kitty lit cigarettes. Gaynor offered one to Wallace. "No thanks. Don't smoke."

"You're a clean-living soul, aren't you? I bet you don't drink, either," Gaynor said.

"No, ma'am. My father did enough of that."

"Gotcha. So, did Kitty tell you her big news?"

Wallace looked surprised. "No. What news?"

Kitty made a face. "Gaynor, it's still too new. It might fall through."

"Nonsense! This child never blows her own horn. They're making a movie of her first book, with others to follow if it does well. Harry Gunn on the screen! Which is absolute gold for Empire and Bloom. If people like the movie, we'll get an avalanche of new readers."

"Wow! Congratulations," Wallace said. "Does Gunner know?"

"No, I haven't told him yet."

"Who's Gunner?" Gaynor asked.

"My dad."

"He's a detective," Wallace added. "And boy, he sure looks like one."

Gaynor's mouth dropped open. "Are you serious?"

"You didn't know?" Wallace looked at Kitty. "I'm sorry. I shouldn't have said anything."

"How come you never told me that, missy? I've always wondered why a young woman would gravitate to stories about murder investigations."

"It was my way of spending my days with him. He was always wrapped up in his job. Not much time for a growing girl. I mean, I knew he loved me, but a person needs more than that, don't they?"

"Oh, hell, Kitty." Gaynor frowned. "I'm sorry. You really have been hiding."

"I kept it private. And now my father and I are slowly repairing our relationship, so I don't resent spending so much time with Harry Gunn instead of my real dad. He's with me, or I'm with him, at the moment. We're having a good time now that Martha's gone. Harry Gunn can go back to being just another character."

Gaynor looked confused. "Martha? I thought she was your mother-in-law?"

"She is."

"Then why..."

"Did she live with my dad? She was his live-in housekeeper, and I thought they were an item because she never moved out of his house when Kurt and I left."

"Kurt lived in your house?"

"Yep. He and Martha moved in when I was seven, after my mom died. She was a great housekeeper but a lousy companion."

"You've known Kurt since you were seven?" Wallace said. "I know you said you were young when you met, but he lived in your house?"

Gaynor rubbed her temple. "If you gave this to me in a manuscript, I'd tell you to stop being so far-fetched. Hells bells, what a tale of woe. And now I can see why Kurt is so upset about you leaving him. Not that he doesn't deserve it, but he's probably just as emotionally attached to you as you are to him, growing up in the same house together."

"Now that you say that, I guess that's why I've always given him the benefit of the doubt. He was my first friend."

Kitty saw Gaynor and Wallace look at each other. "Stop it! I'm not going to change my mind. I'm ending my marriage."

"I think you have a lot do with that, Wallace," Gaynor said.

Kitty and Wallace gave each other a quick, guilty glance.

"What do you mean?" he said.

"You and your family. When she spent time in the company of people who have a happy home life, she took a long hard look at her own. She needed that."

They couldn't linger at the table any longer. There was a line of people waiting. Wallace offered to pay and Gaynor refused. "This is what we call a business lunch. I write this off on company expenses."

Out on the sidewalk, Gaynor shook Wallace's hand. "I really enjoyed meeting you, Mr. Bailey. I can see why Kitty thinks you're wonderful. Well, actually, she thought you were a rotten louse when she first came back, but that has obviously changed. Goodbye, dear. Talk soon." She gave Kitty one of her brief half kisses and marched off up the street with her cookie tin.

Kitty grabbed Wallace's arm once more. "Well, what did you think of my intrepid editor?"

"I'd get a massive headache if I had to spend all day with her."

Kitty smiled as they started down the street. "She's something, all right."

"She thinks the world of you, so she's all right in my books. Get it? Books."

They strolled along Sainte-Catherine Street and went into Ogilvy's. Wallace wanted to pick something up for his mother. "Something I can pack in a suitcase."

Kitty picked out a very pretty ivory dressing gown. She held it up. "What do you think?"

"I think she won't wear it. It'll get dirty around the wood stove and the dogs will slobber all over it."

"That doesn't mean you shouldn't get her something nice."

"I know! She always said she wanted something called a bed jacket. I have no idea what that is."

"Perfect. It keeps you warm when you're in bed at night reading. No dogs or wood stoves in her room."

The one they picked was a quilted pink satin with tiny white flowers. Kitty made sure it was in an extra-large size.

When they found themselves out on the street again, Wallace holding a green tartan bag, Kitty said, "Where to now?"

"Could we go home and see the dogs?"

They got back on the bus and Kitty saw Wallace's eyes closing as he stood holding the metal post by her seat. It wasn't easy being in a different environment. He wasn't used to hectic.

After supper the phone rang. It was Gaynor.

"Simon is in tears over Bertha's baking. We tried not to eat the whole thing but alas, we were weak. Please thank Wallace for us. And my god, honey, for the record, what a specimen he is!"

"Goodnight, Gaynor." She hung up and sat back down in her father's chair. Wallace was on the chesterfield with the two dogs hugging him closely.

"Gaynor says to thank your mother very much for the baking. They ate the entire tin."

"What's her husband like?"

"Eccentric. Excellent professor of English at McGill. They don't have children, by choice, but dote on a bassett hound named Jersey May. She's a sweetie."

"McGill is near here?"

"A hop, skip, and a jump."

"I always wanted to take a university course in philosophy, but I don't think I'm cut out for it. Reading from home seems to be my way of doing things."

"Don't sell yourself short."

"Kitty, I can tell after only one day here that I'm not meant to be around crowds of people or small spaces. The taxi, the bus, the elevator, the restaurant, I felt my heart racing. I've always thought of myself as a calm person, but that's because I live exactly where I need to. I'm a fish out of water here, and not just here. I think any city would bug me. I'm happy to get home after I've been in Sydney, so what does that tell you? The thought of sitting uncomfortably at a small desk in a classroom of young people gives me the willies."

"Well, now you know. Would you rather not go sightseeing?"

"I think I can manage for two days. It would be slightly pathetic if I came here and saw nothing."

For the rest of the trip Kitty drove them to the locations she wanted him to see: Notre-Dame Basilica, Mount Royal, Saint Joseph's Oratory, Chinatown, along the waterfront of the St. Lawrence River, down by the old port and through Old Montreal, with its narrow-cobbled streets. He liked Old Montreal the best.

"I can't get over the architecture here. All these old brick and stone buildings with elaborate stonework just for beauty's sake. I always loved the old town hall in Glace Bay. This is what it reminds me of."

"On our way home, I can show you Westmount, where the rich live. The higher up the mountain you go, the bigger the houses."

"I believe you, but I'm pooped. Can we go home to the dogs?"

※※

It was their last night together, and Kitty's father called to say he'd be late for dinner, not to wait, but he hoped to be home around nine.

"Do you think he's staying away on purpose? Maybe he doesn't like me."

Kitty doled out their cheeseburgers and fries. "Nonsense. It's just the nature of his job."

Wallace wasn't sure if he believed her, because she appeared to be a little anxious. Or maybe she was tired, too, after dragging him around for three days straight.

They enjoyed their meal and took their tea and slices of spice cake into the living room. The dogs mooched for the cake so Kitty gave them a slice too. Once that was finished, she cleared her throat and held her hands in her lap. It seemed to him she was preparing to say something she'd rehearsed.

"Wallace, I want you to tell me honestly why you came on this trip. I know you said it was to see if I was okay, but it's a long journey for someone who's never travelled for fun, and an even longer one for someone who's never left the nest."

"Left the nest?"

"Sorry, your mom's words, not mine."

Sometimes living with a mother wasn't great. He rubbed Pearl's ears. "What else did she say in her infinite wisdom?"

"That she's proud of you. That I'm lucky to have such a wonderful chum. She's totally right. I'll never find a better one. But why did you come?"

He could tell she was begging him to tell her the truth, whatever that truth was. He took a deep breath. "You told me right away that you didn't want to talk about Kurt or your marriage, so that's a lot not to talk about. Especially when we agreed that if we wanted to figure out us, you had to go home and deal with it one way or the other. Well, it seems like you've made your decision, so I guess I wanted to find out where I stood. I told myself I was coming to make sure you were okay. You told mom in your letter that you were missing your friends. So here I am. Your friend. But I suppose I also want to know if I'm more than a friend."

She lowered her head and let out a long sigh. "That's what I thought. Thank you for being honest." She chewed her thumbnail and stared into space.

"It's okay, you can tell me. I have a feeling I know the answer anyway," he said.

She ran her hand through her hair and sat up straight. "I'm going to be just as truthful. When I first saw you, it felt like all the people I've been missing in South Head were standing there with you. That world I love. Sometimes it still feels like a dream. I was so very grateful to be able to touch it again. If you'd asked me in that moment to go back with you, I probably would've. That's how much it meant to me."

"I've always had lousy timing."

"These last three nights I haven't been able to sleep much. My brain keeps clicking over. My honest answer is, I don't know where you stand. But standing up for myself is where I need to begin." She leaned forward and clasped her hands together. "Honestly, I can't think about you. I have to worry about the little girl who's been missing her mother and brother and father. Who wanted a normal family like you enjoy and who ended up with a very odd one."

She looked down and hesitated, before raising her head. "And that has taken a big toll on me. I have no idea who I am or what I want, but everything I need to fix is here. The movie project is going on, I'm trying to sort out my relationship with my father, and that needs a lot of work because it's not going to fix itself. I have to be here and make sure he's holding up his end of our bargain. Not to mention helping him transition into the next part of his life. Either fix this place up or buy another. Hire him another housekeeper, because I won't be living with him forever. I have a divorce to finalize." She sagged back against the chair. "God, there is too much taking place to even think about us. I left in December and it's only March. Not a lot of time to figure out something this big, wouldn't you say?"

"You are totally right, and I can't believe I even thought that you'd have an answer for me. I'm ashamed—"

"Knock it off. You're the best person in my life. After Pip and Pearl, naturally, and I suppose I should throw in Dad for appearances' sake."

"I'm very glad I came, because now I get to picture you at home and at work. To meet your friends and your father has given me a bigger sense of you. I'll be able to picture what you're talking about when we write to each other."

"I'm so very glad you came too, Wallace. It's the nicest gift I've ever received. And I'll never forget it."

Leo came in at nine and looked done in.

"Bad day?" Kitty asked him.

"Don't ask. I have to leave early in the morning, so I might be gone before you leave, Wallace. Have a safe trip home and thank you for coming to see Catriona. She did need a pal." He approached him with an outstretched hand.

Wallace took it and almost flinched at the strength of it. "Thank you for your hospitality, sir. I appreciate it."

Leo pulled his hand closer, leaned in with an unsmiling face, and said under his breath, "Back off, son."

Saying goodbye to the dogs was hard. Saying goodbye to Kitty was tougher. She took him to the station and insisted on waiting around until his train was called.

"Please thank your mother and make sure to tell Ethel and Winnie that I loved their gifts and as soon as I go home, I'm putting the pictures of the kids and the dogs on the fridge so I can see them every day."

"I can't wait to see how my snaps came out."

They did that thing people do when they know they have to say goodbye to someone but don't want to. They looked around and made awkward small talk.

"You've got everything?"

"I think so."

"Charlie's picking you up?"

"Yeah. What are you doing today?"

"Not much. I'll take the dogs for a walk."

"I looked at your backyard. It's not big, but if you put a fence around it, it's enough for the dogs to enjoy under the tree. Plenty of shade in the summer. Wouldn't cost that much."

"Good to know."

His train was announced, and the people waiting at the gate with their suitcases got up off the few seats that were available. Those who had been milling around organized themselves into a crooked line for the conductor to check their tickets before they descended down the stairs to the railway platform below.

"So, this is it," he said. "Thanks for everything. I had a great time."

She gave him a huge hug and pressed her cheek against his chest. "Thank you. Thank you."

He knew he had to go. He gave her a quick smile and joined the line. She looked like she was going to stay until he went through, but suddenly she blew him a kiss and hurried away.

He got himself sorted in coach. It was easier because he wasn't carrying a box. No one sat next to him, probably because he took up too much space, and he was glad. He waited in the darkened tunnel, the sounds of the train getting ready for its journey occupying his mind because he didn't want to think. He watched as conductors walked up and down the platform directing people still trying to find their cars.

Eventually the first jolt of movement and the slow forward motion of this iron horse pulling out of the tunnel began. The rail-yard was a confusing labyrinth of tracks with railcars parked on both sides. The back end of the city behind the street facade looked dirty and grimy. Industrial. But as they snaked out from the station and away from the shadows of the surrounding structures, the light shone and the glistening office towers with their many windows came into view and the beauty of the city revealed itself once more.

Wallace could appreciate this vibrant world, but he knew he didn't belong here.

He didn't read on the way back either, content to watch the world go by out the window, his head resting on the pane of glass. He dozed for most of the journey and slept deeply at night when the windows were dark and the carriage lights turned down. He didn't have any appetite. As the world outdoors became more familiar and he knew he was in Nova Scotia, his breathing got deeper, easier.

What is it about the body? It recognizes home.

When he disembarked, the air was immediately familiar. He was very happy to be walking towards Charlie, who held up his hand in greeting and thumped the back of his shoulder. "How's she goin', b'y? Good time?"

"Yeah, it was great. Took lots of pictures. Thanks for the camera. How's Mom? Did she cope okay?"

"Believe it or not, we managed to keep her alive and well while you were gone. But we're not sure if Argus and Pride will ever be the same. They just about drove her nuts with their whining and staring out the windows."

"I can't wait to see them." Wallace put his suitcase in the back of the truck and got in as Charlie turned the key and put it in drive.

"So how's Kitty? Glad to see you?"

"Oh yeah. She was very surprised, and we did a lot of sightseeing. Her father's a little scary. He's a police detective, a murder investigator. Think Dragnet."

"Shit. You better be on your best behaviour, little brother."

"And get this. Her first novel is being made into a movie."

"You're pullin' my leg."

"Nope."

"She writes novels? A movie?"

"Yep."

"What the hell is she doing running around with your sorry ass?"

"Beats me."

His mother was very happy to see him, but not as happy as the dogs. It's quite the experience to be lovingly assaulted by two furry giants at the same time. They would not leave him alone, and of course his mother twittered around him, wanting to know everything.

"Mom, I'm taking the dogs for a walk to clear my head. I've been sitting down for two days. I'll be back and tell you all about it."

"I've got Salisbury steak, gravy, and mashed potatoes for supper."

"Great."

Out he went, the dogs prancing around him in a glorious reunion. He headed across the field down to the water, breathing in the ocean air as if he'd never have enough. The water was navy blue with whitecaps, the wind brisk. He stood on the shore and held out his arms, letting the gusts almost blow him off his feet. The anxiety that had seeped into his skin when he stepped off that train in Montreal and filled his senses with dread was now being battered by this blessed sea breeze. He was coming back to himself.

Wallace knew he was important to Kitty, but that was all. His life was here and hers was there. Knowing that made it easier to let her go.

Chapter Twenty-Five

As it turned out, Kitty the writer couldn't write to Wallace. She tried to, but every time she did, she'd squish up the paper and throw it out, so she called him instead, keeping the conversation light. Just checking in. He called back on occasion, but there was really never anything to say. She got more information talking to Bertha, but even then, it was never anything personal because of Myrtle Lovett.

One day Kitty decided to phone Ethel as a surprise and almost called her Myrtle instead.

"M-Ethel? It's Kitty."

"Titty? KITTY! You've called the wrong number."

"No, I wanted to see how you and Winnie are doing. I hope everything is well."

"Oh, yes, dear. The weather's warming up a bit. Blackie sits on the step now after hibernating all winter. He scratched my ankle the other day when I went to the post office. Didn't even feel it, so that's a bit worrisome. Winnie wants me to go to the doctor to check my circuits."

"Your circulation?"

"Yes. She's a worrywart."

"I hope you do. Any gossip for me?"

"Dolly tried to hire Wallace to put in her new kitchen sink and was some miffed when he said he did everything but the kitchen sink. Ya gotta hand it to her. She never gives up."

"How's Wallace doing?"

"Fine, fine. Always busy. Putting stakes in the ground the other day. Probably going to build another shed when the ground softens up. Bertha's expecting another great-grandchild, so she's knitting herself silly. Everything okay with you? How's that divorce coming along?"

"It's chugging away. Nothing to do but wait for a private Act of Parliament."

"Parliament? As in Ottawa? What do those ruffians have to do with it?"

"It's the law in Quebec, but it's safely in the hands of a lawyer. I'll keep out of it until I sign on the dotted line and it's done."

"I never knew a divorced woman before. What do they call you? A floozy?"

"Floozy sounds about right. I'd better go, Ethel, someone might want to use the line."

"Probably that Donna one. Always sticking her nose in everyone's business."

"Goodbye, Ethel! Give my love to Winnie!"

"If I see her I will. Goodbye, dear."

Kitty hung up and leaned back in her chair. Talking to Ethel was a boost to her spirit.

That first month she and her father learned a few things about each other. Like how they were both stubborn mules. Every night after work, if he came home at a decent hour, she'd have supper for him and a list of things to work on, or decisions to be made.

"I hate that notebook," he growled when she produced it at the kitchen table over a plate of liver and onions.

"Never mind. It's my only chance to talk to you, unless I accompany you to a crime scene, which I might do now that I'm trying to write this first draft. When I spent three days with that screenwriter Claude set me up with, he made it sound effortless. It's driving me mad."

"Make it easy for yourself. Kill me off in the first ten minutes."

"That would make a brilliant movie. The hero dies after the opening credits. Okay, first I want to know with absolute certainty that you want to stay in this house. You don't want to move, find a smaller place? Remember you're getting old."

"Damn it, I'm fifty-five. Not quite ready for the slag heap yet. And no, I don't want to move! I want to stay in this house until someone drags me out of here feet first, which will probably be you. Keep hounding me and I'll have a heart attack."

"Okay. You're not moving. But this place needs to be spruced up. Nothing has been done to it in twenty-five years. The whole place needs a fresh coat of paint, new curtains, the carpets ripped up, the kitchen linoleum definitely needs to be replaced, and your appliances are on their last legs. The kitchen wallpaper has to go—"

"You said you'd wallpaper long ago, but you've been too busy. How are you going to get all this done, with the screenplay eating up your time?"

Kitty looked at him with incredulity. "DAD. You honestly have no clue about anything. I'm not going to do all that. And since you don't do anything but chase bad guys, you're not doing it either. I'm hiring professionals."

"That costs money."

She pointed at him. "You have spent nothing on this place since Mom died. How do you think she'd feel if she knew how badly you've neglected this house? One she loved, or so you keep saying. She'd be ashamed, that's what. You're spending the money and that's that. You're also building a fence in the back, so the dogs can go outside. It won't cost much. I'll be here to oversee things, but not for long."

"What do you mean?"

"I love this house because I love you and Mom, but I hate this house because of Martha. I can't sleep here. I'm going to buy my own little house with a fenced-in yard. Somewhere close by. Signing that movie contract will let me do that."

"But—"

"I'm not living here, Dad. But before I go, I'm interviewing housekeepers, who will definitely not be living here either. I know what you want and need and I'll make sure I find someone suitable."

"When did you get so goddamn bossy?"

"You just never noticed. Remember, we have a lunch date tomorrow."

"But we're seeing each other now. Are we still doing lunch dates if you live with me?"

"Yes. It's practice. Father-daughter time, like you promised. And you did promise."

"Fine. Pea soup?"

—◦◦—

It took Kitty a week to organize the manpower for the renovations. She ended up conducting her first interview for a housekeeper on April Fool's Day in her bedroom, since they were ripping up carpets in the living room and stripping wallpaper in the kitchen. They'd even started to paint in the hallway and bathroom. She perched at the edge of the bed, a dog on either side, and the first lady sat on her desk chair.

"I apologize for this. We're obviously having work done. So my father is looking for a housekeeper. He doesn't want anyone to live in."

"Good. My husband will appreciate that."

"He wants the place clean, laundry and ironing done, and a meal at the end of the day."

"I'm a housekeeper. Not a cook."

Next.

This woman was such a chatterbox, Kitty knew that even limited contact with her would drive her father foolish, so she thanked her, and the woman was still talking as she went out the door.

The one after that seemed promising. Until she asked what her father did.

"He's a detective."

She stood up. "I ain't workin' for no stinkin' cop. My Larry's in jail because of those bastards."

Kitty couldn't help it. "And what did Larry do?"

"He robbed a bank, but he only drove the getaway car. He wasn't carrying the gun."

Pip growled.

A close call.

It was late in the afternoon when the last woman for the day arrived, a neat little bird. She had on a hat, gloves, and a flowered scarf tucked around the neck of her coat. Her grey hair was perfectly done and she even wore small gold earrings. She could be a church organist. A definite lady.

The workmen had gone for the day, so Kitty took her into the kitchen. "I'm sorry the place is a bit of a tip. We're having work done. Please sit. And don't mind the dogs. They obviously like you."

"Thank you. I love dogs." She reached out and patted their heads before she put her purse on her lap and folded her hands over it. She had a lovely Irish brogue.

"Your name again?"

"Mary. Mary Brennan."

Kitty looked up at her. Her name was Mary. Whenever Kitty ran into someone named Mary, she always lingered by them, as if the name itself meant that her mother was close by.

"It's nice to meet you. My mother's name was Mary."

"Oh dear. She's no longer with you?"

"No. She died when I was seven."

Mary tsked and shook her head. "What a terrible shame for a little girl."

Kitty felt like she was talking to an Irish Bertha. "Mary, I'm conducting this interview for my father. He owns this house. I'm staying with him temporarily, but hopefully I'll find a place of my own soon. He works crazy hours, so you probably won't even see him. He wants someone to make the bed, dust and hoover, wash and iron his clothes, keep the bathroom clean, do the dishes, even scrub the floors and windows when necessary. And he'd like to have a meal on the table when he gets home. Because his hours are so unpredictable, you could make him supper and leave it in the fridge for him to heat up later. He only drinks coffee in the morning and grabs a bite downtown for lunch, so there's no other meals to worry about."

"That sounds fine."

"And I know this sounds crazy, but if you agree to work here, could you leave the lights on when you go for the day?"

"So he feels like someone's home when he returns from work."

"Exactly."

Just then the door opened and the dogs ran out to greet the man himself. She didn't expect him so soon. "Dad? Come in the kitchen. I want you to meet someone."

"It better not be a new housekeeper."

Kitty reached out her hand to Mary. "It's okay, it's a private joke."

He appeared in the doorway and took off his hat.

"Dad, this is Mary Brennan. She might be your new housekeeper if you don't scare her off."

He crossed the floor and shook her hand. "Nice to meet you, Mary. I'm Leo Faulkner. Henpecked father."

Mary smiled. "You have a lovely daughter, Mr. Faulkner. She wants what's best for you."

"Indeed."

"She tells me you have an unpredictable work schedule. Something I was very used to. My late husband was a detective here in the city. I know all about it."

Her dad took a step back and looked completely shocked. "Paddy Brennan? You're Paddy's Mary?"

Her face lit up. "Yes! Did you know Paddy?"

"I guess I did! I worked under him years ago."

"You're a detective too?"

"Yes. Paddy was only five years older than we were, but he was always the one we looked up to and asked for advice. He had a fatherly way about him that made you feel safe."

"That's my Paddy. Such a fine man. I miss him."

"Well, my god. This is fantastic. Let me make you a cup of tea, Mary. Do you like spice cake? Kitty has a few slices left in the freezer." He took off his coat and buzzed around filling the kettle and getting cups.

"That would be lovely, Leo. Thank you. I can't believe you knew my Paddy. I miss talking about him."

Kitty left quietly. She was obviously not needed. She took the dogs for a walk just so she could smile and gloat to herself. She literally clapped her hands as the two Ps had a pee. Sometimes the world turned out exactly right.

❦

Kitty spent the next month looking for a place to live, but it had to be near her father, near Mount Royal Cemetery, near Gaynor's home and office, and have a fenced-in yard. She could tell her real estate agent was fed up with her. Nothing was quite right; everything was too far away.

"If you want a single dwelling, you have to be prepared to move further out from the city centre, like maybe the NDG area. The single houses here are out of your price range. Are you sure you don't want to look at a row house or a duplex?"

"Look, all I want is a little house with a kitchen, living room, bedroom, and bathroom. And a loft."

"A loft?"

"Never mind."

He called up very excited one day. "I think I've found it! It's just a mile outside your preferred area, a small bungalow on a cul-de-sac. A bit rundown and no loft or fence, but it's the closest I've seen to your requirements."

She took one look at it and the surrounding dwellings and sighed. "I don't want to leave the house for groceries and be killed by a stray bullet. Something that will happen thanks to the drug mules who obviously live on this street."

"I'll keep looking."

Kitty pulled up behind her father's Volvo and parked in front of the house. She was tired, discouraged, and getting nowhere. What was she going to make her father for supper? All she wanted to do was crawl into bed with a bowl of Cheerios and sulk.

She walked into the house to be greeted by two happy dogs. That's when she realized the workers had packed up and left. Without the equipment around she finally had a sense of the total package. The place was unrecognizable. She'd obviously seen the progress, but because it was in such a jumble for so long, she'd stopped looking. Just changing the paint from a beige to a warm ivory brightened up the entire space, and the shiny wooden floors that had been covered for years with old carpet made it seem like an entirely new house.

Then she realized a wonderful aroma was coming from the kitchen. She poked her head in and there was Mary at the stove stirring something in a pot. Her father was at the table reading the paper.

"Mary?"

"Hello, dear."

"Did you forget she was starting today, now that the renovations are finished? Notice how clean everything is?"

"It looks fantastic. And this new floor is so shiny. The whole place looks like a different house. I told you it was a good idea, Dad. Look how this wallpaper cheers everything up. Of course, the new appliances help with that."

"I have to admit it looks good," her dad said, taking in the turquoise fridge and stove.

"What's on the menu?" Kitty leaned over and took a sniff.

"Irish stew, of course."

"I hope you'll join us for dinner. Seems a shame to make this and then leave," her dad said.

"Oh dear, thank you, but I must get home. I have two fat cats to feed." Mary took off her apron and gathered her things.

"Would you like a drive home? Obviously this doesn't happen often, but I'd be happy to when I'm here. It will save you a ride on the bus. You live in Saint-Henri, as I recall. I drove Paddy home one day. Are you still in the same place?"

"Oh yes. I can't leave my Paddy's house."

"I know just how you feel."

They left without a backward glance. Forgot all about saying goodbye to her. Kitty looked at the dogs. "Can you believe that?" She turned off the stove and took the dogs for their walk while she waited for her dad to return.

When she walked back in the front door, she had the same reaction. It wasn't Martha's house. She was nowhere in these rooms. Kitty went downstairs to Martha's bedroom, just to make sure. The paint had transformed this level as well. She'd thrown out the pillows, sheets, and blankets on Martha's bed, but she'd left the things in Kurt's room alone.

When her father came back, he seemed chipper. "You know, hearing Mary talk about Paddy brings back a lot of memories. Those were good years on the force."

Kitty ladled the stew onto plates and put them on the table. They blew on their forks and took a mouthful, then grinned at each other.

"You did a hell of a job finding the right person, Catriona."

"As soon as she said her name was Mary, I knew she was, even without knowing your connection. I hate to ask, but did her poor husband die on the job?"

"No, thank God. He found out he had cancer and ten days later he was dead. Everyone at the station was devastated. No one could believe it happened so fast. But I'm glad for his sake. He wasn't the type of man who would tolerate being sick or pitied."

"Did they have kids?"

"No. It was always just the two of them. He talked about Mary all the time. And I talked about my Mary constantly. The guys would get sick of it. I didn't care and Paddy understood."

"Well, this is at least something I can be happy about."

"What's wrong?"

She leaned back in her chair and groaned. Both dogs lifted their heads to make sure she was okay. "I'm having a miserable time finding a house."

"I could've told you that. You keep saying you want to be near me, near the cemetery, near Gaynor and Empire & Bloom. That leaves only one place. Here."

"But I want to move because I keep thinking this is Martha's house."

"Does it look like Martha's house? You've done a hell of a job erasing her, too. And by the way, it was never her house."

"She made sure I thought it was."

"You're not a little girl anymore, and she's not the boogeyman. She can't hurt you. You don't need to move, Kitty. Your home is right here."

Now she got upset. "But if I stay here, you won't need Mary, and now that we've found her, I don't think you should let her go. She's going to make this place so much nicer for you to come home to. You've talked to her more in two days than you did to Martha in two decades."

"Why does she have to leave if you stay?"

"Well, I can obviously cook for you, and clean. Not as well as she does." She held her head up with her hand, but took another bite of stew anyway.

Now her father put down his fork and crossed his arms over his chest. "Let's look at the facts. I have a career. I don't have time to clean and cook. You have a career. You don't have time to clean and cook. Mary will be needed more than ever. You are more than welcome to contribute to her raise in pay for the extra work involved taking care of two people, not one. Living under this roof doesn't mean you're just my Catriona. C. J. Faulkner lives here too. The writer and screenwriter. A grown woman I am extremely proud of. This will work. And your mother would be very happy."

Kitty jumped up and landed in his lap, crying her eyes out. "That's the nicest thing you've ever said to me!"

"What?"

"I have a career! I'm not just fooling around in my study to keep myself from dying of boredom and loneliness. I've always felt like a fraud saying I'm a bestselling author. Like someone made a mistake. But this is a career. Gaynor's been trying to tell me that for years and I wouldn't listen. I've been so obstinate."

"You can stop crying now."

"No! Get used to it, old man. I'm giving myself permission to burst into tears at a moment's notice. It feels wonderful. You should try it."

"Ah, no thanks." He passed her a napkin. She took it and went back to her seat. They resumed eating their meal. Then she held up her finger. "Wait. If I'm living here, I want that fence built, like, yesterday."

"When did you get so goddamn bossy?"

Chapter
Twenty-Six

It was the first week of July when Kitty remembered she needed business cards, now that she knew her permanent address and phone number. And the only reason she did remember was because she had a meeting at the end of the week with Miles at Un Film Bien, and she wanted to surprise him with one.

The day before the meeting, she took the bus downtown to pick up the cards. The printer told her to order at least two hundred, they were cheaper that way. The thought of giving out two hundred cards seemed preposterous, but hey, she liked cheap. The cards themselves were a linen colour instead of white. She'd never liked white business cards; they were too stark in her mind. The card had her professional name, *C. J. Faulkner, Writer*, with her phone number along with Gaynor's office number. "Dolores is always here. She can take a message when you're walking the dogs."

It was a glorious summer day, not a cloud in the sky. Almost too hot on the pavement. There was no time like the present, so she hopped on another bus and got off on Mansfield, hurrying up the stairs to Gaynor's office. Dolores had a big smile for her. "Hi, Kitty. Lovely day."

"Yes, indeed. I keep popping in, but I should make an appointment. Is Gaynor available?"

"She's here, but she's in a meeting. If you don't mind waiting."

"Not at all. Thanks. Oh, you'll be the first person I give my new business card to. I'm a real writer now."

She held out the card and Dolores took it. "Nice."

"That sounds like I'm showing off, but I'm trying to get over that mindset. Gaynor hates it. Here's one for you too, Iris. Just because."

"We're a matched set. Thank you."

At that moment Mel came out of his office. "Hey, you! What are you doing here?"

"I've come to give Gaynor my new business card. Would you like one?"

"Certainly." He looked at it. "Come on into the office for a second. I have news."

She sat across from him as he took his seat. "Firstly, how's the screenplay coming?" he asked.

"It's done. I have a meeting with one of the producers tomorrow to discuss it." She sat up straighter, crossed her legs, and adjusted her skirt. "It's a very different beast, writing a movie script. You're writing by committee. Everyone has a hand in it and you have to keep them happy for one reason or another. There's no just doing what you want, more's the pity. One page equals one minute of film, so you're constantly aware of that. Ninety pages only for an hour-and-a-half movie. Yikes!" She tossed her head back and laughed. "Not only that, but you have to think visually. A lot of dialogue can be eliminated with an actor's one glance. I've had the script editor send it back with whole pages crossed off." She slashed her hand through the air. "*Not needed. Not needed.* I did tell them I'd never done one before and it didn't seem to worry them, but I doubt there will be a lot of my writing left once the professional gets his hands on it."

"Still, what an opportunity. Not many authors get to write a screenplay for their own novel."

"Very true. I need to remember that. So, what's your news?"

"*One Long Ring Around the Rosey* will be released in the middle of October, just in time for Christmas sales, and we've got a big campaign planned. And we'll know more about the film's release by then."

"They haven't even cast it yet. Isn't that premature?"

"I've been in touch with Claude Racine of Un Film Bien. He says he'll keep me in the loop. They are obviously anxious to capitalize on all your loyal readers as a built-in audience for the film. It's going to be a win-win. And it's never too soon to start promoting in this business."

There was a brief knock at the door and Gaynor appeared. "You've kidnapped my author. Is the ransom me taking everyone to lunch?"

"I'd love to, but I'm up to my neck. Take Kitty somewhere nice." He reached over his desk to shake Kitty's hand. "Congratulations, my dear." He held up her business card. "Your future is very bright indeed."

Somewhere nice turned out to be a hole in the wall that served Montreal hot dogs known as steamies, with fat crispy french fries and bottles of Coke. They sat in the corner away from the crowd on stools at the counter and made a complete mess trying to keep the toppings on the dogs. Gaynor even wanted sauerkraut on hers.

"I think Mel was thinking more along the lines of Moishes," she said, wiping her mouth with a napkin.

"This is perfect. I love steamies. I'm exactly like my dad. I hate fuss, and sitting through a three-hour lunch is torture, no matter how good the food is."

"Simon and I are the exact opposite. We'd live in a restaurant if we could. Multiple courses with perfectly paired wine. Delicious. How is your dad, anyway? What's it like living together?"

Kitty had to put down her hot dog. "My dad has always been like this." She held her hands about six inches apart. "And now he's like this!" She opened her arms and accidently smacked a waiter's empty tray out of his hand. "Oops! Excuse-moi!"

He picked it up, gave her a curt nod and left.

"I can't take you anywhere, missy!" Gaynor said laughing.

"Ow, that's going to leave a bruise." Kitty rubbed her skin.

"Sorry, what were you saying about your dad? I'm so glad he's in your life again."

"What's happened to me is happening to him. He got lost in the gloom of that house when Martha was there. I truly believe that some people have an energy about them, either good or bad. I'm not saying the woman's evil, but she's so repressed and selfish and intolerant that Dad retreated into his den and stayed there, not even realizing that his world was becoming incredibly small."

Kitty picked up her bottle of Coke and took a big sip through the straw before continuing. "And I didn't help matters by staying away. I'd get sick to my stomach whenever I had to go to that house because she was like a guard dog at the door. And I was so angry with him for not seeing it." She took another bite of her hot dog and savoured it. "But now he has a friend. A lovely spirit who keeps the house for us and nourishes us with delicious food. And her name is Mary! Can you believe it?"

Gaynor dipped a fry into what was left of her ketchup. "Your mother's name, right?"

"Yes. And my dad knew Mary's husband. They worked together as detectives years ago. She's delighted to talk to Dad about Paddy and he's delighted to talk about his old friend. She's so lovely. I've noticed Dad is coming home a little early now on occasion so he can drive her home instead of her taking the bus. She even stayed for dinner the other night."

Gaynor scraped the last of her coleslaw out of the paper cup. "You don't think there's a possibility of..."

Kitty shook her head. "Romance? Not on your life. Dad is still in love with mom, and Mary is still in love with Paddy. Just because their spouses died doesn't mean their relationships ended. For some people, there's only ever one love."

"True."

"And not only that," Kitty said, wiping her mouth with her napkin. "I think all the renovations to the house have lifted his spirits. We even went out and bought a new living room set. My father has never shopped for furniture. And now, instead of watching television after supper with a glass in his hand, he takes the dogs for a long walk, or we go together, which is even better."

"You look happier." Gaynor said. "The dark circles under your eyes are completely gone."

"It seems like ages since I tracked you down at the hairdresser's, and it's only been a year."

Gaynor offered Kitty a cigarette. "Because I know you don't have any."

She took it. "I don't have any because I'm tired of smoking. Except when I'm with you. I don't like the smell of it on my clothes. Every once in a while is fine, but I don't need them anymore. Very strange."

"I will always need them. You can't have wine and good food without them. No doubt Simon and I are headed for an early grave, but we've sure had fun." Gaynor lit her cigarette and shook the match. "Not to change the subject, but how's Wallace?"

"He's fine. Busy."

Gaynor blew her smoke over her head. "Wow. That's as boring an answer as you'll ever get. Are you not talking to each other?"

"Not really. I've been busy."

"There's that boring word again. You know that huge man loves you, right?"

"Just because I'm spilling my guts to you doesn't mean you get to pry."

She made a funny face. "Of course I can. I'm me."

Kitty lit the cigarette, took a deep drag, and finished off her Coke instead of answering. Gaynor waited.

"Oh okay! I know he does."

"And?"

"And what?"

"You feel the same way."

"Look, he's my wonderful friend..."

"You are in love with him, honey. You are so in love with him you can't see straight, because if you could, you'd be on the first plane out of here."

"Gaynor, I seriously think you've lost millions of brain cells thanks to your love of red wine. In case you've forgotten, I'm rather busy. And anyway, just where is Wallace supposed to fit into my world? He had several panic attacks while he was here, just going on the bus and in an elevator. He'd curl up and die if he had to come here again."

"So go to him. You love South Head. Go for a couple of weeks this summer. Take your dad to show him the place. That's rebuilding your relationship. Get out of your routine. Can you still rent the house?"

"I suppose so."

"And you miss Bertha and Myrtle—"

"Ethel."

"Her too. You've gone through a hell of a lot. Take some time off."

"But it'll be hard to see him."

"So what? Were you delighted to see him in March? Did you survive? Were you never going to go back? That place makes you happy. It started this journey for you. Don't use Wallace as an excuse to never access that world again. Think about it, that's all I'm saying."

She thought about it on the bus home, remembering Wallace's grim face as he swayed above her. She thought about it while drinking Mary's lemonade out in the fenced-in backyard with the dogs under the shade of the red ash tree. And she thought about it while getting ready for bed in her bedroom. It was now a relief to be in here, as she had completely changed the configuration of her new bed and grown-up furniture. Her study was now in her brother's nursery next door. She'd asked them to paint the yellow room a soft blue, and she'd put everything in exactly the way she'd had it in the apartment.

Kitty was still thinking about it as she drove to her meeting with Miles. She left her name at the reception desk and he appeared moments later to take her to a conference room.

"Please, sit. It's lovely to see you again, Kitty."

"You as well." She held out her hand. "Here's my business card."

He gave a delighted laugh as he looked at it. "Fantastic, you remembered. Very classy."

They sat at the conference table. "Would you like a coffee or water?"

"No, thanks. Are Claude and Pierre joining us?"

"No. They're out of town, so I get the pleasure of informing you that we have received the funding we were looking for and the movie is a go. It's still a long way off, of course, but now that the wheels are turning, we can get started with the fun stuff, like casting."

Kitty didn't say anything.

He smiled. "Aren't you pleased?"

"I'm sorry. I'm stunned. I've been working on this project for months, but I always thought it would fall through. That it was a nice idea but it wasn't real."

"It's real." He held up her card. "This says so."

She shook her head as if to clear it. "Okay. What now?"

"You'll be relieved to know your part is over."

"And what's the status on my screenplay? Were you able to use any of it?"

"Of course! That's why we got the funding."

"You're going to use all of it?"

"No. We're still bringing in someone for the second draft, but the bones are there and we liked some of the changes you made. You didn't seem to mind playing around with the story, which surprised me, frankly. Most authors would want their original story to be followed as closely as possible."

She looked down at her hands. "You're talking about Harry Gunn's new younger partner? The mouthy, brash know-it-all who's secretly insecure? The handsome one who has a way with the ladies and who Harry loathes but helps in the end?"

"No guesswork here. You wrote it for Robert."

"It's my parting gift."

He tapped his fingers on the table. "You know there's no guarantee he'll get the part."

"I know, but why ever not? He's perfect for it. You said yourself that he's a great actor. And his looks will bring in a female audience who normally don't flock to detective flicks. I think you'd be wasting a great opportunity."

He didn't look completely convinced.

"Look, Miles, if you want to know the truth, I'm not just doing it out of the goodness of my heart. I wrote the whole Harry Gunn series in our house. Robert was there, when he wasn't on a movie set. I feel it belongs to him too. Sometimes we'd discuss a scene I was having trouble with and he'd suggest things. I think if this adventure becomes a series of movies, he'd be heartbroken to be left out of the process. He owns some of it, just by being with me when I conceived it. And I know I've been paid for this, but I think my opinion should hold some sway. I wrote the book. I wrote the screenplay that got you the funding. I won't say you owe me, but I'd greatly appreciate it if you'd consider my proposal. You don't have options for the other books, which might have been a mistake on your part, so Sophie Blanchette tells me."

Miles sat up in surprise and looked at her card. "Well, well. Not only are you a writer, you're a businesswoman as well."

She kept her mouth shut so she wouldn't mess up.

"Duly noted. I will consult with my partners and the casting director, but I still can't say with certainty that it will happen. It has to be our decision."

"Well, you know how I feel about it, Miles."

"I do indeed."

He walked her to the front door.

"Thank you. We'll speak soon," she said.

"I look forward to it."

She turned away.

"He doesn't deserve you."

Kitty looked over her shoulder. "I know."

⋙ ⋘

That week was as hot as blue blazes and it was only early July. She and the dogs baked in the sun out back despite the tree's shade, and her thoughts returned to the ocean. Why wasn't she swimming? Dad needed to go swimming with her, to see the beautiful shoreline and have a feed of lobster.

The dogs were panting. Who cared how difficult it would be to see Wallace? She wanted Pearl to jump in the waves at Mira Gut beach. Pip pranced at the water's edge, but that's as far as she'd go. Kitty was sure Pearl would dive right in, like Argus and Pride. This was ridiculous. She and the dogs marched into the house and looked at her father, who was at the kitchen table with the fan blasting on him. He had the salt and pepper shakers holding down the top edges of his newspaper.

"We're going to Cape Breton for two weeks. You and me and the dogs. You haven't had a vacation in twenty years, and you deserve one. I need to get out of here and go swimming. I'll call Gaynor and get the number for the Campbell guy in Toronto about renting the cabin. I'm positive no one's booked it."

"I can't just go on vacation. And our cars are too small to stuff two dogs in the back seat. Especially that one!" Pearl cocked her head when he pointed at her.

"Then I'm trading my car in for a station wagon. I can do that since I'm not buying my own house. And you'll go to your boss and say your daughter's having a breakdown and needs therapy at a rural retreat. They owe you for all the times you've covered for everyone else over the years."

"Now wait a minute…"

Mary came into the room with a load of laundry to fold. "You're going on a retreat?"

"Yes! I'm taking Dad and we're spending two weeks in Cape Breton."

"Oh my, how wonderful. When?"

"The first two weeks in August, hopefully. I'll melt if I don't go by then."

"That's three weeks away!" her father shouted. "I can't be ready in—"

"Oh, fantastic!" Mary jumped up and down and clasped her hands. "My sister wants me to go with her to Calgary to visit her grandchildren. I've never met them. She wants to pay for my plane ticket and everything. I didn't dare hope I might get some time off this summer to go."

Kitty watched her father squirm and delighted in it. He might say no to Kitty, but Mary was another matter.

"Well, sure, Mary. You can always take time off if you need to. Don't even hesitate to ask."

"Oh, thank you, Leo! May I use your phone in the den? I have to call her right now." She ran out of the kitchen and accidentally knocked the laundry basket off the table. Kitty picked it up and started to fold the clothes.

"Don't think that means we're going. We can cope without her for a few weeks."

"Nope. We're going. You're taking your little girl on a summer vacation to make up for all the summer vacations she missed when she was a kid because you were too bloody busy. Have you got that?"

"When did you get so goddamn bossy?"

Kitty drove to the car dealership the next day in her Morris Minor and drove home in a boat. Her father was walking up the street with the dogs on his lunch hour (a new habit) when she honked and waved at him. He had no idea it was her. She pulled up to the curb in front of the house and jumped out, running to the sidewalk to point to the car as he approached, being dragged along by Pearl, who was determined to get to her first.

"TA-DA!"

"What's this?"

"My new car."

"I've seen smaller apartments. This is nuts."

"Not nuts. It's a 1956 Chevrolet Two-Ten Townsman station wagon. Crocus yellow and laurel green over a charcoal interior. Isn't it beautiful? Plenty of room for us and the dogs."

"And forty other people, but we don't have that many friends. How can you afford this?"

"I have a career. The one you're proud of?"

"Still..."

"Dad, for the love of Larry, please be happy for me. I'm excited about this, in case you haven't noticed, and it's now your job to notice when your daughter is happy, remember."

He gave her a genuine smile. "You're right. This is terrific. Let's take the girls and go for a drive around the block."

Chapter
Twenty-Seven

Bertha was feeding laundry through the wringer washer with only three grandchildren at her feet when the phone rang. Drat, one long three short, it was hers. It never failed. She wiped her hands. "Hold on, hold on."

She went into the dining room, picked up the earpiece, and didn't even get a chance to say hello.

"Bertha?" Kitty shouted.

"Kitty! Hello, dear, just a minute." She put the phone receiver against her chest. "You sweeties stay away from Nan's washing machine, do you hear me?"

"It's okay, Nanna," Ruby answered. "We'll go weed the garden with Walrus."

"Thank you, sweetheart. Kitty? What a surprise to hear from you during the day. You normally call in the evening. Is anything wrong?"

"NO! Everything is right. Dad and I rented the Campbell place for the first two weeks of August! We'll be there in seven days!"

"Oh, my land! What wonderful news. Isn't it, Ethel?"

There was silence on the other end.

"Can you believe it?" Bertha said. "She's not listening in."

"I hope nothing's wrong," Kitty worried.

"I'm fine," Ethel said, coughing. "Had to swallow my candy."

"Well, this is the best news," Bertha said. "Wait until I tell everyone."

"Oh, Bertha, you're busy," Ethel said. "I'll tell everyone."

"I meant my family, but certainly, tell the rest of Homeville, Round Island, and Black Brook. And don't forget Morien."

"I can't wait to be there. We should be arriving around supper-time on the first. We can't know for sure; it might take longer with the two dogs."

"Oh, that's right. We get to meet Pearl. I'll have something nice ready for your dinner."

"It won't be five o'clock sharp."

"I can forgo the rule for one day."

"Could you ask Wallace to mow the lawn? But don't worry about cleaning the place up. I'll do that when I get there. Donna's going to bring down the key."

"Okay, dear. Drive safely and we'll see you soon."

"Bye, Bertha! Bye, Ethel."

Ethel had already hung up to get straight back on the line.

Bertha hurried out into the garden. Wallace now had three helpers on their knees, unfortunately pulling out not only weeds but actual plants.

"Wallace! You'll never guess. Kitty and her father have rented the house for the first two weeks of August. They're coming next week!"

He sat back on his haunches. "What?"

"She was just on the phone and sounded so excited. She wondered if you wouldn't mind mowing the grass but said don't bother cleaning the house up, she'll do that when she gets here."

"Okay."

Bertha waited for him to say something else but he didn't, just went back to showing the kids the difference between a weed and a carrot top, so she went back to her wringer washer to sneak peeks at him. The excitement she'd initially felt was extinguished a little. She hoped he wouldn't get quiet again, like he had when he first got back from Montreal.

He wasn't that quiet when he was mowing. The grass was long and the ground uneven. It needed to be ripped out completely and backhoed level. It took three hours in the heat to finish it. Donna had dropped off the key, so he went inside to get a glass of water. It was rusty and the place was dusty and full of dead ants like before. She couldn't come back to this, not with her scary father coming to see it for the first time. He took the mower back to the house and gathered up cleaning supplies. He was in the middle of it when his mother came in from the clothesline.

"She said not to clean anything."

"Kitty has no idea what she's talking about. That place is not exactly airtight, and the local ants had a high old time in there until they all croaked. People from away have no idea what happens to an old bungalow when it's left empty all winter. I don't want her to be embarrassed in front of her father."

"That's awfully nice of you."

"No, it isn't. It ticks me off that I have to do it. I have my own work to contend with."

"Then let me help you. I'll get Ethel too. We'll have it looking great in no time."

"No, Mom, you do enough."

She put her hands on her hips. "When did you get so darn bossy?"

It was six o'clock before they finished. The three of them dragged themselves home and only had the strength to make soup and sandwiches for supper.

"I've never cleaned my own house like that." Ethel used a napkin to fan herself. "I doubt Mrs. Campbell would recognize her own place, God rest her soul."

Bertha cut pieces of cold ham off the bone to put in between her slabs of homemade bread. "Once you start a job like that it takes over. You clean one part and the rest looks so shabby you have to keep going. Thanks for the help today, Ethel. It's greatly appreciated."

"Well, if it wasn't for you, I doubt Winnie and I would be alive, what with all the meals you give us. And my doctor said I needed more exercise. Me? I'm already a scrawny chicken. Why should I exercise?"

Wallace didn't dare look at his mother.

❧

They were about halfway through New Brunswick and her father was driving. "I've never seen so many goddamn trees in my life."

"Quebec has trees."

"Maybe it's because there are such long stretches between any kind of community. I didn't realize how big this province is. It's one thing to see it on a map, and it's another to be driving behind someone who refuses to go the speed limit. I should've put a police light and siren on this rig."

"We've still got the other half of the province to get through, so don't start moaning now."

"How did you not go crazy driving all by yourself?"

"Pip was with me."

"No doubt sitting in your lap, like now." He glanced to his right. Pearl's head was hanging over the middle of the front seat like a vulture, afraid to miss something.

"I thought you bought a big car for these two mutts. There's a bowling alley of space behind us, and neither one of them is taking advantage of it. You could've kept the Morris Minor after all."

"I've decided I'm a station wagon kind of gal. Now pull over and let me drive this baby. You've been behind the wheel long enough."

"I gotta say, it drives like a dream."

He drove into a gas station and pulled the car up to the pump, but the attendant kept motioning him to drive forward. He wasn't used to such a long car, so he miscalculated where the gas cap was. Kitty got out to take the dogs for a piddle, and when she opened the door a whole cloud of white fur came with her.

The attendant, who at this point was washing the front windshield, waved some of it away. "Whatcha got in there, a polar bear?"

"That's about right."

It was quite late when they stopped for the night between Woodstock and Fredericton. A little motel by the side of the road. The minute they unlocked the room, a wave of hot, stale air hit them. It was wood panelled and dark, the twin beds covered with bedspreads the colour of straw.

"When was the last time someone opened a window in here?" her father griped. He pushed the heavy red curtains aside and had to almost pry the window open to get some air, but it wouldn't stay up without help, so he reached into the bedside table drawer, took out the Bible, and used it to prop up the window. "Thank you, Jesus."

It's never easy to sleep with a parent in the same room. Pearl spent all night trying to get up on Leo's bed and he was having none of it. It was one in the morning when he shouted, "Does this dog do this all night?"

"She sleeps with me on my double bed, so there's usually room. She's not used to having you here. It's a treat for her. She loves you."

"She can love me from the floor."

"Come here, Pearl. He's a big meany."

Then Kitty was awake because of the snoring. And her father talked in his sleep. She tried to understand what he was saying, but the only word she caught was "warrant."

After a hot, sticky night, they were both awake at five thirty. Dad hopped in the shower first and she took the dogs for a stroll around the motel, staying away from the front office, in case they weren't supposed to have dogs in here. They'd never mentioned dogs, so Kitty had never asked, which was deliberate on her part and she felt guilty. Pearl was quick, an expert in the field of pee and poop, and did her mother proud. Pippy was still a fusspot and spent too much time trying to decide where to water the flowers.

Kitty was getting ready to feed them when her dad emerged from the bathroom. "The water in that shower comes out in a stabbing spurt. Don't put your face up to it. You'll lose an eye."

They were glad to see the back end of that place and drove for twenty minutes until they came to a small diner. They parked in the shade and put all the windows down halfway so it wouldn't get hot in the car.

"On second thought," Kitty said. "Maybe you should go in and order coffee and egg sandwiches to go and I'll stay here."

"And have these two mooches drooling inches away? No thanks. They'll be fine for twenty minutes. They aren't kids."

"Oh yes they are, but all right."

They were in the middle of their bacon and eggs when they heard a car horn beeping. Everyone looked out the window to see what was going on, but there didn't seem to be a commotion. It continued and the owner went out to see what was up. He came back in laughing. "Anyone here own a big white dog? It's out there in the driver's seat pressing on the horn. I guess you've been in here for too long."

The next night they spent in New Glasgow, another roadside motel, nothing special but the shower was nice. And this time they did get breakfast to go from a local diner. Her father drove to the causeway, and there they switched.

"I want you to look at the scenery," Kitty said.

Her father might have growled about a few things on the trip, but Kitty could see a difference already. His shoulders weren't so close to his ears. He always looked like a cop giving you a speeding ticket, stern, no-nonsense. Most people were wary of him, but as he looked out the window while they drove through the hills and dales of Cape Breton and he saw the shining blue water, a big grin appeared on his face.

"I told you. Isn't it beautiful? Smell the sea air. It's a tonic."

Pip was on Dad's lap when she sniffed the familiar scent and began to wiggle.

"That's right, Pippy! You remember this place."

She started to yip, which set Pearl off, and her barks were serious. Her dad put his hands over his ears. "Pearl! Knock it off. Or at least go to the back of the bus."

Because they had to stop every so often to let the dogs out for a stretch, they pulled up at a look-off site that had a few picnic tables and a toilet. They munched apples as the wind rushed up the hilltop from the ocean and gave them blessed relief from the heat. Kitty looked at her watch. "I have a feeling we'll be pretty close to Bertha's five o'clock sharp deadline after all."

Dad threw his apple core away and naturally Pearl found it and ate it. "You're absolutely sure this whole adventure is a good idea?"

"A hundred percent. And the fact that you came with me makes it extra special."

"But the place is small, you tell me. Think of the motel. Two weeks of that?"

"Anyone can put up with anything for two weeks. I'm sure you've faced more dire circumstances than Pearl trying to get into your bed."

"I don't know about that. Pearl was a rather insistent woman."

She clapped her hands with delight. "You made a joke! My dad made a joke!"

Kitty was so excited when she turned down South Head Road, she could hardly contain herself.

"Where the hell are we going?" her father asked.

"I know, it takes some getting used to, but once you get to Bertha's table, it'll be worth it. Oh, I forgot to mention that Wallace has two huge Newfoundland dogs."

"Of course he does."

She honked the horn as she passed Ethel's place and announced their arrival in the Baileys' yard the same way. Pippy was frantic and she jumped right out the window when she saw Argus and Pride, who were tethered to the shed. They were delighted to see her. She ran around and drove them mad.

"Keep Pearl on the leash for now. Oh, everyone's here. Smile, Dad. No cop face."

Bertha, Ethel, Winnie, and Rita holding a much bigger Ben emerged from the front porch, Wallace and his brother George sauntered from around the back of the house, and Georgie and Elizabeth jumped off the rubber tire swing in the yard. Kitty hardly recognized Wallace. He'd shaved off his beard and mustache and cut his hair. How dare he hide that face, with his high cheek bones and cute dimples? Kitty hugged them all, but when she reached Wallace she slapped her own cheeks and grinned stupidly like a cat looking at a bowl of cream. "You look ten years younger! I love it."

"Thought it was time for a change."

Her dad stood to the side holding a rather subdued Pearl. He ended up having to poke Kitty in the ribs to get her to stop staring at Wallace. "Oh, everyone, this is my father, Leo Faulkner. Dad, you know Wallace."

Wallace came forward and shook his hand. "Nice to see you again, sir."

"You too, son."

Wallace reached down to pat Pearl. "And you, Pearl. You've grown."

"Dad, this is Wallace's mother, Bertha Bailey, her friends Ethel and Winnie, and this is Charlie Bailey and his family, Rita, Georgie, Elizabeth, and baby Ben, who's not a baby anymore!" She reached for him, but he hid his face in his mother's shoulder. "Maybe later."

Bertha shook Leo's hand. "So nice to meet you, Leo. We're very happy to see Kitty again and I hope you'll enjoy your stay."

"I'm sure I will. Hello everyone, thank you for being so kind to my girl. I'm grateful."

"She's easy to love," Bertha said. "Supper will be ready in fifteen minutes." She glanced at her watch. "For goodness' sake. At five o'clock sharp."

It took about that long for Kitty and her dad to introduce Pearl to Argus and Pride. Wallace kept them in check as they sniffed her. Pearl was submissive around these two older animals. Pip bounced between them, thrilled to see her friends again. Wallace eventually let them off their ropes and Leo took the leash off Pearl, but he stood right by her very protectively, Kitty noticed.

The four of them did a little reel around, but Pearl wasn't too adventurous at this point, so she stayed close to her father. Argus and Pride were none too happy about being excluded from the kitchen as the others went inside. They whined until Wallace told them to be quiet and they laid down on the front step and sulked.

Bertha did herself proud, serving crispy salt cod cakes, fried onions and scrunchions, black-eye baked beans, green tomato chow-chow, tea biscuits, warm rolls, and coconut cream pie for dessert. She used her tea set, and Kitty was delighted with how good it looked on the table.

Her dad drank the last of his tea. "That dinner was simply amazing. Do you eat like this every day?"

The family laughed and nodded.

"Ethel and I are very lucky to live so close to this splendid cook," Winnie told him. "She's always sending over food."

"Bertha, any chance you could mail some?" Leo asked.

"Another joke! Dad, who are you?"

They didn't linger. They had to get to the house before dark. After many thanks, the four of them piled in the station wagon. Wallace stood with his dogs and watched. "Like your new car. You could open your own touring company."

364

She smirked. "Very funny. Goodnight."

He waved and went inside.

When she pulled up to the house, Kitty got emotional. "Here it is."

Her father didn't say anything.

"I know. It takes some getting used to."

"It's not what I expected, but whoever mowed the grass did a nice job."

They let the dogs out and they sniffed around. "The dogs can't be left alone outside. Coyotes or eagles could eat them."

"I'd like to see the size of the eagle who flies off with Pearl."

Kitty led the way, opened the unlocked door and let the dogs in. The smell of lemon furniture polish was in the air. "I told them not to clean it!"

There were wildflowers on the table, and a tea towel was draped over a plate of what she knew would be molasses cookies. She walked around in a daze. "It's so clean! Look, Dad, here's the wood stove I told you about, and the little pantry, and look in here, the loft in the living room, and through here is the bedroom, and oh, my god, my tub!!!"

She buzzed around like a honeybee, touching everything. "It's so wonderful, don't you think?"

"Some of this furniture is from another era, but if you like it, that's all that matters."

"You don't like it? Say you like it, old man."

"I like it, I like it. Give me a minute to get over the fact that it's about the size of our living room."

"Don't be a city snob."

"I'm stating a fact, that's all."

"You and your facts." She ran over to him and gave him a big hug. "I've got to call Wallace to thank him."

"He did all this?"

"He did the last time. Watch how the phone works."

She cranked one long ring and three short rings. Wallace answered. "Hi, I knew you'd call."

"You incredible man! This place is spotless!"

"Hey, I helped too. And so did Bertha."

"Thank you, Ethel. Thank you, Bertha. Thank you, Wallace. Dad said whoever mowed the lawn did a nice job, and I know that was you, so thanks for that too, unless you did it, Ethel."

"No, dear. Don't want to break my hip and be eaten by a bear."

"Gotta go and help Dad unpack the car. Talk to you later."

That night as Kitty laid her head against the curve of the porcelain tub and felt the hot, soapy water lap against her weary bones, she realized how far she'd come in the past year. Truthfully, she hardly recognized herself.

Or her dad.

She insisted he sleep in the bedroom on the lumpy mattress while she took the lumpy chesterfield. They said goodnight to each other and she turned off the lights. Ten minutes later she heard the bedroom door open and her father slowly make his way through unfamiliar territory.

"What's wrong?"

"Gotta get more of those molasses cookies. Damn, they're good."

Pearl was restless all night in this new space, thanks to the wind moaning, the branches of the trees scraping the sides of the house, and sound of scampering on the roof at some point. Instead of staying curled up on the rug beside her, by the middle of the night Pearl was lying on top of her. They finally found a spooning position, until Pearl managed to hog all the space and Kitty rolled over the side and landed on the floor. She grabbed her blanket and pillow and stayed put. It was easier. Pip and her father were dead to the world, judging by their deep, steady snoring.

Her father was still making a racket while she puttered around all morning and couldn't believe it when he finally crawled out of bed just before ten.

"What happened?" he said groggily as he schlepped out to the kitchen in his slippers. "I feel like I've been drugged."

"That's Cape Breton air. You haven't had real air in years. Want some breakfast? I've made porridge, and there's Bertha's homemade bread and strawberry jam, and thanks to the Baileys' chickens, fresh eggs. Even coffee."

"Did Bertha harvest the coffee beans too? I wouldn't put it past her."

"Country women are superheroes. They can do anything and make it look easy."

She was determined to take her dad to the beach, so they went to the one in Big Glace Bay and planned to stop in Morien for groceries on the way back. She packed more thick sliced bread with butter and molasses for lunch. They still had apples from the roadtrip, but she did make a quick run into the store for ice cold Orange Crush, two bags of chips, and penny candy. Hopper welcomed her back.

"Where's the little dog?"

"She's in the car with my dad. I'll bring her in one day. But I can't carry in the new dog. She's too big."

"She'll be eaten by the bear, then."

That would always be their joke.

It was a great day. Kitty was very happy to walk down to the beach, both dogs on a leash just in case, but there was hardly anyone here, so she let them off and they ran along the sand to a more out-of-the-way spot. She and her dad followed them. When they'd gone far enough, she reached into her beach bag. "Did I show you the gift Gaynor gave us?" She brought out two plush beach towels. "It was her suggestion that I take you here, and when I actually listened to her, she dropped these off as a reward for good behaviour."

"Very nice. Look, Pearl's nervous of the water. That's a surprise, I'd better go help her." Her dad took off his trousers and shirt. He had his swim trunks on underneath.

"My god, Dad. How long has it been since your body saw the sun? Your skin is the colour of Gyprock."

"It's a good thing I'm a confident guy, Catriona. You can be a little too mouthy."

"Sorry. But you're so cute."

"Cute? Now that's an insult." He rushed off to join Pearl, who was now digging to China in the sand.

They spent almost the entire day there, getting in and out of the water as the sun shone. She'd remembered to bring an umbrella, which the dogs took advantage of, and a bowl for their water. Most of the chips went to them as well, but both father and daughter polished off the penny candy.

They were in bed by eight.

❧❦

The next two weeks flew by. Kitty and her father went over the Cabot Trail. They'd planned to spend a night in Ingonish, but when he found out about their famous golf course, they stayed an extra night so he could play eighteen holes badly while Kitty lolled on Ingonish Beach with the dogs.

Another day they took to the road and went all the way to Inverness, staying overnight there as well.

"This is what I've always imagined Scotland would look like. I can't get over how beautiful it is here."

He said that everywhere they went—back to Baddeck, Louisbourg, Kennington Cove, the Mira River, and Main-à-Dieu.

And then they got tired of driving and stuck closer to home, having a huge feed of lobsters with the Baileys, again Kitty's treat. She insisted. They even had a beach fire one night down at the shore, the choking smoke and sparks flying up towards the stars while the water lapped on shore. They baked clams and mussels and ate them hot out of the shell.

By the end of it her father's arms and face were quite dark. His body was still ghostly, but he claimed it was his English rose complexion. Kitty was thrilled to see how he got along with Wallace and the gang. He talked to them easily when the fellas asked about his line of work. He mentioned the usual things people know about detectives from the movies, never the real horror that he'd seen over the years.

"To tell you the truth, it can be incredibly boring. Watching someone's home for hours at night, trying to stay awake. There's a reason cops love coffee. Then there's going through boxes and boxes of evidence. There's a lot of paperwork and checking and re-checking the facts."

"My father loves facts."

"As I matter of fact, I do."

"Another joke! I can't get over this new guy!"

Kitty had obviously not spent a lot of time with Wallace, and without saying so, she had a feeling he preferred it that way, so she respected his wishes. She did catch him looking at her from across the bonfire. He gave her a quick smile before he turned away. She couldn't get over how young he looked without a beard. She wouldn't have recognized him like this on the streets of Montreal. She was used to thinking of him as sort of a scruffy old bear, like his dogs. This good-looking man was now someone who seemed like he meant business. And that was a bit unsettling.

By the last day, Kitty and her father had done everything they wanted to. They sat at the kitchen table eating Cheerios before they were to leave.

"This was the trip of a lifetime, Kitty. I'm so grateful you talked me into it. I've had the best time with you. I'll never forgive myself for not doing this sooner."

She grabbed his hand. "No. Don't do that. I've forgiven you. I mean, really forgiven you. Now you have to forgive yourself. We both know why it happened, but we've crawled out of the hole. Let's enjoy it, not wallow in the past."

"You're right. It seems you're always right."

"Don't forget that."

They got in the car and drove to the Baileys'. Only Wallace and Bertha were there. It seemed they were all determined to keep their composure.

"Goodbye, Leo," Bertha said. "Let me hug you. I hope you had a grand time."

He gave her a big hug. "It's been the nicest time I've had since my Mary died. I'm very grateful to you both for that." Her dad reached over and grasped Wallace's hand with both of his. "You are a fine young man. I'm very glad to know you, Wallace. I'm sure we'll meet again."

"Goodbye, Leo. Take care of Kitty and the dogs."

Bertha and Kitty hugged each other. That's all they could do. She hugged Argus and Pride and then Wallace. "Last, but not least," she said. "Thank you. Thank you."

They turned and got into the car where the dogs were waiting. As they drove away, they waved out the open windows, Pip and Pearl barking until they were out of sight.

Chapter Twenty-Eight

Kitty had to get out of the car. She walked and walked, the dogs with her, her breath coming too rapidly. She started to run, and was still running towards the shore when she saw him turn around, alerted by his loyal bodyguards.

"Kitty?" Wallace shouted. "What's wrong? What did you forget?"

She stopped in front of him, winded. The four dogs greeted each other like they hadn't just seen each other an hour and a half ago.

"I'm so sorry. Please forgive me."

"For what? Where's your dad?"

"I took him to the airport."

"That makes no sense. You're driving home alone? You just said goodbye to us."

"And I feel terrible about that, but there are reasons. If you don't mind sitting with me, I can explain."

He looked upset, which was what she'd been afraid of, but he sat on the log. "You've got to stop jerking me around. Friends don't do that to each other. If you're going, go! Don't come back when I'm...trying to not miss you."

She held up her hands. "I know. I apologize. There was no other way to do it."

"Your dad knew about this? That he was leaving on a plane?"

"Yes."

"And he was okay with that? Why didn't he say anything? I feel like we've been lied to."

"You *have* been lied to! And if you'd shut up for half a second, I'll tell you why."

He grabbed a rock and threw it into the water, since it was obvious he didn't want to look at her.

"When you left Montreal, I could tell you were upset. About what I told you. About me not being ready to make up my mind. Despite saying you understood, I knew you were hurt. And you have to admit, we haven't really made much of an effort to be in touch with each other, so I assumed I was right. I had no idea of the reception I'd get here when I arrived. I knew you'd be polite and kind, obviously, but I wasn't sure about where I stood."

He threw another rock.

"Just like you know your life is here, I know my life is in Montreal. My work commitments, my father's house that I can live in now without heartbreak, my mother and brother's resting place. I need to be there. But I also need to be here. In Cape Breton. This place sings to me. It cries out to me. I can't imagine my life without it."

"Are you telling me you're going to show up here for two weeks every summer and then fuck off back to Montreal?"

"I bought the Campbell place. I'm living here from May until November."

"Say that again."

"You're going to help me fix it up, show me how to plant a garden, and use my new double bed."

He finally looked at her. "Don't mess with me."

"I don't want to marry you, Wallace. I don't want to marry anyone. And I don't want you to stop living your life with your mom. I want to be a single woman who spends half of her life at her writing retreat in Cape Breton while being madly in love with the man up the road, and half of her life with her father and lovely housekeeper and silly Gaynor, who has become a trusted friend, not just my writing partner. That's why I bought that huge car. To haul the dogs and my belongings back and forth. Not to mention it can take nine kids to the store for penny candy and I can drive your mother, Ethel, and Winnie to town for lunch. And think how handy it will be to drag the Homeville Women's Institute members to local events."

He still looked flummoxed. "And your father, Leo Faulkner, detective Harry Gunn, knew about this plan the whole time?"

"I told him what I wanted to do before we left, but asked him to keep it to himself in case we got here and you'd changed your mind. And I couldn't exactly talk to you about it with him hanging around. I asked Junior Campbell to keep the sale quiet, so even Donna doesn't know. I tried to be careful with everyone, and this was the only way I could think of. Flawed, I know."

"You still don't know if I've changed my mind. What if I have? You went ahead and bought the place anyway."

"Well, if you have written me off, you won't care if I'm living down the road. You don't have to speak to me, but I warn you, I won't stop eating at your mother's table, so you'll just have to deal with that. She loves me."

He pointed at her. "Your father told me to back off in Montreal. So that's what I've been trying to do."

"Things were still difficult then, and he didn't know you. He was being protective, that's all. Dad likes you, Wallace. He thinks you're a good sort. His words. And he gave you a two-handed handshake today and he never does that. Over the past two weeks he's seen how kind you are to your family and the dogs. And besides, I'm a grown woman. I get to make up my own mind."

"So, you're staying here today? You're here tonight?"

"Yes. I have to go by the third week of October, because the book is coming out. I'll be busy with readings and signings. But until then I'm as free as a bird."

"Oh."

"You sound hesitant. That's not good."

He looked down at his hands and Kitty's heart nearly stopped. "I won't be available much. I have plans too."

"Do they involve moving away?"

He laughed and pointed at the dogs. Argus and Pride were lolling in the water, with Pearl hesitant to join them but standing farther out than she had before. Pippy was everyone's cheerleader at the edge of the sand. "You know the answer to that question." He kept looking out over the water. "When I came home from Montreal, I took a long, hard look at myself. And you're right. Leaving your life, even for a week, can make you see things from a whole new prospective. I don't have to be the man everyone expects me to be. I know what I love. I want to be a baker."

Kitty grabbed him by his overall straps and shook him back and forth, or at least tried to. "WALLACE! How wonderful. Do you have a job lined up?"

"No. I'm creating my own. That new building on our property I've been working on all spring and summer is going to be my bakery. It's big enough to have four ovens, room for shelves and racks and counter space to bake. When I looked at the money we made with Mom's Christmas orders, it was more than my odd jobs took in, so I thought, why am I wasting my time when I can pour my energy into my own business? Mom already has quite a reputation around here. When people come all the way to South Head from Sydney for a pan of squares, you know they're something special."

Kitty was so happy she was speechless. She kept trying to shake him.

"Bailey's Baked Goods."

"That's so...goods."

He reached over and took her face in his hands. "I was so afraid when I heard you were coming for two weeks. Unsure how I'd live through it, so I told myself that even if you were just a friend, I'm still better off than if I'd never met you. But when you said goodbye today and drove away, I had to come here with the dogs to try and gather up the pieces of my heart. To think that I never have to do that again leaves me breathless. This is such a shock, Kitty. I need time to process it. It doesn't feel real."

"I know. I don't want to kiss you right now, because I know the minute I do I won't stop. Let's sit here for a bit and then go tell your mom. I want to see her reaction. We can reconvene later in my new house. I'm thinking of naming it The Drafty Shack."

She laid her head on his shoulder and he wrapped his arm around her. They stayed like that for an hour and enjoyed their mutts frolicking under the hot August sun.

It was Kitty who moved first. "Okay, I'm famished. I need your mother's bread."

"Actually, my bread is slightly better."

"I'll sample both. I can be your taste-tester from now on. Oh, no. I can't tell Gaynor. She'll wail for a week."

❦

Bertha was washing muffin tins when she heard the screen door slam behind her. "I think I'll make a jellied chicken salad for supper. It's too hot for anything else."

"Sounds delicious."

That was Kitty's voice. She was hallucinating in the heat. She spun around and grabbed her chest when she saw her. "Oh my god. What's going on? Did you have an accident? Where's Leo?"

"I drove him to the airport."

"What? What's going on? Are you staying?"

"Yes, I'm going to live in my new house down the road. It's no longer the old Campbell place. From now on, please refer to it as the old Faulkner place."

Bertha felt like she was hyperventilating. She looked at Wallace's face. "Did you know about this?"

"I just found out myself about an hour ago. How's that for sneaky?"

Bertha took her dishtowel and chased Kitty around the kitchen with it. "You miserable brat! You made me think you were going! Was your rotten father in on this too?" All the dogs got in on the chase around the table.

Kitty held up her hands to ward off the dishtowel as she tried to get away. "We are both very sorry, but I had to make sure that Wallace still loved me before I told everyone."

Now Bertha stopped. "Wallace has loved you from the very first time you came into this kitchen for supper. Are you telling me, please God, that you feel the same way?"

Kitty reached out and hugged him. "Oh yes. Very much."

"But how will you get married if you're still married...for now?"

"We're never getting married."

"Isn't that great?" Wallace beamed.

Bertha was sure she was about to faint. She quickly sat in the nearest chair. "Someone get me some water."

"Are you okay, Mom?" He got water and Kitty sat next to her looking concerned.

"I'm fine. Physically." She drank the water in one go. "Now what do you mean you're never getting married?"

Kitty patiently explained. It made total sense by the time she was finished.

"Be happy," Wallace said. "That means I won't be leaving home."

"Maybe I want you gone. Ever thought of that?"

The look on his face made her feel bad. "I'm joking, you great goat. So as far as the rest of the world goes, meaning Ethel, you two are just friends and neighbours?"

"Until my divorce comes through. And then we'll be dating when I'm here. Before long it will be yesterday's news."

It started to sink in. Her Wallace had a love of his own. This extraordinary woman had come into his life and now she was his.

He was hers. Bertha couldn't contain herself any longer. She put her hands up to her face and sobbed tears of relief and joy. Her last chick was leaving the nest without leaving the nest. A perfect solution for them both.

Once she grabbed the tissues they handed her, she got out the chair and squeezed them. Then she collapsed in her chair again. "More water, please."

Once she drank that, she started to feel a little more normal. "This has been a shock to my system, let me tell you."

"Want another shock?" Kitty grinned.

"Not really."

"Okay. Tell you later."

"Tell me now! I don't want any more surprises from you."

"But you can't tell anyone."

"Oh, for the love of Pete. It's a good thing I love you. You're as irritating as my own kids."

"You know C. J. Faulkner?"

"Who?"

Wallace piped up. "The author who writes Harry Gunn novels. The murdering tuba and the opera singer?"

Kitty slapped her hands on the table. "For the last time, the tuba was the murder weapon, not the killer!"

Bertha was confused. "What about him?"

Wallace pointed at Kitty. "He's her."

"He's who?"

"Kitty is C. J. Faulkner. She wrote all those books."

Bertha's mouth dropped open. "I was reading your book when you walked into our lives. That must be fate. Hold on! Harry Gunn is based on your father? I had Harry Gunn in my house and you didn't tell me?!"

"I've only told you because you read my books. I don't want the community around here to know just yet. At some point, but not now."

Bertha suddenly realized why. "Because of your new scrawny chicken book? I can't wait to read it! But I won't tell a soul. It'll be our little secret."

❦

There was a soft knock.

"If that's you, come in. Everyone else, go away."

Wallace entered the kitchen carrying a beautiful cake with boiled icing swirled on top. "This is for you."

"My favourite."

"You don't know what it is yet."

"It's yours. My favourite. Pip! Pearl! Let him get in the door."

The dogs were determined to have his attention first, so Wallace put the cake on the table and gave them a proper hello.

"I can see this is going to be a problem," Kitty mused. "But I have a solution. Wait! I'll put the cake in the fridge. Pearl can reach the table now."

Once that was done she grabbed Wallace's hand and led him to the bedroom and shut the door. They both tried to ignore the whining. "This solution isn't perfect, but I cannot wait one more second. If you don't kiss m—"

He kissed her. Until daybreak.

Kitty slowly opened her eyes and it took a minute to figure out where she was. The light was streaming in the window, so she knew it was late morning. And then she remembered. She hugged herself and kicked her feet like a little kid. She'd never been loved before. Not like this. Not ever. She hadn't even known what loving was. No wonder she'd never written romance novels. But now she could, because last night would live in her memory forever.

She had a leisurely bath in her fabulous tub, wrapped a robe around herself, and took the dogs outside. It was chilly, going to rain. She brought them back in, gave them breakfast, and started a fire in the stove. Most mornings she put on the electric kettle to heat water for a cup of coffee, but today felt damp, so she wanted to hear the fire crackle. She decided that maybe Wallace would come by, so she made a batch of blueberry pancakes just in case.

She was at the kitchen table reading, eating a syrupy stack with her coffee, when Wallace's truck pulled up. When she saw him get out of his truck with a fantastic array of flowers, she yanked open the door and hopped up and down.

"Oh, my word, thank you so much!" She threw her arms around his middle and hugged him tight. "What a thoughtful thing to do. You are the best."

When she tilted her chin and looked up into his face, she saw his cheeks redden. Oh no. She peeled herself off that solid, warm torso.

"They're not from you, are they?"

"I'm sorry. They came to our house instead, so I said I'd bring them over. I'm not sure why delivery men are so reluctant to go past our place."

"Afraid they'll get lost, I'm sure. Well, thank you for bringing them. No doubt they're from Gaynor." She put them down. "Good morning, Walrus."

He took her in his arms. "Good morning, Kitty."

When the kiss didn't end soon enough, both dogs jumped up on them. "This is going to be a problem. But I cannot stop kissing your fabulous soft face." She caressed his cheek. "Would you like some breakfast?"

"No thanks. I have to make a quick trip to town to pick up some shelves for the bakery."

"Isn't that amazing? How does it feel to say that?"

"Pretty darn good."

"I'm taking the gals for lunch. Winnie is no longer a hermit. Will you be back by one?"

"Should be."

"Would you take the dogs when we go? Is it too much with the four of them?"

"They're no problem, they actually listen to me, unlike you. See you later, beautiful."

She kissed him again, waved from the door, and hummed as she went back to the table, grabbing another forkful of pancakes before she picked up the flowers.

"Thank you, Gaynor."

She opened the card. They weren't from Gaynor.

Dear Kitty, I got the part. The part you wrote for me. Because that's who you are. I will always love you. Be happy. Kurt. xoxo

Her eyes filled with tears. "My first friend."

Chapter Twenty-Nine

Three months later Kitty pulled up in the station wagon to the front curb of her father's house. Her house. It was good to see the place again. And it looked different. Her father told her he'd painted the front door, but never in her wildest dreams did she think it would be blood-orange. It looked very inviting with Ted's yellow door on one side and the Dions' blue door on the other. "Good job, Dad. Okay, girls. We left home and now we're home. Aren't we lucky?"

She was aware, after three days in the car, that she should've bathed Pearl before she left. She smelled like ninety pounds of seaweed and saltwater. Once she got used to the ocean, she never stayed out of it. Argus had even had to use his Newfoundland dog–rescue skills and grab her by the scruff of the neck to pull her to shore one day.

It would take an hour to get all the stuff out of the car. Thank God she didn't buy a smaller one; she could barely get her belongings in as it was. It was a puzzle to figure out what she would leave and what would stay. She'd figure it out eventually.

The three of them ran up the stairs and burst in the door. No more wiping paws and feeling unwelcome. "We're home!"

"Wonderful!" Mary came out of the kitchen and looked very happy to see them. The dogs wiggled around her as she patted them. "Oh, we've missed you very much! Your dad said he'd be home early because he wants to help you unpack the car."

"Sounds like a plan."

"It's only three. I just put pork roast in the oven. Would you like some scones and a cup of tea?"

"Would I! Thank you. Okay, you guys, out in the backyard for now. I've got to wash Pearl. She stinks to high heaven."

"She is a tad ripe."

They sat in the kitchen and had a nice chinwag. "Did you have a good time with your sister in Calgary?"

"Oh my, I sure did. The grandchildren were sweet. My sister is very lucky. She has four children, three of them in and around Montreal and the one girl in Calgary. I've always been very close to my nieces and nephew. That's what happens when you can't have children of your own. You happily borrow everyone else's."

"I know. I'm in the same situation, which is why my puppies are so important to me."

Mary reached over and patted her hand. "Oh, dear. Then you know the heartache."

"I always wanted them, but not every woman is the same. My friend Gaynor is very happy with her decision never to have kids. She and her husband and dog are a content trio."

"Families are an endless variety of combinations. Whatever works."

"Being a part of a happy family has always been my dream. I had a perfect one until I was seven and then lost everyone, including my father."

Mary put down her teacup. "Yes. Your father has talked a lot about that."

"Has he?" Kitty took another big bite of her scone and apple jelly.

"He feels great remorse over your upbringing. Not only his role in it, but for bringing the other housekeeper into your world. He wants to spend the rest of his life being the dad he should have been when you needed him."

"Aww. I'll always need him, so that's nice to hear. I can't quite believe he told you all that. Thank you for letting him talk. I'm so glad you're his friend. We all need someone to listen to us, and my dad shut out the world when Mom died. I'm finally seeing the real him, and I have to say I rather like him."

Mary put her teacup up to her lips. "Me too."

Hmmm. It was the way she said it.

Dad came home and the dogs went crazy. He got down to their level and Pearl knocked him over. He laughed as she climbed on top of him. He had to hold her face away so she wouldn't lick him to death. "Pearl! You stink!"

They unpacked the car and then gave Pearl a bath in the downstairs tub, which was an incredible ordeal. Kitty resorted to taking her out in the yard to dry her off and brush her for an hour until her hands got too cold. She had a gigantic mound of dog fur by the end of it and she saved it in a paper bag in the shed, something Wallace mentioned he did with Argus and Pride's fur. Saving it until spring for the birds to line their nests.

There was no rushing off for Mary. She stayed and ate the pork roast, garlic mashed potatoes, peas, and homemade apple sauce with them. If Kitty had been meeting these two for the first time, she'd think they were an old married couple, the way they talked and laughed together over their meal. Kitty offered to do the dishes while her dad drove Mary home.

When he came back in, Kitty was curled up on the new chesterfield reading a book, Pip beside her and Pearl out cold on the floor recovering from her hairy ordeal. He stood in the doorway and made a face. "Now I smell wet dog."

"It's going to take a while for all her fur to dry."

"Keep her off the new furniture."

"She is off the furniture, as you can clearly see."

He joined her, wearing his slippers, as he sat in his favourite new chair and lit his pipe. He held his legs out in front and crossed them at his ankles, settling in with a sigh, his elbows on the chair's arms. He looked incredibly good.

Kitty stared at him. "There's something missing in this picture. What is it?"

"Darned if I know."

"I've got it. You don't have a drink in your hand."

"I've stopped drinking."

Kitty's book fell out of her hands. "Repeat that."

"I've stopped drinking. Mary didn't like it."

"When would Mary see you drinking? Isn't she usually gone by the time you get home?"

"Not always." He cleared his throat. "We've been spending some time in each other's company."

Kitty kept her smile hidden. "Oh."

He rushed to reassure her. "Not a lot. Just on occasion we'll go to the movies or a restaurant. We went to a concert once featuring Irish dancers. They're a frantic bunch."

"That sounds nice, Dad. I'm glad you're doing things together. You could both use the company."

"I was worried it would bother you."

"Why?"

"Your mother."

"Dad, Mom has been gone a long time. She would want you to be happy. If being with Mary makes you happy, then I'm thrilled."

"We're never going to live together or anything like that. She loves her house and her cats and I love it here. But it's so nice to come home and have a lovely smile greet me. We make each other laugh."

"That's perfect, Dad. Look at us, sitting here together in Mom's house, so happy and content. Can you believe what's happened?"

"You should write about this. It's a good story."

❧❧

Gaynor was happily lying on a beach in Maui, the hot sun baking the back of her neck. The roar of the ocean filled her ears as she drifted off. A lovely calm overtook her frayed nerves. This was just the ticket.

And then some kind of hermit crab kept pinching her shoulder. Her eyes flew open and she sat up, hitting her forehead on the front of the hairdryer with a thwack. "OW!"

Gaynor pulled up the dryer and gave the young woman in front of her a look. "Kitty! What the hell are you doing here?"

"I told you I was coming home last week."

"I mean, *here* here."

"Dolores said you wouldn't mind."

"Well, Dolores is getting full of herself. I do mind."

"Really?"

"Of course not. Dolores is my rock. Wait over there and I'll take you to lunch. Dunn's?"

"Perfect."

"Want a smoke?"

"No, thanks."

"Bitch. And stop looking so happy while you're at it."

They settled down at the same table they had when Wallace was in town. After they placed their order Kitty sighed and looked out the window. "I miss Wallace."

"How is the big man?"

"He's heaven."

"I'm so sorry your life is shit."

Kitty laughed and laughed. "I love you, Gaynor. Thank you for being my friend, as well as my editor."

"Don't get sappy. So, how's he going to occupy himself while you're here selling thousands of books? Oh, by the way, here's a copy. I happen to have one in my handy suitcase purse. I was taking it to a buyer after my hair appointment, but I'll get another one."

Kitty had known what the cover would look like, but it was always a thrill to hold a new book in her hands for the first time. On a bright yellow background, which was quite striking, it featured a large, wall-mounted crank phone with the earpiece dangling, as if someone had rushed off in the middle of a call. C. J. Faulkner was at the top in its usual font, with *Bestselling Author of the Detective Harry Gunn Series* over the name in a smaller font. The title was at the bottom, with a blurb: *C. J. Faulkner has done it again! Only this time add humour to the riveting mix. A rollicking good time! A non-murder murder investigation gone wrong…and oh, so right.* —Amos Jones, author of the Murder Club trilogy.

"Wow. You got Amos to do the blurb. That was kind of him."

"His endorsement on a book is always stellar."

"It's lovely. I really like it." She thumbed through it. "You know, I'm thinking I might just put my picture on the flap of the next Kate Higgins book."

Gaynor bit her knuckle. "Be still my heart. I was hoping you'd say that. Have you got a plot yet?"

"Just a half-baked idea of Kate becoming a P. I. and her first client is a woman who thinks her husband is cheating on her, so she hires Kate to get evidence on this guy. I know a little about that. But it could be something else tomorrow."

The waiter brought their smoked meat sandwiches, coleslaw, and dill pickles. They stopped talking and tucked in. While Gaynor munched, she said. "I don't see why we shouldn't use your picture in the future. Especially for a female detective series. You're established now, but of course it's Mel's decision."

"That's fine."

"While I'm thinking of money rolling in, Simon and I wondered if you and your dad would like to come and visit us in Florida for a week this February."

Kitty quickly took a swallow of her Coke to get rid of her

mouthful. "Are you serious? I'd love to! Thank you so much! But I doubt Dad would go."

"I understand. He's a bit of a loner."

"No, he won't want to leave Mary behind."

Gaynor started to cough and now she had to take a drink to make sure she didn't choke. "WHAT? I thought you said—"

"What do I know? At this moment they're rediscovering how nice it is to have a companion. They go to dinner and the movies. It's unbelievable to me that he's actually enjoying his life. I can see it on his face. He's no longer Harry Gunn. He's Leo again."

They finished their lunch and had coffee. Gaynor lit her cigarette while Kitty sucked on a mint, but she pointed at it. "Every so often I'd love to have a puff."

"Hold fast! You can do it. I can't, but you can."

"Sometimes I have to pinch myself. Am I dreaming? Literally everything has changed for me. For us."

"Well, I hope you remember that it was little old me who suggested you get out of town. That started the whole ball of wax."

"It was Simon's idea about the writing retreat, but you're right. I have a gift for you both."

"I was wondering what was in that bag."

Kitty took out a big white box wrapped in string from her carry bag and put it on the table. Gaynor still had a cigarette in her mouth. It bobbed up and down as she spoke. "Is this what I think it is? Bertha's baking?"

"No."

"Rats."

"It's Wallace's baking. That's what he'll be doing while I sell thousands of books. He's built his own bakery called Bailey's Baked Goods and he's already overwhelmed with orders. Bertha declared it will be the death of her, but she insists on getting underfoot. Wallace wants to hang her up on a hook by her apron strings so she can talk to customers but keep out of his way. That's when she reminds him, she taught him everything he knows. Now, keep in mind these treats are four days old."

Gaynor crushed out her cigarette. "I'd eat them if they turned into petrified wood. I don't dare open them now; Simon would kill me. Could you please thank Hercules from the bottom of my heart?"

"I've got something else, too."

"I'm not sure my nervous system is equipped for this much excitement."

Kitty took out a manila envelope and extracted a small painting. "My neighbour Winnie made this for me."

"A bunch of animals? Cute, but so what?"

Kitty pointed at each one. "These are my dogs, these are Wallace's dogs, there's a little walrus, and there's a kittycat. And a chicken."

"Okay."

Now she took out another picture. "Look again."

The next picture had only three animals, and it was entitled, *Walrus and Kitty have an Adventure.* There was a larger and more detailed picture of a baby walrus and a fuzzy black-and-white kitten on a sailboat. There was a very plump chicken wearing an apron, perched on the mast looking out to sea, squawking, with its wings stretched out in alarm.

She pointed to the chicken. "This is their sidekick, Bertha, who always has to get Walrus and Kitty out of trouble."

Suddenly Gaynor looked at it like it was the cover of a book. She started to say something, but Kitty interrupted her.

"Now, I know my sampling of readers was a little biased, seeing as how their nanna is the chicken and their uncle is the walrus and the kitty is the woman who's always mooching at their nanna's kitchen table, but judging by their reactions when I read them the story, I think we might have a winner here. Walrus and Kitty can go on lots of adventures. Winnie is over-the-moon excited to do the illustrations, and I don't think you'll find a more delightful artist. I love the way she's drawn Walrus. Her love for him is obvious. And I have to admit the kitty is really cute too. But my favourite has to be Bertha. Bertha and her big chicken breast."

Gaynor kept looking at it and shaking her head. "I don't believe it. It's perfect. Charming and perfect. Of course, it'll be a lot better once I get my hands on the story. Not that I know anything about children or their books, but we have a whole department for that. And putting your pretty face on the back cover will only be a plus."

"So, you like it?"

"I love it. I love you. I love your books and your South Head baking giant. You are officially Gaynor Ledbetter's best friend. And I have not said that to anyone but Simon. Not even my three sisters, who all need to take a dose of castor oil. But I'll tell you now, you'll never take Dolores from me. You'd have to kill me first."

"I can do that. My dad knows people."

They walked arm and arm back up Metcalfe Street towards Empire & Bloom to talk to Mel about many things. Gaynor glanced at Kitty's lovely face as she smiled and turned her face to the sun.

Catriona Jane Faulkner wasn't hiding anymore.

Acknowledgements

Many thanks to Port Morien's own historian, Ken MacDonald, for always being available on the phone and over email to answer my endless questions with not only facts but also pictures and documents. Thank you to Bucky MacLeod and Richie Jerrott for their insight. I'm grateful to Yvonne Kennedy and Mary and David Ferguson for delivering and lending me the original W. I. Minute Books from 1951 to 1961 that David's mother, Effie, kept in her possession. Thanks to the gang who belong to the "You Know You're from Port Morien When" Facebook group for answering my inquiries, and especially Catherine Fergusson for taking me to her property along a very bumpy South Head Road to show me the glorious view she gets to look at while having her morning tea.

And because this book is about a writer and her publishing company, I'd like to thank for the first time this writer's team at Nimbus Publishing in Halifax, Nova Scotia. A writer needs more than a half-baked idea when she sits in front of her keyboard typing up a storm while endless characters play havoc with her mental health and precious time. She needs to know that there is a knowledgeable and loyal team behind her who want the best for her. Who have, over the years, become her dear friends. Who have taken this journey with her and made all of her stories so much better.

I had no idea how lucky I would be when I hitched my star to Nimbus and their new Vagrant Press fiction imprint. *Relative Happiness* was one of their two inaugural novels. Fifteen books later, we're still together.

Thank you Terrilee Bulger, Heather Bryan, Whitney Moran, Kate Watson, and the office gang for, quite literally, everything.

And to my own Gaynor Ledbetter, known as Penelope Jackson, or Sweet P, as I've always called her, my unending gratitude for being the one I share a first draft with. Yours is the only opinion that matters at that stage because I know that whatever you tell me is the absolute truth and I trust your instincts. You've never steered me wrong. When you say you love something, I know it's good.

I love you all. xo